*New York Times* bestseller Jill Shalvis is the award-winning author of over four dozen romance novels, including her sexy, heart-warming contemporary 'Animal Magnetism' and 'Lucky Harbor' series. She won a RITA for *Simply Irresistible* and is a three-time National Readers Choice winner as well. Connect with Jill on her website www.jillshalvis.com for a complete book list and to read her daily blog, where she recounts her Misplaced City Girl adventures, or visit her at www.facebook.com/jillshalvis or @JillShalvis for other news.

**Praise for Jill Shalvis:**

'Packed with the trademark Shalvis humor and intense intimacy, it is definitely a must-read . . . If love, laughter and passion are the keys to any great romance, then this novel hits every note' *Romantic Times*

'Heartwarming and sexy . . . an abundance of chemistry, smoldering romance, and hilarious antics' *Publishers Weekly*

'[Shalvis] has quickly become one of my go-to authors of contemporary romance. Her writing is smart, fun, and sexy, and her books never fail to leave a smile on my face long after I've closed the last page . . . Jill Shalvis is an author not to be missed!' *The Romance Dish*

'Jill Shalvis is such a talented author that she brings to life characters who make you laugh, cry, and are a joy to read' *Romance Reviews Today*

'What I love about Jill Shalvis's books is that she writes sexy, adorable heroes . . . the sexual tension is out of this world. And of course, in true Shalvis fashion, she expertly mixes in humor that has you laughing out loud' *Heroes and Heartbreakers*

'I always enjoy reading a Jill Shalvis book. She's a consistently elegant, bold, clever writer . . . Very witty – I laughed out loud countless times and these scenes are sizzling' *All About Romance*

'If you have not read a Jill Shalvis novel yet, then you really have not read a real romance yet either!' *Book Cove Reviews*

'Engaging writing, characters that walk straight into your heart, touching, hilarious' *Library Journal*

'Witty, fun, and sexy – the perfect romance!' Lori Foster, *New York Times* bestselling author

'Riveting suspense laced with humor and heart is her hallmark, and Jill Shalvis always delivers' Donna Kauffman, *USA Today* bestselling author

'Humor, intri[...] ' Suzanne Forster, *New [...]*

# Jill SHALVIS

# head over heels

**headline**
ETERNAL

Published by arrangement with Forever,
a division of Grand Central Publishing.

First published as an ebook in Great Britain in 2014
by HEADLINE ETERNAL
An imprint of HEADLINE PUBLISHING GROUP

First published in paperback in Great Britain in 2015
by HEADLINE ETERNAL
An imprint of HEADLINE PUBLISHING GROUP

1

Cataloguing in Publication Data is available from the British Library

ISBN 978 1 4722 2263 3

Offset in Times by Avon DataSet Ltd, Bidford-on-Avon, Warwickshire

Printed and bound by CPI Group (UK) Ltd, Croydon, CR0 4YY

Headline's policy is to use papers that are natural, renewable and recyclable
products and made from wood grown in well-managed forests and other
controlled sources. The logging and manufacturing processes are expected
to conform to the environmental regulations of the country of origin.

HEADLINE PUBLISHING GROUP
An Hachette UK Company
338 Euston Road
London NW1 3BH

www.headlineeternal.com
www.headline.co.uk
www.hachette.co.uk

*To another youngest sister. To my youngest, Courtney,
whose heart is the biggest of all.*

*And also to Lance Tyler, my real life inspiration for the
Lance in my story, who I know is sitting on a cloud
somewhere, amused at my attempt at giving him a
Happy Ever After. For additional information
on cystic fibrosis, go to www.cff.org.*

# Acknowledgments

To Melinda, who read the rough draft and lent me her husband Todd's expertise on being a cop. And to Todd, for answering the endless questions. All mistakes are mine.

To Gena, who asked for a big, tough, stoic hero. Sawyer's all for you.

And last but definitely not least, to Jolie and Debbi, because without you two, this book would still be on the floor in little bits and pieces, and me alongside it. :)

# head over heels

# Chapter 1

*"If at first you don't succeed, destroy
all evidence that you tried."*

CHLOE TRAEGER

It wasn't often that Chloe Traeger beat her sisters into
the kitchen in the morning, but with Tara and Maddie cur-
rently sleeping with the town's two hottest hotties, it'd
been only a matter of time.

And in the name of fairness, Chloe hadn't actually gotten to bed yet, but that was just a technicality. With a wide
yawn, she started the coffee. Then, gathering what she
needed, she hopped up onto the counter—hissing in pain
from her throbbing legs. The quiet in the kitchen soothed
her as she mixed ingredients together for her natural an-
tibacterial cream. Given how loudly she lived her life, the
silence was a nice start to the day.

Especially today, which promised to get crazy quickly,
though not much could out-crazy last night. Later in the
afternoon, she'd be doing her esthetician thing at a high-
end spa in Seattle, but first she had to put in some time

here in Lucky Harbor at the B&B that she ran with her sisters.

The fact that her days were centering around work instead of play had her shaking her head with a rueful smile. Oh, how things change. Only a year ago, she'd been free as a bird, roaming happily from spa to spa at will, with no real ties. Then she and the half-sisters she'd never really known had inherited a dilapidated, falling-down-on-its-axis beach inn. With absolutely no knowledge of what to do with it.

Hard to believe how far they'd come. They'd renovated, turned the place into a thriving B&B, and now Chloe, Tara, and Maddie were real sisters instead of strangers. Friends, even.

Well, okay, so they were still working on the friends part, but they hadn't fought all week. Progress, right? And the fact that Chloe had been gone for four of the past seven days working at a five-star-hotel spa in Arizona instead of here in Washington didn't count.

Chloe looked down at the organic lavender oil she'd just "borrowed" from Tara's stash for her cream and winced.

Probably she could work harder on the friend thing...

Out the window, waves pounded the rocky shore in the purple light of dawn as she yawned again and stirred the softened beeswax and lanolin together with the lavender oil. When she was done, she carefully poured the cream into a sterile bottle. Then, still sitting on the counter, she tugged the legs of her sweat bottoms up to her knees, cringing in pain as she began to apply the antiseptic to the two long gashes on each of her calves. She was still sucking in a pained breath when the back door opened.

Sheriff Sawyer Thompson.

He practically had to duck to come in. He was in uniform, gun at his hip, expression dialed to Dirty Harry, and just looking at him had something pinging low in Chloe's belly.

He didn't appear to have the same reaction to her, of course. Nothing rippled Sawyer's implacable calm or got past that tough exterior. And he did have a hell of an exterior. At six feet three inches, he was built like a linebacker. But in a stunning defiance of physics, he usually had a way of moving all those mouth-watering muscles with an easy, male, fluid grace that would make an extreme fighter jealous.

*Stupid muscles*, Chloe thought as something deep within her tightened again from just looking at him. Some complicated combination of annoyance and reluctant lust. Last she'd checked, they had developed a sort of uneasy truce, meaning he lived by his rules and she lived by hers. Mostly this meant two different roads to the same conclusion, but there'd been some... misunderstandings.

Not wanting to explain last night—which would undoubtedly lead to another misunderstanding—she quickly yanked her sweatpants legs down to hide her injuries, shooting him the most professional smile in her repertoire. "Sheriff," she said smoothly.

The guarded expression that he wore as purposefully as he did the gun at his hip slipped for a single beat as he looked around. "Just you this morning?"

"Yep." Her smile turned genuine as Chloe enjoyed achieving what few could. She'd knocked that blank expression right off his face. She knew that was because he hadn't been expecting her. It was usually Tara who made the coffee every morning, coffee so amazing that Sawyer routinely stopped by on his way to work for a cup instead of facing the station's crap.

"Tara's not out of Ford's bed yet," she informed him.

The mention of his best friend and Chloe's sister in bed together made him grimace. Or more likely, it was Chloe's bluntness. In either case, he recovered and strode to the coffeemaker, his gait oddly measured, as if he was as tired-to-the-bone as she.

The county police and sheriff departments played weekly baseball games against the firefighters and paramedics, and they'd had one last night. Maybe Sawyer had played too hard. Maybe he'd had a hot date after. Given how women tried to get pulled over by him just to get face time, it was possible. After all, according to Lucky Harbor's Facebook page, phone calls to the county dispatch made by females between the ages of twenty-one and forty went up substantially whenever Sawyer was on duty.

His utility belt gleamed in the bright overhead light. His uniform shirt was wrinkled in the back and damp with sweat. She was wondering about that when he turned to her, gesturing to the coffeepot questioningly.

Heaven forbid the man waste a single word. "Help yourself," she said. "I just made it."

That made him pause. "You poison it?"

From her perch on the counter, she smiled. "Maybe."

With a small head shake, Sawyer reached into the cupboard for the to-go mugs Tara kept there for him.

"You're feeling brave, then," she noted.

He lifted a broad-as-a-mountain shoulder as he poured, then pointed to her own mug steaming on the counter at her side. "You're drinking it. You're a lot of things, Chloe, but crazy isn't one of them."

She suspected one of those "things" was a big pain in his very fine ass, but she shrugged.

Sawyer leaned his big frame against the counter to study her. Quiet. Speculative.

Undoubtedly, people caved when he did this, rushing to fill the silence. But silence had never bothered Chloe. No, what bothered her was the way she felt when he looked at her like that. For one thing, his eyes were mesmerizing. They were the color of melting milk chocolate but sometimes, like now, the tiny gold flecks in them sparked like fire. His hair was brown, too, the sort that contained every hue under the sun and could never be replicated in a salon. At the moment, it was on the wrong side of his last cut and in a state of dishevelment, falling over his forehead in front and nearly to his collar in back. The lines in his face were drawn tight with exhaustion, and she realized that he probably hadn't been headed in for his shift as she'd assumed, but just finishing one. Which meant that he'd been out all night, too, fighting crime like a superhero.

And yet somehow, he still managed to smell good. Guy good. She didn't understand it, but everything about him reminded her that she was a woman.

And that she hadn't had sex in far too long. "Seems a little early, even for you," she noted.

"Could say the same to you."

Something in his voice caused the first little niggle of suspicion in her brain and put her on alert. "Got a lot of things to mix up for the day spa I'm running later," she said.

His eyes never wavered from hers. "Or?"

Crap. Crap, she'd underestimated him. He was onto her, and the nerves quivered in her belly. "Or what?" she asked casually, shifting to get down off the counter, not looking forward to the pain at the contact. But Sawyer moved before she could, blocking her escape. His hips wedged between her legs, one hand on her thigh, the other on her opposite ankle, holding her in place.

"Romantic," she said dryly, even as her heart began to pound. "But I should get breakfast first, don't you think?"

"You're bleeding through your sweatpants." He shoved the sweats back up her legs to her knees, careful to avoid the wounds. As his eyes fixed on the deep gashes, the only sign he gave that he felt anything was the bunching of his jaw.

Chloe tried to pull free, but he was twice her size and tightened his grip on her thigh. "Hold still." He looked over the injuries, expression grim. "Explain."

"Um, I fell getting out of bed?"

He lifted his head and pinned her with his sharp gaze. "Try again, without the question mark."

"I fell hiking."

"Yeah," he said. "And I have some swamp land to sell you."

"Hey, I could be telling the truth."

"You don't hike, Chloe. It aggravates your asthma."

Actually, as it was turning out, *living* aggravated her asthma.

Sawyer bent to look more closely, pushing her hand away when she tried to block his view. "Steel," he said. "Steel fencing, I'm guessing. Probably rusted."

Her heart stopped. He knew. It seemed impossible—she'd been so careful—but *he knew*.

"You need a tetanus shot." He straightened his big frame but didn't move or let her go. "And a keeper, too," he added tightly. "Where are the dogs, Chloe?"

"I don't know what you're talking about." Except that she did. She knew because she'd spent the long hours of the night with her best friend, Lance, procuring the very six dogs he'd just mentioned.

AKA stealing them.

But in her defense, it had been a matter of life and death. The young pit bulls belonged to a guy named Nick Raybo, who'd planned on fighting them for sport. What Chloe and Lance had done had undoubtedly saved the dogs' lives, but had also been good old-fashioned breaking and entering. And since B&E wasn't exactly legal...

Sawyer waited her out, and for the record, he was good at it. As big and bad as he was, he had more patience than Job, a result, no doubt, of his years behind the badge and hearing every outrageous story under the sun. And like probably thousands before her, Chloe caved like a cheap suitcase. "The dogs are with Lance," she said on a sigh.

He stared at her for one stunned beat. "Jesus, Chloe."

"They were going to die!"

His expression still said one-hundred-percent cop, but there was a very slight softening in his tone. "You should have called me," he said.

Maybe, she thought. "And you would have done what? They hadn't begun the fighting yet so you couldn't have taken the dogs off the property. And they were going to fight them tonight, Sawyer." Even now it made her feel sick. "They were going to pit them against each other. To the death." Her voice cracked a little on that, but he didn't comment as he once again bent his head and studied the gouges on her legs.

He was right about how she'd gotten them. It'd happened when she'd crawled beneath the fence behind Lance as they'd made their escape. She held her breath, not knowing what Sawyer might do. He could arrest her, certainly. But he didn't reach for his cuffs or cite her Miranda rights, both good signs in her book.

"These are deep," was all he said.

She let out a breath. "They're not so bad."

"You clean them out?" He ran a long, callused finger down her calf alongside one particularly nasty gash, and she shivered. Not from pain. Maybe it was her exhaustion, or hell, maybe it was just from having him stand so close, but the stoic, tough-guy thing was sort of doing it for her this morning. He was a little on edge and sweaty, and a whole lot hot and sexy, and utterly without her permission, her brain rolled out a "Stern Cop and the Bad Girl" fantasy...

"Chloe."

She blinked away the image of him frisking her. "Yeah?"

His expression a little wary now, he repeated himself. "Did you clean these out?"

"Yes, sir."

He slid her a look, and she smiled innocently, but clearly she needed to have her hormone levels checked when she got her tetanus booster for this injury because she was *way* too aware of the heat and strength of him emanating through his uniform. Not to mention the matching heat washing through *her*, which was especially annoying because she had a personal decree that she never dated uptight, unbending men—particularly ones with badges.

The back door opened and Chloe jumped. Not Sawyer. Nothing ruffled him. Hell, he probably had sex without getting ruffled.

No, she thought, glancing up into his eyes. That wasn't true. Sawyer would have no qualms about getting ruffled, and a little shiver racked her body just as her sister Maddie walked into the kitchen, followed by her fiancé, Jax.

Not too long ago, both Tara and Chloe had nicknamed Maddie "the mouse," but she'd outgrown that moniker in spades since coming to Lucky Harbor. Now Maddie took one look at Sawyer wedged between Chloe's thighs and stopped short so fast that Jax plowed into her back. "What's this?" she demanded.

Chloe couldn't blame anyone for the shock, as typically she and Sawyer didn't share space well. In fact, usually when forced into close proximity, they resembled two tigers circling each other, teeth bared.

"Whatever it is," Jax said, taking in the scene, "it looks like fun." Jax was tall, lean, and on a mission as he poured himself a coffee and came directly toward Chloe, reaching for the drawer beneath her right thigh. "Can you move her leg?" he asked Sawyer. "I need a spoon, man."

Mouth still agog, Maddie plopped down into a chair. She waggled a finger between Chloe and Sawyer. "So you two are...?"

"No!" Chloe said and shoved at Sawyer, who still didn't budge, damn him. The two-hundred-plus lug was bent over her left calf again—the worst one—his hair brushing the insides of her thighs. She told herself *not* to think about how the silky strands would feel on her bare skin, but she totally did, and shivered again.

Sawyer looked up at her and she did her best to look cold instead of turned on. "You might actually need stitches," he said.

With a horrified gasp, Maddie hopped up to come look. Seconds later, Chloe had her sister, her sister's fiancé, and the man she didn't quite know how to categorize at all, standing far too close, staring at her injuries. She tried to close her legs but couldn't and tossed up her hands. "They're just scratches!"

"Oh, Chloe," Maddie murmured, concern creasing her brow. "Honey, you should have called me. What happened, and where else are you hurt?"

Sawyer's gaze ran over Chloe's entire body now, as if he could see through her sweats. A very naughty part of her brain considered telling him that the scratches went all the way up just so he'd demand a more thorough inspection.

Bad, *bad* brain. Because at just the thought, her chest tightened, and she had to reach for her inhaler, thanks to the asthma that always kept her slightly breathless.

And sexless. "It's nothing," she said. "I'm fine, all right? Back up."

Sawyer gave Jax a light shove away from her. "She and Lance rescued six dogs from the McCarthy place last night," he said to Maddie, ratting Chloe out without qualm.

Maddie shook her head, clearly horrified. "Chloe. God. That was...crazy dangerous."

Hearing the worry in her voice had guilt tugging at Chloe. She couldn't believe how much she'd grown to care about the two strangers that were her half-sisters, or for that matter, about Lucky Harbor and the people in it. The fact that she'd let down her guard enough to care at all was new.

For most of her childhood, it had been just Chloe and her mom, and the lessons had been clear: Connections weren't meant to last past the overnight camping pass. Only traditionalists let themselves get trapped by things like boring relationships or full-time jobs. The special people were destined to spread their wings and live life fully and freely.

Like Chloe and Phoebe.

"Raybo is crazy," Maddie said, moving to get coffee. "It could have gotten ugly."

Chloe wished Sawyer would move, too, and gave him a nudge with her foot. Actually, it might have been more like a kick. Didn't matter, he was a mountain and didn't move.

"It's awfully hot in here," Maddie said, and opened the window.

"It's called sexual tension." Jax sent an eyebrow wiggle in Sawyer and Chloe's direction.

Humor from the peanut gallery.

Sawyer sent Jax the sort of long, level look that undoubtedly had bad guys losing control of their bowels, but Jax just smiled. "If *I* was going to make that move on a woman, I'd at least have bought her breakfast first."

Chloe nodded. "That's what I said."

Maddie plopped into Jax's lap to cuddle up to him. "You made *plenty* of moves on me before you ever bought me breakfast."

"I'm not making moves," Sawyer said. Maddie and Jax

stared pointedly at his position between Chloe's thighs. He lifted his hands from her as if he'd been burned, backing up with his hands in the air. "Okay, I'm going to bed now. Alone."

"You know what your problem is?" Jax asked. "You don't know how to have fun. Haven't for a long time."

"Does this"—Sawyer pointed in the general vicinity of Chloe's lower body—"look anything like *fun* to you?"

Jax choked back a snort, and even Maddie bit her lower lip to hide a smile.

"Jesus," Sawyer said with a small head shake. "You know what I mean."

Yeah. He'd meant the sorry mess Chloe had made of her legs, as well as the risks she'd taken last night, but she said "*hey*" anyway in token protest. Because dammit, her lower half could be lots of fun.

If she ever got to use it, that is.

# Chapter 2

*"If things don't seem right, try going left."*

CHLOE TRAEGER

One week later, Sawyer Thompson walked into his bedroom, dropped his gun and cell phone onto the nightstand, and glanced at his bed. It'd been a hell of a day, and the only thing that could have saved it would have been a woman waiting for him.

Naked.

With nefarious intentions in mind.

He should have thought ahead when he'd broken it off with Cindy a few months back. But after four dates, the sweet, quiet, unassuming middle school teacher had already been unhappy going out with a guy who was on call just about 24-7.

He couldn't blame her. But nor could he change for her.

Needing a hot shower, he stripped and stood beneath the spray. Pressing his palms to the tile wall, he dropped his head and let the water bead over his aching neck and shoulders. Today should have been a day off, but the county was perpetually understaffed, and fellow sheriff Tony Sanchez had taken a personal day to help his wife take their newborn twins for a checkup. This left Sawyer covering not just Lucky Harbor but two neighboring small towns as well.

By midmorning, he'd faced a dead homeless guy slumped on a park bench—natural causes, according to the ME—and delivered a newborn out on Highway 37 from a woman in labor who somehow thought it was a good idea to drive herself to the hospital with contractions only one and a half minutes apart.

After that, there was still time left in his day to break up a barroom brawl, deal with a domestic dispute call, and his favorite, rescue a five-year-old and his puppy from a muddy storm drain.

The shower removed the residual dirt clinging to him from that last call, but it didn't revive him or numb the unrest coiling in his gut. A pizza and a beer might make a dent, but he didn't have time for that. Earlier he'd heard a rumor that Nick Raybo had procured more dogs and was planning a midnight event. Sawyer was going to make sure that didn't happen. Maybe he'd get pizza and beer afterward with Ford and Jax. Either of his best friends would join him no matter the time, but Sawyer knew he'd be shitty company tonight.

And in any case, what he really craved was a woman to bury himself in, and it wasn't sweet Cindy who came to mind as he soaped up. Nope, against all the reason and logic that he prided himself on, he wanted the one woman whose favorite pastime seemed to be pushing his buttons.

The thought of it, of having Chloe, was about as crazy

as his week had been. She was obstinate, impulsive, trouble with a capital T…and damn. *Hot*. She was also a walking-talking reminder of a part of his life he'd given up—the wild part. There was a lot of sexual attraction, but no future. Because while he was a permanent fixture in this town, Chloe was just a sexy little tumbleweed blowing through.

The day after the dog-nabbing incident, there'd been an article in the opinion section of the local paper about recent vandalisms and petty theft in the area. The anonymous writer had gone on to include a list of people in town known for trouble seeking, and Chloe had been on it.

Not a big surprise.

He wondered if she'd been disturbed or upset by it. It wasn't in her nature to worry about what people thought of her. But he bet her sisters had been. They were trying to generate *good* press for the B&B, not negative.

Of course, if he'd arrested her for trespassing, B&E, and theft, *that* would have been negative press. And a personal hell for him since Tara and Maddie would have skinned him alive. Which was not why he hadn't arrested her, he told himself. He hadn't arrested her because…shit. Because for the first time in his adult life, he'd chosen to look the other way, and it didn't sit well.

He'd seen her several times this week. Once when she'd been coming out of the urgent care with a Band-Aid on her arm from her tetanus shot, and then again riding her Vespa on the highway, her long, wild red hair billowing out behind her, her helmet and Hollywood-style sunglasses hiding most of her face.

And yesterday he'd run into her at the grocery store

just as she was pulling a bottle of vodka from the shelf, which she'd assured him was for work.

He'd laughed. He'd only been in the store to grab a sports drink on the way to his weekly baseball game, but he'd immediately forgotten about that, standing there in the aisle feeling...alive. "Work," he said. "The vodka's for work."

"It cleans glass like nobody's business. And if applied topically, it works as a great preservative. And did you know that used as a *non*-topical application, it's the perfect man cure?"

"How's that?"

"A few shots, and you're cured of wanting one."

He shook his head now at the memory. How in the hell she managed to make him want to both kiss her and run like hell was beyond him. He stepped out of the shower, dropped his towel, and pulled on fresh clothes before going back out. When he was on duty, he drove a department marked SUV. His personal vehicle was a truck. Both were equipped for whatever came his way, and tonight, going low profile, he took the truck. Lucky Harbor was basically a tiny little bowl sitting on the rocky Washington State coast, walled in by majestic peaks and lush forest. It was all an inky shadow now.

Nick Raybo had ten acres of land out at Eagle's Bluff, deep into the forest. It was rugged and isolated out there, perfect for all sorts of illegal dealings and a favorite place for partiers.

But that's not where Sawyer headed first.

At this time of night, his truck was the only vehicle on the road as he headed down the hill into town. The moon peeked through the clouds, hanging low and wan. It cast a pale glow over the Pacific Ocean churning against the rocky terrain off to his left. The pier was dark, the town was dark, and his thoughts were darker still.

He'd been raised here, though he used the term "raised" loosely. It'd been just him and his father, Nolan Thompson, a blue-collar union man who believed in hard work, Jim Beam, and ruling with an iron fist.

Or in Sawyer's case, a wicked long leather belt.

It hadn't helped much. Sawyer had been just about as wild as they came, which made it all the more amusing to those who knew him best that he now wielded a badge.

He drove through town and onto the narrow road that led to the Lucky Harbor Beach B&B. The inn was a Victorian, freshly painted and renovated, lit up warm and welcoming for guests. Pulling around to the back of the property, he idled in front of the small owner's cottage where Chloe lived.

The lights were off.

Sawyer hoped like hell that meant she was sleeping and *not* up at Eagle's Bluff with Lance in the middle of another Two Stooges act that could get them killed this time, but his luck wasn't running that way. A quick swipe of his flashlight didn't reveal her Vespa.

*Shit.*

Exhausted and doing a slow burn at the thought of what Chloe might be up to, he got out of his truck to check around. To his relief, he found her Vespa parked on the side of the cottage.

On the way back to his truck, he flicked his light to the front door, taking in the potted plants thriving there and the yoga mat leaning against the wall. When she was in Lucky Harbor and not working at a spa somewhere around the country, Chloe liked to do yoga on the beach at sunrise. He'd seen her on that very mat, lit by the morning sun glinting off the waves, her tanned, toned limbs bent in impossible ways that made him think of other, better ways to bend them. Chloe on her mat was not only a huge turn-on, but an anomaly. She was blithe and breathless, literally, both from her free-spirited nature and from her severe asthma—the one exception being when she was doing yoga, the sole thing in her life that required a deep, calm stillness. Most likely that was what drew her to it.

He had no idea what drew him to her.

Okay, not true. She had a sharp mind, an even sharper wit, and used both to drive him up a wall as often as she could.

She was good at it.

He was good at letting her.

Shaking his head at himself, Sawyer turned to go just as someone cried out, the sound cutting through the night. He was at the front door, gun in hand, when the cry came again.

Not a pain-filled scream, he realized. Not one of terror either, but of passion. *Loud* passion, he corrected as she did it again.

Chloe.

Jesus. Closing his eyes, Sawyer dropped his head to the door, wishing like hell he wasn't here, listening to Chloe in the throes of what sounded like wild animal sex.

When the scream came a third time, a ridiculously over-the-top porn-star wail of epic proportions, it was accompanied by a low, husky, unmistakably male voice.

Definitely time to get the hell out of there. Sawyer

turned on his heel to do just that, but the porch light suddenly flickered on, fully illuminating him to whoever was peeking out the peephole. A second later, the bolt clicked and the front door whipped open.

"*Sawyer?*"

Grimacing, he turned back. Chloe stood in the doorway, her best friend, Lance, at her side, both fully dressed, thank Christ.

Lance ran the ice cream shop on the pier with his brother, Tucker. He was in his mid-twenties like Chloe, but painfully thin and pale from the cystic fibrosis that had been ravaging his body all his life.

Next to him, Chloe seemed to glow, the embodiment of health and exuberance. Her shiny, dark red hair was in wild waves tonight, loosely flying past her shoulders except for the few long bangs that framed her face. She was beautiful enough to be a model, but missing the compliant gene. Chloe had never met a direction or a command that suited her.

She wore a soft, black hoodie sweater that clung to her breasts and dark, hip-hugging jeans tucked into high-heeled boots that gave off a don't-fuck-with-me air but made him ache to do just that. There was a wildness to her tonight, hell, every night, and an inner darkness that he was drawn to in spite of himself.

It called to his true inner nature, the matching wildness and darkness within *him*, which he'd tried to bury a long time ago. Ridiculously relieved that she wasn't having sex, Sawyer backed up to go. She was home, safe and sound, and that was all he cared about.

"Sawyer? What are you doing here?"

Good question. He opened his mouth with absolutely

no idea exactly what he planned to say, but Lance suddenly staggered and put his hand to his head.

Chloe instantly slid an arm around Lance's narrow waist to steady him. "What's the matter?"

"Nothing," Lance said, pushing free. "Got up too fast, is all."

"Here, sit." Ignoring his resistance, Chloe gently pushed Lance back inside, to the couch in the small living room. With a hand on his shoulder, she lifted her face to Sawyer, leveling him with her dark green eyes.

A jolt went through him, a zap of something he didn't care to name.

"What can I do for you, Sheriff?" she asked.

*Yeah, Sawyer, what can she do for you*? He searched his brain. "You can explain breaking the noise ordinance."

Lance laughed softly.

"Noise ordinance?" Chloe asked. "I broke the *noise ordinance* with my pretend orgasm?"

"You did sound like a mule stuck in a tar pit," Lance said helpfully.

"A mule—" Chloe choked on a laugh. "Okay, no one who's heard the real thing would ever even *think* of comparing me to a mule."

This information didn't help Sawyer *at all*. "Is that right?"

Chloe's gaze locked on his. In the sudden charged silence, Lance cleared his throat. "This is weird. I'm going to the kitchen now, while the two of you finish...whatever the hell this is. Call for me if you're going to need bailing out, Chloe."

"Sure," she said, her gaze never leaving Sawyer's. "I'll let you know if I end up in cuffs."

Lance grimaced. "Okay, never mind. *Don't* call me."

Chloe laughed, but Sawyer was stuck on the mental image of her in his cuffs. If he'd been half the cop he liked to think he was, it wouldn't, *couldn't*, cause such an erotic rush.

Something came into Chloe's eyes that told him she knew exactly where his mind had just gone—and that just maybe hers had gone there, too. The temperature in the room seemed to shoot up, but the sound of a harsh coughing in the kitchen, hard and relentless, like someone was dying, sent a chill down Sawyer's back.

Chloe rushed into the kitchen, instantly all soft, warm, caring woman, in a way that Sawyer had never seen directed at him. When he followed, he found her murmuring something for Lance's ears only, reaching for him.

Lance, clearly not willing to be babied, held her off, pounding a fist to his own chest to try to catch some desperately needed air. When he'd finally recovered, he looked over Chloe's head at Sawyer. "If you're here to make sure she's not going to Eagle's Bluff tonight, the coast's clear. She's *not* going."

"Wait— What?" Chloe said, dividing a look between both men. "Nick has more dogs?"

Lance's face went blank. "*Had.*"

Sawyer sighed. "You took them already."

"That would be breaking and entering, and stealing," Lance said.

Ah, Christ. Sawyer didn't know whether to be relieved that Lance hadn't dragged Chloe into it again, or be pissed off that he'd once again taken matters into his own hands instead of letting Sawyer handle it. He settled on pissed off because it was easier. "It has to go through proper channels to get it stopped permanently. You know that."

"Proper channels are too slow for the dogs," Lance said unapologetically.

"If you get caught with them, Raybo will press charges."

Lance shrugged. He didn't care. And why should he? The guy was already facing a virtual death sentence with the CF, which left him hell bent and determined to say "fuck you" to karma whenever possible.

Chloe was giving Lance a dark look. She was pissed. But Lance just shook his head. "Like you needed another mention in the paper as a troublemaker."

"I don't care what people think, Lance. I care about you. And those dogs."

"You care what people think of the inn. You care that people whispering about you might keep the inn from getting good word of mouth. You care that it could hurt your sisters."

Chloe let out a breath. "Yeah. I do."

The sudden scent of acrid smoke had Sawyer frowning, and turning on his heel, he headed back outside. Beyond the inn and the cottage was the ocean. He couldn't see it in the dark, but he could hear it pounding the shore. Off to the left was the marina building and dock, and beyond that, woods. The trees were thick as feathers, growing right up to the waterline in some spots. He couldn't see a fire, but he could sure as hell smell it. It was illegal to have a campfire without a permit, not to mention they were in the middle of high fire season, but suddenly from somewhere beyond the tree line came an undeniable glow.

Sawyer turned back to the door, nearly plowing over Chloe, who'd come out after him. It was automatic to reach for her, to grip her arms until balance was restored, but for a beat, they were plastered to each other. Her hair brushed his jaw, her soft breasts pressed against his chest, and as tended to happen with her, he felt something stir inside him other than a frustrated indifference.

She murmured a soft, nearly inaudible apology but didn't pull away.

"My fault," he said, looking down in her face. "Who's in your woods?"

"Tucker and some of his friends," Lance said from behind her.

Tucker was Lance's older brother, which meant the friends with him were Jamie and Todd, and aside from the fact that Todd and Sawyer went way back, to a time Sawyer preferred not to think about, the combo of those four guys usually spelled mayhem. "They have a permit?"

Lance laughed.

Right. No permit. "They doing anything illegal out there besides the campfire?" Sawyer asked.

"Maybe drinking beer."

Perfect. When Todd drank, he became the King of the Terminally Stupid. The others were never far behind. Sawyer stepped off the porch, stopping when Chloe followed him. He grabbed her wrist, his thumb brushing the very small tattoo she had there at her pulse point, an Asian symbol he didn't know the meaning of.

"I want to come with—"

"No," he said, knowing the smoke would bring on her asthma. "Wait here."

At the command, her face closed, and for a moment he wished...

Hell. He had no idea what he wished when it came to her. She twisted him in fucking knots. It used to be they just rubbed each other the wrong way, but lately he'd been extremely caught up in rubbing her the right way. Which actually, when it came right down to it, made *him* the King of the Terminally Stupid.

# Chapter 3

*"It's always darkest before dawn. So if you're going to steal your neighbor's newspaper, that's the time to do it."*

CHLOE TRAEGER

Chloe held Sawyer's steely gaze with one of her own, though she got a crick in her neck doing it. He was big, armed to the teeth, and if the flash in his eyes meant anything, his irritation level was on the rise.

Nothing new when it came to her.

To be fair, she'd certainly earned his wrath on several occasions, back when she'd first arrived in Lucky Harbor. But she'd grown up over the past year and was learning— or trying anyway—to curb her impulsive, reckless behavior. Having grown up with a mother whose only consistent passion had been following the Grateful Dead, Chloe hadn't learned a whole lot about roots or long-lasting relationships. Or long-lasting *anything* for that matter. But she was working on it, on becoming more aware of both herself and how her actions affected others. And also what it meant to care. There was no doubt that she was still a work in progress, but then again, she'd never claimed to be anything but.

And slightly tamed though she might be, she could still dig in her heels with the best of them. So when Sawyer commanded her to "wait here," the urge to do the opposite was strong.

It would appear that she wasn't quite as grown up as she thought.

In response to her unspoken reaction, the very corners of Sawyer's lips twitched. Not quite a smile. More like a grimace to go with the faint lines of stress around his eyes and mouth and the tension in his shoulders.

He was tired. From the look of it, he'd already had a hell of a long day, which only added to the ruffian edge to him. He wore a button-down untucked over the gun at his hip, and jeans that fit him perfectly across the butt. Yes, she'd checked.

And let's not forget the testosterone and pheromones and all around general air of badassness. He was a man always ready for anything, anytime, and he wasn't someone to tangle with. Something she knew all too well. He was intense, hard, unyielding, and—

"The smoke, Chloe. Stay back because of the smoke."

—and uncompromisingly fair. With a sigh, she nodded.

He gave her one last long look and walked toward the woods. She'd never been drawn to ridiculous displays of naked courage or sheer brawn, but Sawyer really brought it to a whole new level.

"You're drooling," Lance said dryly, having stepped up to her side.

She ignored him, not taking her eyes off the spot where Sawyer had vanished. No, she wasn't drooling, but something just as bad. She was tingling. It's okay, she told herself. A woman would have to be dead not to feel anything when she looked at Sawyer Thompson, and Chloe wasn't close to dead.

*Yet*, she thought wryly, feeling the smoke begin to invade her lungs. Twice a day, she took meds to control her asthma, but she also carried a fast-acting inhaler for the in-between times when she hit trouble—like now. She pulled it out of her pocket and took a puff. Then she looked over at Lance. "Where's your sweatshirt? Your lips are blue."

They both knew his lips weren't blue because he was cold, but Lance obligingly went back inside for his sweatshirt. "You're so predictable, Chloe."

Chloe was many things. She was a sister, a friend, an esthetician. She was a wanderer and an adventurer. She was also hard-willed, stubborn as an ox, and quick to temper. But one thing she wasn't, was predictable. "Take that back," she said.

"*Predictable*," he repeated. "Among other things."

"Such as?" She stepped off the porch but stopped when Lance grabbed her wrist.

"You're staying," he said. "I don't want to get arrested tonight for aggravating an officer."

"He won't arrest you for that." But he was right, there was no reason to piss Sawyer off. And yet, dammit, staying went against the grain. Like so many other things in her life. It was her asthma's fault. It held her back, and because of it, she tended to push the envelope too far in other ways. She understood that, from the outside looking in, it might seem like she had a secret death wish, but she didn't. It was just that when she was in the midst of an asthma attack, she often felt so close to death that she, well, *dared* it. But she just wanted to run or dance or laugh hard, or have sex without needing an inhaler and possibly an ambulance.

Not exactly a common problem, but one that often left her straddling a fine line between socially acceptable behavior and the wild yearnings her mother had always encouraged. Her sisters wanted her to stop pushing those boundaries and settle down a little. And it was that which bothered Chloe more than anything. The message was simple: If she wanted to be accepted, even loved, by those she'd come to care about, she'd need to change. But dammit, she wanted to be accepted just as she was, imperfections and all. "Predictable," she said like it was a dirty word.

Lance sighed and put a hand over hers. "Okay, maybe not predictable so much as . . ."

"Crazy?"

He laughed softly.

He got her, and always had. So it really sucked that they had no chemistry together. "Lance?"

"Yeah?"

She squeezed his fingers. "I'm really annoyed that you aren't sexy."

"Gee, thanks," he said dryly.

"To me, I mean." She nudged her shoulder against his. "I want to want you. You know?"

Lance slid a hand to her ass. "Give me ten minutes and I'll change your mind— *Oof*," he said when she elbowed him, but he laughed good-naturedly. He knew. They both knew. First of all, he was like her brother and had been since the day they'd met. And second, he was totally, completely, pathetically hung-up on one of the cute nurses at the medical center where he spent far too much of his time.

Not that he'd ever do anything about it.

"What woman would be attracted to a sick guy with a looming expiration date?" he'd asked her once.

Which left it just the two of them against the world.

Not having sex.

A low-lying fog was rolling in off the water, slipping through the night toward them like silvery fingers. Through it, several shadows appeared, materializing into the outlines of men. Todd, Tucker, and Jamie, with bad attitude in every line of their bodies.

Sawyer was behind them.

As they came closer, Chloe saw that Todd was holding a piece of paper. Normally he was also one of those easy charmers who could convince a nun to give up her habit. He'd certainly turned it on her as often as possible—not that it'd ever gotten him anywhere. But now he displayed none of that charm, passing by the porch without a word, heading around to the side of the marina where they'd parked. Jamie went with him.

Not Tucker. He stopped and looked up the porch steps at his brother, an odd tension simmering between the siblings. "You okay?" Tucker finally asked, and when Lance nodded, he gestured the way Todd and Jamie had gone. "Then let's go, we're out of here."

Lance's gaze slid to the retreating stiff shoulders of Todd and Jamie with unease, and Chloe grabbed his hand. "You promised to stay and try out my chest rub to see if it helps you breathe easier, remember? I'll drive you home after."

When Tucker left without another word, Lance

squeezed her hand, then dropped it. "I'll be inside," he said, and with one last look at the still silent Sawyer, vanished into the cottage.

Chloe turned to the sheriff. The shimmering tension between them certainly wasn't sibling-like. Nor was it going to disappear anytime soon, which meant she had two choices: Get used to it or fight it.

Because Sawyer was the last man on earth that she should ever get involved with, option number two was the smart route.

Returning her gaze evenly, he waited. He never spoke more words than absolutely necessary, and this drove her batshit crazy. "What happened out there?"

"I ticketed Todd for the illegal bonfire."

"Just Todd?"

"He was the one who started it."

She paused. Todd was one of those guys who could talk his way into a bank vault with nothing but a smile, and then walk out with all the money, leaving the bank manager happy to have been ripped off. He was also a native Lucky Harbor guy, and the residents were very fond of their own, troubled son or no.

Sawyer was native too, and just as well liked, if not more so. "You ticketed him even though everyone lights illegal bonfires out there?"

"Not in a high fire hazard season, they don't," he said.

"It's almost October."

"Fire season," Sawyer repeated.

"So...if I lit a campfire, you'd arrest me?"

"Ticket," he corrected. "Not arrest. Not for a first offense."

What was wrong with her that the stern cop thing he

had going on was doing it for her? Huh. Maybe she didn't want to fight this attraction so much as test its boundaries. "What if it was my second offense? Would you frisk and cuff me then?"

His eyes darkened. "What is it with you and my cuffs?"

"Well, if you don't know," Chloe said as demurely as she could, "I don't want to corrupt you." She made to go inside, but Sawyer snagged her sweater and tugged her back.

"Not so fast," he said and studied her, giving nothing of his thoughts away. "You're playing with me," he finally decided.

"Trying."

"I don't like games, Chloe."

No shit. She'd known him for nearly a year now, and yet she didn't know him at all. He kept everything extremely close to the vest, which she could admit made her quite envious, as she was completely incapable of doing the same.

"What were you and Lance up to earlier?" he wanted to know.

"Popcorn. Chatting. Stuff."

"I mean with the Meg Ryan orgasm impersonation."

She hesitated. This was going to be embarrassing. "I'm not sure you're going to understand."

"Try me."

"Okay, well, sometimes the cottage creaks at night, you know?"

"It's probably the wood and joints settling."

"Yes, but it's the 'probably' part that gets me. At night, it's...loud."

"And you sleep here alone now."

"Yes." Maddie had moved in with Jax, and in fact,

was marrying him in two months. Tara had moved out as well to live with her boyfriend, Ford. The three sisters worked out shifts when they had overnight guests, but for the most part, Chloe took care of anything that came up because she was the one without a life. "Sometimes it sounds like there's a...ghost." She waited for him to laugh, and even gave some thought to all the ways she might hurt him if he did, but he didn't.

He just looked at her meditatively. "You could tell your sisters you don't like sleeping here alone."

Hell, no. She'd already managed to stir up negative press; she wasn't going to bring more chaos. "They have more on their plates than I do. I'm not going to add worry or grief to it by telling them I'm afraid." And she wished like hell that she wasn't telling him either. "It's no big deal. It's just that I read one Stephen King too many, and sometimes, I get a little freaked is all. Lance knows that and comes over, and we make up funny stories to go with my ghost."

"Stories."

"Tonight we decided the ghost died here at age ninety-nine. A virgin."

"A ninety-nine-year-old-virgin ghost."

"Hey, it's not as unlikely as you might think. Anyway, she can't go on to her afterlife until she has an orgasm. So she stays here, granting wishes. Tonight Lance wished for a long, normal life, and..." Her throat tightened because Lance could wish all he wanted but it wasn't going to happen for him. And God, how she hated that, hated it so damn much that sometimes she couldn't breathe just thinking about it. "So assuming the ghost grants his wish," she said softly, "in return, we were trying to give her the orgasm she'd never had."

His mouth twitched. "A *fake* orgasm."

"Yes, well, it's the best we had." She didn't know how she felt about Sawyer catching her silly show, or what the hell he could have possibly thought when he'd heard her screaming.

Or why she cared...

But she did. And in return, he nodded in understanding. It didn't exactly go with the tough, unflappable cop image she'd always had of him, a guy who followed the rules and a set path for life like a map, no veering. Black and white, always.

He certainly wasn't someone who would get her need to live saturated in color.

Lance poked his head out and showed her that he was holding the chest rub. "Ready to take me home?"

Nodding, Chloe turned from Sawyer.

"Chloe," he said. "You're staying away from Eagle's Bluff tonight."

She glanced back, not surprised he'd bring it up again, and even less surprised that it was a command and not a question. "Sure."

"I mean it, Chloe."

He was back to being all cop. It defined him. It suited him. It must be nice to know what defined you, what suited you. "I know you do, Sheriff."

He let her go, and she got on the Vespa, putting on her helmet. Lance got on behind her and slid his arms around her waist. Chloe revved the engine and hit the gas, glancing into her side mirror.

As they pulled away, she could see Sawyer standing there watching them go in the growing fog.

# Chapter 4

*"Why was man created before woman? Because you always need a rough draft before the final copy."*

CHLOE TRAEGER

Chloe got up before dawn, when the sky was still inky black. Every October was fire season but this October, drier than any in recent history, made it all the more dangerous. Still, there were some benefits to a dry fall, and taking advantage of it, she dressed in yoga pants and a long-sleeved tee and took her mat to the beach to work out. When she was on the road, she did yoga in some of the fanciest hotels in the world, but here, with the rhythmic pulsing of the waves crashing onto the rocks, the seagulls squawking, the sand crunching beneath her mat—this was her favorite.

Afterward, she walked. She didn't usually do that, couldn't if her chest was too tight, but she had the time this morning and needed to burn some energy.

Everything was quiet, not a single soul stirring except the seagulls and the pounding surf, but she knew her way well enough by now to get along in the predawn. Lucky Harbor was a picturesque little beach town, nestled in a rocky cove with an eclectic mix of the old and new. The main drag was lined with Victorian-style buildings, most painted in a variety of bright colors. There was a long pier that jutted out into the water, lined with a café, a few shops, an arcade, and a Ferris wheel. Since Chloe wasn't ready to face her day, she walked the pier to the end, standing in one of the far corners between two benches so that she could feel surrounded by the ocean below.

She gave herself a *Titanic* moment, closing her eyes, raising her face to the salty, still chilly air. To the east, the dark sky was tinged slightly purple with the coming day.

It was hard to believe that she was still here in Lucky Harbor. A year ago, she, Tara, and Maddie had been living their own lives, rarely connecting, so different. Whether that was due to the mysteries of genetics from their three different fathers or simply the fact that they'd been raised separately, Chloe didn't know. Their mom, Phoebe Traeger, had been the embodiment of a true, free spirit. She'd kept to the road, found love—often—then had moved along. Nothing had stuck to Phoebe, not even her two eldest daughters. Nothing except Chloe. Chloe had been her one concession to a traditional life, if you could consider being schooled in the back of a VW bus and eating most of their meals in soup kitchens traditional.

Tara's father had taken Tara with him when he and Phoebe's relationship had deteriorated. Maddie's father had done the same when she'd come along a few years later. Chloe couldn't say what her own father had done or felt, as she'd never known him. Phoebe hadn't talked about him and had always dodged Chloe's questions by claiming Chloe was a gift from a life well lived.

Ahead of Chloe, the Pacific Ocean was a deep, choppy sea of black, meeting the metallic sky. The entire vista was framed by rocky bluffs, misty and breathtaking. She stood there and wondered at her fondness for this place, which seemed to anchor her like no other. She'd been fond of places before, lots of them, but she'd never had a connection like the one she'd had with Lucky Harbor.

When she heard footsteps come up behind her, she instinctively grabbed her inhaler like it was Mace and whirled around.

Sawyer stood there all rugged and damp from exertion and looking damn gorgeous. He took in her ready stance and then the inhaler, held out like a gun. "Going to shoot me with that?"

Chloe shoved the inhaler back into her waistband. "What are you doing?" It was a stupid question, born of nerves. He was dressed in sweatpants and a T-shirt, breathing heavy but not overly labored. Clearly he'd been running, which caused a yearning to well up within her to do the same. But running would be like stepping out in front of a speeding car—deadly.

"You okay?" he asked.

"Of course." It was easier to think of Sawyer as a badge. A sanctimonious authority figure, and an irritating one at that. But whether she liked it or not, there *was* more to the man, much more. Yeah, he was tough, stoic, and impenetrable, but once in a while he'd reveal more, like the way his eyes filled with concern when he'd seen her injuries after rescuing the dogs, not to mention how he'd let her stretch the letter of the law that night. "I'm always okay," she said. "Tell me what happened last night at Eagle's Bluff."

He gave her one of his patented "yeah right" looks.

Okay, so he was still more irritating than intriguing. Good to know. "Come on, Sheriff. It'll be on Facebook if anything went down, so you might as well spill."

The threat was legit. Lucille ran the local art gallery and Lucky Harbor's Facebook page with equal enthusiasm. In fact, her updates were practically required reading for Lucky Harbor residents. She reported on the happenings in town, each detail joyfully chronicled, the juicier the better.

"We found no dogs on the premises," he said.

He shifted to go, but she asked the question that was tweaking her curiosity. "So why did you stop?"

"Excuse me?"

"Why didn't you just keep running when you saw me out here?"

Not a blink. Not even a shrug.

"Sheriff Sawyer Thompson," she murmured. "Communication master."

The very corner of his mouth turned up slightly. It knocked her off balance a little.

A lot.

"Let me guess," she said. "You couldn't resist me." She couldn't say why she was poking the bear, but maybe it was her version of running . . . with scissors. "You saw me, and you couldn't resist me, and so you stopped to . . ."

"To . . . ?"

"Well, that's the question, isn't it?" she asked. "I mean, we don't like each other. We don't have anything in common. Whatever would we do with each other?"

His eyes heated at that, and in reaction, her nipples contracted to two tight beads. Hmmm. Apparently they could do plenty. But before she could process that, he took a step back as if to go.

"I scare you," Chloe said.

"Hell, yeah," he admitted, shocking a laugh from her. He wasn't afraid. Nothing scared him. But she'd learned not to tangle with the good sheriff unless she was on her A-game, and that wasn't the case at the moment. Being in Sawyer's presence took all of her concentration so that she didn't accidentally give herself away. Because the truth was, in spite of the overwhelming odds of the two of them being a major train wreck if they ever got together, she wanted him.

It was the most ridiculous thing she'd ever wanted.

After all, he was rigid where she was flexible. He was black and white, and she was all the rainbow in between, and they didn't go together.

Not that her body cared about logic. He was the most virile, potent, testosterone-filled guy she'd ever met. Sex with him would be fireworks, thunderstorms.

*Magic.*

But even she knew that she wasn't ready for prime time with Sawyer Thompson. "I have to go."

"Now who's scared?"

"No, I have to get back to the inn." It was nearly seven, and she needed to beat her sisters there. They hadn't had any guests last night, but Tara was adamant that someone always be available, even at the ass crack of dawn.

Someone being Chloe, naturally.

"Know what I think?" Sawyer asked.

"I have no idea. I never do."

He was leaning against the back of the bench, all six feet three inches of brawn at rest. "I make you nervous."

"You don't make me nervous." Okay, he *so* made her nervous. She turned to the water and tried to take a deep, relaxing breath. With the ocean in front of her—a much more relaxing view than the one of the gorgeous, smug bastard behind her—it should have been no problem. But it took a few tries, and she had to close her eyes. When that didn't work, she added a stretch, rolling her shoulders, then lifting her arms high.

A low sound of male appreciation came from behind her in mid-stretch, and she turned to face him.

Sawyer's eyes lifted from the vicinity of her ass. "What are you playing at now?" he asked softly.

And wasn't that just the thing. "I don't think I'm playing," she said back, just as softly.

He studied her carefully, clearly searching for half truths.

But she never dealt in half truths. Or lies for that matter. Too much to remember. Nope, she liked her life dealt straight up. Possibly the one thing they had in common.

Sawyer stepped toward her, something in his stance making her feel like Little Red Riding Hood facing down the Big Bad Wolf. With the pier rail at her back, she tilted her head up to meet his gaze. "What?" she whispered.

"Is there something going on with you and Lance that I should know about?"

"No. Why?"

"Just trying to figure out if last night's fake caterwauling was a warm-up."

"For the real thing? No." She paused. "Caterwauling?"

He was giving her a complex. "It happens, you know. Screaming during sex." Although not to her, dammit.

"Does it?" he wondered. "Moaning, I get." He stepped even closer. Since she had nowhere to retreat to, his body touched hers. "Panting? Definitely." His voice dropped an octave. "Some dirty talk? Oh hell, yeah. But not that horrendous sound you were making, no."

He was warm, so deliciously warm. "It happens," Chloe repeated, having to lock her knees so they didn't wobble. She put a hand on his chest because he'd moved into her personal space and suddenly there wasn't nearly enough air.

"When?" he asked, his hand circling her wrist, and as he'd done once before, he let his thumb brush over the tiny tattoo there. "When does it happen?"

"Well...in books."

His eyes softened slightly at this and so did his mouth. "What kind of books are you reading, Chloe?"

"Er..." Okay, so *maybe* she'd been reading a lot of romances lately, so what? And maybe some erotica, too. There was nothing wrong with that, or daydreaming about being those women in the stories, the women who had enough breath in their lungs to scream in passion. "Not the point," she said, no longer certain what the point was.

And why the hell was he standing here teasing her instead of running? And..."Why did you ask about Lance?"

Sawyer stared into her face for a long, speculative moment. "So that I could do this." He cupped her jaw, then lowered his head until their lips nearly met. Not hesitant, not uncertain.

The opposite, in fact.

There was a beat of stillness, during which his gaze held hers prisoner while all her parts came alive and her eyes drifted shut. Their mouths brushed lightly, then not so lightly, and when his tongue touched hers, she moaned. At the sound, he threaded his hands in her hair and deepened the kiss.

She melted into him. There was no other word for what happened. One minute her bones were there and then in the next they were gone. Then as quickly as it'd started, it was over, and she was blinking up at him, her breathing nowhere close to under control. "Okay, what...what was that?"

Sawyer shoved a hand through his hair, leaving it tousled. "I don't know. You drive me crazy."

Just what a girl wanted to hear. She used her inhaler, and he frowned. "Come on," he said. "I'll walk you back."

"I can walk myself."

Her phone vibrated. She pulled the cell from her pocket and stared down at the ID. Todd. Because she hung out with Lance so much, she ran into Todd often. Occasionally he called her to see if she wanted to go out—his euphemism for hooking up.

Chloe might have earned the moniker the "wild child" here in Lucky Harbor, but she wasn't the "stupid child." Everyone knew there was simmering tension between Sawyer and Todd, and she wasn't going to be the cause of seeing it burst into flame. She hit ignore and shoved her phone back in her pocket.

"Problem?" Sawyer asked.

"Nope."

Their gazes met and held. He didn't say anything more

but stubbornly stuck by her side all the way back to the inn. He waited at the bottom of the steps while she climbed them and reached for the front door, making the mistake of looking back at him.

He was quite a sight standing there, muscles tense and gleaming from his run, sweats riding low on his hips. He looked dangerous, alluring, and hotter than sin. "I'm going to pretend that didn't happen. The kiss," she clarified.

"Can you?"

Her nipples were still hard so she sort of doubted it. It'd been a hell of a kiss. "It doesn't matter. The fact is that we experimented, got it out of our system. We're done with that now." She paused. "Right?"

"Yeah."

Not even a nanosecond of a hesitation. *Ouch.* "Okay, good," she said, lifting her chin. "Good, then."

Sawyer turned and began jogging back the way they'd just come. She watched him until he'd vanished from sight, then let herself drop to the top step, completely unsettled. Because for two people who valued the truth over all else, they'd both just lied their asses off.

# Chapter 5

*"When you don't know what you're doing, fake it."*

CHLOE TRAEGER

Chloe stepped inside the inn and came face-to-face with
a pissed-off Tara. "What?" Chloe asked, still a little off
her game from kissing Sawyer. *Sawyer.* Holy smokes.

"Where were you?"

"On a walk." Making out with the sheriff. "Why?"

"Because you were supposed to be here."

"I was gone for an hour before sunrise. We didn't have
any guests."

"No, but when a family of four stopped by, who'd been
driving all night, you weren't here. They were just leaving when I drove up."

"So you caught them in time."

"They didn't stay," Tara said. "They said they didn't
feel comfortable staying in a deserted inn."

"Shit. I'm sorry, I—"

Tara held up a hand. "If it's too much, sugar, just say
so. You can't fake your way through this."

"It's not too much." Goddammit. She swallowed the urge to get defensive. "I'll do better."

Tara nodded and went into the kitchen, leaving Chloe alone to wrestle with that promise.

\*         \*         \*

A few days later, Sawyer was off duty and running errands, which rated right up there with paperwork on his hate-to-do list. It didn't help that he'd spent the last twelve hours on a special task force working for the DEA. Under Agent Reed Morris, they'd tracked and rooted out a known drug dealer who'd holed up in Alder Flats, a particularly isolated, rugged area on the edge of the county. Ric Alfonso had been just one piece of a bigger puzzle they were working on, but despite their best efforts, it had ended badly.

Ric was now on a slab in the morgue, and Sawyer was questioning the sanity of his chosen profession. It wasn't the first time he'd been present at a death shot, and it probably wouldn't be the last, but Christ.

Ric had been nineteen years old.

At nineteen, Sawyer hadn't been dealing drugs, but he had been on the fast track to becoming a criminal. Which begged the question—what made the fragile difference between a life lost and a life won? Was it sheer guts and determination? Hard work? Karma? The question was too deep for him at the moment, stuck at a red light when he'd rather be flying over the water on Ford's boat, or lying on a warm beach with a woman, skimpy bikini optional.

Neither was in the cards for him, not today. He got some food, picked up his mail, and then drove to the heart of town, to a square block of small, ranch-style homes built back in the 1970s. Most had been repaired and reno-vated. Sawyer pulled into the driveway of one that hadn't. The garage door's springs were broken. The owner said he was having a guy take care of it, and though the owner's only living relative, a son, had offered to fix it nu-merous times, the offer had been firmly rebuked.

Tough. Sawyer spent the next half hour doing it him-self in spite of the fact that he wouldn't be thanked. The grass needed mowing again as well. He stretched the kink out of his neck as he went for the ancient lawn mower on the side of the house. It was a stall tactic, and he usually wasn't much for stalling, but he mowed the entire lawn and side yard, and finally, with nothing left to do, turned to the front door.

Nolan Thompson stood in the doorway. Sawyer's fa-ther was dressed today, which was an improvement over last week, when he'd faced Sawyer in his underwear. It was hard as hell to take the old man's righteous anger seriously when it was delivered with plaid cotton boxers sagging over a body ravaged by alcohol and fifty-plus years of physical labor.

"I told you I'd hired a kid to do this shit," his dad growled in the same low, gruff voice that once upon a time had struck terror to the depths of Sawyer's trouble-making soul.

It'd been that way until the day he'd realized he was bigger and badder than his father. Instead of taking his punishment for whatever stupid thing Sawyer had done that day—and Sawyer had no doubt it *had* been stupid—he'd shoved back.

He'd been sixteen. After that, the two of them had re-sorted to stony silence for Sawyer's last year in the house.

Contact had remained rare and estranged until Sawyer's twenty-fifth birthday, which he'd spent in the hospital at his father's side after Nolan's first heart attack. That had been ten years ago. Now their visits were still spent in silence, but there'd been two more heart attacks and a new frailty in his father that Sawyer hated.

Because it meant that every time Sawyer looked at him, he had no choice but to feel. Compassion, regret, guilt, whatever emotion bombarded him, he hated every minute of it. He looked around his father's yard. "So where is this paragon of virtue you've hired?"

"He'll be here."

"Uh-huh."

"Look, if he said he'd come, he'll come. He shows up on time, doesn't give me attitude, and doesn't rip me off."

Sawyer had stolen a twenty off his father's dresser exactly once. He'd been twelve and an idiot, but he'd been *twelve*, for God's sake. His father had never forgotten about it. But at least that infraction had been real.

Yeah, Sawyer had been a rotten-to-the-core kid and an even worse teenager. But Jesus, he'd been working his ass off ever since trying to make up for it, which should count for something.

It didn't.

Time had stopped for Nolan as far as Sawyer was concerned. "The garage door is fixed, so you can park in there again. And the grass needs watering."

Another gruff sound, maybe one of grudging appreciation, but that was probably wishful thinking on Sawyer's part. He took a peek inside the house. It was a mess again. Odds were the housekeeper that Sawyer had hired was chased off by Nolan's bad temper. Since the woman had also brought in the groceries, this meant his father was undoubtedly eating crap, not good with his restricted diet. "Didn't Sally come this week?"

"She's out of town."

Bullshit. Sawyer brushed by his father into the house and was bombarded with unhappy memories. He checked the fridge—nearly empty. Pulling some money out of his wallet, he set it on the kitchen table and turned to leave.

His father was blocking his way, eyes bright with anger and something else. Shame.

Shit. "I'll be back tomorrow with groceries and someone else to clean up," Sawyer said.

"Don't bother. I have the kid."

"Fine."

"Fine," Nolan snapped, then paused uncomfortably. "I, uh, have to get another angioplasty."

Sawyer's own heart skipped a beat. "When?"

"Friday."

"I'll be there."

"It's just a routine thing, no big deal."

"I'll be there, dammit."

Sawyer left feeling like shit. Nothing new there. Needing a caffeine kick, he parked at the convenience store, and for just a moment, leaned back and closed his eyes. He needed something, and caffeine wasn't it.

Balls-to-the-wall sex had a nice ring to it.

A shout interrupted the thought. Glass shattered, followed by running footsteps, which was never good. Sawyer straightened just as a guy came barreling out of the convenience store, hugging his sweatshirt close to his body as if protecting something.

A piece of paper fluttered from the sweatshirt.

Aw, Christ on a stick, Sawyer thought, catching a flash of green. Not paper.

*Money*.

The guy hopped into a banged-up Celica and sped away with a show of squealing tires and smoke.

*Goddammit*. Sawyer hit the gas to follow as he called dispatch to report that he'd caught a robbery in progress. The piece-of-shit sedan in front of him turned right at the end of town, obviously headed toward the open high-way. At the freeway entrance, there were two delivery vans, moving slow as molasses. The car swerved around them, heading directly into a small, quiet neighborhood filled with midsized houses, hard-working people, and kids. Lots of kids.

Sawyer swore again and kept on the car's bumper while simultaneously keeping dispatch abreast of their coordinates. Thankfully it was midday, both a work and school day, and the streets were relatively empty.

At the corner, the sedan went up and over the sidewalk and popped the two right tires. By the middle of the next street, the car was slowing, then drifting to a complete stop.

"Don't run," Sawyer said under his breath, pulling up behind him. "Don't fucking run." He *hated* foot chases. But, of course, in the next second, the suspect had abandoned his car and was hauling ass down the street.

"*Fuck*." Grabbing a spare set of cuffs, Sawyer shoved them into the back of his jeans and hit the pavement. "Stop," he yelled. "Police."

The suspect didn't stop. Of course not. Goddammit. Sawyer shook his head and followed with the ease that running five miles every day afforded him. He didn't run for pleasure. Hell no. He ran every day, rain or snow or shine, so he didn't lose assholes like this one. He chased the guy through a yard, over a fence, and into some bushes, yelling at the few curious people poking their heads out to "get back inside!" Closing the distance, Sawyer made a swipe for the guy's sweatshirt and hauled him to the ground.

They landed hard, the suspect on the bottom, limp as a rag doll. Great, Sawyer thought. He'd killed him.

But then the guy groaned, and Sawyer was glad for it. Less paperwork if he was alive. He put a knee in the guy's back and reached for his cuffs. "What the hell was that?"

The suspect shook his head. *"No Ingles."*

*No problemo*. Sawyer had some Spanish. He could say "give me a beer," "throw down your weapon, asshole," and lucky for this idiot, he could also recite the Miranda rights.

\*     \*     \*

It took another two hours and more paperwork before Sawyer could go. He had aching knees from the take-down and a mother of a headache brewing, but it was the adrenaline flowing through him that sent him straight to the gym.

Working out wasn't his first choice for letting down the adrenaline. That honor would still go to the balls-to-the-wall sex he'd wished for earlier, but that wasn't in the cards for him today.

The gym he went to was small but new, and state of the art. A friend of his met him here several times a week. Matt Bowers was a district supervisor forest ranger, and Sawyer's sparring partner.

Sawyer changed and found Matt beating the hell out of a punching bag. "Why don't you try someone who'll fight back?" Sawyer asked.

Matt turned and looked Sawyer over. "I'll get more action out of the bag. You're looking soft, Thompson."

Sawyer smiled. They both knew Sawyer was in top fighting shape himself; he made sure of it. He let out a sound mimicking a chicken clucking.

Matt smiled, one of the few people in Lucky Harbor not intimidated by Sawyer's size. With good reason, since Matt was an ex-cop from Chicago, and deceptively laid-back. "Having a bad day?"

"Yeah, I broke a nail."

Matt grinned. "Pussy."

They beat the shit out of each other for the next thirty minutes before finally dropping to their backs on the mat, gasping for breath.

"You going to tell me what crawled up your ass?" Matt managed to ask.

"No." Wheezing, Sawyer studied the ceiling while he waited for his heart to stop drumming in his ears.

"I know it's not a woman," Matt said. "You don't have one. You've scared them all off."

"Fuck you."

Matt chuckled. "Not my type, man. I like 'em soft and pretty." He paused. "Is it work?"

It was his life, Sawyer thought wearily.

"I'd try to beat it out of you some more, but I can't feel my legs," Matt said.

"So *who's* the pussy exactly?"

Matt snorted and managed to get to his feet. "I'm hitting the shower."

Sawyer lay there for another moment. He'd definitely gotten rid of the excess energy and adrenaline. His body was letting down now, or so the level of pain indicated anyway. Dripping sweat and holding his sore ribs, he staggered to his feet and came face-to-face with Chloe.

She was dressed for a workout in black, cropped yoga pants and a yellow sports bra that he needed sunglasses to look at. Not that *that* stopped him.

"You got your ass kicked, Sheriff."

"Fuck if I did."

"I don't know." She cocked her head to look him over. "Your hot friend got to his feet much easier than you."

"Hot?"

"Mmm-hmm. Your lip's bleeding, Sheriff."

Sawyer swiped at his lip and resisted the urge to grab a ridiculous amount of weights and do an arm curl. "I'm fine."

"Okay," she said doubtfully. "If you're sure…"

Jesus. A minute ago he'd doubted that he could drag himself to the shower, but now he sat heavily on a weight bench and reached for the weights.

Chloe raised a brow but said nothing more as she put in her earphones and sat on a weight bench facing away from him.

"What about your asthma?"

"This isn't cardio. I'm good as long as I go slow." Then she began to work her arms, moving that taut, curvy body to some mysterious beat.

Sawyer watched her. He couldn't help himself. She'd piled her glorious mass of red hair into a ponytail that swung back and forth with her every arm curl. Her shoulders were straight, the lean muscles in her back sleek and feminine. She had the best ass he'd ever seen. Sure there were other cute butts in the gym, but Chloe's was right there in front of him, drawing his gaze. He was very busy attempting to see as much of it as he could when she turned her head and caught him.

He hurriedly pushed up the weights and was relieved when his arms obeyed and he didn't totally humiliate himself.

Chloe was watching him, something new in her eyes now, something hot and lethal and dark.

And just like that, as if she'd let out a mating call, the matching hot, lethal, dark place inside *him* reared its head. Good thing he'd long ago beaten that part of him back, trading it in for a different kind of life. One he could depend on, no matter what obstacles he faced. Which, of course, didn't stop him from pushing the weights up again. He would have decapitated himself for sure if two big hands hadn't appeared to stop him.

Matt.

Hair wet from his shower, he looked down at Sawyer and smirked as he pulled all but twenty-five pounds of the weights off. "There," he said patronizingly. "*Now* you can go ahead and show off for the pretty lady." He shot a warm smile and a quick wink Chloe's way.

Chloe smiled back.

And Sawyer wished he'd pounded Matt into the floor when he'd had the chance.

# Chapter 6

*"It may be that your sole purpose in life is
simply to serve as a warning to others."*

CHLOE TRAEGER

Chloe had always loved traveling for her work, meeting
new people, going from place to place. It was reminiscent
of the wanderlust gypsy life she'd had growing up with
Phoebe, and in its own odd way, was comforting.

But now there was Lucky Harbor and her sisters, and
against all odds, these things gave her comfort, too. It'd
taken months to figure out exactly why, but sitting on the
counter in the B&B's large, homey kitchen, stirring up a
bowl of avocado and mayonnaise, she finally got it.

It was because for the first time in her entire life, she
had a sort of home base. It was extremely new, and if she
was being honest, not as claustrophobic as she'd imagined. She was at war with herself over it.

Luckily she didn't have much time to dwell on it. Later
today, she'd be giving spa treatments at an upscale Port-
land boutique hotel, and since her products were all made

up of fresh ingredients, she had a hell of a lot of work to do to prepare. "That smells...interesting," Tara said. She was at the center island, cooking away. As the oldest, she'd gotten the lion's share of imperturbability. Neatness, too. Despite getting ready to cook breakfast for the three guests they'd had show up last night, there wasn't a hair out of place or a crumb or speck on her pretty black wool trousers and crisp white blouse. And how she cooked and served in those heels was beyond Chloe.

Chloe eyed her own feet, comfy in ballet flats. Everything she wore was built for comfort: leggings, long cami top with a cropped sweater open over it. "How do you stay so neat all the time?"

Tara smiled. She was doing a lot more of that now that she was getting laid regularly by Ford, one of the sexiest guys Chloe had ever met.

"Well, I'm not mixing up a batch of"—Tara peered into Chloe's bowl—"stinky green stuff for spa clients."

"It's avocado and mayonnaise hair conditioner, and it's not stinky. It works better than your fifty-dollar conditioner."

"Avocado and mayo?" Tara's Southern accent was faint and charming when she was amused. "Your fancy clients are going to put that in their hair?"

"It's 'au natural.' Back to basics and all that. Plus, it's loaded with all sorts of good fats and oils. People love it."

"You know what I'd love, sugar? Help with the dishes."

Better than cleaning toilets, Chloe told herself, and she did plenty of those as well. "I really miss Mia."

At the mention of Tara's teenage daughter—whom Tara had when she was a teen herself—Tara smiled. "I miss her, too."

Last summer, Mia had worked here at the inn, helping with the cleaning and whatever was needed, giving Chloe a welcome break. But Mia was in Spain now, spending her senior year of high school as an exchange student.

Setting her bowl down, Chloe ran hot water in the sink and was halfway through the pile of pots and pans when Maddie came into the kitchen. She was carrying an armful of dishes that she must have collected out of the guest rooms, all of which she set into the sink with a sweet smile.

Dammit. Chloe added more hot water to the sink.

"Oh, and hey," Maddie said, turning back to her. "I'm nearly out of that face mask you made me, the one with strawberries, oatmeal, and honey. Can I get some more?"

"Sure." Chloe would be making up a batch today anyway. "Did you like the scent? Because I can switch the strawberries with—"

"No, don't change a single thing. Jax says it makes me glow."

Tara and Chloe exchanged a look. Good as Chloe's mask was, and it *was* good, it wasn't the ingredients making Maddie glow.

That would be the sex.

Maddie looked into the bowl of avocado conditioner, swirling the spoon around, sniffing curiously. "Dip?" She grabbed a bread stick from the counter and scooped up a dollop of the hair treatment.

"Chloe, don't you dare let your sister eat hair conditioner," Tara said, not looking up as she expertly flipped her omelet.

"Hair conditioner?" Maddie narrowed her eyes at Chloe and threw the bread stick at her.

Chloe ducked and grinned. "It's just avocado and mayo. And you need it, too. It'd fix your frizz problem."

Maddie's hand flew to her hair. She had a mass of brown curls, rarely tamed unless it was tied back. Today was no different. It fell in curls to her shoulders, looking full and thick, and, well, frizzy.

"And your shirt's inside out again," Chloe noted.

"It is not." But Maddie stretched out the collar of her tee to see it and eyed the stitching on the outside. "*Crap.*"

"You still dressing in the dark, or what?" Chloe asked.

That was what Maddie had tried to tell them last week when she'd shown up at the inn all flushed, mussed, and wearing her shirt inside out.

Maddie whipped her shirt off to turn it right side out. She was wearing a pink bra and a hickey on her collarbone.

Chloe burst out laughing. "Go, Jax."

"He didn't— We weren't—" Maddie sagged. "Oh, forget it." She clapped her hands to her cheeks. "I jumped him on the way over here."

"While *driving*?" Tara asked in horror.

Maddie was beet red now. "We…pulled over." A ridiculous grin escaped. "I just always want to eat him up. Does it ever stop?"

"I don't know," Chloe admitted. "But for your sake, I hope not." If anyone deserved happiness, it was Maddie. Before coming to Lucky Harbor, a bad experience with an ex had put Maddie off men entirely. Then she'd met Jax. With a little bit of patience, along with his easy, outgoing personality, Jax had woman-whispered Maddie right out of her shell. Now they were getting married.

Given the long-enduring and heated love that Tara and

Ford also shared, Chloe had no doubt that they'd soon be following suit down the aisle as well.

It was wonderful for them. And exciting, too. But Chloe wasn't quite sure what it all meant for her. What her plan would be, or what kind of future she'd have...

"You'll find it, too," Maddie said softly, watching Chloe. "Love."

"Oh," Chloe said, shaking her head. "No. I don't need—"

"You will," Maddie promised and hugged her. "Maybe after you settle down a little."

Ah, there it was. The problem. The *real* problem. In order to find that elusive acceptance that she craved, Chloe had to "settle down," had to stop being who she was. Grow up. No more letting her sister eat hair conditioner...

But dammit, hadn't she taken on her share of the responsibility for this place? Hadn't she cut back drastically on the constant traveling to help with the inn? Shifted her schedule so that most of the trips she took were only day trips now, and doing so only when she could, between guests?

Chloe had done everything asked of her. And yet it still wasn't enough. Feeling a tightening in her chest that might have been anxiety or an oncoming asthma attack, she pulled out her inhaler and took a puff.

"Already?" Maddie asked with some concern. "You're having trouble breathing today already?"

Chloe shrugged. In times of stress, they all had their ways of coping. Maddie mainlined potato chips. Tara cooked. Chloe used her inhaler. "Maybe I don't want to settle down."

"Everyone does eventually," Maddie said.

"I don't think it's for me." Not looking at either sister, Chloe added more soap to the hot water and dug into the pile of dishes, searching for happy thoughts. Chocolate. Puppies. Rainbows.

*Guys.*

Yeah, guys always worked as a nice distraction. She thought of Matt Bowers, the sexy forest ranger she'd seen at the gym. Then there was Dr. Josh Scott, the ER doc. She'd met him during a particularly rough asthma attack when she'd landed in the ER on his shift, and they'd since run into each other several times. He'd asked Chloe out but she'd been too busy balancing her travels with the inn. Maybe it was time to sync their schedules and play doctor together.

And then there was Cute Guy. She didn't know his name. He was a new Lucky Harbor resident and a real mystery. He'd moved into a house on the bluffs, an expensive one. Even the Facebook mavens had been caught by surprise. No one knew what Cute Guy did or who he was, but Chloe had seen him at the grocery store, and he was H-O-T.

And yet as she washed the last pot, it was a different man entirely who popped into her head and made her breath catch—the one who wore both a gun and a bad attitude with such wild sexiness that he'd begun to haunt her dreams.

As had their kiss. Yowza, that kiss. She'd been ignoring him just fine before that. "Damn sheriff," she muttered, scrubbing hard at the reticent pot.

"Sawyer?" Tara asked.

Chloe closed her eyes. "No, that's my point. *Not*

Sawyer. I want Matt. Or Josh. Or Cute Guy. Hell, even Anderson at the hardware store. *Not* the sheriff, thank you very much."

What followed was such an awkward silence that Chloe could feel it blister her back. With her stomach knotting on itself, she turned to face the room.

Sawyer stood in the back doorway, in uniform, armed, silent, filling up the entire room with his presence.

There was a long beat during which nobody breathed.

"Nothing personal," Chloe said to Sawyer with as much dignity as she could muster, which wasn't much. But hell, she had to be the last woman on the planet that he'd pick, too, so no harm no foul, she figured. Except their gazes were locked now, reminding her of how his mouth had felt slanted over hers, hot and hungry, and a sudden, rather powerful longing filled her.

Okay, time to get the hell out of Dodge. She needed to think. Preferably alone, on top of a mountain somewhere. As for what Sawyer needed, it was hard to tell. He was a rock when he wanted to be.

Tara handed him a mug of coffee to go. "Guess you're wishing you'd stopped at Starbucks this morning, huh?" she quipped, clearly trying to lighten the tension.

"Can't go into places like that in uniform," Sawyer told her.

"Why not?"

"Sometimes people spit in the food or drinks when they see a cop."

"Well, in all my born days," Tara murmured, her accent thickening with her temper as she spoke into the horrified silence.

Chloe shut off the water and stared at Sawyer, her

unhappy awkwardness replaced with something that felt like possessive protectiveness. "Why would you do it then, be a cop, just to be treated like that?"

"You mean besides the glory?" he asked dryly, then shrugged. "I'm good at it."

She knew he was. He was doggedly determined and aggressive behind that calm veneer, which served his job well. It probably served him well in other areas too.

Like in bed.

Sawyer looked into the bowl of avocado/mayo mix. "What's that?"

"*Not* dip," Maddie said quickly.

"It's hair conditioner," Tara told him. "For the frizzies."

Everyone looked at Sawyer's wind tousled, fawn-colored hair. It fell thick and silky to his collar. No frizzies, the bastard.

"I think I'm good," he said. He was leaning back against the counter, clearly right at home, feet casually crossed, long legs at rest, the muscles of his thighs pressing against the material of his uniform.

Yeah, he was good... "Your skin's dry." Chloe nodded to the bottle next to the conditioner, which held a special blend of vitamin E and tea tree oil in a petroleum jelly base. "That'd cure your problem." Though she had nothing to cure the big, bad, broody thing he had going on. "That is, if you're not still afraid I'm going to poison you..."

He looked at her steadily, then picked up the bottle, which looked small and feminine in his big hand. Very gingerly, as if maybe he was holding a bomb, he lifted the lid and took a sniff. "Smells like flowers."

"Does that threaten your manhood?" Chloe asked.

Tara opened her mouth to object, but Sawyer laughed, the sound low and slightly rusty, as if he didn't have a lot of reason to laugh lately.

"Use it twice a day," Chloe said. "And you'll be glowing in no time. Just like Maddie here."

He looked like he wanted to say something about Maddie's "glow" but he squelched it. Smart man.

"I heard about what's been going on," Tara said to him. "You okay?"

"Yeah," Sawyer said. "It's another angioplasty. He'll be fine."

Tara paused. "I meant at work. Who's having an angioplasty?"

Sawyer sighed. "My father. It's just routine. He's too ornery to let a heart problem slow him down." His face was calm and blank. The cop face again, which meant he didn't want to talk about it.

"Tell us about the robber," Maddie said.

"What robber?" Chloe asked.

Maddie looked at Sawyer, who just sipped his coffee.

"He single-handedly caught the convenience store robber," Tara told Chloe. "You didn't see it? It was all over the papers. I e-mailed you the link."

Hmm. Maybe she should've checked her e-mail last night instead of hanging out with Lance. "The convenience store got held up?"

"And Sawyer was outside the store when the thief made a run for it," Tara said. "Money falling out of his pockets as he went."

Sawyer shook his head, like he still couldn't believe the stupidity of the guy.

"Sawyer chased him in his car," Tara went on. "And then on foot, with innocent people getting barreled over by the suspect. The librarian broke her ankle."

Chloe gasped. "Ms. Bunyan?"

Tara nodded. "Finally Sawyer pulled his gun and got a few shots off before tackling the guy to the ground. By the time the rest of the cavalry came, Sawyer had the guy subdued and cuffed."

Chloe stared at Sawyer, who was looking mildly annoyed. "Really?" she asked him.

"No. Ms. Bunyan broke her ankle when she came running out of her house looking at her cell phone instead of where she was going, trying to record a video for YouTube. She was nowhere close to the action."

"But there *was* action, right?" Maddie asked. "Gunshots?"

"*No* gunshots," he said.

"Well, damn," Maddie said, disappointed. "I like Tara's version better."

Chloe didn't. Not at all. She was glad there'd been no shots fired, but that still left the chase, the tackle, the wrestling... It wasn't the first time she'd been forcibly reminded of how dangerous Sawyer's job could be, but she marveled just the same at the ease in which he faced it all, day in and day out. "Are you okay?"

Sawyer met her gaze. Right. He was always okay. And if he wasn't, no one would ever know otherwise because he'd keep it to himself. The thought made her wonder if maybe they didn't have more in common with each other than she'd imagined possible.

"The paper said that the perp was in the middle of a divorce, and he just snapped," Tara said. "His ex is taking him to the cleaner's, and he's going around stealing money to pay his lawyers. Takes all kinds of crazy."

Sawyer nodded, and Chloe had to laugh at the resigned look on his face. Clearly he had seen the "all kinds of crazy."

"You were definitely the talk of the town yesterday," Maddie said. "Our hero." She grinned as he grimaced and pushed away from the counter.

"But that's not all that happened to you yesterday," Tara said.

Sawyer slanted her a look. "Yes, it is."

"Nope. You also got called to Mrs. Abbott's house."

"Which turned out to be nothing," Sawyer said.

"Not exactly nothing," Maddie broke in.

"Maddie." Sawyer's voice was meant to scold, but he actually sounded patient and maybe slightly amused. Definitely gentle.

Chloe was fascinated by this glimpse of a gentle Sawyer. But then again, Maddie inspired that in a man.

Chloe sure as hell didn't. "What happened? Is Mrs. Abbott okay?"

"Mrs. Abbott's fine," Sawyer said.

"Only because you rode in on your white horse to save the day." Maddie turned to Chloe. "Her smoke alarm went off, and Sawyer got there first."

"Oh no," Chloe said, genuinely dismayed. Mrs. Abbott was a favorite of hers. Chloe made her a special moisturizer weekly, the only thing that helped ease the older woman's psoriasis symptoms. They had tea, and Mrs. Abbott would regale Chloe with tales of her wild youth. "Was there a fire?"

"No." Clearly trying to get out before Maddie finished her story, Sawyer moved to the door.

Chloe tore her gaze off his very fine ass and glanced at her sister.

"No fire," Maddie assured her. "And not twenty minutes later, the smoke alarm went off again. And then again, with Sawyer responding each time."

Sawyer stopped with a sigh. "Only once more, not twice."

"I have *got* to start reading Facebook," Chloe said. "What was wrong?"

Maddie grinned. "Her smoke alarm needed a new battery."

"Aw," Chloe said. "Those things are a bitch."

"No, the 'aw' is that Sawyer went to the store for her and bought a battery," Maddie said. "Then he came back and put it in for her. So sweet."

Sawyer looked pained. "Not sweet, a necessity. I was tired of driving out there."

"*Sweet*," Maddie repeated.

Chloe snorted, and Sawyer's eyes cut to hers. "Like *you'd* want to be called sweet," he said.

"Not me," she said. "But then again, I'm not even halfway close to sweet."

And truthfully, neither was he, she thought. He was big and bad and alpha and gorgeous and smart and brave and loyal...

But not sweet. *Hell*, no.

"It's okay," Tara told him, patting his shoulder. "Your secret's safe with us."

"Bullshit if it is," he grumbled. "You'll tell Ford and Jax. And Jax's such a girl that he'll tell...everyone."

"And what'll happen then?" Chloe asked. "Will they revoke your man card?"

In tune to Maddie's and Tara's laughter, Sawyer muttered something beneath his breath about the entire female gender and was gone.

# Chapter 7

*"Always remember, you're unique.
Just like everyone else."*

CHLOE TRAEGER

The next day Sawyer was sitting in the hospital, waiting to hear how his father's surgery had gone. The TV was tuned to some soap opera, and there was no remote in sight. After two hours, he was feeling a little trigger happy and might have shot the thing, but Chloe showed up. She plopped down next to him.

"*All My Children?*" she asked. "Didn't peg you as the type."

"I'm not watching it."

She made the exaggerated motion of checking out the room.

He was the only one in it.

He pinched the bridge of his nose. "What are you doing here?"

She handed him a bag. "Bringing you pick-me-up

muffins from Tara. Banana–chocolate chip. She says they can fix anything."

Well, that explained her presence. Tara had sent her on a Good Samaritan errand. There were four muffins in the sack. He handed one to her and started in on the other three, finishing them before she'd finished hers.

"Hey. How's that a fair division?" she asked.

"Weight ratio."

She slid her eyes over his body, and if he wasn't mistaken, she also sucked in a breath, but all she said was "Hmm."

She finished her muffin before she said, "Oh! Almost forgot!" and pulled out a thermos from her huge purse. "Milk."

He offered her the first sip, and when she shook her head, he downed it.

"Better?" she asked.

He nodded, and she laughed softly. "Don't hog all the words, Sheriff." Not appearing overly insulted, she settled in next to him, leaning back in the uncomfortable chair, her legs stretched in front of her, crossed at the ankles.

"I figure we can do this one of two ways," she said. "Awkward silence, or I could keep talking and you can pretend to listen."

"Or you could leave."

"Yeah, but it's much more fun to stay and make you squirm."

"You don't make me squirm."

Her fathomless green eyes met his. "I make you something."

Yeah. She sure as hell did. "Annoyed?" he offered. "Irritated? Frustrated? Infuriated?"

"Horny."

He shook his head, but hell if she wasn't right. "Option two."

"Irritated?" she asked.

"No. You talk."

She laughed, then talked about her last trip to Belize, where she'd gotten the small tattoo on the inside of her wrist, which apparently meant "Be Yourself." "Hurt like a bitch," she said. "And Tara's certain that I'll never land a corporate job because of the location—it's hard to cover it up. She'd probably freak if she saw my other tat, but she won't because it's ... discreetly placed," she said, flashing a grin.

Sawyer thought about that for a very pleasant beat, enjoying the distraction of picturing where and what that might be. "Do you anticipate wanting a job in the corporate world?" he asked, unable to envision her in an office setting, all tamed and subdued.

She laughed. "Sitting behind a desk making nice? No, I'm not sure I have that in me."

"What *do* you have in you?"

Chloe looked surprised at the question. "Well, I'd like to get this natural skincare line I'm creating off the ground."

"That sounds ... surprisingly corporate."

"Bite your tongue," she said.

He found himself smiling.

"Wow," she said. "You should do that a *lot* more."

He ignored that. "You like what you do."

"Well, yeah. Isn't that the point?"

He opened his mouth, then closed it again, conceding with a nod. "Did you always know what you wanted to do?"

"Yeah. When I was little, I camped with my mom all the time. Did you know that?"

He shook his head. He didn't know much about her past at all. He'd known Phoebe though, and she hadn't exactly been the mothering type.

"Maddie and Tara grew up with their dads, but I was with Phoebe. Camping," Chloe said. "Mostly we traveled from one Grateful Dead concert to the next; sometimes we'd go off for another adventure. But I always had everything I owned in a little *Saved by the Bell* backpack."

He felt something tighten in his chest, and it took him a moment to speak. "That must have been hard for a little girl." His childhood had been a world away. He'd had a house, a *miserable* house, but a roof over his head regardless.

"Oh, I liked it," Chloe said. "I mean, we were poor as dirt, of course, but I didn't know that. We made the things we needed when we could. Soap, shampoo, stuff like that. I loved figuring out which scents went best with which ingredients."

Of course, she would have made the best of the cards she'd been dealt. But the nomad life had to have been rough. He had no idea how things would have been different for him without Ford and Jax, who'd given him a taste of stability. And then, after getting arrested, he'd found a different, even more stabilizing force in his arresting officer, of all people. Sheriff Allen Coburn had been the first adult to take the time to show interest. To care. He'd straightened Sawyer's ass out by checking on him weekly, and had until his death a few years back.

It didn't sound like Chloe had had any such stabilizing forces, at least not until this past year. "Moving around like that," he said. "How did you go to school and make friends?"

"Phoebe homeschooled me for the most part, until high school. We settled in San Francisco for a while because she had a boyfriend who was a theater stagehand. I went to school there."

"You and your mom lived with the boyfriend?"

"No, he lived in his car in the theater lot. We camped then, too, a lot." She shrugged, like no big deal; it was what it was. "I made friends wherever we were; that wasn't really a problem. It's easier now, of course, having a home."

So the B&B with her sisters was the first real home she'd ever had, which tightened the knot in his chest.

"What about you?" she asked.

"What about me?"

"You grew up here."

"Yes."

She gave him a long look, waiting impatiently for him to open up. "Come on," she said. "Give me something. Do you have any tattoos?" she asked. "Childhood stories? Something you want to share with the class? Anything?"

"I thought the deal was that you talk and I sit."

She shook her head. "I looked you up, you know." She nudged her shoulder to his. "And for a town that loves gossip more than Walmart, there's not a lot about you out there. Actually it's kind of nice that the people here are so protective of their big, bad sheriff."

Protective? He shook his head, but he should have known she wasn't going to let it drop. "Is that no, you're just boring as sin?" she asked. "Or no, you're being obtuse simply because you can and it's what you do best?"

He laughed just as the surgeon came out. Suddenly somber again, Sawyer got to his feet and braced himself for the worst, but the doctor assured him that his father's procedure had gone well. In sheer relief, he sank back to the chair. Why he gave a damn was a complete mystery. Nolan Thompson thought his son wasn't worth his time. That wasn't going to change because of an angioplasty. A heart replacement, maybe...

Chloe sat, too, and slipped her arm around him, resting her head on his shoulder. She didn't speak, just gave him a moment. Which was another surprise. She was always in such perpetual motion, always working so hard at driving him up a wall. Or hell, maybe it wasn't hard work at all, maybe it came easy to her.

But now, right this very minute, she was here. For him. Soft and warm and caring. What the hell was she doing here anyway? And why did it feel so damn right? Unable to resist, he gathered her in close. Just for a minute he told himself, pressing his face into her sweet-smelling hair, absorbing the quiet comfort she was offering.

Finally they rose from their chairs, and in another surprise, she stared up into his face. With a satisfied nod that he was apparently looking okay in her book, she went up on tiptoe and kissed his jaw. And then she walked out of the room just as mysteriously as she'd arrived, leaving in her wake an odd void that he couldn't name.

\* \* \*

Three nights later, after a helluva day, Sawyer dragged his sorry, aching ass into the Love Shack, the bar co-owned by Jax and Ford. That morning, it had snowed for about five seconds, just enough to screw up the roads. Which meant that every call Sawyer had gone on after that had been a life-or-death situation just getting out of his damn SUV. Twice he'd been out on the highway handling traffic control, and twice he'd been nearly hit by some idiot going too fast for the conditions.

But it had been his last call that had gotten to him—a fatal accident just outside Lucky Harbor. A twenty-year-old kid drinking and driving had wrapped himself around a tree.

Once upon a time, Sawyer had nearly been that kid. On that long-ago night, Sawyer hadn't been driving but he'd been just as drunk as the driver when they'd hit a pole.

Sawyer had managed to live through that accident, and while he'd like to think that it had straightened his ass out, it had actually been several more years before that happened.

Now, icy cold to the bone, he headed toward the bar's front door just as another man came out.

Todd, whose eyes narrowed at the sight of Sawyer. Sawyer returned the look evenly. Saying something unintelligible beneath his breath, Todd shoulder-checked Sawyer hard and headed out into the night.

Sawyer was in the mood for a fight and nearly followed Todd to get one. But common sense prevailed, and he let Todd go. He headed into the bar, hoping to warm up.

The Love Shack was done up like an old Western saloon. The walls were a sinful bordello red and lined with old mining tools. Exposed wooden beams high above supported lanterns, which hung over the scarred bench-style tables, now filled with the rowdy weekend crowd.

Sawyer walked straight through the bar to Ford's office in the back. He'd changed out of his dirty uniform at the station and was in plainclothes now, but still armed. He locked his utility belt and the majority of his weapons into an empty locker that the guys kept for him and moved back out to the bar.

"Well, if it isn't the local hero," Ford noted when Sawyer sat at the bar. "Change any smoke alarm batteries lately?"

"Shut up." Sawyer watched him pour his usual soda. "Make that a beer."

Ford raised a brow as he hit the tap. "Fucked-up day?"

"Fucked-up day." Sawyer took a long pull from the beer, still seeing the kid's sightless eyes as he lay forever still on the asphalt forty-five feet from where he'd been flung from his car.

Not five minutes later, Maddie waltzed out from the storage room looking a little tousled, which meant Jax was undoubtedly close by. She smiled at Sawyer and helped herself to an ice water while Ford called out to one of his servers, "An order of fish and chips for the sheriff," he said. "Double the chips." He looked at Sawyer. "Anything else?"

It was a well-known fact that Sawyer ate like a truck driver. He shrugged. "I'm not real hungry."

Ford's brow rose again. "Should I hold the fries?"

"Just the double part."

Maddie and Ford exchanged a worried look, and then Maddie slipped onto the stool next to Sawyer. "You okay?"

It used to be that no one ever asked him that. People just assumed that he was, or at least that he would be. Then the three sisters had come to town. Two of them had snagged his best friends, and now one or another sister was forever asking him if he was okay. "Just not that hungry is all."

Jax came out of the storage room. He pulled Maddie off her stool, sat in her place, then tugged her into his lap, nuzzling at her hair, one hand sliding to her ass. "Hey, babe. Feeling a little better now?"

Jesus, Sawyer thought. They even had Jax asking about feelings.

But Maddie melted against her man. "Much. Sawyer's had a bad day, though. He says he's not hungry."

Jax looked at Sawyer, brows up.

Sawyer ignored him, and when his food came, hunkered in to eat to prove he was fine. Jax leaned close to help himself to a fry. "Since you're not hungry— *Hey*," he grumbled when Sawyer stabbed him with his fork. "Well, there's nothing wrong with your reflexes anyway." Giving Maddie a smacking kiss, Jax went back to work.

Maddie watched him go with a dreamy sigh. "I'm going to marry him."

"God knows why." Sawyer reached for the ketchup, and Maddie laughed.

"He makes me happy," she said. "He makes me…everything. You know?"

Sawyer looked into her warm eyes and nodded, not wanting to disappoint her. She smiled and hugged him, then kissed his cheek. "You're sweet to humor me."

He nearly choked on a fry. There was the *sweet* again. He should have killed someone this week; that would have taken care of that.

A few minutes later, Chloe came in. Sawyer took a deep breath that he hadn't realized he'd been holding. Forget killing someone. He wanted…her.

He'd been thinking about that ever since she'd surprised him at the hospital. Dreaming about it, too. Dreams hot enough to singe his sheets.

She pulled off a black leather jacket, revealing an eye-popping red sweater, a tiny denim skirt, tights, and knee-high boots. And Christ, the boots gave him ideas. Not that he needed more. Her glossy, dark red hair was wind tousled and cascading over her shoulders, making him think of those dreams he'd had. In detail.

Or maybe that was just her. *She* made him think of sex. Hot, wild, no-holds-barred sex...

Chloe came up to the bar and met his gaze for a long, timeless beat. She didn't ask him if he was okay. She didn't weigh him down with her worry. She didn't even give him her usual I-don't-give-a-shit sardonic smile. No, she just looked at him with those deep green eyes, and he found himself wanting to fall in and drown.

He also wanted another drink, and possibly a vacation. Definitely he should get laid. Maybe a tall, stacked blonde who didn't give a damn about his feelings, who's only words would be "Harder, Sawyer, fuck me harder."

Except he didn't want a tall, stacked blonde.

He wanted a petite, curvy, wild, redhead. He wanted *this* petite, curvy, wild redhead.

"After a tough day," Chloe said softly, "I always need something a little...crazy. Something a little off center to nudge me back into place."

He was much farther gone than he'd thought if that made perfect sense to him.

"But maybe that's just me," she said to his silence. "Probably an Eagle Scout doesn't feel the need for crazy."

"Eagle Scout?"

She smiled. "Did I say Eagle Scout? I meant an officer of the law, sorry."

Bullshit she was sorry. She thought he was a straight arrow. He knew that. He'd let her think it because it suited his purposes. They needed distance between them.

Lots of distance.

But tonight he wasn't feeling so straight arrow, and he sure as hell wasn't feeling distant. "Sometimes crazy works."

"Don't tease me," Chloe said. "We have very different ideas of crazy. I mean like zip-lining over snapping alligators." She nudged the drink in front of him. "You mean having a single beer."

"You have no idea what I mean."

She lowered her head slightly in acknowledgment and might have spoken but some guy shoved his way between them and slammed his hands down on the bar. Obviously already two sheets to the wind—hell, make that four sheets gone—he waved a drunken hand in Jax's direction. "Hey, dude, hurry the fuck up. We need another pitcher at our table, pronto!"

"That's the last thing you need," Sawyer said.

The guy whirled on him, eyes flashing with ready-made temper. Sawyer lifted his shirt to reveal the badge hooked on his belt, then pointed for the guy to go back to his table.

"Impressive," Chloe said when the guy did just that. She waited a beat. "You've had a long day."

Sawyer lifted a shoulder.

"Heard about the fatality."

He didn't reply. Nothing to say. But she just kept looking at him, with something far too close to sympathy in her gaze. He didn't want sympathy. He wanted her, wrapped around him, chanting his name as he pounded himself into her over and over again.

She didn't break eye contact, and as tended to happen when he got sucked into her vortex, everything else seemed to fade away. The general din of the bar, the music, the faces of the two men who were more brothers than friends, everything…it was just him and her.

She touched him, just a light stroke of her fingers over his shoulder, and though his body tightened, he felt himself breathe a little easier.

Her mouth slowly curved. Her eyes were warm, with a hint of challenge and quite possibly concern.

He didn't want the concern.

But the challenge…yeah. He'd take that.

"You're tense," Chloe said. Standing up, she moved behind him, putting her hands on his shoulders. She dug her fingers into his tight muscles, working them with a surprising strength, until he melted into a puddle at her feet.

"Better?" she murmured against his ear, making him nearly groan when she pressed her breasts against him.

Was she kidding? The only way for this to be better would be for them to be alone and naked. But someone called her name, and she moved away to talk to friends, leaving him staring after her while pretending not to be. Yeah, they were playing at something new these days, some sort of cat-and-mouse game, and he was pretty sure that he didn't have a complete set of the rules.

She was laughing at something someone said, her red hair gleaming like fire beneath the lights. Her gaze drifted to his. Yeah, definitely something had changed between them. Again. At first he'd thought it was his imagination. After all, she had always baited him, and he'd done the same to her. But he'd always been able to shrug it off, knowing they were just messing with each other.

Nothing more.

Never anything more.

But now they were one spark away from a fire that could burn them both to cinders, and that couldn't happen. He'd worked too damn hard to make this life of his. Every day, every single day, he had to walk the straight road. Discipline was the only thing that he could count on. Not even his friends could help him if he went off the rails as an adult. Coburn was dead, his father didn't count, and Ford and Jax were busy starting new lives. They deserved to be happy and not have to worry about him. That was logic and reason.

But whether it was exhaustion, or the memories stirred from tonight's fatal accident, logic and reason didn't make a dent in his insatiable, drumming, unrelenting need to have Chloe Traeger.

# Chapter 8

*"A closed mouth gathers no foot, though that's
hard to remember in the moment."*

CHLOE TRAEGER

Normally Chloe loved being at the Love Shack when it
was full like this. She loved the warmth and connection of
the people that lived here in Lucky Harbor. She enjoyed
the easy camaraderie, especially after being gone for the
past few days working. Usually sitting on a barstool listening to stories filled her with a sense of calm. Like she
could belong in this place.

Not tonight. She'd been in San Francisco for a few
days, and it'd gone well. She had new orders for her skincare line, and she'd even managed to work in some fun,
visiting friends she hadn't seen in a while. They'd wanted
her to stay a few more days, and she could have easily
stretched the work to justify it. But for the first time, she'd
been anxious to come back to Lucky Harbor.

Home.

On the drive, she'd started to think of ways to stick

closer to home next time and alleviate some of the travel time.

The idea wasn't new. It'd first come to her a few months ago, and it wouldn't leave her alone. She wanted to be more to the inn than just the token dishwasher or night watch for their guests. She wanted more than just filling in. She wanted to be a part of the place in the way Maddie and Tara were. She'd even thought of a perfect way to do that—open her own day spa at the B&B. Several times in the past she'd treated the occasional guest to a complimentary facial in the sunroom, but this would be different. Every day. Officially.

No doubt her sisters would remind her how much time she spent away, but why couldn't she come up with a compromise? Why couldn't she have it all? There was nothing to say she couldn't slowly ease into it, proving she could pull it off. Hell, she could still travel on the days she didn't have anything booked. That would be the best of both worlds, keeping one foot here in this place but being able to get out and spread her wings when she needed.

She'd like that.

Sawyer's name pulled her attention back to the bar. Jax was serving Lucille, telling her a story about his own wild, misguided youth, one that happened to include Sawyer. Apparently the good sheriff had also been a wild, misguided youth, which shocked Chloe. But at the tender age of fourteen, Sawyer had been running a little fake ID business. He'd made both himself and Jax a pair of fake IDs, which they'd attempted to use to buy alcohol.

It hadn't ended well.

Lucille, wearing her customary eye-blinding, neon-pink sweats and white headband, cackled in her been-smoking-for-seventy-years voice. "Oh, honey," she said to Jax. "Do I remember that. Sawyer's daddy was furious. He gave the both of you boys a stern what for."

"Yeah, more than a what for," Jax said with a remembered wince.

Sawyer appeared to be paying no attention to the story. He was finishing up his French fries with singular concentration, chasing them down with the last of his beer.

Chloe had never seen him drink alcohol before.

And she'd sure as hell never thought that the guy behind the badge would have once upon a time had a fake ID business going, stupid kid or no. It was hard to reconcile the two very different images she had of him.

Sawyer pushed his empty plate away, nodding at the waitress who took it for him. Clearly distracted, he rose to his feet and moved behind the bar, vanishing into the back room.

Chloe watched him go, then saw Ford exchange a look with Jax. Obviously, they knew something was up, which was good because she didn't feel that tangling with Sawyer tonight would be the wisest move. And dammit, she was trying to make wise decisions.

And yet...hell. Neither Ford nor Jax were going after him. She waited another minute, remembered the careful blank look on Sawyer's face and knew that it meant he needed the mask tonight. Heart squeezing, she drew a deep breath and went herself.

He stood alone in the far corner of the back office, in front of an open locker. She remembered Maddie telling her once that the guys kept a locker for him so that he could come from work and unload his weapons in a safe place and be off duty.

Which he'd clearly done earlier in the evening, as he was now in the middle of entering a combination. He opened the locker without turning in her direction, though she knew damn well that he'd heard her come into the room. He was a cat when it came to that stuff, seeing behind his back, sensing things.

She watched as he pulled his utility belt from the locker and slid it around his waist, clicking it securely in place. Next he bent over and clicked the leg strap around his muscular thigh. Selecting his gun next, he carefully held it up and eyeballed something on it. Satisfied, he placed it into the holster on his hip, snapping the small band in place to secure it.

Chloe stood rooted to the spot, shocked to find that watching him arm himself to the teeth was turning her on.

Still not acknowledging her in any way, Sawyer pulled out a knife, sheathed it on his leg, and then slipped another gun into the small of his back.

Whew. Suddenly it felt a little hot in here. "Isn't that a bit of overkill for the kind of calls you get here in Mayberry, USA?" she asked, her voice annoyingly husky. "I mean, sure the traffic jams are irritating, and the occasional drunk stumbling along the pier probably takes up time, but are they really *that* dangerous?"

Sawyer didn't start at the sound of her voice in the quiet room. He merely slid a jacket over his entire ensemble that had DEA in bold white letters on the back. He shut the locker, spun the lock, then slowly turned to face her. "I've been doing extra projects as part of a special task force."

Dangerous projects, from the looks of things, and she felt a prickle of fear for him. "Oh. So you..."

"Like to be prepared."

She nodded, keeping her concern to herself because he wouldn't want it. She liked to be prepared as well, or at least the semblance of it. And at the moment, she wasn't even close to prepared for what just looking at him was doing to her, so she backed up, right into the door. Wincing, she grabbed the handle. "Well," she said, far too brightly, "sweet dreams." She left the room without another word. She walked straight through the bar, got onto her Vespa, and rode to the B&B in the dark, dark night.

*Sweet dreams*? Had she really told the man to have sweet dreams? What was going on with her? And dammit, she hadn't even asked about his father. She'd been too busy being distracted by his job, and how good he looked doing it.

Only when she was on the porch of the little owner's cottage behind the inn did she take a deep breath. She was all alone. Alone was good. She really liked alone...

An SUV pulled around the back of the B&B and parked next to her Vespa.

Sawyer, of course. He exited his vehicle and strode up the steps to the porch, looking especially big and bad in the dark. Her knees did an odd little wobble, and she locked them in place, leaning back against the porch railing. "What are you doing here?"

"Wanted to make sure you got home okay."

"Do you follow every woman home from the bar, Sheriff?"

"No. Just the ones who are most likely to go sneaking around late at night near Black Ridge." He braced an arm on the railing at her side and leaned in. "Since I'm too tired to go after you tonight, I thought I'd head you off at the pass."

"You saw us," she murmured, refusing to be intimidated by the size of him looming over her. However, her body didn't fail to get a little thrill from the close proximity. "Lance and I, the night before I left for San Francisco." They'd gone up there because the old Whitney house was scheduled for demolition next Monday. It was out there on thirty acres of thick, remote woods and hadn't been lived in for decades.

Except for the homeless. There was always a small number of them seeking shelter in the place, especially in late fall like this, when the nights got cold. Chloe and Lance, and several others from town, including Lucille and her blue-haired posse, had driven them to various neighboring shelters, to make sure everyone had a place to go before the house came down.

"Got there just as you were leaving." His gaze was hooded. "You help everyone find a place to go?"

Something inside her got a little mushy, which she ruthlessly squelched. "Yes." She drew in a sharp breath as he stepped even closer. For someone who'd been working all day long, he still smelled delicious, like whatever masculine soap he'd used, and man. All man. "So we're back to that Eagle Scout thing," she said. "Stalwart and charitable, worrying about the homeless and women getting home safe and sound."

He gave her a single head shake. "There's nothing stalwart or charitable about how I feel for you, Chloe."

"Well, that's a relief." Her every nerve was on high alert screaming: *Run don't walk*! But there was also something else. The man willingly put his life on the line every day in a thousand different ways, for people like her. It was an odd and uncomfortable realization. But he *was* dangerous, if to nothing other than her heart. She should go inside and lock the door, not because she was afraid of what he might do, but because she was afraid of what *she* might do.

Instead, she found herself taking that last step, closing the gap between them, so that they were toe to toe, only a breath away from each other.

He looked down into her eyes. "What are you up to?"

"No good."

He shook his head and ran a finger along her temple and down her jaw. A little startled by the power of his touch, she covered his hand with hers and held it in place against her. Something flashed in his eyes, an aching hunger that held her captive.

Because it matched hers. She was shocked at the strength of it, at how difficult it suddenly was to breathe. But she wasn't shocked when he nudged her backward until she bumped up against the door. His mouth skimmed her jaw, then her throat, his teeth grazing her skin as he pressed a thigh between hers.

Heat skittered through her belly, then directly south. "Sawyer."

In answer, he brought his head up and kissed her. Deep, hungry, tasting her in a purposely slow, thorough manner before pulling back to once again look into her eyes.

Oh, God. "Sawyer, what are we doing?" she whispered.

He shook his head. "No fucking clue."

She let out a low laugh. "Maybe we should do it some more."

He obliged, pulling her in for another kiss, which grew rougher and more demanding, until she was *vibrating* with need, making little whimpers in her throat for more.

When he stepped back, eyes black as the night, she staggered for balance. "What?" she managed. "Why did you stop?"

"Your phone's going off."

Right. *That* was what was vibrating. Touching her still tingling lips, she pulled her cell phone from her pocket and read the incoming text.

> *Can you come relieve me at the B&B?*

Tara. "I gotta go," she said, blood still rushing through her veins.

Their gazes met. Disaster averted, at least for now. And sleeping with him *would* be a disaster. Well, it'd be an *amazing* disaster. And possibly an out-of-body-experience disaster to boot. And now that she was thinking about it, she'd really like that...

"Behave tonight," he said.

That made her laugh, and even he smiled. "Yeah," he said. "I figured that might be a stretch."

"I do occasionally behave, you know."

"Is that right?"

His voice was low, husky. Playful. It was almost as much a turn-on as big, bad Sawyer had been. With the silent night all around them, she tapped her iPhone screen and accessed her Magic Eight app. "You heard the man," she said to it. "Will I behave tonight?"

\*   \*   \*

The iPhone screen went foggy for a moment, then cleared, and two words floated to view.

*Absolutely not.*

With a low, mirthless laugh, Sawyer shook his head. Of course, Chloe wasn't going to behave. She didn't know the meaning of the word.

Chloe smiled a little apologetically, like the odds were completely stacked against her, and some of the tension created by that mind-blowing kiss dissipated into the night. But relaxing around her was just as dangerous as whatever had been crackling between them. Sawyer took another look at the screen of her phone to see if it'd changed its mind. A strand of Chloe's long hair stuck to his stubbled jaw. Her scent filled his nostrils, and he shifted closer so that her shoulder bumped into his chest.

He liked being close to her. Way too much.

"Ask it a question," she said.

"Like what?"

"I don't know. Anything. You could ask if you'll catch another idiot convenience store robber, or have to replace any more batteries for Mrs. Abbott anytime soon. Hell, ask it if you'll be getting lucky—I always ask it that. It's good at giving love advice." She turned to the phone and said, "Magic Eight Ball, will Sheriff Sawyer Thompson get laid anytime soon?"

"Jesus, Chloe."

She grinned at him over her shoulder and peered at the screen, which clouded and then cleared, and two more words appeared:

*Not likely.*

Chloe laughed out loud with what Sawyer thought was a rather nasty glee. "Same question," she told it. "For me this time. Will *I* be getting laid anytime soon?"

Sawyer didn't know what he wanted the answer to be, but before he could decide, the screen came into focus, and two crisp words floated:

*Outlook good.*

Chloe burst out laughing again, bending at the waist with amusement, which thrust her ass directly into his groin.

As that part of his anatomy was still cocked and loaded from their kiss, it was also now aimed. His hands went to her hips to step back, but somehow his brain mixed up the signal, and he held her still instead.

In the heavy silence, all he could hear was her suddenly accelerated breathing. "Well," she said straightening. "The Magic Eight app has never paid off quite so fast before."

Sawyer was dizzy. He was certain it had to do with the fact that he no longer had any blood in his brain.

"Sex stirs up my asthma."

Sawyer blinked. "What?"

"Yeah. I probably should have told you that sooner."

He shook his head, trying to catch up. He couldn't.

Turning to face him, Chloe grimaced. "Every time. And then I end up overusing my inhaler. But they're expensive, and I have this really crappy catastrophic insurance, and the inhaler isn't covered at all." She drew in a breath. "So I have this thing I do before sex. A test. An 'Is He Inhaler Worthy?' test."

He just stared at her. "There's a test. Before sex."

"Yes. And I should tell you, not many pass."

Somehow they'd ended up tangled in each other again, and she rocked against him, her actions at odds with her words. "There's a test," he said inanely.

"A guy has to pass it before I'll—"

"Have sex with him."

She nodded, her gaze locked on his mouth. He could tell she wanted it on hers, and for once, they were perfectly in sync. Having no idea what he was doing, he kissed her again, another no-holds-barred, tongues tangling, rock-his-fucking-world kiss that left him staggered and her apparently unable to speak as they tore apart for air and waited for the world to right itself.

Didn't happen.

She was breathing hard but not wheezing. Good sign, he thought. He stared at *her* mouth now, still wet from his, and just barely managed not to take a bite out of that full lower lip. It took a hell of a lot more control than he thought possible. Her hands were gripping his shirt, and also a little bit of his skin and some chest hair to boot, but he didn't say anything. Mostly because he wasn't sure if she meant to push him away or pull him closer, and if it was the former, he didn't want to remind her. "Chloe?"

"Yeah?"

"I'd be worth the inhaler," he said, then forced himself to walk away into the night.

\* \* \*

Chloe busied herself with work, which wasn't hard to do. It was early, and she sat in the inn's kitchen with her sisters preparing for their day.

The B&B was thriving. More and more, their weekends were booking up, and people were beginning to schedule during the week as well. Maddie continued to run the inn with supreme efficiency, handling the books, the staffing, the supplies, and the equipment. Tara, as always, handled the kitchen.

And Chloe did her best to pick up the slack. But the restlessness within her was still building, and cleaning and filing and answering phones weren't doing it for her. She had a talent, dammit, and it was time to bring it up. "I've been thinking about a way to get the B&B some publicity."

"Oh, good Lord," Tara said. "Don't tell me you're in the paper again. I mean, your motives with the homeless thing was sweet, but they always refer to you as some sort of troubled rebel. And who the hell is going to want to stay here with a troubled rebel, Chloe?"

"It's okay, I didn't get in the papers again."

Tara let out a sigh of relief and turned back to Maddie. The two of them had spent the past ten minutes arguing over towels. Towels. "Blue," Tara drawled to Maddie. "Blue's soothing as right rain."

Maddie shook her head. "Pale green. Soothing *and* on sale." She turned her laptop to reveal the site that she was looking at. If Maddie gave the place its heart, then Tara added the practical logic. Tara's practical soul was big...and cheap. The word *sale* was one of her favorite words, and she nodded her agreement.

Soothing on-sale green it would be.

"Hey," Chloe said. "About my idea…"

"If you suggest red towels," Tara said, her south show-ing, "I'm going to hurt you."

"It's not about the towels." Chloe stood up. "And it's more a plan than an idea."

Tara frowned. "The last time you said that, you were calling me collect from Tijuana, needing me to wire you money."

"Okay, first of all," Chloe said, "that was a *long* time ago. And second, this is an actual *good* idea." She drew in some air and held it. "A day spa. Here."

"You already do day spa stuff here," Tara said.

"Yes, I *prepare* here. And sometimes I do freebies for the guests," Chloe agreed. "But I'm talking about making it official and charging for the services."

Tara had turned away from the computer to her island. She was whipping eggs in a bowl now, her whisk moving at the speed of light. "As in a schedule where you set up appointments for our guests?"

"Yes," Chloe said, nodding, feeling the excitement flow just talking about it. "Facials, skin treatments, all the stuff I do for other spas all over the place. But here. Right here."

"What if you're gone on a trip when people want an appointment?" Maddie asked.

"I'd keep a schedule. Like we do for the inn. People would book in advance."

"But you take off on a whim all the time," Tara said. "I wouldn't want to have appointments booked and you off for parts unknown."

"I never take off on a whim anymore," Chloe said, try-ing not to get defensive. "I go when I get bookings. And I wouldn't leave if there was a booking here."

Neither sister spoke. In fact, there was no sound except the eggs sizzling on the stove, and the heavy weight of Tara and Maddie's misgivings. "Wow," Chloe said, failing at not getting defensive after all, as a ball of hurt clogged her throat. "All I hear are the crickets and doubt."

Tara flipped the eggs with the precision of a brain surgeon. Maddie was head down, forensically examining her fingernails as if they held the secret to the universe.

Chloe stared at them, then let out a mirthless laugh. "You know, all the faith you guys have in me is staggering." She strode to the door with absolutely no idea where she was going.

"Chloe," Maddie said softly, regretful, and Chloe stopped.

"There's a track record to consider," Tara said firmly, not caving to sentiment.

"You think I'd flake on you?" Chloe asked. "When have I ever flaked on you?"

"Well, let's see." Tara turned off her eggs. "Easter. July 4th. My birthday. Maddie's birthday, Mom's service—"

"Hey," Chloe said defensively. "I came to the service." A day late, but she'd had a good reason. She hadn't been ready, not to say good-bye to her mom, nor to face the fact that with Phoebe gone, Chloe had been truly alone. If she'd gone to the funeral, she'd have completely lost it. And she didn't "lose it" well. Truthfully, she didn't do deep emotion well. And birthdays, holidays, and funerals were all about deep emotion. "I've never made an appointment and not shown up."

Maddie, ever the peacemaker, got up and took Chloe's hand. "Why don't we all just think about it? Okay?"

No. No, it wasn't okay. They didn't believe in her. Angry words settled on her tongue, but her chest was too tight to voice them. "I can handle a schedule," Chloe repeated. "I can make us some good money, too. I'd be contributing."

"Honey, you're contributing now," Maddie assured her. "You're a huge help. We couldn't do this without you."

"Yeah, all that taking out the garbage is invaluable," Chloe said, heavy on the sarcasm. "Look, I can do this," she said again, hating that she sounded vulnerable.

Hating that she *felt* vulnerable.

And because she knew that they wouldn't give her what she wanted, the acceptance and the belief she needed, she grabbed her keys and cell phone. Her ever-present inhaler was already in her pocket.

"Chloe," Tara said. "Where are you going?"

"Out. On a whim."

# Chapter 9

*"Sisters. Love 'em or fight 'em, but no matter
how hard you try, you can't ignore 'em."*

CHLOE TRAEGER

Frustrated and mad at herself, Chloe rode the Vespa hard. Okay, so there was no riding any Vespa hard, and not for the first time, she wished she could afford a Duc. Or a Harley. Something fast and bad.

She was feeling the extreme need for both.

In substitution, food would work. She'd stop for breakfast, but she didn't have any money on her. Note to self—next time you leave in a diva fit, bring money. Thankfully, it was warmer than it'd been in weeks, which was good, since along with her wallet, she'd also forgotten a jacket.

Okay, so buying food was out. Sex. Sex would be lovely. She didn't need money or a jacket to jump someone's bones. *Sawyer's* very fine bones . . .

But he'd laid low for days. He'd given her that smoking-hot kiss—*kisses*—that had melted all resolve and reason, and then nothing. Maybe he'd simply had better sense than she. After all, he was a stable fixture around town. People had respect for him. Getting mixed up with her would undoubtedly put a check mark in his demerit column.

Whatever. She was better off on her own.

Always had been.

She sucked in a calming breath, annoyed with the jitter in her belly. Residual anger. No one could disappoint her quite like the sisters that she hadn't meant to let into her heart. If she'd been thinking straight, she'd have told them about the offer that she'd had two weeks ago in San Diego. The owner of the spa at a luxurious boutique hotel there had asked Chloe to take a permanent space in her salon, where Chloe could work and sell her products on consignment. What would Tara and Maddie think of that? A business acquaintance had more faith in her than they had.

But she hadn't told them, hadn't told anyone, because a little part of her wanted to have a reason to stay here in Lucky Harbor. To be *needed* here…

Dammit. She drew as deep a breath as she could and rode. She rode between mountains smothered in forests so thick it was like being swallowed up by a green comforting throw. Above her, the sky was a rare brilliant blue, streaked with a few white, puffy clouds. About fifteen miles out of Lucky Harbor, on a narrow two-lane road that she wasn't exactly sure of the name of, she caught sight of a sign for Yellow Ridge, and then another for some mud springs. She'd heard about the mud springs from Lucille, who knew everything about every square inch of the entire county. Years ago, beavers had created a meadow when they'd chewed their way through the surrounding forest and inadvertently flooded it. Early settlers had then discovered it and come to bathe nude in the mud for its healing effects.

Intrigued, Chloe turned off the highway, riding through a canyon lush with giant moss-draped trees. A mile or so up the road, she parked in the small clearing, in front of the trailhead to the mud springs. She pulled out her phone to text her sisters that she was alive, but she couldn't send it because she had no cell service.

This didn't stop her. It was a fairly easy climb, which was a good thing. Not anxious to have an asthma attack out here all alone, she didn't push herself. The trail was wet, meaning there was no pesky dust rising as she walked, which helped. The trail branched off several times with no rhyme or reason, or further sign. Staying to the right so that she wouldn't get lost going back, Chloe took it all in. The way was lined with wildflowers and offered up spectacular views of the peaks towering over her. Awe-inspiring, and very effective at clearing her head.

Twenty minutes in, the forest suddenly opened up, and she stood in the small meadow Lucille had told her about, filled with pockets of the promised mud springs.

She sure could use some healing effects right about now, she thought, slipping out of her shoes and socks. And hey, this was research. If the mud was good stuff, well, then she owed it to her clients to check it out before incorporating it into a product. Stepping to the edge, she dipped a toe into the mud.

It was warm.

And she wanted in. Taking a careful look around, she realized just how alone she was. "Crazy," she said out loud. "This is crazy." But she had to admit, she'd done far crazier. Her knit top was long, well past her butt so she stripped out of her jeans and told herself she was still decent if anyone happened upon her. Then she stepped into the mud up to her shins, and it oozed between her toes, toasty and oddly comforting. Wading in a little farther, she sighed in pleasure. The temperature of the mud gliding up her legs was so incredibly soothing that she went out even more, up to her thighs now.

All around her, the woods pulsed with life. Birds, insects, leaves dancing on the light breeze, and she felt... alive. If only she could bottle this feeling, with the sun on her face, the forbidden sense of being outside in her shirt and panties, with the mud soothing her skin in a way she hadn't expected, she'd be a millionaire.

She bet her sisters would take notice then...

She wished she was better prepared, because she would've liked to strip down even more and treat herself to a good soak. But she didn't have a towel or water to wash off with afterward, so she turned back to shore and...

Her foot slipped.

Chloe did a perfect imitation of a cat scrambling for purchase on linoleum, but it was no good. A second later, she was on her butt. She gasped but didn't bother to scramble up. It was too late now; she was in up to her belly button. Never one to waste an opportunity, she took another look around, then carefully pulled off her half-muddy shirt and tossed it to the shore to join her jeans. Relaxing, she soaked in her bra and panties beneath the wide-open sky.

As the mud worked its magic, she finally admitted to herself that what she'd felt earlier was more hurt than anger. She'd honestly tried to fit in, to pick up the slack around the B&B. And just because her mother's death and going into business with her sisters had forced her life into a one-eighty, it didn't mean she could ignore her other responsibilities. Dammit, she'd been serious about the skincare line she'd been working on, and her client list hadn't been developed overnight. Didn't that alone prove she'd grown up some?

But with some distance—and warm mud—she could admit to herself that she understood her sisters' concern. Renovating the sunroom would cost time and money. And yes, they were right, Chloe's track record *was* spotty. But there had to be a compromise. She could promise to commit to a certain number of days a week where she'd stay in town, for instance. And they could promise to believe her. With a resigned sigh, she rose and walked out of the mud.

She looked around, then with a philosophical shrug, she stripped out of her bra and panties, rubbed the excess mud off the best she could, and put her clothes on.

Commando.

Then, with the mud drying on her skin, she moved gingerly back down the trail, telling herself she was merely amplifying the healing affects by keeping the mud on so long. Hell, she'd probably look like a movie star after this. By the time she got to her Vespa, she'd talked herself into believing it. Hard to do when she felt like she'd been wrapped in concrete, but she managed.

That's when she discovered problem number two. Her Vespa wouldn't start. Okay, this was more than a minor setback. With no cell service, she had little choice. She walked down the road to the highway. Unfortunately, by the time she got there, her lungs had had enough. The two long walks had tightened her chest uncomfortably. Her inhaler helped with that, but she still didn't have cell service. She was going to have to flag someone down off the highway while looking like a swamp thing.

So much for being a grown-up.

In less than five minutes, a shiny black truck pulled off to the side of the road. Todd's baby.

"Hey, cutie," Todd said with his good-old-boy smile as he leaned over and opened the passenger door. He wore a Mariner's cap on backward, a ratty T-shirt, equally ratty jeans, and steel-toed boots, none of which took away from his easy good looks and tough build. A roofer by trade when he chose to work, he was clearly on his way to or from a job. "Problem?" he asked.

He didn't blink at the mud. This was probably because he wasn't looking at her limbs. Nope, that honor went to her braless breasts, now outlined with extra-special clarity thanks to the mud acting like an adhesive. "My Vespa's battery is dead," Chloe said. "And I don't have cell service."

"No one does right here." He didn't say a word about the fact that her Vespa was nowhere in sight. "You know what this means, right?" he asked. "You're at my mercy." He grinned, and she sighed. One hundred thousand sperm and *he'd* been the fastest.

"Come on," he said. "That was funny."

"Why are you out here?"

He shrugged. "On my way home from work."

"Isn't this way out of the way?"

Another shrug, and he stared out his windshield. "Sometimes I like to be alone, to hear myself think."

More like he'd gone somewhere remote to get high. But he didn't look buzzed.

"You getting in?" he asked. "Us outcasts need to stick together."

"Outcasts?" She shook her head. "You're not an outcast."

"Misfits, then." Something came and went in his eyes when he said this, but she couldn't read him. "You know what I mean."

"Yeah," she said, softening. Because she did know. Exactly.

He had a duffle bag on the passenger seat, which he took and stuffed behind them instead. Then he patted the passenger seat.

He was Jamie's brother. And Jamie was Tucker's friend, and Tucker was Lance's brother—but six degrees from trouble was still trouble, and she'd been trying so damn hard to stay *out* of trouble. But she was cold now, and getting even colder. Sawyer would hate this, but she couldn't help the extenuating circumstances.

"Come on, sweet thing. I've got somewhere I've gotta be."

Guilt didn't begin to cover how she felt about getting into his truck, but she did it anyway. She glanced over her shoulder and saw his open duffle bag.

She thought she caught sight of ziplock baggies stuffed with—

Todd reached back and shoved the duffle bag farther down so she couldn't see into it. "You're going to owe me," he said, shoving the truck into gear and speeding back onto the highway, flashing her a grin. "Big."

She straightened and looked at him. Was he carrying

drugs? She hadn't gotten a close enough look, and she sure as hell wasn't going to ask him while they were out in the middle of nowhere. Besides, she could admit that she hadn't gotten a good enough look to accuse him of anything. "I'll pay for gas."

"Not the kind of payment I was banking on."

"Shut up and drive, Todd."

He grinned again. Ignoring him, she huddled into herself for warmth, staring out the window. Clouds sifted through the trees like wood smoke, distracting her for a while. Out here, the growth was extravagantly thick with spruce and hemlock. Moist air rode in from off the coast, something her lungs liked but made her even more cold.

Twenty minutes later, she sat up straight. "Pull over."

"Yeah, baby," Todd said, and braked.

"Not for that! Lucille has a flat."

"Hell no," Todd said. "I'm not helping that old bat. She's always calling the damn cops on me."

"We can't just leave her there."

"Hell, yeah, we can."

"Todd, goddammit, pull over!"

Todd shook his head and slammed on the brakes as he pulled onto the shoulder. Dirt rose. "I'm not changing her tire. She told Kelly Armstrong I was a menace to society, and her husband, Manny, fired me. Cost me three weeks of work."

"We can't just leave her out here. It's chilly, and she looks cold. I'll help her myself." Chloe swung out of the truck.

"I'm not waiting," Todd warned, revving his truck. "I'm late."

"Then don't wait." She slammed the door, not surprised when he peeled out and was gone, leaving her literally in his dust. "Idiot."

Just as she walked toward Lucille, another truck pulled up.

Sawyer Thompson ambled out of his truck, then stood there in low-slung Levi's and a soft-looking, thin black sweater over a black T-shirt, eyes hidden behind dark, reflective sunglasses.

Off duty, Chloe thought as a violent shiver racked her.

"My white knight," Lucille said, dusting off her hands. "I called him a few minutes ago."

*       *       *

When Sawyer walked up to Lucille's little Prius, the older woman was giving the flat a kick. He glanced at Chloe, who was very busy studying the highway. "Hey," he said, taking in the mud all over her. "You okay?"

"Perfect."

Okaaaaay. He watched her shiver and handed her his keys. "Go wait in my truck; crank the heat." He headed toward Lucille, not all that surprised when he heard Chloe follow him. "Nice job on listening," he said.

"Maybe I'd listen if you ever asked."

"I ask."

She snorted.

Lucille had stopped kicking her tire and had picked up a lug wrench.

"You didn't mention you had a passenger when you called me," Sawyer said.

"I didn't." Lucille glanced at Chloe. "She just got dropped off."

Sawyer turned to Chloe, who was back to studying

the highway like her life depended on it. "What does she mean, you just got dropped off?"

"I believe I have the right to remain silent," Chloe said.

Shaking his head, Sawyer crouched at Lucille's side by the back rear tire and took the lug wrench.

Lucille backed up and smiled knowingly at Chloe's condition. "Mud springs, right?"

Chloe nodded.

Sawyer narrowed his gaze on Chloe. "You were at the mud springs?"

"Yes."

"How did you get here?"

Before she could answer, Lucille cut in with, "I used to take my stud muffin up there, back in the day. That mud has healing effects, you know. And also, it's an aphrodisiac. Not that you need an aphrodisiac with this one," she said to Chloe, gesturing to Sawyer with a sly smile.

Sawyer grimaced, but Chloe cocked her head and studied him. "You don't think so?" she asked Lucille doubtfully.

"Honey, just look at him."

Both women studied him now, and Sawyer, afraid of nothing except possibly these two, found himself squirming.

"Where's your uniform?" Lucille asked. "I like looking at you in it."

"I'm off duty," he said.

"Aw, and you still came out to help me instead of calling someone else to do it." She patted him on his arm. "Such a sweet boy."

Chloe made an indistinguishable sound, but when Sawyer looked at her, she was all green-eyed innocence.

"I talked to Suzie today," Lucille told Sawyer. "She told me what you did for her boy this week, how you stepped in for him."

Suzie Tierman worked with Sawyer in dispatch. She was a single mom, and she had an eight-year-old terror named Sammy who'd gotten caught last week cutting off a girl's ponytail in class. Her parents had wanted to press assault charges even though their little "princess" had been mercilessly tormenting Sammy for months about being a "stupid loser."

At Suzie's request, Sawyer had stepped in and mediated. Sammy would be doing hard time pulling weeds, and the girl had written an apology for calling Sammy names. Sawyer would have liked to see her do some hard weed pulling as well, but the letter would have to do. "I didn't do much."

"According to Suzie, you're being a father figure to the boy. You call him and take him to your baseball games, and last week you went to his class for career day. She says she couldn't do the single-mom thing without your help."

Uneasy with the praise, Sawyer shrugged. "Being a single mom's hard."

"And you don't want her to give up," Lucille said softly.

"Sammy's a good kid," he said and fixed his attention to the flat.

Lucille and Chloe talked amongst themselves. He wanted to talk to Chloe about the mud springs, but she was doing a damn good job of avoiding the subject. He had no intention of letting it go, but somehow she and Lucille had gotten on the subject of Sawyer at the age of eight. Lucille was telling Chloe about the time when he and Jax had urinated their names in the snow in front of the pier and gotten caught by none other than Lucille herself. And then how several years later, the two of them had moved on to delivering flaming bags of dog poop to the residents on Mulberry Street—until one of the bags had tipped over and caught Mrs. Ramos's dead rosebush on fire. The flames had leaped up to her awning and nearly burned her house down.

Sawyer finished with the tire just as Chloe asked about his teenage years. Christ, that was the last thing he wanted her to hear about, and he tensed.

But Lucille gave him a reassuring smile, a glint of understanding in her kind eyes as she shook her head at Chloe. "He figured things out," she said. "He had a big heart, even then."

Bless her for lying through her teeth.

"He's one of the good guys," Lucille said, and patted him again.

"Lucille," he started.

"What? It's true. Yesterday alone you saved the peace in town at least twice."

"What happened yesterday?" Chloe asked.

"Honey," Lucille said with exasperation. "Facebook! I have all the good stuff up there, including today's blog on Cute Guy. Someone got a picture of him jogging shirtless on the beach this morning. I'm telling you, if I were thirty years younger—"

"Okay, we're all done here," Sawyer said, gently but firmly ushering Lucille to the driver's side of her car.

"Lucille," Chloe said. "Could you give me a ride?"

"Of course, dear. I can't believe Todd just left you on the side of the road like that. I—"

"I've got her, Lucille," Sawyer said, giving the older woman the bum's rush, shutting Lucille's door on whatever it was that she was going to say. He turned to Chloe, every line of his body saying pissed-off cop.

Well, crap. "You just chased off my ride," she said casually as Lucille drove off.

"Yeah. You're coming with me. Are you hurt?" he asked.

"No."

He pulled off his sunglasses and looked her over for himself, taking in the way that every inch of her skin was covered in mud except for her clothes, which were relatively clean. She knew the exact second when he came to the realization that she'd been skinny-dipping because the carefully blank look vanished. "You and Todd were in the mud springs together."

A logical assumption, she supposed, but she'd had a rough enough day that it pissed her off. "No. I—"

"He's dangerous, Chloe. *Stupid* dangerous."

No shit. She thought about mentioning what she might or might not have seen in Todd's truck, but Sawyer cut her off.

"I realize you like the dangerous part," he said. "But I never pegged you for stupid."

Oh no, he didn't. She reached for the Zen calm she'd found at the mud springs. It was a total stretch. "I don't know exactly how *stupid* I look, but even I know Todd's nothing but a player."

He didn't bend an inch. "Lucille said you were in his truck."

"He gave me a ride."

"So you *were* with him."

"Oh my God!" So much for Zen calm. He was like kryptonite to her Zen. Whirling from him, she stomped along the highway with no concern for how she must look, only knowing that she could feel the steam coming out of her ears. Maybe it'd melt the mud from her body. "Moronic man," she muttered, prepared to walk all the way back to town to avoid talking to Sawyer. "Moronic *men*, all of them, the entire gender is a complete waste of good penises—"

A big, warm hand grabbed her arm, and she spun willingly around, stabbing Sawyer in the chest with a muddy finger. "And you—"

"Moronic," he said mildly. "I know." With a firm grip, he pulled her back to his truck and stopped at his passenger door. "Stay," he said.

"Oh, hell no. I don't *do* 'stay.' I—"

But she was talking to air because he'd moved to the back and pulled a blanket from his emergency kit. Which he wrapped around her shoulders. It was thick wool, and she snuggled into it even as she shook her head. "I'll get it all dirty."

"Done deal," he said. "Get in the truck."

"What about my Vespa?"

"Did you crash it?"

"No. I think the battery is dead. Which is how I ended up in Todd's truck, you . . . you Neanderthal."

He ignored that. "Your Vespa can wait. You need to get dry and warm. Get in."

She was really quite over the ordering around. "I'm walking." Even to her own ears, she sounded ridiculous, but the words were out. She realized that she was completely contradicting her commitment to being more mature and grown up, but she decided that a few mistakes along the way never hurt anyone.

Sawyer considered her for a brief moment. She'd seen him handle a variety of situations without ever appearing so much as rattled, without even the slight indication that his patience was stretched, yet it seemed ready to snap now. It was in the grimness of his mouth, the narrowing of his eyes. Oh, and his jaw seemed to be bunching and unbunching at random.

"You're not walking," he said.

She took a page from his own book and said nothing.

"Jesus." He pinched the bridge of his nose, then drew in a deep breath. "Just get in the damn truck."

"I'll get it dirty, too."

"It's seen worse." He pulled open the passenger door, bodily picked her up, and plopped her onto the seat. Leaning in, he yanked the seat belt across her and stabbed it into the buckle at her hip. He didn't slam the door. Exactly.

Chloe could have gotten out, but it was warm. And it smelled good. Like Sawyer good. It'd be counterproductive to leave, she decided, and leaned her head back and closed her eyes, ignoring Sawyer when he slid behind the wheel. She went into radio silence as he started the truck, maintaining that quiet as he cranked the heat and aimed the vents at her, and then finally began to drive.

He gave her a full five minutes before he spoke. "You going to tell me what's going on?"

"Thought you had it all figured out," she said.

"Christ. You drive me insane, you know that?"

Yeah. She knew that. She drove everyone insane. It was a special talent of hers.

# Chapter 10

♥

*"Just when you think you've hit rock bottom,*
*someone'll throw you a shovel."*

CHLOE TRAEGER

Extremely aware of the pissy woman in his passenger seat, Sawyer drove back to Lucky Harbor, occasionally glancing at her. She was no longer shaking, he noted with what he told himself was clinical and professional interest only.

But it wasn't clinical or professional interest that also took in the fact that she looked better covered in mud from head to toe than any woman had the right to look. Her shirt had once been white but was now streaked with mud and sheer as a second skin. Through it, he could see every dip and soft curve, every nuance of her, including two perfect, mouthwateringly tight nipples threatening to burst through the cotton. "Chloe."

Nothing.

"Fine. Let me know when you're done pouting."

Turning her head, she leveled him with yet another

icy stare. "Pouting? You think I'm pouting? I'm...
*furious.*"

"At the Vespa?"

She stared at him like he'd grown a third eye. "At
you!"

"Me? What the hell for?"

"You..." She choked, as if she could hardly speak.
"You actually think that I'd fuck Todd? In the mud
springs? Or anywhere outside of hell freezing over, for
that matter?"

Sawyer clenched his jaw. "I found you caked in mud
but your clothes are mostly clean. Which means you
stripped down to skin. Plus, you're not wearing any underwear. What the hell else am I supposed to think?"

"How can you tell that I'm not wearing any underwear?" she demanded.

"God-given talent."

She closed her eyes and counted to ten. "I was alone in
the damn mud springs. I slipped in, then had to ditch my
bra and panties. They were...uncomfortable. I didn't see
Todd until I got back to the highway to hitch a ride when
the Vespa wouldn't start. Halfway back we saw Lucille
and I made him pull over to help. He didn't stick around.
Not that I should have to explain myself to you."

He was quiet a moment. "I had to ask."

"Why?"

"Why? Christ, Chloe."

"No, I mean it, Sawyer. In the past week, you've made
it abundantly clear that we're...well, I don't really know
exactly what we are—were—but whatever it was, it
clearly wasn't worth your time. So I have to know. What
if I *had* been with Todd? What would it matter to you?"

Sawyer reminded himself that she didn't, couldn't, know his history with Todd, or the level of resentment and escalating violence that Todd directed toward him.

Or how the thought of Todd's hands on her twisted him in knots. "It'd matter," he said grimly.

"Why?"

"You don't want to know."

"I *do*."

No way was he going to tell her that once upon a time he and Todd had been fellow thugs. That he and a group of other equally stupid thugs had terrorized the entire county together and had, in fact, outdone themselves on several occasions. The most memorable time being when the four of them had gotten drunk—God so fucking drunk—then stolen a car for a joyride. That had been the night that they'd reduced their gang by two when they'd hit a telephone pole.

Sawyer had earned a trip to juvie.

Todd, the driver, hadn't been as lucky. He'd turned eighteen the week before, had been tried as an adult, and had been convicted for involuntary manslaughter. "There's an old grudge between us," Sawyer finally said.

To say the least.

"What kind of grudge?"

Todd had done some hard time, and when he'd gotten out, he wasn't the same easygoing troublemaker he'd once been.

And even though they'd each made their own decisions, Sawyer had never been able to shake the guilt. This was because he knew without a doubt that if he'd been smarter that night, the accident wouldn't have happened.

Two guys wouldn't be dead.

Todd wouldn't be on a one-way street to Loserville.

And Sawyer wouldn't still be trying to straighten Todd's ass out. "Let's just say that Todd blames me for the way his life has turned out," he said quietly.

"Well, that's ridiculous," Chloe said. "And not your fault. We all make our own path."

"Yes, and his is to fuck with me. I want you to stay away from him, Chloe."

She looked pissed off again. "Look, I understand you're trying to offer me advice, but—"

"Not advice," he said. "I'm flat out telling you. Stay away from him. He's trouble."

She kept her voice low and even, but her eyes were flashing pure fire. "He's a friend of my closest friend's brother. So staying away from him won't always be possible. I get that you have some sort of pissing match going with him, but he's not *that* bad a guy."

"Are you sure about that?"

She had no answer for him, but huddled farther into the seat with a shiver.

Sawyer blew out a breath and checked the heater output, but it was already on full blast.

Chloe sighed. "I need to tell you that Todd maybe had drugs in the back of his car."

He slowed down and looked at her. "Maybe?"

"I can't be sure. He had a duffle bag, and it was filled with small ziplock bags. I couldn't quite see what was in them." She shook her head. "Forget it. I shouldn't have said anything."

"No, I'm glad you did." He fought with what to tell her. "He's under investigation and being watched. If he's got drugs, we'll catch him."

She nodded.

"And no one in Lucky Harbor knows that information."

"Understood."

He glanced at her again, and told her the other thing bugging the hell out of him. "And for what it's worth, I stayed away from you all week because some distance seemed in order. Chloe…" He let out a breath. "We both know damn well we could give each other something we need, but it's a real bad idea."

Her gaze darted away from his, but not before he caught the flicker of unmistakable hurt. "Yes, all the kissing proved that," she said to the window. "It was awful."

He opened his mouth, shut it again, and waited for the traffic to get moving.

\* \* \*

Chloe tried unsuccessfully to ignore the mud that had tightened uncomfortably on her skin. As she squirmed, Sawyer slid her an unreadable gaze. She ignored him, too, and he put the truck into gear, pulling back onto the highway.

She wasn't mad at him anymore. She'd tried to hold on to it, but it was just too hard to stay mad at a guy who stopped to change a woman's tire, not to mention rescued another woman from turning into a mud popsicle. "Tell me the truth," she finally said. "You can't drive and talk at the same time, right?"

He didn't say anything, but his mouth quirked slightly, and she sighed. The ability he had to keep everything to himself drove her nuts. But only because she wanted to be able to do the same. It was another big reason to stay away from him. He wasn't the yin to her yang; he was the Batman to her Joker.

And Batman was fully in his zone right now, complete with the dark reflective sunglasses and the blank face. "So...Lucille says you're sweet."

"She wears rose-colored glasses for everyone."

This made her take a second look at him. "You don't think you're sweet?"

He grimaced and didn't answer.

"It's a compliment," she said, amused. "Sweet is a positive quality."

"Yeah," he said. "In puppies."

Chloe laughed, a little disconcerted by how easily and effectively he disarmed her, every single time. "Don't worry, Sheriff. I won't tell anyone."

His concentration was on the road. Apparently he'd exhausted his word usage for the day. "So does this happen to you a lot?" she asked, perversely determined to make him talk. "The rescue thing?"

He shrugged. "It's my job."

Maybe. But he wasn't on the job at the moment. "Tell me about the calls yesterday, the ones Lucille brought up."

"They were nothing."

"Fine. I'll just go read Facebook. Probably it's not too overly embellished."

He glanced over at her. "Do you ever use your powers for good?"

"Not if I can help it. Tell me."

He blew out a breath. "I got called out to Mrs. Perez's house because she was shining a light in her neighbor's windows. Apparently the neighbor—Mrs. Cooper—had cheated at bunco earlier in the week and pissed Mrs. Perez off, so Mrs. Perez was retaliating by scaring Mrs. Cooper."

"What did you do?"

"I took the batteries out of Mrs. Perez's high-powered flashlight."

"Fast thinking," Chloe said, impressed. "What else happened?"

"I got called to the Sorenson house."

"Bill and Joanne, with the eight daughters?" she asked.

"Yes. Bill had plowed a pile of mulch in front of his neighbor's driveway."

"Why, had the guy been cheating at bunco too?"

"No," Sawyer said. "The neighbor's son got caught...in a compromising position."

"Compromising position?"

"Pants at his ankles, in the company of one of Bill's daughters."

"Uh-oh. In that case, you're lucky there weren't gunshots."

"No luck involved," he said. "I took Bill's rifle from him two weeks back when I heard the two teens were dating."

She laughed. "You took his rifle? Are you allowed to do that?"

"*Borrowed.* And then accidentally disposed of it."

"How do you accidentally dispose of a rifle?"

Sawyer turned and flashed her a heart-stopping grin, full-wattage. "You go sailing with Ford and dump it three miles out at twelve knots."

Ford had been a world-class sailor, with an Olympic medal and many other awards for his efforts. He didn't go out on the racing circuit so much anymore, but he did sail with Jax and Sawyer on their mutual days off. Chloe had seen them on the docks at the marina. Hell, she had a permanent kink in her neck from all the times she'd stared out the marina building window at the three of them wearing board shorts and nothing else.

The truck's heater was decadently warm on her chilled skin, but the dried mud was still a huge irritant and she squirmed some more.

"What's the matter?"

"You ever go naked on the beach and get sand in places that no sand should go?" she asked.

"Ah. I take it the same applies for mud."

"Little bit." Plus, she'd never worn jeans without underwear before, and it wasn't nearly as fun as she'd thought it might be. The center seam kept riding up, and the zipper was cutting into her. She looked out the side window to distract herself, but all she could see was Sawyer's reflection next to her. *He* wasn't fidgeting. Of course, that was because he didn't have mud in his cracks and crevices. But even if he had, she doubted that he'd fidget. He never wasted a single ounce of energy. He was driving, relaxed—maybe a little too amused at her dilemma—all his carefully controlled energy at rest.

Though he hadn't been so relaxed when Lucille had been recounting the story about how he'd helped Suzie because she was a single mom. Chloe turned to look at him in profile. His hair was windblown, his face tanned. He hadn't shaved that morning, and his square jaw was scruffy. She liked it. But there were lines of tension along the outside corners of his eyes.

He wasn't as relaxed as he appeared to be.

He worked hard. He always did. From what she knew of him, he'd gotten that from his father, a hard worker himself, and a single dad. And it hit her. "How old were you?"

"When?"

"When your mom gave up being a mom."

For a brief beat, he took his gaze off the road and looked at her before turning back. "Eight."

Her heart squeezed. "You were eight when your parents divorced?"

"They were never married. Or together, for that matter. I went back and forth between them until I was around eight." His hesitation was brief. "That's when she left town." He lifted a shoulder, like life happens, no big deal.

But it was a big deal. Chloe knew all too well what it was like to have only one parent, a parent who wasn't always so keen on being one in the first place. It had left its mark on her, and the older she got, the more she was beginning to understand how deep the wounds went. Or maybe being here in Lucky Harbor with her sisters was what had stirred the pot, but all her relationships seemed to be affected by her childhood. Not only that but also her search for stability, for a home, and the ironic fear of those very same things.

Which left her to wonder what the loss of his mother had done to Sawyer. "You ever hear from her?"

"No."

He said it easily enough, but something made her throat tighten a little. Maybe it was the thought of him at eight years old being utterly abandoned by the one woman in his life who he should have been able to count on. She knew what it felt like to be without a parent, too. It was possible, she supposed, that her own father hadn't known about her at all, but she thought it far more likely that he'd known and simply hadn't wanted her. "Are you close to your dad?"

He let out a low laugh.

"I'll take that as a no."

"There's bad history. I haven't exactly been a model son."

"You were a motherless little boy," she said in his defense.

"I was a complete shit," he corrected. "A holy fucking terror. My father did what he could." He gave a slight shrug. "At least you and Phoebe were of like minds. She was the original wild child." A small but fond smile crossed his lips, taking any of the possible sting out of his words.

"You liked her," she said in surprise.

He glanced at her. "Is that so odd?"

"Well, yeah. You're not always so fond of me, so..."

"Says who?"

She opened her mouth, then closed it again.

"Wow. I just made you speechless. That's new. I like it." He paused. "And yeah, I liked Phoebe, too. She did as she pleased, lived the life she wanted to live."

"Sometimes," she said, staring at him, "you surprise me."

He shot her a rare smile. "So what about your dad?" he asked after a minute. "I've never heard anything about him."

"No? Me either."

"You don't know him?"

"I don't even know who he is."

Again he glanced at her, and she once again turned to the window, annoyed at herself. She never told people that. First of all, it was embarrassing, and second...

Second, it brought out something she hated.

Pity.

She didn't want pity. Most of the time, she didn't give a damn about her father. He was a nonentity. It was only since coming here and being around Tara and Maddie that she'd realized his absence had had such an impact on her. She shifted yet again and sucked in a breath of discomfort.

Beside her, Sawyer made a sound of his own, but when she looked at him, he was watching the road, calm as can be. "Still cold?" he asked.

Fair question. Her nipples were two tight pebbles, so visible that she might as well have been naked. "Yes." She shifted around some more.

"Jesus, Chloe. Stop doing that." He shoved his sunglasses to the top of his head and sent her a look so heated that she nearly went up in smoke. "Get the blanket back on you," he said, reaching behind him, where she'd tossed it to get out of the truck earlier. He threw it over her, including her face.

"Oh for God's sake, they're just nipples," she said, tugging the blanket down so she could breathe. She leaned as close to the vents as her seat belt allowed. "Just let me off in town at Lance's."

"What's with your place?"

"My sisters are going to give me shit about this. We had a fight this morning." A stab of remembered hurt hit her low and deep, but she ignored it. "Among other things, I told them I was all grown up. Which obviously," she said with a mirthless laugh and a gesture at her ensemble, "was a complete lie. Seeing me like this isn't going to help my cause. If you drop me at Lance's, I can check on him and also borrow his shower. And maybe get Tucker to help me fix the Vespa."

"Lance's mother was with him when I talked to him. In your condition, you'll give her heart failure. Hell, *I'm* nearly in heart failure." He pulled off the highway just before her exit.

"So where are we going, then?" she asked.

He drove up a steep street, then turned a couple of times, and pulled into a driveway. The house was the last on the block, a midsized ranch on a bluff overlooking the ocean. Chloe had never been up here, but she knew Sawyer had bought the place earlier in the year.

He turned off the engine and faced her, laying his arm along the back of her seat. "It wasn't a lie, what you told your sisters," he said. "About growing up. You've changed a lot since you moved here."

"Yeah? Then why am I still making stupid moves? Look at me, Sawyer."

He did just that, appearing to like what he saw in spite of the mud. "Just because you're unconventional doesn't mean you're not a grown woman."

It was possibly the nicest thing anyone had ever said to her. "So...is 'unconventional' the new 'sweet'?"

He laughed, and she liked the sound, very much. "Why do we always fight?" she whispered.

"You know why."

Yeah, she did. "It's science."

"Combustible chemistry," he agreed. "Dangerous." His voice was pitched so low as to be nearly inaudible and sent tingles down her spine. Clearly mistaking that for a chill instead of desire, he got out of the truck and came around for her. He held out his hand, but she just stared at it while the fresh fall air slid into her taxed lungs.

"Scared?" he asked.

"Of course not." And she wasn't. Scared. Nope, she was something else entirely, and it was making her breathless, and her chest was tight. She slid out of the truck, and since Sawyer didn't move out of her way, she bumped directly into him, her body pressing close to his.

Given that she could feel him hard against her, she was guessing he wasn't scared of a little combustible chemistry either. "What are we doing?"

"Come on. I'll show you." He pulled her toward the house.

"But I'll get your house as dirty as your truck."

"No, you won't," he said, and that's when she realized that they weren't moving toward his front door but around to the side of the house. Then they were in his backyard, which was nothing more than an open patch of wild grass. Stairs cut into the cliff that led down to the beach about a hundred feet below.

"I run along the beach sometimes," he said. "Or climb the rocks. Clears my head."

She walked to the edge and looked over. The cliff was rocky, jutting out in spots, creating little pockets where trees stuck out like porcupine quills. An entire elemental world of rock, trees, and water that made her itch to explore. "Does it work?" she asked. "The clearing of your head part?"

"Yeah."

She could imagine him climbing to one of the alcoves there on the cliff, staring out at the churning ocean, inhaling the salty air, the wind in his face as the waves crashed on the rocks. "It's a good place," she said.

"It is. And after a run, I come up here." He walked her to the very far corner of his house. "Maybe I'm not muddy, but definitely sandy and sweaty." He gestured to the wall. There was an outdoor shower there, like the ones at the public beaches. But this one wasn't grimy and gross. Instead, it was clean and tiled, and, as she discovered when he leaned in and flicked the handle, equipped with hot water.

She watched the muscles play across his back and shoulders as he straightened, and when she saw what he had in his hands, she paused. "A removable showerhead?"

"For those hard-to-reach spots."

# Chapter 11

*"I've always wanted to be somebody.
I should have been more specific."*

CHLOE TRAEGER

Chloe stared at the pulsing showerhead in Sawyer's hand. Half an hour ago, they'd been furious at each other. Apparently they were going in an entirely different direction now. "Lance would've let me inside his house, you know. Of course, I'd probably have had to strip naked to get past the front door."

"Feel free to strip naked now."

She narrowed her eyes at him. Yeah, okay, they were definitely over their mad. New direction coming at her. Was she ready? And good Lord, that smile should be registered as a lethal weapon, because surely it was as dangerous as anything else he was carrying. She stuck her right jean-covered leg beneath the spray, then moaned against her will as the water soaked past the mud-stiffened denim and warmed her skin. "Ahhh. So warm."

"I might be a—what was it you said? A waste of a penis? But I'm not a complete ass."

"Hmm," she said noncommittally. She kicked off her tennies, then bent over to use her hands to rub her feet beneath the water. The caked-on mud washed away easily, which was nice. She could see this stuff in a really great body mask—

The water suddenly hit high on her thighs and made her jerk upright and squeak in surprise. "Hey!"

"Looked like you could use some help," Sawyer said mildly.

"I've got it, thanks." Because if he stepped in and "helped" by running his hands over her body, getting clean would be the farthest thing from her mind. Her breath hitched just thinking about it, and she thought of her inhaler, which she'd left on the seat of his truck. She considered going back for it, but she felt oddly compelled to stay right where she was even as she grabbed the showerhead from him.

"Don't trust me?" he asked.

"Hell no."

His soft laugh danced along her nerve endings and gave her goose bumps. Or maybe that was the chill that the water left in its wake. In any case, she had a sudden urge to wipe the smirk off his face. She'd been working hard on curbing her impulses, but she decided that not all impulses should be curbed.

So she aimed the water at his chest. "Whoops."

He didn't react other than to narrow his eyes and step directly into the spray. In less than two seconds, he'd wrestled the showerhead from her, twisted her around so that her back was to his chest, and held the showerhead inches from her as he pressed his mouth to her ear. "Are we playing?"

"No!" Laughing and gasping for breath, she squirmed and fought with all her might, but he had her easily restrained against himself. Not a bad place to be—if her chest hadn't felt like it was contracting, the first and most annoying sign of an impending asthma attack. She went still for a beat to mentally assess herself.

"Oh, no you don't." Clearly thinking she was trying to figure a way out of his grasp, Sawyer tightened his grip and lowered the nozzle, letting the water hit her.

She gasped, but couldn't deny the excitement driving through her. There was something to be said for being held captive against a hard, warm chest, completely at his mercy.

With a flick of his wrist, the nozzle shifted higher, near her face.

"Don't you dare," she said.

"I always dare." He nipped her earlobe with his teeth. "But maybe if you beg me real nice..."

Beg, her ass. Besides, she hadn't exhausted all her options yet. She still had some dirty fight left in her, and without qualm, she let her backside grind into his crotch.

He sucked in a breath and instantly went still, his grasp on her slackening slightly. It was enough to whip around, grab the shower handle back, and get him.

Right in the face.

He simply opened his eyes and gazed at her steadily. Calm. His entire body relaxed. *Ready.*

Uh-oh. "Okay," she said, backing up a step. "I got it out of my system."

"My turn, then."

Oh shit. Dropping the showerhead, she whirled to run, but he reacted so fast that all she got out was another squeak as he propelled her forward with his big body, until she was planted cheek against the wall of the outdoor shower. Holding her there with his considerable brawn, he reached up and replaced the showerhead in its bracket. Then, with the hot water now raining down over them, he turned her to face him.

She was breathing hard. "Look at you," she managed. "Now you're as wet and dirty as I am."

His big hands came up to cup her face. "I've told you—I like wet and dirty."

Good thing, since they were plastered together by drenched clothes and warmed-up mud.

"You're still shivering," he said.

"Not from cold." She could feel him, hard beneath his wet denim. No longer playing, she rubbed up against him.

"Chloe." The warning in his voice only turned up the flame on the slow burn in her belly, spreading both north and south now, beyond her soaked clothes all the way to her core.

She moved against him again. "You started it."

His eyes met hers, dark and hungry. With the mist from the hot water swirling around them, he dipped his head and let his lips slide down her throat, igniting flames along each nerve ending. "Stop me now if you're going to," he murmured against the hollow at the base of her throat where her pulse pounded frantically. His voice was thrillingly gruff, and his hands encircled her wrists on either side of her head, slowly sliding them up the wall, holding her pinned as he nibbled at her.

Stop him? Was he kidding? Instead she arched against

him, eliciting a rough groan from deep in his chest that reverberated through hers. "Too many clothes," she complained.

In response, he stripped off his sweatshirt and shirt together, and then her top, tossing everything aside. She looked at him and lost even more air. He was sheer perfection, all perfectly toned muscles, with that hint of danger still vibrating from him even now. It was enough to make anyone think twice about making a move on him, but she was fearless, or at least knew how to pretend to be.

His mouth covered hers again, which worked for her because he kissed like heaven on earth. His hands were cold, sending a quick thrill through her when he cupped her breasts, his fingertips teasing her nipples before his fingers slid down her torso on their way to the next barrier. She felt the button on her jeans give, the zipper go down, and then he was pushing the jeans off her legs.

"Kick them off," he said, cupping her ass, pulling her tight to him as she obeyed the quiet demand.

"Yours, too," she panted, annoyingly short of breath. Still ignoring the warning signals dancing in her head, she lent a hand to the cause, helping until they stood facing each other.

Naked.

Wet.

Sawyer was always cool, calm, and utterly in control, but that control was being tested now. She could see it in the line of tension between his eyes, in his tight jaw, and most of all, she could see it in what was quickly becoming her favorite body part of his—the one bouncing happily at the sight of her.

She licked her lips, a nervous little gesture. Sawyer said her name again, voice definitely strained. No more cop face, that was for sure, though his body was hard, strong, and rippling with power. It made her feel her own power, and incredibly sexy. He could probably make any woman with a pulse feel sexy, but she also felt safe, like she could say anything. Do anything.

*Temporary*, a little voice said. This is just a *Twilight Zone* intermission, and when they were done and once again dressed, they'd return to their separate universes.

But that was a worry for later.

For now, the steam continued to swirl around them, like fog on a humid night. Sawyer's flesh gleamed before her in the weak sunlight, his big body sleek and drenched, taut like a warrior's. Such a beautiful body, she thought, and used her mouth to learn him, tracing her tongue over a pec, flicking at a nipple.

Drawing in a sharp breath, he threaded his hands into her hair and tipped her head up to kiss her. It was long and wet and deep as his hands roamed down her sides, over her hips to her backside again, pulling her in tight, leaving no room between them for so much as a single drop of water.

She tried to suck in more air but couldn't. Dammit. *Not yet.* "Hurry." They had to, because her chest was way too tight. Hell, her airway was already closing. Knowing she was on borrowed time, she dropped to her knees. Sawyer was a big man, *everywhere*, and humming her pleasure, she lightly scraped her nails up the backs of his thighs as she ran her tongue along the length of him.

From above, he hissed in a sharp breath, his fingers tangling in the wild mess of her hair. Not surprisingly, he took over, pulling her away from him, tugging her up to her feet again, pressing her to the tile wall.

Then he dropped to *his* knees. She let out a startled "Wait. What—"

"Ladies first."

Oh, God. She could probably come from his voice alone. "I can't," she whispered, but the words backed up in her throat when he pressed his mouth to the spot just beneath one hip bone, right over the top of her tiny hummingbird tattoo.

"Free as a bird?" he whispered with a smile.

She nodded, her heart pounding in her ears, her breath caught in her throat. And she knew damn well that it wasn't the good kind of can't-catch-your-breath, that she wasn't just near the danger zone but *in* it. She didn't care. He was there, *right* there, looking at her, and it'd been so long. So frigging long..."*Sawyer*—"

If he responded, she couldn't hear over the roar of blood in her ears and the water hitting the tiles around them. Then it didn't matter because his hands were on her hips, holding her steady, his thumbs gliding down her quivering belly, then over her trimmed mound. "Pretty," he murmured.

It took her a moment to get enough breath to speak. "Are you going to just look?"

He laughed softly against her, his warm breath caressing her, making her moan. Her hands went to his hair, trying to draw him in close.

"Spread your legs," he said, then took care of it himself with a big, hot hand wedged in between her thighs. Her hips rocked helplessly, and her toes curled. Her heart was going to burst out of her chest, she was certain of it. And, oh God, she really needed air. Little spots were dancing around the very edges of her peripheral vision, but hell if she was going to pass out before she got to the good stuff. No way. "Now. Oh, please now."

Probably thinking she was just impatient, he slowly trailed a finger over her, letting out a raw sound of sheer male appreciation at how wet she was. And then barely, just *barely*, slid it into her, all the while her body racing with equal speed toward the edge of an orgasm *and* an asthma attack.

And still he wasn't hurrying. Pushing him so that he sat back on his heels, she dropped to straddle him right there on the shower floor.

"Chloe—"

She rocked her hips until she had what she wanted, his erection poised at her entrance. "I'm on the pill," she panted.

He ran his hands up to her breasts, then to her ass, yanking her in, angling her so that they were better aligned, the whole time kissing her to the point of madness.

And breathlessness.

But breathing was completely overrated, she assured herself, and then he slid home with one sure, shocking push of his hips, filling her to the hilt, and she didn't need to breathe at all.

They gasped in tandem pleasure. God, the pleasure. He rasped his thumb over her, just above where they were joined, and then again. She cried out, arching against him as the orgasm hit her hard and fast and utterly unexpectedly. Shuddering, she writhed against him in exquisite torture, her body completely under his control.

Heaven.

For one beat, there was such incredible heaven, but in the next, the tightness in her chest spread and completely shut off her air supply, and the dots that had been dancing at the edge of her vision closed in. She heard Sawyer's sudden and urgent "Chloe!" but it was far too late. She'd already faded to black.

# Chapter 12

*"A guilty conscience needs no accuser."*

CHLOE TRAEGER

Sawyer spent the next half hour in a state of unaccustomed panic. After Chloe had passed out, he'd run with her to his truck, where he'd found her inhaler on the seat. She'd come to enough to use it several times, and now sat in the passenger seat insisting she was fine.

Ignoring her, Sawyer drove toward town, intending to take her straight to the ER.

"Don't," she said. She was wearing sweats—his. He'd grabbed dry clothes from his house. "I'm okay."

"Chloe—"

"Look, I'm still paying off my last two ER visits." Her voice was rough and ragged, and she didn't look nearly steady enough, but she put a hand on his arm. "Please, Sawyer. Just take me home. I have a portable nebulizer there and can give myself a breathing treatment."

He opened his mouth to demand why the hell she

hadn't had her inhaler *on* her, but he decided to save that fight for when she didn't look like a slight breeze could knock her on her ass. Against his own instincts, he drove her home and settled her in on the cottage couch, watching as she gave herself a breathing treatment.

At least she had some color back to her lips. That helped, but Christ, he'd never forget the way they'd turned blue, or how she'd gasped, hands at her throat, fighting to draw air into her lungs.

*His fault.*

"Mr. Magic Eight was right on once again," she rasped over the rumble of her nebulizer.

"What?"

She let out a low, wheezy laugh. "The Magic Eight app. The love advisor, remember? It said you wouldn't get laid, and that I would. Of course, I didn't get *laid* laid, but close enough. I mean, I finished and you didn't get to..."

"Christ, Chloe."

"And now you can confirm I don't sound like a mule in a tar pit, right?"

"You *stopped* breathing."

"Only for a minute."

Head spinning, he dropped it into his hands. "Only for a minute," he repeated dully.

"Yeah." She paused. "Too soon?"

He'd been mentally flogging himself, and she was joking around. He shoved his fingers through his hair and resisted pulling out the strands by the roots.

"Yeah," she murmured. "Too soon. Sorry. Sawyer, look at me. I'm fine."

He gently pushed the nebulizer mouthpiece back in

place. She'd passed out from lack of oxygen, and *she* was comforting *him*. "Why wasn't your inhaler on you?"

"Because nothing was on me. We got naked, remember?"

"Fuck, Chloe."

She had the good grace to look sheepish. "Okay, so I didn't exactly realize what was going to happen, or that I'd need it. I told you, I'd been on a sex moratorium."

"No, you absolutely didn't tell me that."

"Oh." She grimaced. "Well, I started to. I told you I couldn't."

Okay, she *had* told him that. And he'd mistakenly— and cockily—believed she'd meant that she couldn't orgasm with a man.

Which mean that he was an ass. A complete ass.

"And technically, it's not that I *can't* orgasm," she said, waving the mouthpiece. "*Obviously*. It's just that the experts recommend measuring your peak oxygen flow and having a portable nebulizer handy."

"Okay. So why didn't we do that?"

"Well, for one thing," she said, "that doesn't exactly scream spontaneity and excitement, and second, I didn't plan on having sex in your shower, it just happened. Which proves point number one."

"Never again, Chloe," he said flatly. "I don't want you to ever again be without that inhaler. Do you hear me?"

She gave him a smart aleck salute that made him narrow his eyes and open his mouth, but before he could say a word, the front door opened and Tara and Maddie came rushing in. Maddie was in the lead, wearing jeans and a USC sweatshirt that Sawyer recognized as Jax's. She sat at Chloe's side and hugged her. "You avoided the ER this time."

*Barely*, Sawyer thought grimly.

Tara, cool and calm as ever, squeezed in past Sawyer to get closer to Chloe, patting him on the arm as she did, probably assuming that he'd rescued Chloe. If she'd known the truth, he knew he'd have been on the receiving end of a blistering verbal and well-deserved attack. No one did pissed-off-Southern-belle slash protective-mama-bear better than Tara.

But for now, Tara leaned over Chloe and kissed her cheek. "I should have sat on you earlier when you left all half-cocked, making yourself as scarce as hen's teeth. You were wheezing even then."

Chloe left the nebulizer mouthpiece in but rolled her eyes as her two sisters continued to mother and baby her, while Sawyer wondered if they had any idea just how strong she really was.

"Can you tell us what happened?" Tara asked Chloe. "What were you doing, and why in God's name are you streaked with...*mud*?"

A faint blush tinged Chloe's cheeks, and her eyes locked on Sawyer. Slowly she pulled the nebulizer mouthpiece out to speak, but before she could, Tara pushed it back into place.

"No, don't." She fussed at the blanket over Chloe's legs. "It can wait, especially if you're going to tell me you were rock climbing or—"

"She was with me," Sawyer said.

Three sets of eyes landed on him. Maddie's and Tara's were both curious and completely nonjudgmental.

They trusted him, and right now, the weight of that trust sat like an elephant on his chest. He worked so damn hard to earn the respect and trust of the people of his town, and this was a perfect example of why it was all a sham. He knew full well that he'd had no business touching Chloe, and he'd done it anyway.

Coburn had warned him, all the way back when he was eighteen and scared spitless, that all it took was one step out of line. One extra drink before he got behind the wheel. One reckless word, and his whole world could implode. He knew that, and yet when it came to this, he lost it.

Chloe's eyes were narrowed, clearly trying to tell him to keep his trap shut, but he refused to let this be her fault. "I was giving her a ride home from the mud springs."

"The mud springs," Tara said with a frown. "Those are *way* out there. How did she get to your house? When you called me, you said you were bringing her here from your house." She turned to Chloe. "Oh, sugar. What did you do this time?"

Chloe yanked the mouthpiece out. "Nothing!" It wasn't quite a yell, but only because she was clearly still hampered by her inability to breathe freely.

Tara shoved the mouthpiece back in Chloe's mouth. "And yet here you lie, struggling to breathe."

Chloe slapped a hand on the nebulizer power button, and the room went quiet. "You're right," she said. "I did do something. I rode to the mud springs, then hiked all the way back to the highway when I couldn't get the Vespa to start. I tried to hitch a ride, but Sawyer came along and played hero."

"All that hiking," Maddie murmured. "That could have brought on the asthma attack."

Clearly wanting answers, Tara whirled on Sawyer. "Tell me what happened."

"Hey," Chloe said before Sawyer could open his mouth. "Talk to *me*."

Tara reached back and hit the power button of the nebulizer again. "I was asking *him*," she said, eyes on Sawyer. "You picked Chloe up from the highway and then brought her back to your place, and..."

"And I forgot my inhaler," Chloe said. "I left it on the seat of his truck."

"Chloe." Tara's voice was full of censure and dismay.

Maddie looked equally upset with her.

Sawyer met Chloe's intense gaze. Obviously she'd rather them think she was completely irresponsible than blame him.

But she wasn't. Reckless, maybe, yeah. Impulsive, too.

But not irresponsible. So...was she trying to protect him? The notion was unexpected, as was the way it made him feel, but he didn't need her protection. "She's okay," he said to a suspicious Tara, knowing that a good amount of her anger came from a gut-wrenching fear for her sister, the fear that someday they wouldn't get to her in time, and she'd suffocate during an asthma attack.

It also came from the fact that Tara considered Chloe hers. And no one messed with anything that belonged to Tara, even if that possession was a full-grown woman with her own needs and passions.

"He's right, Tara," Chloe said. "I'm okay, like always."

Thankfully, not five minutes later, Sawyer was paged into work by DEA Unit Chief Reed Morris. An ongoing drug investigation that he was working on had some movement, and his presence was required at a task force meeting. From there, he had to go by the hospital to talk to one of the ER docs on staff. The guy had treated a suspect they needed to interview, but he couldn't tell Sawyer anything new about the case. He was just leaving the ER, intending to go check on Chloe, when a nurse came running by, stopping short when she saw him.

Mallory Quinn. Sawyer had dated her in high school. Well, not dated exactly. She'd written his English papers, and in turn, he'd done her science and math. He'd also had a big crush on her, but she'd never returned it, preferring the boys who didn't get arrested when they got bored.

They were friends now and occasionally ran into each other professionally. Seeing him, Mallory skidded to a stop, the relief evident in her eyes. "We need help restraining a patient in bay three."

He didn't waste time asking questions but ran ahead of her. In bay three, two orderlies were struggling with a man on the bed.

"Paranoid schizophrenic," Mallory said. "And off his meds."

He wasn't big, maybe five foot seven, and one hundred forty pounds, but given the odd light in his eyes, he was deep into an episode. When the guy swung out with a fist toward Mallory's face, Sawyer grabbed him, restraining him while Mallory produced a syringe.

It was over in ten seconds, the patient out cold.

"Well, that was fun." Mallory shoved back her hair. She was sweating. They were all sweating. "Thanks. That was about to get ugly."

Sawyer ran a finger over her wrist, where already the bruise in the shape of the man's hand was starting to show. "Get some ice on that."

She laughed shakily. "Will do." She squeezed his hand

and smiled at him. "Anything you need in return?" She smiled. "Maybe I can help you out in study hall or something?"

"I've got a Vespa that needs a rescue and a once-over. Possibly a new battery. Your brother still working at the auto shop?"

"Yes." Mallory glanced down the hallway. "I'll call Joe on my break. Would this be Chloe Traeger's Vespa?"

There were no secrets in Lucky Harbor, so he didn't bother to sigh. "Yes."

Her smile went a little teasing. "I suppose she gives better...English than me?"

Sawyer grimaced, and she laughed. "No worries, Sheriff. I won't tell Lucille if you won't."

He walked outside the hospital toward his truck, pulling out his cell to check on Chloe. She didn't answer, so he headed toward the inn, stopping by the Love Shack first because Ford and Jax had texted him ten times. Each.

They were both little girls that way.

Ford was behind the bar. Jax was there as well, not serving but sitting on the counter in the corner, thumbs flying over his phone. They both looked at Sawyer expectantly.

"What?" Sawyer said.

"You know exactly *what*," Jax said. "Start with Chloe being taken home by you in *your* clothes. No, wait. Start just before that."

From beside him, Ford's mouth twitched as he served Sawyer a tall soda. "Way to ease into it, man."

Sawyer tossed back the soda and gestured for another.

Ford refilled him. "Let me save you some time. Tara and Maddie ratted you out. Here's what we know—Todd gave Chloe a ride and dumped her on the side of the road with Lucille. We know this because he came here and knocked a few back, muttering about the idiocy of women. Then somehow you showed up and saved the day with the flat. You gave Chloe a ride and then you two went at it. She had an asthma attack. Oh, and you should watch your back. The sisters are pissed off at you for sleeping with the wild child."

"She's not a child," Sawyer said. "And there was no sleeping involved."

"Nice," Ford said. "But you probably shouldn't mention that in front of my girlfriend—"

"I meant," Sawyer said through his teeth, "that I didn't— *Fuck*. Never mind."

Jax laughed softly. "You didn't...fuck?"

"That's *not* what I said."

Jax looked at Ford. "He's all pissy, too. He didn't get his."

"Hey," Sawyer said. "I was a little busy making sure she didn't die."

"Ah," Ford said with a sage nod to Jax. "You're right. He didn't get his. Which explains the bad attitude."

When they both laughed, Sawyer headed to the door. "You guys are assholes."

"Aw," Ford called after him. "Don't go and get your panties in a wad. That's not good for a guy in your condition. If things get too tight down there, you might do some real damage."

Without looking back, Sawyer flipped them both off and went out into the night. He drove to the B&B and parked in front of the small owner's cottage between Tara's car and Chloe's Vespa, which Joe had indeed rescued and fixed at Sawyer's request.

Tara opened the door, and it was a good thing that looks couldn't kill or he'd be dead on the spot. "She okay?" he asked without preamble.

"Yes."

A tension that he hadn't realized was gripping him released slightly. "I want to see her."

"She's sleeping."

A silent battle of wills commenced, and Tara was good. She had thirty-five years of staring people down and winning, but Sawyer was better, and he held his ground.

She caved with a small sigh and a shake of her head and moved aside to let him in.

He'd have gone in search of Chloe but Tara's hand on his arm stopped him.

"She thinks she's a real tough cookie," she said.

"She is."

"Not when it comes to you."

He met her gaze. "What does that mean?"

"You're going to have to figure that out yourself. I like you, Sawyer. I like you a lot, but hurt her and I'll hurt you."

He stood in front of her armed to the teeth, trained in hand-to-hand combat, outweighing her by seventy-five pounds minimum, and raised a brow.

"Okay," she said. "So I know how ridiculous that sounds, but I mean it."

"We're on the same side," he said.

"No. I'm here for her, always. You're here because there's something going on between you two, something physical and clearly out of control. But when that's done..."

He understood what she was saying. He was temporary in Chloe's life, and Tara was not. "I just want to see her," he said. "I want to see for myself that she's okay."

Tara stared at him for a long beat, clearly fighting the urge to tell him to go to hell. "Fine. I'm going to the inn to check on things. But I'll be back in fifteen minutes, you hear?"

He stopped in Chloe's doorway, propping up the doorjamb with his shoulder. The room was pitch-black, but if he strained, he could hear her breathing and just that sound soothed him. As a few minutes passed, he slowly felt some more of the tension drain out of his body.

Earlier, in his shower, her breathing had started out quiet like this, but then she'd gone up in flames for him. He'd loved it, loved the way she'd panted for more, clutching at him as if she was afraid he'd stop. It had gone straight to his head, more potent than any alcohol or drug.

And then in the very next beat, when she'd started to suffocate, all he'd wanted to do was breathe for her. God, he could still taste the bitter helplessness, and he hated, *hated*, that she'd suffered. That she'd almost died.

There was a chair by her bed, and feeling oddly wobbly, he straddled it. Reaching out, he messed with the shades so that they let in slats of pale light from the moon's glow, enough to see her by.

Chloe lay on her side, a hand tucked beneath her cheek. Her lips weren't blue. He wasn't sure if he'd ever get that image out of his head.

The stuff of nightmares.

The covers had slipped to her waist. She wore a thin camisole top, and one of the straps had slipped off her shoulder, nearly exposing a breast. The thin material was caught on her nipple, and his mouth actually watered.

The hem of the cami was bunched high on her waist, and with the blanket at her hip, several inches of smooth skin was bared. He watched her stomach rise and fall with each easy breath. No wheezing.

She'd showered. He could smell the scent of her shampoo and soap, and he leaned in for a better whiff. Yeah, he'd completely lost it.

Careful not to wake her, Sawyer ran a finger up her arm, intending to nudge the strap of her cami back into place. But murmuring something in her sleep, Chloe rolled, flopping to her back, covering her eyes with a flung-up arm.

Her breast escaped its confines, and in the cool night air, the nipple puckered into a tight peak.

He bit back a groan and closed his eyes. Not looking didn't help, so he stood and pulled the covers to her chin, hiding her from his gaze. Then he sank back down to the chair, not moving from the spot until he heard Tara return, and then he left like the hounds of hell were on his heels.

# Chapter 13

*"Smile. It's the second best thing you
can do with your lips."*

Chloe Traeger

Chloe awoke with a start and sat straight up, startled by
her cell phone vibrating at her bedside table. "Sawyer?"
she whispered. The sun was shining in through the
shades, the ones she'd shut the night before.

But she was alone in the room. No Sawyer. Which was
odd only because she…*felt* him. Blowing out a breath,
she lay back and grabbed her phone. "Hello?

She'd missed the call. Squinting, she accessed her
messages and listened to someone just breathing. She
hit delete. The next message was the same, more of her
heavy breather.

Delete.

The third message, she finally got a voice. "Hey, sweet
thing." Todd. "We need to talk."

No, they didn't. Delete. She sat up and looked around
for Sawyer. But of course he wasn't here. Why would he

be here? Just because yesterday they'd—and she'd—and he hadn't—

*Don't think about it.*

Happy to be the Queen of Denial Town, Chloe flopped onto her belly and closed her eyes, but instead of going back to sleep, she relived yesterday with aching acuity. Sawyer giving her a ride, stopping to change Lucille's tire, his hands moving economically and capably, his shirt stretching taut over the bunch and play of the muscles in his back and shoulders.

Mmm, those muscles. But it had been the fact that he'd helped Lucille that had grabbed her by the heart. He wanted her to think he was so badass, but the truth was, he *was* that good guy Lucille had accused him of. Way too good for the likes of Chloe. Sawyer's world was black and white, and if any gray popped up, well then, he arrested it.

A lot of her life had been spent in the gray. Nothing illegal. At least not *too* illegal. She may not have been raised the way most kids were, but Phoebe had taught her about doing the right thing for the right reasons. That's who she was. At least, that's who she tried to be.

And she wanted to be loved for being that person.

She could play with Sawyer all she wanted but the fact was they were too different, and eventually it would go bad between them. Even if he could put up with her asthma issues—and those were pretty huge considering she couldn't have sex without a tactical plan—he wouldn't be able to put aside his code of conduct, not for the long haul.

He was bound by duty. He hadn't caught her and Lance freeing the dogs, or trespassing, or any of the "gray" area things she did, but what if he had? What would it do to him if someday he had to make a choice between the law and her?

Realizing sleep was nothing but a distant memory, Chloe tossed back the covers and forced herself to get up. After a long, hot shower that only brought more memories, she dressed and went outside.

And came face-to-face with her Vespa.

Confused, she pulled out her cell phone and called Lance. "Hey. You okay?"

"That's my question for you, babe," he said, sounding just as wheezy as she'd been yesterday. Her heart kicked hard. He'd had a long hospital stay last month, complicated and awful, and he'd never quite recovered.

She was deathly afraid this was as good as it got for him. His doctors were starting to discuss lung transplants. "I'm serious, Lance."

"Me too," he said, breath rattling. "I'm good. I'm better."

She wanted desperately to believe that. "Did you fix and bring home my Vespa?"

"No. Sawyer said he'd take care of it."

So he *had* been here...

"Chloe? You still there?"

"Yeah." She shook off the image of Sawyer caring enough to remember her stranded Vespa and getting someone to retrieve it. "Want lunch later? I'll bring you something yum from Tara and also make you some more of that decongestant balm."

"Sure. Hey, did you really go au natural at the mud springs?"

"Not quite but close enough."

"Would have liked to see that," he said wistfully. "How 'bout I make us a mud patch in my backyard?"

Chloe was laughing when she hung up, and her gaze snagged on the Vespa. Sawyer had come through for her. Again. She rubbed at the ache in her chest that had nothing do with asthma and headed inside the B&B. She found Tara cooking and simultaneously muttering to herself as she wrote something on a recipe card. Maddie was at the table with a stack of paperwork, probably organizing inventory and scheduling for both the inn and her wedding, as evidenced by the handful of bridal magazines spread across the table.

"Hey," Maddie said to Chloe with a smile. "You're up."

Tara turned off the stove, pushed Chloe into a chair, and served her a plate of food. "Feeling better?"

Chloe stuffed her mouth with a bite of something cheesy and moaned in delight. "If I say yes, are you going to yell at me for yesterday?"

"No one's going to yell," Maddie said with a stern glance at Tara.

Chloe tried to tell if Sawyer had come by for coffee yet. She was staring at the pot when her sisters exchanged another glance.

"Let me save you a neck crimp," Maddie said. "The sheriff hasn't been here yet."

"Nope," Tara said. "Not yet." Her grip was tight on her spatula, like maybe she was hoping to hit him upside the back of his head when he did show up.

Maddie shoved an open magazine at Chloe. "What do you think of this dress?"

It was a long-sleeved chiffon in an absolutely hideous Easter-colored floral print that looked like something a great-grandmother would wear. "Um..." Chloe searched for tact. "Thought you wanted a more traditional bridal dress."

"It's for you," Maddie said, beaming with pride. "As my bridesmaid."

Chloe blinked, then slid a cautious look to Tara for help.

"You don't like it?" Tara asked innocently. "Because we've already ordered it for you. You should see the hat that goes with it."

Chloe was chewing on her lower lip, trying to find something tactful to say about the dress from hell when Maddie let out a snort, her face mottled red with the effort of holding in her laughter. "Okay," Chloe said. "That's just mean."

"Sorry," Maddie said, looking anything but. "I was hoping to scare you half as bad as you scared us yesterday."

Chloe ran a finger over the god-awful dress and shuddered in relief. "Yeah, well, consider it done."

Maddie flipped the page over. "*This* is more what I have in mind for you."

This dress was a beautiful spaghetti-strapped sundress the color of a perfect summer sky.

"I can just see you walking along the dock in it," Maddie said, beaming.

The wedding was going to take place here at the marina, right on the water, with the reception inside the inn. Lucille, who'd become an ordained minister online, was going to do the honors.

Chloe, Maddie, and Tara *ooh*ed and *aah*ed over the dresses for a few minutes before Tara went back to the stove and Maddie to her notes. Chloe ate and watched them both. Her sisters were happy, content to be here in Lucky Harbor doing something with their lives. And she...she needed to find *her* happy. If she couldn't do that here with them, she wanted to know. "I meant what I said yesterday," she said. "I want to do more around here than just fill in. I think I have more to offer than that."

"Well, of course you do," Maddie said.

"Then give me a chance. Look, I understand that over the years I haven't exactly been the model of responsibility or reliability, but you have to admit I've gotten better. And we could start slow, a few days a week. See how it works out." She took Maddie's hand and pulled her up. Then turned off the stove and grabbed Tara's hand as well.

She tugged them into the sunroom and pointed to the windows lining the wall. "There's where I'd put the spa bed, so the client could look out while getting a facial, or whatever they've chosen. The sea is one of the most Zen things you can look at, and we have a helluva view. And I'd put a chair there," Chloe said, pointing to a corner. "For mani/pedis. A pretty table too, where a guest could be served a delicious lunch prepared by our very own chef—" She smiled at Tara. "It's endless. We can do bridal parties, women's retreats, girls' weekends, all with the promise of being far away from the hustle and bustle of real life. Can't you see it?"

"I can," Maddie said and looked at Tara.

"If I ask you a question," Tara said slowly, "will you get all mad and run off and get naked and muddy with the sheriff again?"

"Jeez, *one* time!" Chloe sighed. "Ask."

"What you're suggesting is a major change in our marketing strategy and planning. It also changes your daily grind, *hugely*." She lifted her hand when Chloe opened her mouth. "I'm not saying it doesn't have potential," she said. "Because it does, but I have to know. If we do this, if we invest and get on board, do you really see yourself happy here, locked in one spot? Because you would be, Chloe. Even if we start with just a few days a week, that's *every* week. You'd be locked in. This is one of those things called a root, sugar—which you've avoided like the plague your whole life. And it's a biggie. We'll be depending on you."

"I know," Chloe said. "And yes. I really see myself doing this." Trying not to get defensive, she stood her ground. "And it's not like it's a cement block attached to my feet for crissake. It's a schedule, and I can work it out to suit me."

"Not if we put a ton of money into it," Tara said. "If we do that, you're going to have to put the clients first, ahead of your need to ... whatever."

Chloe swallowed, willing herself to stay calm. "I'll pay for the necessary renovations and marketing," she said, and bit back her retort when Tara didn't look overly impressed at that. Because the truth was that Chloe hadn't been able to put in as much capital for the B&B's renovations as her sisters had. But she was finally starting to make money and was trying to make up for lost time.

"Why don't we draw up plans and get an estimate on what it'd cost to get this room ready?" Maddie suggested with her ever-present mediatory skills. "And like everything else, we'll decide together. Majority rules."

Tara nodded. "Sounds good to me. Chloe?"

Not seeing much of a choice, Chloe nodded. Her sisters went back into the kitchen, and she stayed in the sunroom and let herself envision the spa room. When it was as clear as the ocean outside the window, she sat in the corner and drew her plans. Then she pulled out her cell phone and called the only contractor she knew. "Jax," she said. "Question."

"Me first. You breathing today?"

She had to laugh. "Yes."

"Good. Keep doing it."

"Believe me, I intend to," she said. "I have a new client for you."

"I love new clients. Who is it?"

"Me."

He was quiet a moment. "Why do I have the feeling I'm about to get myself in trouble?"

"No trouble. You know I want to turn the sunroom into a day spa. What I need is an estimate to install a really plush client bed, an industrial sink, hidden speakers, a wall fountain, and a pretty oak wall cubby for storage. Oh! And a soaking tub and a shower for body wraps and things like that. I'll need to know how fast you could get to it, and how much."

Jax promised to get back to her as soon as possible, and satisfied that she was at least on her way, Chloe headed out the back door.

\*　　\*　　\*

Their property was about an acre, and though they were off the beaten path, they backed up to the ocean. It was remarkable, really, and Chloe could still feel the shock that had hit her last year when her mother had died and a will had surfaced.

Growing up with Phoebe as Chloe had, she would have sworn on her own life that Phoebe didn't have a spare dollar to her name. After all, they'd lived in tents, or on friends' couches, or even in their car for most of Chloe's childhood. Always at the mercy of Phoebe's need to be free.

Looking back on it brought mostly fond memories, and she'd never suffered for their distinct lack of luxury, but there'd definitely been lean times. Lean enough that a tiny germ of resentment had found its way into Chloe's heart. She'd never admitted it out loud. To do so felt...disloyal. But the feelings of resentment sometimes surfaced regardless.

Why hadn't her mother raised her here in Lucky Harbor?

There'd been two short visits, but Chloe had been very young, too young to understood that her mother's parents owned this place. All Chloe remembered was her excitement over having a real bed with a soft mattress and more food than she could eat. When she'd lost her first tooth, it'd been here. The tooth fairy had found her sleeping in a spare bedroom and slipped a crisp new dollar bill under her pillow. After that, there'd been no more dollars, and her young mind had concluded that the tooth fairy must have lost track of her.

Chloe sighed at the jumble of emotions swirling inside of her. She glanced around the property and hoped like anything that she was doing the right thing, and not being influenced by long-ago childhood yearning. Just because she'd felt safe here as a kid once or twice didn't mean this was right for her. She'd always found her own security, her own way.

Still, it felt right, living with the sisters she'd never really known.

With her name on the deed.

Granted, just last year that hadn't meant much. When they'd arrived, the inn had been mortgaged to its eyeballs and in massive disrepair, practically falling down on its axis.

They'd fixed it up, and it was now the three sisters mortgaged to their eyeballs, but it was home.

Home.

Chloe marveled at that and shook her head. On the far side of the property was the marina, which consisted of eight boat slips and a small marina building—basically a one-room warehouse. It held kayaks, canoes, and various other equipment for the marina, and a small office area where Maddie usually worked the books for the B&B, when she wasn't in the kitchen looking at wedding magazines.

As she walked across the yard to the marina building door, she suddenly stopped. The building was always kept locked, with a code lock. But the lock was broken, the door half open.

She took a step back and peered around the corner of the building to the docks. Normally she'd see the fishing boat and houseboat that had come with the inn, and the two boats that Ford kept at the dock as well.

But there was nothing, no boats. Heart stuttering, Chloe whipped out her cell phone.

*       *       *

The police came, including Sawyer. All four watercrafts were found floating within ten miles, with insignificant damage.

Someone had set the boats loose.

There was no real property damage beyond the broken lock on the marina door, for which Chloe was hugely relieved but still completely unnerved.

"Kids," one of the cops decided.

Tara shook her head. "We've never had problems before."

"And this seems personal," Maddie murmured.

If Sawyer agreed with that, Chloe couldn't tell by his expression, but he stayed back when the other uniforms left.

"We'll make extra drive-bys," he told her quietly. "But you need to think about getting some security. An alarm. A dog."

"I don't want to scare the guests with a big old guard dog," Tara protested.

"Safety is far more important than worrying about what anyone else thinks," Sawyer told her.

"You're right, of course." Tara looked at her sisters. "We'll think about both an alarm and a dog."

"We can borrow Izzy from Jax," Maddie said.

"Sure," Tara said. "And she can lick the next bad guy to death."

When she and Maddie left Sawyer and Chloe alone, Chloe met his gaze. "What are you thinking?"

"That I like the sight of you breathing. How are you feeling?"

"Fine. And don't deflect. Do you think this is just a random vandalism by a kid?"

Before he could answer, his cell phone vibrated. Simultaneously inside his open SUV, he was paged over the radio. He swore and looked at her.

"You have to go," she said.

"Chloe." He put his hand on her jaw and tilted her face up to his, his gaze searching hers.

"I'm fine," she said again. "They need you. Go."

She waited until he'd driven away and then headed inside the marina building. She looked around, hating the fact that someone had invaded their space. She settled at Maddie's desk and booted up the computer. Sometimes being able to compartmentalize was a benefit, and now was no exception. She put the vandalism out of her mind, occupying it instead with thoughts of her day spa.

They needed brochures, a social networking plan, and a schedule. She worked for several hours, even updating their website, posting a survey to see how many people would be interested in coming into the inn for a day spa.

She took a lunch break to whip up some chest balm for Lance, bringing with it some of Tara's Not Your Granny's Homemade Chicken Noodle Soup and a Don't Call It Just a Grilled Cheese Sandwich. She bullied him into using the balm and into eating, not liking how thin he was. "Lance—"

"I'm *fine*," he said, leaning back on his couch. He lived in a rental duplex with his brother, Tucker, and the decor was late-nineties frat boy. Todd and Jamie lived on the other side of the duplex, though they were at work with Tucker at the moment, which Chloe was glad for. Todd had left a couple of messages reminding her that she still owed him, and that he wouldn't be averse to collecting.

The doorbell rang, and Lance opened the door to a pretty petite blonde holding a plate of brownies. She beamed at him, leaning in to kiss his cheek. "Hey, baby."

*Baby*? Chloe looked at Lance, who blushed and shrugged. "Renee, this is Chloe."

"Your best friend!" Renee smiled sweetly at Chloe. "I've heard so much about you!"

Huh. Chloe slid another look Lance's way because *she'd* heard nothing about Renee.

"Renee's a nurse and works at my doctor's office," Lance said.

Ah, now it made sense. The crush. Thrilled and amused at Lance's rare shyness, Chloe took a brownie, then left them alone. Hopefully when Lance got lucky— and given the way Renee was looking at him like he was lunch, he was going to get *very* lucky—he wouldn't end up passing out like she had.

She headed back to the marina office and found a happy surprise—there were already hits on the inn's website survey, all of them positive and requesting further info about her spa services. She was working her way through them when the office door opened.

"Whatcha up to?" Maddie asked innocently.

Too innocently. Chloe looked at her, but Maddie had quite the inscrutable face when she chose. "Selling swampland in Florida."

"Or...?" Maddie asked.

"Or organizing Santa's naughty-and-nice list."

Maddie laughed. "Or...?"

"Okay, let's play a different game." Chloe leaned back in her chair. "The one where you tell me what you really want to hear."

"Okay, how about this—when were you going to come clean about hiring Jax to renovate the sunroom?"

Chloe sighed. "He tattled."

"He *mentioned* it."

"That man is *so* whipped."

"Honey, you asked the man I sleep with every night to help you," Maddie said. "Of course he's going to tell me. I thought we were going to do this as a team."

"We are. And I didn't hire him. I only wanted to get an idea of the damage before we worked on the overall business plan. I put a short survey up on our website, just so we could get some feelers about who might be interested." She had to work hard at sounding cool, calm, and collected, when she wanted to grin triumphantly. "Several people have already inquired about booking for day treatments. Two of them are interested in overnight stays at our full rate."

"I like the full rate part," Maddie said.

"I bet Tara likes it even more."

"Let's go get some food and find out."

"Is Tara cooking?" Chloe asked hopefully.

"Not tonight. We have no guests, and we were thinking Eat Me."

Eat Me Café was the diner where Tara had worked up until they'd gotten the B&B running. It was still a quick go-to when they were starving, though lately they'd been too busy to eat together. Well, technically Tara and Maddie had been too busy with their full lives. Chloe not so much. "What's the occasion?"

"Nothing. Just a together meal. And maybe…" She pulled Chloe to her feet. "A certain sister feels like she could have been more supportive, but she's too Southern and mule-headed to admit it so she's buying dinner instead."

"Mmm," Chloe said, grabbing her purse. "I love it when Tara feels the guilt."

\*      \*      \*

Chloe, Maddie, and Tara had just ordered their dinner when a group of guys entered the diner, laughing and talking so obnoxiously loud that the entire diner went quiet. It was Todd, Jamie, and two others that Chloe had seen around, Dan and Mitch. Filthy from head to toe, they'd clearly just gotten off a job, but that wasn't what made Chloe's gut clench.

It was the look in Jamie's eyes, the one that said he'd been drinking. Mitch too. She was glad Lance and Tucker weren't with them.

The diner was still quiet, the uncomfortable kind of quiet as Jamie gave them all a mocking bow. Next to him, Mitch started laughing into the silence.

"Sit down," Todd said to them uneasily, locking gazes with Chloe.

Arms still wide, Jamie straightened from his bow and knocked the glasses off the table closest to him. "Oops."

Seated at that table was Lucille and her blue-haired posse. Lucille put her hands on the table and rose, her tight bun all aquiver. "Jamie Robinson," she said sternly. Even with her tower of hair piled on top of her head, she was barely five feet tall, but she got right up in Jamie's face, waggling a bony finger. "You can't afford any more trouble, do you hear me? You boys get out of here, and don't come back until you're sober, all of you."

She spared a scathing look at Todd. "And you. You should be ashamed of yourself. People are rooting for you to get your life together."

The four guys stared at her like she was an alien, and then Mitch burst out laughing again as they took an empty table.

Amy was the waitress on shift, and she was new to Lucky Harbor. Mid-twenties, she was tall and leggy and tomboy pretty in low-riding cargos, a tank top, and some ass-kicking boots. She was standing behind the bakery counter, gazing at Mitch, clearly unhappy to see him. When she'd first come to town, he'd gotten a little aggressive in his attempt to date her, until she'd actually Maced him one night.

Still laughing, Mitch looked her over and winked lecherously.

Lucille pulled out her cell phone. Probably calling the police, Chloe thought. She wondered if Sawyer was on duty, and how he'd feel about having to face down these drunken idiots.

"Jan should have refused them service," Tara murmured. Jan was the diner's owner and had a zero monkey business tolerance. "They're obviously intoxicated, and they're making Maddie as nervous as a long-tailed cat in a room full of rocking chairs."

"I'm fine," Maddie said. A lie. She was vibrating with nerves. Confrontations did that to her, for good reason. She'd once told Chloe that her ex-boyfriend had been a bully, much like Jamie and Mitch. Smooth and charming on the outside, mean as a snake on the inside.

From the kitchen, the cook dinged his bell. Someone's food was ready, and Amy loaded up a tray. As she walked past the guys' table, Mitch reached out and patted her ass. "Hey, baby. Miss me?"

Amy gave him an eat-shit-and-die look. "Get your hand off my ass."

He laughed like a hyena. "Or what?"

Amy dumped the tray over his head. Soup rained down his hands and face, noodles clinging to his wet skin. "Jesus, that's hot!" he yelled, pulling his shirt away from his body.

Amy glowered at the others as she bent to pick up the fallen dishes. Chloe got up to help her, as did a man from a table behind them.

"Hey, asshole!" Mitch bellowed at the man crouched next to Amy. "Back away from my girlfriend."

Amy stood up. "Are you kidding me? Get out of here, Mitch."

Eyes completely soulless, Mitch merely smiled. "Make me."

# Chapter 14

*"They say money talks, but all mine
ever says is 'good-bye, sucker.'"*

Chloe Traeger

Earlier that morning, Sawyer had given some serious consideration to staying in bed. He was tired, and already knew his desk was nothing but a mountain of paperwork waiting for him. He hated paperwork with the same passion that he hated errands, cooking for himself, and mowing his dad's lawn—which reminded him, he needed to go by there, as he'd been doing every few days.

For all the good it did him.

Hell, Sawyer wasn't even sure the man was eating the food he brought. Nolan Thompson was probably tossing it out soon as Sawyer left, then ordering himself pizza.

Sawyer would've liked a pizza. He thought about it all day, and five minutes from going off duty and getting himself that loaded thick crust, the call came in—overly rowdy customers at the diner. He drove over there wondering what the odds were that he'd get pizza tonight after all.

Not good, he realized in the first two seconds of walking through the diner's front door.

"Who the fuck called the pigs!" Mitch bellowed at the sight of Sawyer. Swinging out, Mitch punched his fist through the bakery display.

Glass shattered to the floor in a slow, musical wave.

He pulled back his arm for another swing, blood blooming brightly from shoulder to wrist as he snagged a surprised Amy around the neck and pressed her against him. "Who did it? Who called? You?" he demanded of Amy, giving her a shake. "You?"

"No," Chloe said, rising from where she'd been crouched on the floor picking up fallen dishes. "I did it. I called the police. Don't hurt her."

"Chloe." Without taking his eyes off Mitch, Sawyer gestured for her to sit back down. "Mitch, let her go."

Mitch shook his head and tightened his grip on Amy.

"Amy didn't do anything to you," Chloe said to Mitch, *not* sitting down.

"Chloe, goddammit," Sawyer said softly. "Sit."

Mitch was glaring at Chloe, clearly wishing he had enough arms to grab her, too.

Lucille stood up next to Chloe. "Mitchell Tyson, if you hurt that girl, I'll tell your mother. Do you hear me?"

Jesus Christ. Sawyer's fingers itched for his gun, but he couldn't pull it. The place was too crowded, each person being an unpredictable variable in this shitty situation.

And Chloe knew that, dammit. Anyone with any common sense would have just let him handle this. But he'd been in enough bad spots to know that common sense wouldn't come into play, not during a time of panic.

And people were panicked, he could practically smell it. The most panicked of all was Mitch. Sawyer watched the blood run down Mitch's arm and wrist to drip on the floor. With any luck, he'd pass out from blood loss. "Let her go, Mitch," he said again.

"No way, man. I watch those cop shows. I know what happens to a guy like me."

Sawyer would have liked to evacuate the diner quickly and quietly, but no one in Lucky Harbor did anything quickly or quietly. "Nothing's going to happen to you if you let her go." He took a few steps forward, stopping only when Mitch tightened his grip on Amy, cutting off her air supply.

Amy clawed desperately at Mitch's bloody arm.

"Stop it," Chloe yelled. "You're strangling her. Stop it!"

Mitch eyed the front door, but Sawyer was blocking it. "Let her go," Sawyer told him. "And I'll let you walk free and clear." He spoke the lie smoothly, without blinking an eye.

"Fine." Mitch shoved Amy hard at Sawyer, but before he could make his escape, Chloe whirled and executed a badass roundhouse kick to Mitch's family jewels.

Mitch let out an unholy scream but didn't go down. He reached for Chloe, but Sawyer was already lunging forward. He vaulted the table between them, hitting Mitch in the middle of the back. They crashed into the center of Chloe's table. The Formica table cracked and broke beneath them, sending them to the floor hard.

Sawyer pulled Mitch's hands behind his back and cuffed him just as the front door opened.

Everyone craned their necks to see what now.

Matt Bowers walked in. Though he was wearing his

forest ranger uniform and obviously armed, he was looking loose and relaxed, sipping on a Starbucks coffee. He took in the room with his sharp eyes, not missing a thing. "Aw," he said to Sawyer, taking a slow sip of his coffee. "You get all the fun."

\*    \*    \*

Chloe, Maddie, and Tara helped Amy and Jan clean up the diner. Chloe did so with an ear half bent toward the action outside, where Sawyer had hauled Mitch.

The parking lot was cop central. Chloe could see Sawyer in profile, looking particularly badass in his uniform and various weaponry, his face the usual impassive blank as he directed Mitch toward the back of an ambulance. Odd how one man could evoke so many emotions within her. Lust? Oh yeah, much of the time. The urge to smack him upside the back of his head? Yep, that was often there, too. Affection? She'd have said no. He didn't need her affection, everyone admired and loved Sawyer, who was just about the most composed, self-assured, capable man she'd ever met.

But there was something suspiciously close to affection filling her now, which had her shaking her head at herself.

Todd, Jamie, and their other pal were out there, seated on the curb being questioned. Inside the diner, things were nearly back to normal, but Chloe didn't think she'd forget anytime soon the way Sawyer had looked facing Mitch. Her stoic sheriff had been steady and calm, his body at ease but ready for anything.

Willing to put his life on the line.

It'd been that willingness that had really brought home

the realities of his job. He wasn't playing at getting a thrill, the way she did when she went rock climbing or hang gliding.

His job was real. And potentially lethal.

There'd been that one horrible moment when Mitch's arm had tightened over Amy's throat and Amy had made that little involuntary squeak as she'd used up the last of her air. Terror. More than anyone, Chloe knew what that terror was like, and she'd never felt so helpless in her life, so she'd interfered. She'd just been so afraid that Sawyer's help would come too late.

She'd made it worse, but Sawyer had handled it. He'd had an entire diner full of scared customers, and yet he'd resolved the situation with minimal damage.

Amy came up next to her at the window.

"You should go home," Chloe said gently.

Clearly made of sterner stuff, Amy shook her head. "I'd rather be here and keep busy. Besides, the police said I'll need to answer some questions for their report in a few minutes. I wanted to thank you for helping. We've got customers pouring in now. Lucille must have put it up on Facebook already."

The cook's bell dinged from the kitchen, and with a tight smile at Chloe, Amy moved off.

Chloe stayed at the window. Without looking, she knew when her sisters closed in and flanked her. A year and a half ago, they'd been complete strangers to each other. Now she could sense their presence without a single glance, just as she also knew that Tara was frowning in concern and Maddie was waiting for the right moment to hug her tight. That was Maddie's thing, hugging. Kissing. Throwing the love around.

Chloe could appreciate that the three of them were very different, that they each had their own way of expressing their feelings, but she herself was of the show-don't-tell school. She showed her feelings through actions, which she thought she'd done over and over again for her sisters by laying down roots here. It certainly hadn't been for herself. At least not at first. "Close call," she murmured.

"You've had a few of those in as many days now," Tara said.

"I'm fine."

"You always say that."

"It's true."

Tara nodded. "You're resilient," Tara agreed. "But we still worry."

"Not necessary."

Together through the window they watched Sawyer, though Chloe was probably the only one whose good parts twitched at the way his uniform fit his big body.

"Let's go home," Maddie said after a few minutes, slipping an arm around each sister.

Tara nodded.

"I'll meet you there," Chloe said.

"'Kay." Maddie squeezed them both, then kissed Chloe's cheek. "Love you."

"You too," Chloe said, and though she didn't take her eyes off Sawyer, she still felt it when Maddie rolled her eyes at Tara.

Tara didn't hug Chloe, waiting instead until Chloe looked at her. "And you love me, too, right?"

"Sure," Chloe said. Hello, wasn't that implied?

"One of these days," Tara grumbled, "you're going

to say it to me, and I'm going to be too old to hear you."

"You're too old now."

Tara sighed. "See you at the inn."

"Mm-hmm." Chloe could see inside the ambulance. Mitch's arm was being wrapped, with Sawyer watching closely. When Mitch shifted as if to run, Sawyer put a hand on his shoulder.

He had big hands. Capable of subduing suspects. Equally capable of taking her straight to ecstasy. He was also of the show-don't-tell persuasion, which she appreciated.

"Hey," Amy called out to Chloe as she strode by, her thin but toned arms straining under the weight of a heavily loaded tray. "No drooling on the glass!"

\* \* \*

Sawyer drove himself to the ER. He'd sliced one palm and also had a cut above his left eye. Regulations required him to go for a hepatitis shot and to get checked out whenever blood was shed.

It took less than an hour. No stitches, just another boatload of paperwork. He was just walking out of the ER when a Vespa pulled up. He watched as Chloe parked illegally and walked to the entrance, stopping when she caught sight of him standing there beneath the overhang.

"Hey," he said. "What are you—" He was deeply startled and stunned when she wrapped her arms around him and squeezed him tight.

When she'd interfered at the café, fear and fury had fought for equal space in his brain. With the fear for her safety gone, it left more room for the temper.

"I just heard you were hurt," she said.

"I'm fine. Chloe—"

She reached up and touched the bandage over his brow. He grabbed her wrist. "We need to talk."

"Okay, so I butted in and I shouldn't have."

"Damn right you shouldn't have."

She glanced up at him, eyes fierce. "He was hurting her. And I was closer." Her eyes settled on the bandage over his brow. "I'm sorry you got hurt."

"It's nothing. You're the one who could have gotten hurt."

"You had a gun."

He gaped at her. "The diner was full. I couldn't pull my gun. There are rules, protocols—"

"*He was hurting Amy!*" She looked at his cut and frowned.

"I'm *fine*." If this whole thing wasn't an example of their basic differences, he didn't know what was. He'd never actually had to choose between his job and a woman before, and he never wanted to. He closed his eyes and found that his temper couldn't hold up against the feeling of her warm and safe in his arms.

"I was scared," she murmured.

"You're safe now."

"Not for myself! For you!" She took a breath. "But it's your job. I get that, because your job is a part of you. No one gets that more than me."

He'd lost his last girlfriend because of his job. And the one before that, too, now that he thought about it. He'd figured no woman could get it, but he'd forgotten.

Chloe wasn't just any woman.

"I imagine it takes some time to learn to deal with the worry," she said.

He felt an ironic smile twist his lips. "Want a lesson on how to deal with someone in your life who makes you worry?"

She stared at him. Then smiled. "Do you worry about me a lot?"

"Twenty-four seven."

Her smile warmed. "We could start a club." She found the bandage on his palm, and taking his hand in hers, turned it over to inspect it.

"Just a scratch," he said.

Chloe nodded, then kissed the skin just above the bandage. He'd known that she enjoyed baiting him. That she'd also enjoyed driving him nuts. That she was sexually attracted to him.

All those things were mutual.

But this... this felt like more. It felt like a level of caring he hadn't realized existed.

For either of them.

*        *        *

After the brief ER visit, Sawyer went back to the station to finish up the paperwork before finally dragging his sorry ass toward home.

He probably shouldn't go so far as to call the house he'd purchased earlier in the year *home*. He actually wasn't sure why he'd bought it in the first place, other than Jax had been on his ass to buy instead of rent for years now.

Sawyer had liked renting, liked not being responsible. But now that he'd gone and put his name on the dotted line of a mortgage, he was getting used to it. Plus he had to admit, owning a house gave him an air of unexpected stability, even respectability. It took him one more step away from that reckless guy he'd nearly turned out to be. Like Mitch. Like Todd. Like the thug his father had been so damn sure he'd end up being, rotting in jail somewhere.

But Sawyer hadn't. He'd turned himself around. And he'd bought a fucking house to prove it.

The place needed work. A lot of work, actually. The house was older, built in the 1970s. The color scheme was early Partridge family. A month ago, he'd bought paint for the living room, dining room, and kitchen, and it'd been sitting in his garage ever since. His *garage*. Christ. At least he didn't have a white picket fence and two-point-four kids.

When he'd first told his dad that he'd bought the house, the old man had frowned. "You gonna keep it up?"

No, he'd just spent $250,000 to let the thing rot away. Grimacing, Sawyer ignored his still pea green walls and went straight to the kitchen. The refrigerator held beer, a questionable gallon of milk, something that had maybe once upon a time been cheese, and a leftover...something.

Stomach growling, he took a beer, pulled out his cell phone, and called the diner, surprised when he heard "Eat Me" in Amy's usual brisk cheer.

"Amy, it's Sawyer," he said. "You should have gone home after this evening."

"Are you kidding? Retelling my near-miss is making me some serious bank in tips today. You need a late dinner, Sheriff?"

"Yeah. You have anyone making deliveries tonight?"

"For you, yes. Let me guess—a bacon blue burger,

extra blue, side of fries, and a dinner salad with no tomatoes, because tomatoes are a vegetable and despite the fact that you're six feet three of pure man, you eat like a little boy."

"Hey," he said. "Salad's a vegetable."

"Iceberg lettuce is a single step up from water. Doesn't count."

"Good, then forget the salad," Sawyer said. "And make it *two* burgers and double the fries."

While he waited for his dinner, he went into the garage and eyeballed the buckets of paint. "Fuckers," he said to them, but picked one up and carried it into the dining room. "You ready?" he asked his walls.

They didn't have an opinion.

He'd taken a second beer and rolled two very nice plain "ecru" stripes when the doorbell rang. He answered while reaching into his pocket for money to pay the delivery kid.

But it wasn't a delivery kid at all.

It was Chloe, wearing a short denim skirt, emphasis on short, and a black angora sweater that was slipping off one shoulder, revealing a little black strap of something silky. And holy smoking hell, was she a sight for sore eyes.

"Hey," she said.

Ever since their little playtime in his shower, their encounters together had vacillated between awkwardness and their usual lust-filled animosity. Right now it was a little of both. He cleared his throat. "Hey."

"I forgot to say thanks at the hospital earlier, for getting my Vespa back to me."

"Thanks for not dying on me in my shower."

She snorted. "You're just glad you didn't have to explain *that* to Tara."

He felt his brows knit together and his stomach clench.

"I'm kidding." She flashed a smile. "Gonna have to lighten up, Sheriff, otherwise life sucks golf balls." Looking like sin on a stick, she held up two large bags from the diner. "I went back to the diner to get dinner to go for Maddie and Tara and found Amy bagging your order. She got someone else to deliver to the inn and sent me here with enough food for two normal guys. Or for one starving sheriff." She tried to come in, but he stopped her forward progress.

"Inhaler?" he asked.

"In my pocket, Sheriff. Sir." She added a salute. "Can I come in now?"

This was a very bad idea, of course, but she simply pushed past him, her sweet little ass moving seductively in that skirt as she walked through his nearly empty living room and into the dining room.

She looked at the few swipes he'd taken with the roller. "Coming right along, are we?"

"Been busy."

She'd been busy, too, he knew. Everyone and their mother in Lucky Harbor had felt free to keep him up-to-date on her every move. She'd been taking care of Lance, working at various hotel spas in the state, giving geriatric yoga classes at Matt's studio to Lucille and her cronies, and planning a sunroom renovation at the inn for a day spa.

And if she'd trespassed, done any B&E, or anything else illegal, he hadn't caught wind of it. Or maybe she'd laid low. No doubt she still had that rowdy untethered spirit that he was so inexplicably attracted to. But she'd changed over the last few months. Not settled down—not in any way, shape, or form, but she'd done something else, something better.

She'd found a place to belong.

He wondered if she even knew it yet. Best not to ask. Best not to keep her here one second longer than necessary, as they clearly didn't have themselves under control around each other.

Or maybe that was just him. *He* didn't have himself under control, not when his hands were shoved deep in his pockets to keep them off her. It was getting hard to remember why they were a bad idea.

*Because she's the opposite of your type.* She was crazy unpredictable, spontaneous…

Okay, that was a load of bullshit. She spoke to the part of him that he kept locked down tight. And that. *That* was why this was a bad idea. He wasn't ever going to be the man she wanted or needed, one who'd fly off a mountain on a hang glider simply for the thrill. One who'd open a vein and bleed out his emotions at the drop of a hat. Or crawl under a fence into private property to rescue a couple of dogs.

He wasn't that guy. He'd committed himself to the obligations of duty and discipline. His job swallowed him whole, and that was just how it was. So he stood in the doorway of the dining room waiting for her to set down the food and leave.

Instead, she turned to him with a little smile that was disarmingly contagious. "You may not know this about me," she said. "But I'm excellent with a paint brush."

Oh, Christ. He was a goner.

# Chapter 15

*"Never drive faster than your guardian angel can fly."*

CHLOE TRAEGER

Sawyer shook his head at Chloe. "I'm not going to ask you to help me paint."

"Don't ask. I'm offering." She took a second, longer look around at his nearly empty living room, the completely empty dining room, the equally sparse kitchen.

He knew what she saw. She saw what he'd just been thinking himself...it was a house. Not a home. "You need to go before the paint fumes aggravate your asthma."

She merely moved to open the windows and turn on his two ceiling fans.

"Is that enough?" he asked.

"For now. There's good cross ventilation." She picked the food back up and moved to the middle of the dining room floor and dropped to her knees.

"What are you doing?" he asked, voice a telltale hoarse, causing her to glance at him, but he couldn't help it, he'd just flashed to her making that same move in his shower.

"Making you a picnic." She leaned over to pull food from the bags. "Come on."

He didn't budge, riveted by the way her skirt was riding up the backs of her thighs.

"If you don't sit," she said, not looking at him. "I'm going to eat all of this by myself. And trust me, I totally could. I'm starving."

Sawyer sat. She handed him a plate loaded with two burgers and double fries, and then pulled a large bottle of wine from the depths of her huge purse.

"The big guns," he said.

"No, that would have been vodka. But I wanted to relax you, not put you out of commission. Though you're so freaking stoic all the time, it's hard to tell if you need relaxing. Nothing seems to faze you."

He let out a mirthless laugh. "You think nothing fazes me?"

She smiled a secret little smile. "Well, except when I'm naked. You were pretty fazed then."

He shook his head.

"No?" she asked.

"Yes." *Fuck*, yes. "But that's not *all* that gets to me."

"What else, then?"

"Seeing you suffocating," he said. "That fazed the hell out of me."

Her smile faded. "I know. I've been told that's damn hard to watch. I'm sorry."

"Don't be." He shook his head. "God. Don't apologize for that." He paused. "You and your sisters make up?"

"Oh. Yes." Chloe shrugged. "Pretty much anyway. It

was my fault. I spent all those years being wild, and then I hate when no one wants to depend on me." She shook her head. "I'm working on that, but the problem is, people tend to assign you the role of the person you are at your worst, you know?"

Yeah. He knew. Exactly.

"Not much I can do about that," she said with a philosophical shrug. "Except hopefully continue to prove them wrong." She set the bottle between her thighs to steady it and went to work the corkscrew, also from the mysterious depths of her purse. When she bent over the bottle, her skirt rose up even more, giving him another quick flash of—yep—something that was definitely black silk beneath. The corkscrew slipped, and with a low breath of annoyance, Chloe ran her fingers up the neck of the bottle to reset its position.

"Keep doing that," he said, mesmerized. "And the top will pop off on its own."

She laughed and handed everything over to Sawyer. He removed the cork, and she took the bottle back, pouring him a glass.

He wasn't much of a drinker, not anymore, and he'd already had the two beers, but she was looking at him with a soft smile. And then there was that sweater, still slipping off her creamy shoulder. Plus she smelled amazing, was wearing black silk under her clothes, and he was suddenly more than a little short on brain power.

They ate and drank in a comfortable silence. After a while, Chloe looked down at his empty plate with a smile. "Better?" she asked.

He'd inhaled everything. Finally full and *definitely* better, he nodded. "Thanks."

"Oh, it's not me." She poured the last of the wine into his glass. "It's the food. And the alcohol."

He was pretty sure it was her, but he kept silent, shaking his head when she pulled a second bottle from her purse. "What else does that suitcase hold?" he asked in marvel.

"Everything."

"Anything worthwhile? Like, say, a house painter?"

"*I'm* your new house painter." She reached for the corkscrew to open up bottle number two.

He stopped her. "Are you trying to get me drunk?"

She tilted her head and studied him. "Is it possible?" she asked, sounding intrigued.

"No." But when she leaned forward, her sweater gaped and he discovered that the black slinky strap belonged to a black, slinky bra. Mouth suddenly dry, he downed the last of his wine, not surprised that he was feeling a nice little buzz.

"I really can paint, you know," Chloe said. "If we keep the windows open, and I wear a mask."

"No way."

"No way?" she repeated in disbelief. "You don't get to tell me what I can and can't do, Sawyer."

He sighed and swiped a hand over his face. This was his own fault for demanding instead of asking. He located one of the paper masks that the paint store had given him with his purchase.

It covered her mouth and nose, and when she got it into position, she looked at him. "I know you're just concerned and not trying to be a domineering asshole," she said benignly through the paper.

"Do you?" he asked, amused in spite of himself. She looked adorable.

And sexy.

"Yes. But I'm a big girl."

And wasn't that just the problem.

Her eyes crinkled so he knew she was smiling as they began painting.

"How's your dad?" she asked.

He watched as she stretched up high as she could with her roller. "Ornery as hell," he said, eyes locked on her bare legs.

"I hear they get that way with age."

He had to laugh. "Then he's always been old."

"You have your moments, too, you know."

That gave him pause. "Are you saying I'm like him?"

"I'm saying that sometimes genetics are annoying."

She was still painting, paying him no special attention, allowing him to look his fill. He wondered if she was referring to Phoebe and the wanderlust lifestyle that had been forced on her, or if she blamed the father she'd never known for not sticking around.

She dipped her roller into the paint tray very carefully. "Sometimes I wonder what I got from *my* dad. If he was…difficult. You know, like me."

Sawyer had liked Phoebe, he really had, but sometimes he wanted her to come back to life just so he could strangle her. How could she never have told Chloe a thing about her father, given her nothing of half of her own heritage—no knowledge, no memories, nothing?

Sawyer had never asked his father much about his own mother. It had hurt that she'd left him, and for a hell of a long time, he'd been positive that he'd been the reason she'd gone. But that was different. Chloe's dad hadn't been there from the get-go. "You're not difficult," he said, meaning it, but when she snorted with laughter, he had to smile. "Okay, maybe you're a little difficult, but I like it."

"You do not. *No one* likes difficult. Which is why I'm so hard to put up with."

It took him a moment to answer because suddenly his throat burned like fire. "If I don't get to tell you what to do, you don't get to tell me how I feel," he said, and watched her eyes crinkle at the corners as she smiled at her own words being tossed back in her face.

Then she scratched the bridge of her nose and left a smudge of paint there, and another just beneath her left eye. Uncharacteristically silent, she turned back to her wall.

They painted in silence for five full minutes.

"You think he'd like the way I turned out?" she asked her wall casually. Too casually. "You know, my father."

God, she was killing him. "I think he'd be proud of you, of your giving nature and spirit, how you live your life. Everything."

She glanced at him. "Including the way I jump in without thinking things through?"

"Proud," he repeated firmly.

She stared at him, then nodded. "Thanks." She nudged him with her hip when they both bent for the paint tray at the same time. "And I bet your dad's proud of you too."

It was Sawyer's turn to snort.

"Deep down," Chloe said, sounding sure.

Maybe deep, deep, *deep* down, but Sawyer kind of doubted it.

"At least he's around," Chloe said softly. "And he visits with you." She shrugged. "So he's a grumpy old fart. Life's short, Sawyer. Sometimes you have to take what you can get and make it okay."

With this deeply profound statement, Chloe bent over to load more paint onto her roller, pulled back her mask, and flashed him those black panties again, distracting him.

At some point, she put down her roller and went for that second bottle of wine. He doubted the alcohol was good for her asthma, but he'd be damned if he'd point that out. He'd drink the whole bottle himself first before pointing it out. "Before you open that, there's beer in the fridge. I'm going to have one of those instead."

She eyed him, a small mischievous smile tugging at her mouth. Had she seen through him? No telling with her. But she put down the bottle, leaving it unopened. "I'm a little bit of a lightweight anyway. Maybe I'll share a beer with you."

"Sure." He got one out of the fridge and offered her the first sip. She passed it back, and he took a big gulp, watching her as she checked out his empty kitchen.

She hadn't been kidding about being a light drinker. She suddenly wasn't seeming all that steady on her feet after two and a half glasses of wine. But then again, he wasn't all that steady himself after the two beers he'd had before she got here, then the lion's share of the wine.

They moved back to the dining room to eye their handiwork.

"Huh," she said, and rubbed at the streak of paint on her jaw.

"What?" He watched her shake her head as if having a private conversation with herself. She laughed.

So did he. Because two walls looked neat, smooth, and orderly.

His.

The other two walls, Chloe's, had been painted in haphazard, uneven strokes utterly without pattern. "Your wall looks...off," he said diplomatically.

"It's your house. Your house's crooked," she said, gesturing to it as she blew a strand of hair from her face. She was paint-spattered and sweaty, and sexy as hell.

He smiled at her. "*You're* crooked," he said, and she burst out laughing, sliding to the floor in a puddle of mirth.

"Probably we shouldn't be painting in your condition," she finally managed, swiping her eyes.

"Your condition is worse than mine."

"Says who?"

"I'm a cop. I know these things. And I know something else, too. We're stopping painting now."

"Yeah?" He heard her breath catch, and when she ran her gaze down his body, she wasn't the only one.

"You have something else in mind, Sheriff?"

"Yeah."

She stared up at him for a long moment, then reached for his beer. He pulled it out of reach, brought it to his lips, and tilted his head back to finish it off in two long swallows.

"Are you drunk?" she whispered.

"More tipsy than I'd like," he whispered back. "You?"

"I don't know." Very carefully, she spread her arms. "Give me a sobriety test, Officer Hottie."

He grinned. "Hottie?"

"Yes, but shh, don't tell yourself that I think so. It'll go to your head. What do I have to do to pass?"

"Walk a straight line."

Affecting a model-on-the-catwalk strut, Chloe headed

straight toward him and tripped over her own feet. "Whoops," she said when he caught her up against him. Her eyes were glassy, and her lips were parted. Damp with exertion and warm to the touch, she was both heaven and hell.

Her hands went immediately to his ass, and damn if she didn't cop a feel. "Sorry," she murmured and gave him a squeeze. "I think I failed the test. You should handcuff me now."

Sawyer would like that. He'd like to handcuff her to his bed and bury himself deep. "Chloe—"

"Uh-oh. Did I scare you off, Sheriff Hottie? Because I can stop talking now. Actually, I—"

He set a finger on her lips, and she smiled. "I talk a lot when I'm wasted," she admitted, her lips brushing against the pad of his finger as she spoke.

"Only when you're wasted?"

"Hey, I'm just trying to figure you out, is all."

"What's to figure?" he asked.

"Well, sometimes you're like...the big bad wolf."

"The big bad wolf."

"Yeah. But then you go to Home Depot to save an old lady from her smoke alarm, and rescue a silly fair maiden from the mud springs, and catch a convenience store robber single-handedly."

"I also paint houses."

"See? You're multitalented." It took her three times to say the word.

He laughed and set her back on her own feet. "Okay, it's time to get you some coffee. I have a coffeemaker somewhere..."

It'd been a housewarming present from Tara, actually.

He'd never used it, preferring to stop by the inn for his coffee instead. He'd never really examined the reasoning for that too closely and didn't stop to do so now either.

"No, not yet," Chloe said, resisting. "I like being just a little buzzed. I don't have bad dreams that way." Turning away, she gathered the empty wine and beer bottles.

"What do you have bad dreams about?"

"Hmm?"

Sawyer stopped her, taking the bottles from her arms, carrying them to the recycling bin. Then he took her hands in his. "The dreams."

"Oh," Chloe said, peering at the walls they'd painted. "They're silly, really. Not nightmares or terrifying or anything like that. They're mostly annoying." She pulled free and squatted before a bucket of paint and stared into the remains.

He crouched at her side. "Tell me."

"Well, they start out differently." She shrugged, and her sweater slipped off her shoulder again. "Sometimes I'm running and getting really tired. Or I'm in a car and almost out of gas. Or I'm on a plane that can't take off... stuff like that. And I know I need to be somewhere, but something always gets in the way. The stupid thing is, in the dreams, I never really know where exactly I need to be, just that I'm late or I'm missing something or..." She shook her head. "I can't explain it, but I wake up frustrated and angry. And feeling helpless." She fell quiet and ran a finger through the paint. "Silly," she whispered again.

"Doesn't seem silly to me." He pulled her back up to her feet, surprised when they both wobbled. She leaned against him with a dreamy little sigh, and he wasn't sure if that was because he'd managed to catch them both or if she liked the grip she once again had on his ass. "Coffee," he repeated, and they let go of each other.

Then he realized that he didn't actually have any coffee to go in his coffeemaker. "I'll call for another delivery."

She bit her lower lip. "That's not a good idea."

"Why?"

"You can't be seen by anyone." She winced. "I sort of maybe just put paint on your ass. On purpose."

"Yeah, I know. Don't worry, you're going to pay for it."

"Uh-oh." She looked both worried and intrigued. "What's the punishment?"

Pretending to consider that, he stepped toward her and she stepped back, reaching the kitchen wall. Her hands slid behind her, covering her own ass. "I'm not into kinky stuff," she said, then hesitated. "At least I don't think I am. What did you have in mind?"

He smiled at her, and she let out a shaky breath.

"Get your inhaler, Chloe."

She took a hit. Then she settled back against the wall again, looking up at him hopefully. "Ready."

God, she was sweet. So sweet and so hot.

"What do you want me to do?" she asked breathlessly.

"Keep breathing. That's your only job, got it?"

She nodded solemnly. "Got it."

"Good." He cupped her breasts in his hands, and she gasped. When his thumbs rubbed over her nipples, she let out a shaky moan, and her head thunked back against the wall. Slowly her legs gave out, and she slithered down to the floor. Somehow, they both ended up on their knees facing each other.

"You okay?" he asked.

"Yeah." She smiled sheepishly. "I guess I just really liked that."

He smiled. "You won't in the morning."

She broke the eye contact and looked down at herself, finding the two large painted handprints, one on each boob. "Hey, I borrowed this shirt from Tara! And when I say borrowed, I mean stole." Reaching past him, she once again dipped her hand in the paint.

"Don't even think about it," he warned.

"Take your medicine like a man, Sheriff."

"Depends on where you're going to put that hand."

She palmed his erection and squeezed, and he let out a soft groan as her fingers did the walking. "Defacing personal property," he managed.

They both looked down at the handprint she'd left on him.

"What's the punishment for that?" she whispered.

"What's with you and getting punished?"

She grinned. "I don't know. I think it's your handcuffs. I can't stop thinking about them. Can I deface you some more?"

"Only if I get to return the favor."

Again she grinned. "We are so drunk."

"This is a true statement," Sawyer said carefully, and she snorted, falling to her back right there on his floor. Staring up at the ceiling fan slowly swirling above them, she said, "We should keep painting."

"That's a really bad idea."

"Why?" she asked. "Haven't you ever pulled a drunken all-nighter?"

"Sure, when I was a teenager."

"Was this before or after the flaming bags of poop?"

"After."

She grinned. "Hard to believe. You seem so..."

"If you say *sweet*," he warned, "I *will* get out the cuffs."

She snorted again, and he pulled her into his lap.

He gripped her ass, feeling the drying paint on the soft material of her skirt. "Hope you didn't steal this, too."

She wriggled a little, and the hem slipped up her thighs to her hips, giving a nice view of her black panties. He slid a finger over the silk, stopping short when he heard her wheeze. "Chloe."

"I'm okay."

Suddenly very sober, he slid out from beneath her. "No, you're not."

"Dammit! One little asthma attack and now you're scared of me." She pushed up to her feet and staggered to the refrigerator. She came back with two more beers and offered him one.

He looked into her eyes and beyond the fresh bravado saw unease. Whatever she said, however she acted, she was no more ready than him to push their luck.

"I thought we were sharing." He took both bottles from her and put one back. She snatched the other one and opened it, even though he hadn't intended on doing so. She took a sip, and he reclaimed the bottle, downing half the beer in one gulp so she wouldn't.

Things got hazy after that.

At some point, Chloe reasoned that since there were no overnight guests at the inn tonight, she was free and clear. She texted her sisters that she'd gone camping and wouldn't be back until morning. And though she and Sawyer kept painting, nothing seemed to get accomplished.

This was probably because Chloe kept stopping to touch him.

Or maybe that was him touching her.

Yeah, probably it was him touching her. He couldn't seem to control it. He, of the famed self-control, couldn't stop and he didn't want to.

# Chapter 16

*"Multitasking means screwing up
several things at once."*

CHLOE TRAEGER

All Chloe knew was that one minute she was blinking sleepily at their handiwork on Sawyer's walls, and in the next, they were on his sole piece of living room furniture—his huge, comfy couch. He was lying lengthwise, and she appeared to be playing the role of his blanket, sprawled over the top of him like she belonged there.

She had no idea how much time had gone by, but it was still dark outside. She lifted her head and met his gaze, and there came the sort of timeless moment that you read about but never really experience. It'd have probably been more classically romantic if Sawyer hadn't had a possessive hand palming each of her butt cheeks, his fingers meeting in the middle, running up and down the Great Divide, but she'd never been all that into the classics.

Their faces were so close that the tips of their noses

brushed, and she hoped like hell that he was extremely far-sighted because she was pretty sure she was a complete wreck.

"You're beautiful," he said, reading her mind.

Chloe ducked her head and dropped it to his chest, but he fisted his hand in her hair at the nape of her neck and tugged until she looked at him again. "You are," he said in his brook-no-argument cop voice.

Actually, *he* was the beautiful one. Not in a pretty boy way, he was far too rugged and weathered for pretty. But there was an absolute beauty to his tough, edgy exterior, and she soaked him up. He always moved with such innate grace and ease that she tended to forget what a big guy he really was.

But his poise was gone tonight, which made her smile dopily. She'd relaxed him, which was quite a feat. "We should have a paint party every night until your house is done."

He took his gaze off her and stared at the walls around them, seeming a little befuddled. It was such a shock to see his expression anything other than his usual imperturbable calm that she looked around, too, and winced. "Do the walls seem to be missing a few spots to you?"

He looked at her, then down at himself. "I think we're wearing the missing paint."

His expression cracked her up. "I've never seen you all discombobulated before," she said.

"I'm not discombobulated."

But he was. His hair was standing on end, cemented into place by some paint that might or might not have come from her fingers. His strong, lean jaw was dark with a full day's growth. And his eyes, those mesmerizing warm chocolate eyes, were glossy. But most telling of all was the adorably sexy, bad-boy smile on his face. She grabbed his face and gave him a smacking kiss. "You're so cute."

"Cute." He repeated this slowly, like what she said didn't compute.

At some point, he'd stripped out of his shirt and gun. Both were on the floor next to the couch, both covered in paint. She had no memory of how any of that had occurred but suspected she was at fault. She really wished she remembered the stripping off of his shirt, but between the wine and beer and her silly low tolerance for booze, she wasn't exactly clearheaded. "You *are* cute," she said with conviction.

"Take it back."

Sawyer looked very serious with his paint highlights, and she struggled not to laugh. "No can do, Officer...*Cute.*"

His grip tightened on her, and he nipped her bottom lip. She heard a ragged moan and realized it was her own. And that her hands had slid into his hair to hold his face to hers.

"Can't do this," he said against her mouth.

"Why?"

"We're drunk."

"Not that drunk."

"So you're completely aware of the fact that you're grinding against me?"

Yikes. She went still with great effort. Then sat up and carefully got off him. It took her a moment to find her sea legs, and she put her hands out for balance.

"Hey," Sawyer said. "Come back." His voice was deep

and steady. A command. She hated commands, but this one suited her. But first, she took a good, long look at him lying there, chest bare, abs hard and flat, jeans slung low. He was so big and bad...

Bad for her, she remembered. She just couldn't quite remember why. "You just said we weren't going to have a drunk make-out."

"We're not having drunk *sex*." He tugged her back over him. Hard arms encased her, and two hands slid beneath her skirt to grope her ass. "Drunk making out is absolutely allowed," he said against her mouth. "In fact, it's required."

She was smiling when he kissed her. He tasted like the beer they'd shared, smelled like wet paint, and felt like warm promise. It was the best kiss she'd ever had. They stopped to breathe for a minute, and she set her head down on his chest. It was the last thing she remembered until some odd and obnoxious pounding sounded between her ears. When it stopped, she sighed and snuggled into the deliciously heated blanket beneath her...

Then came the sound of a door opening, and a low, shocked "Jesus Christ" woke her all the way up. She opened her eyes to Ford and Jax standing in the doorway.

And behind them was...daylight.

This caused her a moment of confusion. She wasn't at home in her cottage. She was still at Sawyer's, and in fact, was still on the couch, wrapped up in him.

And covered in paint.

So was Sawyer. He didn't open his eyes, but he did tighten his grip on her ass. The man definitely had a thing about her hind quarters.

"What the hell are you guys doing here?" Sawyer said

to Jax and Ford without looking. "Besides breaking and entering."

"No breaking. Just entering," Ford said with a laugh in his voice.

"We were supposed to meet at eight to go sailing," Jax said. "Then when you didn't answer your phone..."

Sawyer sighed, then managed to crack one eye and looked at Chloe. "You okay?"

Nodding, she pushed upright and staggered to her feet. When she got her first full-body view of Sawyer, she gasped.

He tilted his head and looked down at himself. He had fingerprints on each pec. A trail of paint across his perfect, washboard abs.

And a full handprint on his crotch.

To his credit, he didn't so much as blink. But Chloe clapped a hand to her mouth to hold in her horrified laugh. She had a few handprints on herself as well. Big handprints, most notably on her breasts.

Ford was wearing a shit-eating grin. Jax looked as if he was trying not to laugh, but he busted up and had to fake a cough.

Sawyer sat up.

Jax, not being a stupid man, backed away.

Not Ford. He pulled out his cell phone, accessed the camera, and aimed it at Sawyer's crotch. "Hold still, man."

Sawyer got to his feet and shoved Jax out the front door, then turned to Ford, who risked life and limb to take the pic before stepping back over the threshold. "Guess you won't be coming with—"

Sawyer shut the door, locked it, and turned to Chloe. "Sorry about the idiots."

"Yes, well, they're not the only idiots." She put her hands to her head, testing. Still on. That was good. Carefully, she took stock of herself. Everything seemed to be in working order. She looked at Sawyer. "I'm going to assume that since your pants are still on, I didn't get much farther than feeling you up. Right?"

Sawyer went still, his eyes serious. "You don't remember last night?"

"Well, I didn't get lucky. Or I'd have had another asthma attack." She smiled.

He didn't. "I took advantage of you." He sounded extremely unhappy about this.

"Look, if anyone took advantage of anyone, it was me, Sawyer. I mean, look at you."

They both looked at his body decor, specifically at the hand on his crotch. Some good humor crossed his face at that. "You are pretty damn hard to say no to," he said.

She bent for her purse and inhaler. "And yet people manage all the time." Crap, she really hated when her mouth disconnected from her brain. She slipped into her shoes and turned to the door, still kicking herself for that revealing statement.

"Chloe."

She didn't look at him. Couldn't. There was something far too serious in his voice, and it tightened her chest. "Yikes, would you look at the time? Gotta run before my sisters call you to send out a search party for me, which would be awkward considering I'm here." She reached for the door. "Plus, I'm giving facials today at the Garden Society lunch and have to mix up my special antiaging blend." She was babbling. She pressed her lips together and told herself to shut up and get out, but when she tried to open the door, Sawyer's hand appeared above her head, holding it closed.

Dropping her head to the wood, Chloe tried not to absorb the warmth and strength of him standing so close at her back, but then it got worse because he turned her to face him.

She felt more exposed than when she'd been naked with him in his shower. "I really do have to go," she whispered.

"In a minute." Sawyer ran a finger over her jaw. "You helped me paint and made my shitty evening a whole lot less shitty. Thank you for that."

She let out a low laugh. "You could be thanking me for something much more fun except for your damn moral high ground."

His eyes met hers, dark and warm. "Yes, but you wouldn't have remembered it." He reached for her, and she realized he was going to kiss her. Horrified, she slapped a hand over her mouth, blocking him. "Morning breath!"

Sawyer stared at her, clearly torn between amusement and frustration. "Stay right there," he commanded and vanished into the kitchen, only to come back a few seconds later with a pack of gum. He popped a piece into his mouth and chewed. When he leaned in again, she slapped a hand to his chest. "Not you, me!"

This didn't deter him. He pushed a piece of gum between her lips. "Chew."

Obeying, Chloe narrowed her eyes. "You sure give a lot of orders."

"Yes. And here's one more. We're both minty fresh now, so kiss me."

Laughing, she pulled the gum out of her mouth, and

he did the same. Going up on tiptoe, she set a hand on his chest and gave him a peck on his warm, firm mouth. Just when she would have ended it, he planted one hand on either side of her head, caging her in. "Again," he said against her mouth. Yet another command—not that she minded this one.

The brush of his lips was soft this time, though not tentative. Not at all. Nope, she could *feel* the barely leashed power, the carefully restrained passion, but for now, with nothing more than their mouths touching, he held it all in careful check, until her fingers curled into his hard biceps and she heard herself moan for more.

He gave it, settling in against her, deepening their connection to a hot, intense tangle of tongues that would have had her sliding to the floor if his arms hadn't been banded tightly around her. When they finally broke apart, she stared at him, happy that he wasn't breathing any steadier than she. "Okay, then," she said, nodding like a bobblehead, and whirled to leave.

And walked right into the door.

Without laughing at her, though she was quite certain he was doing his damnedest to hold it in, he handed her back her gum, which had stuck to his shirt when she'd grabbed on to him with both fists. Then he popped his back into his mouth with a smirk and reached around her to open the door.

"Thanks," she muttered and flew out of there. Two minutes later, she was on the road, smacking her forehead through her helmet, trying to get the brain cells back in working order. "Don't you fall for him," she ordered herself, peeking into the side mirror to make sure she got the message.

Her image didn't answer, but there was something different about her. Dammit. She had the Maddie glow!

Oh, God, this was bad. Falling for Sawyer would be a colossally stupid move. Sure, he wanted her. But she also drove him crazy. She wasn't right for him, and no matter what he'd said about appreciating her as is, there was no doubt in her mind—in order to become the woman Sawyer needed, she'd have to change. Already facing that very problem with her sisters, it felt too overwhelming for her to even go there.

But it was like a damn song in her head all the same. *Change, and you can have acceptance. Change, and you can catch a man. Change, and...*

God, she was damn tired of that song.

In any case, it wasn't as if Sawyer was going to fall for her. He was smarter than that. The man thought things through, never made a misstep, had himself rigidly controlled.

Well, except for last night. She'd gotten him drunk. She hoped he didn't blame her for that—though why not? It had been her doing. It was *always* her doing.

He'd have to repaint, of course. Or maybe not. He hadn't done much with the place in the way of making it a home. Not that *she'd* had a lot of experience with making anything a home, but she did have Tara and Maddie, both of whom were great at it. The cottage was a little messy but it was full of her things. That's what made staying there feel good, seeing the tangible evidence that she belonged. Even something as small as her favorite glass jars for her creams lined up on her dresser instead of shoved into her backpack made her smile.

But Sawyer had nothing of himself in his house, other

than some pretty badly painted walls...A start, she had to admit. He was trying. He didn't have two sisters to show him how. Hell, he probably didn't want sisters. Or a real home for that matter. She actually had no idea. He was quite the puzzle.

All she knew for sure was that he wanted her body.

And that, at least, was very mutual.

*     *     *

For several days, Chloe kept herself busy. It wasn't hard. She taught yoga, worked on a recipe for a mud skin mask, and babysat the inn when Maddie was off doing wedding stuff and Tara attended a culinary conference.

One of the days she brought Sawyer a picnic lunch of Thai food to his station. She found him hunched over his desk scowling at his computer, and he looked so surprised that someone had thought to feed him that she felt an uncomfortable surge of tenderness.

It was incredibly foolish, and she spent two days lying low after that, making sure not to run into him. Because even one more time, her heart told her, and she wouldn't be able to continue to keep things so light and breezy.

It was during those days that she accepted the first four bookings for the following month at their new day spa—the one that didn't quite exist yet. She'd warned the potential clients that they weren't up to full service at this time and hoped that was enough to keep her out of hot water with her sisters. And then she'd called Jax. "We've got a month," she told him.

He hesitated. "Maddie and Tara know this?"

"They will."

"Shit, Chloe."

"I'm not asking for a miracle. Just some basic cosmetic stuff to make the room look warm and inviting. I'll tell Maddie and Tara, I swear, but I need to know what you can pull off and how fast you can do it."

"I'll get back to you," Jax said.

"Thanks." Chloe hung up and buried herself in work once more. She was too busy to think about Sawyer, or so she told herself. But it wasn't true. She thought about him a lot and differently than she used to. Once she'd thought of him as untouchable, but apparently once you finger-painted a man's crotch, things changed in that regard. Plus she'd seen another side to him now, discovered layers and complexity, and learned some more of his past.

He no longer felt untouchable. In fact, he'd become infinitely touchable.

The next night, a windstorm moved in and knocked out power. This wouldn't have bothered Chloe any except that it was a weekend, and they had three of their rooms booked, and she wanted to make sure the guests enjoyed their stay.

With no electricity.

Maddie lit candles throughout the inn, giving it a soft, warm glow for their guests. She used vegetable-based candles so they didn't aggravate Chloe's asthma. Tara barbequed on the covered deck over their brand-spanking-new gas, smokeless grill. "It's older than the mountains and got twice as much dust," Tara had said of their old grill, but they all knew she'd spent a fortune on the new one for Chloe's sake.

Maddie dug a sand pit on the beach and coaxed everyone outside for s'mores. Chloe reminded her that they needed a permit to light a fire on the beach, and Maddie assured her that had been taken care of—and then laughed at Chloe because she'd never been one to worry about breaking any city ordinances before. Maddie's amusement was met with some irritability on Chloe's part, because it was true. Since when did she worry about a city ordinance? "I can't sit at a campfire without getting wheezy."

Maddie handed her a paper surgical mask like the one Chloe had worn at Sawyer's house. "I got a stack from Mallory at the hospital," her sister said proudly. "See if it works."

To Chloe's surprise, it did. Their guests were three middle-aged couples, all friends, traveling together up the coast to Canada. They had a great time making s'mores, and when they'd headed off to bed, Tara stoked the fire while Maddie called the Love Shack. Within ten minutes, the sisters had company.

Ford and Jax, of course.

And Sawyer.

Chloe looked at him from across the fire, and he looked right back. Out of uniform tonight, he was in battered jeans and a CHP hoodie sweatshirt. His eyes were inscrutable, his jaw stubbled, and his thoughts hidden.

Ford had brought beer, which he passed out to everyone except Sawyer and Chloe. "You two kids didn't seem to know your limits the other night," he said.

Sawyer gave him a level look. "This from the guy who once drunk-dialed Tara until I saved his ass by stealing his phone."

Ford winced and offered Sawyer a beer, which he didn't take. Whether he was on call later or had DEA business, Chloe didn't know. What she did know was that

Tara and Maddie were staring at her. She knew this was because they'd thought she'd been camping that night she spent at Sawyer's.

"You said you were with Lance," Tara said.

Sawyer arched an amused brow at Chloe.

Suddenly the annoying mask was her best friend, as it allowed her to hide her expression with ease. "I never said I was with Lance."

"You said you were with a *friend*," Maddie said. "We assumed."

"Lance's been busy lately," Chloe said. "With his new girlfriend. Renee the nurse. She's really great for him. She's given him this new lease on life and—"

"Hold it," Tara said, clearly not interested in Lance's love life. Just Chloe's. "So you and Sawyer are..." She waggled a finger back and forth between them.

"No," both Sawyer and Chloe answered in unison.

Chloe sent Sawyer a long look. It was one thing for *her* to say "no," but she sure as hell didn't like that he felt as strongly about it as she did.

"Okay, but since when are you two friends?" Tara asked. "Friends who have *sleepovers*."

"I like those kinds of friends," Ford said.

"We're not *that* kind of friends." Chloe pulled down the mask to make sure she gave the full-effect glare to a silent Sawyer. "Feel free to step in anytime here and defend my honor."

"Chloe's right," Sawyer said, never taking his eyes off of her. "We're not friends." He was looking at her from dark, brooding, heated eyes, which of course helped not at all.

Tara was clearly unhappy. "What the hell is going on with you two?"

"Nothing!" Chloe said.

"They were fully dressed when Ford and I found them the other morning," Jax offered helpfully. "Well, actually, Chloe was dressed. Big guy here was shirtless. Oh, and he had his hands up her skirt, but—"

Sawyer cut his eyes to Jax, who shrugged.

Maddie was staring at her husband-to-be. "And you didn't tell me?"

Ford *tsk*ed in mocking disapproval. "Rookie mistake," he whispered to Tara.

"For God's sake." Surging to her feet, Chloe stabbed at the fire with a big stick, thinking about using it to whack Sawyer across the back of his big, fat head. But since she didn't want to be arrested tonight, she shoved the stick into the fire and pulled out her iPhone. She accessed her Magic Eight application. "For my sisters' sake," she said to it, "please state for the record whether or not I'm capable of running my own life."

The answer was short and sweet.

*Without a Doubt.*

"Ha!" Righteously triumphant, Chloe sank back to her beach chair. "One hundred percent accurate, as always."

"Actually, statistically speaking," Jax said, ever the lawyer even though he hadn't practiced law in six years, "it has to be wrong fifty percent of the time."

Ford took the iPhone from Chloe. "Magic Eight, will Jax ever learn that he doesn't know everything?"

The screen went cloudy and then cleared.

*Don't Count on It.*

Everyone laughed except Jax, who was trying—unsuccessfully—to pull a resisting Maddie down to his lap. He snatched the phone from Ford. "Hey," he said to it. "I'm still getting married next month, right?"

*Outlook Good.*

Jax let out a loud breath of relief. Maddie gave a low laugh, finally allowing him to pull her down to his lap. "Was that really in question?"

"Just making sure."

"See?" Chloe said smugly. "Always accurate."

"That's because you ask it only the easy stuff," Tara said. "Ask it if you're ever going to settle down."

"I already know the answer to that," Chloe told her. "When I'm old. *Reaaaaally* old," she added, catching Sawyer's knowing eyes. "Like when I'm...thirty-five."

The thirty-five-year-old Sawyer smiled at her but didn't take the bait.

However, thirty-five-year old Tara raised a threatening brow. "Ask it if you'll ever be able to say what you're really thinking."

Everyone smiled at this, because they all knew Chloe *always* said whatever she was thinking.

"Hey, she doesn't always," Maddie corrected. "She never says 'I love you.'"

"Maybe because I don't." Chloe said it teasingly enough, but the silly game suddenly felt too serious. It was so simple for her sisters, she thought, surrounded by the security of the men who loved them.

But for someone like her, who'd never experienced that kind of security and love, it wasn't so simple at all.

"So maybe *that's* the real question," Tara said and took the phone. "Magic Eight Ball, will my sister ever say *I Love You*?"

Ridiculously, Chloe found herself holding her breath as she waited for the screen to clear, which pissed her off. She didn't need a stinking app to give her an answer, but it came regardless:

*Absolutely Yes.*

# Chapter 17

*"Sure, good things come to those who wait—but they're
the leftovers from those who got there first."*

CHLOE TRAEGER

Sawyer watched the reaction cross Chloe's face as she
read her phone's screen. Relief, quickly hidden behind a
scowl and a derisive snort.

"I like the Absolutely Yes," Tara said.

"Well, don't get excited," Chloe told her. "Because
we've finally done it. We've just proven Mr. Magic Eight
Ball completely wrong."

"How can you possibly know that?" Maddie asked.

"Because I don't plan on changing a damn thing about
myself. Which makes it a little unlikely that I'll get someone to fall in love with me as is, wouldn't you say?"

Sawyer's heart squeezed.

"Actually," Maddie said slowly, sounding as if Chloe's
words had made her hurt as much as Sawyer was suddenly hurting. "I meant you telling Tara and me that you
loved us. But I think you're wrong." She said this very

gently, eyes bright, her voice soft but utter steel. "There is someone out there for you. I know it."

"I think so, too," Tara said, and it didn't escape Sawyer's notice that *no one* looked at him. Clearly he was not *the someone* that the sisters had in mind for her. Which, yeah, he already knew, but it still irritated the shit out of him. He was a county sheriff, not some asshole off the street.

Chloe shrugged as if it mattered not one little bit, and it occurred to Sawyer that she had no idea how much she was loved by the people in her life. None.

And *he'd* had no idea that all along she'd been afraid of that love. She hid it well behind that tough, unflappable, hard-edged courage. Not being all that fond of expressing emotions himself, the sympathy coursed through him. With both Tara and Maddie deep in the throes of love themselves, the levels of emotions had to feel like a Hallmark movie at the B&B. He knew because that's how it felt at the bar these days. Kind of nauseating.

Ford snatched the phone again. "Hey, Magic Eight," he said. "Since you're so accurate and all, tell me this—will Tara ever try that one position in the *Kama Sutra*—"

Tara pushed him as everyone cracked up, and just like that, Ford accomplished what he did best and lightened the mood.

"Your turn," Ford said to Sawyer and tossed him the phone.

"Oh no," he said to everyone's expectant face. "Hell no. All I ever get is *Try Again Later*."

"Liar. The odds don't support that any more than Chloe always being right." Jax leaned close and spoke to the phone. "Magic Eight Ball, what about our good sheriff here? Will he ever get a woman and manage to keep her?"

Maddie gave Jax a dark look and a little nudge. Sawyer gave him a nudge, too, one that was actually more of a shove, right off the log he was sitting on, but not before the stupid Magic Eight app answered:

*Try Again Later.*

Everyone laughed but Jax. "What did the love advisor say?" he wanted to know, from flat on his back in the sand. Sawyer considered dumping his beer on him when, from deep in the woods, a flare went off. At least it looked like a flare.

"What was that?" Tara asked with a startled gasp, getting to her feet.

"I'll go look." Sawyer was already on his. A movement at his side had him turning his head and meeting Chloe's gaze.

"Don't," she warned him. "Don't even try to tell me to—"

"*Stay*," he said firmly.

"Goddammit, Sawyer. A 'please' wouldn't kill you."

Sawyer moved to his SUV and grabbed a high-powered flashlight. Their fire was right near the water's edge and nowhere close to the woods. But that flare... They were at an all-time low for precipitation. It would take next to nothing to ignite a catastrophic forest fire. He moved into the woods, Jax and Ford at his side. A few minutes later, they came to a small clearing that Sawyer knew well. He'd come to this very spot as a stupid teenager to get trashed. There was a hastily put out campfire, several empty beer cans, and two cigarette butts.

The three men made sure the fire was out, then headed back to the beach. Chloe stood there, her back to their little circle, lit by the glow of the flames as she squinted to see into the woods. She was waiting, the concern etched on her face.

For him.

That was different. He'd always been the one to look after people and wasn't used to it going the other way. And yet he could see it plain as day. Tough as she was, she let her emotions show, every single one of them.

He wasn't good at that and didn't want to be. He hadn't managed to stay alive on the job by being an open book. Anything he felt, he kept to himself. And actually, sometimes he wasn't sure he even had any emotions to hide.

But all he had to do was look at Chloe and know that he did. He had way too many feelings. It'd been a damn long time since he'd let anything penetrate, but she'd gotten through. In fact, what he felt for her had invaded his life.

Love was a weakness.

Love made a guy soft.

And soft meant mistakes were made. And yet there was Chloe, looking for him. At him. And something turned over in his chest. It was his heart, exposing its soft, vulnerable underbelly. He had no idea what to do with that.

Or her.

\*     \*     \*

Several days later, Chloe was manning the inn. She was sweeping the living room wood floors and watching an old *Friends* repeat.

Lance called. "Working hard?" he asked.

She glanced at the TV wryly. "Very."

"Is that *Friends*?"

Chloe aimed the remote and turned down the volume. "If you can recognize it by sound alone, you know it too well."

"What season?" he asked.

"Well, Chandler's secretly doing Monica, so season five."

Lance laughed. "If you can name the season, *you* know it too well."

She snorted. "Better than being married to my PS3. Haven't seen you in days."

"Been busy, but not with my PS3."

The smugness in his voice alerted her. "Ah. So how's your nurse?"

"Good. *Very* good."

"Are we ever going to all hang out?" Chloe asked.

"Hell, no."

"Afraid I'll tell her all your secrets and scare her off?" she teased.

"Hell, yes. Listen, we have people coming in this weekend, and they want two rooms. You up for it?"

"Depends." Chloe turned to the front desk and brought up the B&B's schedule on the computer. "Are they normal?"

"Define normal."

"Viable credit card and not any of Tucker's idiot friends."

"You're in luck. They're actually my godparents and their teenage kids, and they're nice. *And* they pay their bills."

"Okay, then. I'll book them."

"Thanks. So what's this I read on Facebook about you and the sheriff sending out save-the-date magnets?"

"*What?*" Chloe nearly fell off the chair. Righting herself, she clicked over to the Facebook page on the computer. Nothing except a Cute Guy sighting had been made in the grocery store. He'd been caught buying an expensive cut of steak, and people were wondering which woman in town he was cooking for. "You made that up!"

"Yeah," Lance said on a rough laugh. "When did you get so easy?"

"When did you get so mean?"

"Aw, you know I love you." Then some of the amusement faded from his voice. "And you should also know, Todd has a new crush."

"Jesus. Amy is *not* interested in *any* of them. Tell them just because she's new and beautiful that she—"

"You," Lance said. "He's crushing on *you.*"

"Too bad for him."

"Yeah, well, be careful."

"I'm handling Todd." Mostly by ignoring him, but there wasn't much more she could do.

"He was drunk the other night, Chloe," Lance said. "Talking about snatching you from beneath Sawyer's nose."

Terrific. "I—"

A woman walked in the front door of the inn. "Gotta go," Chloe whispered and hung up. "Hi," she said with a welcoming smile, promptly putting the annoying Todd out of her head. "Can I help you?"

"Um, yeah. I hope so. I don't have a reservation. Do you have any rooms available?" She was a mid-twenties blonde, pretty. And she was nervous as hell. When she clasped her hands together at her chest, her fingers were shaking.

"We do have rooms," Chloe said. "Just you?"

"Y-yes." She squeezed her lips together. "Just me."

Chloe opened a registration page on the computer. "Okay . . . your name?"

"Um." The woman's gaze shifted toward the television, still turned to *Friends*. "Monica."

Chloe paused. "Last name?"

"Do you really need that?"

"Well, I'll need a driver's license and credit card, so . . ."

"Oh, but I'm going to pay cash," the woman said, eyes darting around as if someone might object. "So you don't need an ID, right?"

"Actually, we still ask for ID." Chloe looked at "Monica's" luggage—a garment bag from a haute couture store in Seattle and two wrinkled plastic bags from Target. Quite the contradiction. Another was that "Monica's" makeup was theater flawless, with her hair up in an intricate French twist that had been clearly done by a professional and yet she wore cheap, baggy sweats. On her right breast was a tiny round clear sticker with a small black *S*, the size hadn't yet been removed.

And then there was the big tell—the woman's panic was a tangible, living, breathing thing in the room, and Chloe knew right then she was going to cave. But before she could say so, Tara poked her head in from the kitchen. "I've got groceries to unload— Oops, sorry."

"Excuse me for just a minute," Chloe said to Monica and jogged after Tara into the kitchen. Maddie was just coming in the back door as well.

"Problem," Chloe told them quietly. "We have a guest who doesn't want to show ID."

"We have to have a credit card on file," Tara said.

"She's running away from someone." Chloe cracked the kitchen door to peek at their guest, who was pacing the living room. "I want to let her stay here."

"You asking or telling?" Tara asked.

Chloe locked gazes with her.

"We've got to at least get ID," Tara protested.

"Or we could...forget," Maddie said softly. "Because if the poor thing is hiding, it's for a reason, and we should help her."

Chloe nodded her agreement on that score. "She's scared. I'm going back out there." Back in the living room, she smiled reassuringly at their guest. "Just one night?"

"Yes. I need to be on the road at the crack of dawn."

"Sure." Chloe once again bent to the computer. "So where are you headed?"

She bit her lip. "LA?"

Chloe looked up from the screen. "Okay, but tomorrow night, when you're standing at another front desk in some other inn, don't say it with a question mark. Own it."

The woman winced. "Oh, God. You're right." She seemed to collapse in on herself. "And I don't want to be standing at another inn tomorrow. I've only come from Seattle, and I'm already tired of driving. Can I just book a room here for a week and have you pretend I don't exist?"

"A week might be harder to swing without a credit card."

"Monica" backed to the couch and sat down hard. She was wearing white pumps with her sweats.

Pristine white pumps.

"I know what it looks like," she said. "Like I'm an escapee from the mental hospital, but I'm not."

"Because you're a runaway bride?" Chloe asked softly.

She straightened and stared at Chloe in horror. "I don't—I mean..." She bit her lower lip. "I just like white pumps, a lot. So of course, I'm not a runaway bride. Running away from my own wedding would make me a horrible person." She covered her face. "Oh, God, I'm a horrible person! How did you know?"

"The Target sweats with the wedding pumps were a dead giveaway," Chloe said gently, coming around the desk to sit at her side. "So was stealing Monica Geller's identity." She paused. "Are you okay?"

"Sure. I've only broken the hearts of all my family and friends and groom-to-be, who I've known since I was ten. But other than that, I'm terrific." And then she burst into tears.

Chloe put a sympathetic hand on her shoulder, and she slumped against her like they were best friends and sobbed.

Chloe awkwardly patted her back while staring helplessly at the door to the kitchen. Where the hell was Maddie the Hugger when she needed her? "Um...can I call your family for you? I could tell them that you're safe. They don't have to know where you are, but I'm sure they're worried sick about you."

Maddie came out with some tea, and Tara followed with cupcakes, thank God. The three of them sat on the couch while the woman sniffled and blew her nose. "My name's Allie."

"Cupcake, Allie?" Maddie asked kindly.

Allie nodded and took two, one in each hand.

"Tara calls these Sugar and Spice and Anything but Nice Cupcakes," Chloe said. "She was annoyed at her boyfriend when she baked them."

"Yeah?" Allie shoveled in a cupcake, still occasionally hiccupping and wiping her nose. "What did he do?"

"Oh, she won't tell us," Chloe said. "Whatever it is happened this morning, I think, but she's mum on the subject. He probably left his underwear on the floor. Tara's OCD about that kind of stuff. But then again, I'm still on the fence that Ford actually *wears* underwear." Chloe grinned into Tara's narrowed eyes. Hey, maybe she'd promised to grow up, but she'd never promised to stop poking at her sisters.

"Maddie thinks maybe he's the one who sneaked a piece of Tara's Very Berry Pie without asking, but it wasn't him." She pointed at herself and mouthed "me."

Allie eyed Tara speculatively. "You look so... with it. He had to have done something bigger than leave out his underwear, right?"

Tara gave Chloe a meaningful glare but said nothing. The Steel Magnolia wasn't talking.

"Did you ask him how you look and he said fine without taking his eyes off the TV?" Allie asked. "Or did he ogle a woman in the frozen foods aisle at the grocery store because her nipples were hard from standing in front of the ice cream display? Did he tell you that your mother is a pain in his ass?"

"No," Tara said and paused. "He asked me to elope with him to the Greek Islands on his boat."

"Bastard," Allie said, sniffing, while both Maddie and Chloe gaped in shock at Tara.

"*What?*" Maddie whispered, a hand on her heart, a slow smile curving her mouth. "Did he really?"

"Yes." Still looking calm, Tara took a cupcake, cool as she pleased. "The other night, after the bonfire."

Allie was double-fisting cupcake number three and four, mascara smeared on her cheeks. "It's a lot of pressure, isn't it?" she said, mouth full, inhaling sugar like she hadn't eaten in a week.

"What are you going to do?" Chloe asked.

"Well, I could jump off a bridge," Allie said dramatically. "Or maybe I ought to try being a lesbian for a while."

"No bridge jumping," Chloe said firmly. "And the lesbian thing? Two menstrual cycles and double the PMS. That's a big commitment. But actually, I was asking my sister." She looked at Tara. "Are you going to elope with the sexiest man on the planet, or what?"

"Hey," Maddie said. "My man's sexy, too."

Tara patted Maddie's hand, then followed Allie's lead and grabbed yet another cupcake. "I think I have to."

"No," Allie said, eyes glossy from the sugar high. "You don't have to do anything. You can run away to...here." She laughed softly. "I'll share my room. We can do the lesbian thing together."

Tara shook her head. "Got that out of my system in college, sorry."

Maddie choked on her cupcake, but Chloe just grinned. "And they call *me* the wild one."

The phone rang, and Chloe jumped up to take the call. It was a woman wanting to make reservations for her and her sisters for a long weekend.

"How many rooms would you like?" Chloe asked her.

"All of them."

Chloe blinked. "What?"

"We'd like the whole inn for ourselves. It's a reunion, you see. Two of us have been overseas in the military, and another has just gotten her doctorate, and the baby's getting married. We haven't all been together, the eight of us, in five years."

"The whole inn," Chloe repeated, stunned.

"Yes, for at least four days. I hope that's not a problem. We want to utilize the day spa, too. Oh, and do you have yoga classes?"

"Yes." Or they would...Chloe cleared her throat. "How soon are you looking at?"

"What's the soonest you have?"

"Hold on a sec?" Dizzy with excitement, Chloe covered the phone and turned to Tara and Maddie.

"Problem?" Tara asked, rising to her feet at what surely was a look of shock on Chloe's face.

"No. Yes. I don't know." Chloe laughed. "I have a request for a four-day exclusive stay for a family of sisters who wants the entire B&B and day spa at their disposal. *ASAP.*"

Tara and Maddie stared at her. "Honey," Maddie said gently, "there is no day spa yet."

"Not yet," Chloe said. "But it's coming." She went back to the phone, catching the warning look in Tara's eyes, the one that said don't you dare be impulsive. Chloe grinned at her while calmly telling the woman on the phone that the spa would be open for limited service in two weeks, or they could wait for the full range of services to be offered in a month. She made the booking, not unhappy that the woman had settled for limited service. "No worries," she said to her sisters when she'd hung up. "Jax promised he could handle it."

Allie sighed. "They all think they can handle it. So there's a day spa?"

\*     \*     \*

Thirty minutes later, Chloe had shown Allie to her room, then headed into the sunroom, where she was joined by Tara and Maddie. "I think Allie's going to be okay."

"You were good with her," Tara said. "I might have just given her the room key and stayed out of it."

"No, you wouldn't," Maddie said. "You were the first one on board when I was running away from my life and needed to stay here, remember?" She hugged Tara, then reached for Chloe's hand, pulling her in close, too. "I called Jax. Told him we had reservations coming in, that we need this room done yesterday. He said he'd do it at material cost only, and that I could pay the labor later."

"*I'll* pay," Chloe said, trying to figure out how long was long enough to stay in the group hug without being rude. "Whatever it is."

"I've got it," Maddie said. "No worries."

"No, I—"

"Chloe," Tara said dryly. "I'm pretty sure the debt can't be paid in money."

Maddie blushed to the tips of her toes.

"Oh. Gotcha." Chloe laughed. "Well, then, thanks for paying up, sis."

Maddie rolled her eyes and hugged her again. Jesus. Tara was still right there, too, so that now Chloe was sandwiched between them. "Okay...Well. I have things to do."

"You always do when we're having a mushy moment," Tara said, not letting go.

Dammit. "Seriously?" Chloe asked. "Because we *just* mushed all over each other a few months back when Maddie got engaged, and I'm still recovering from that."

"That was a year ago," Maddie said. "And now Tara's engaged. It's definitely mush time."

Tara shook her head. "No, first we mush on this." She looked at Chloe. "We owe you an apology."

"Whoa. Can you repeat?"

Tara sighed. "You might be the youngest, but you're not a baby. You've really changed, Chloe. Grown up."

"Okay, thanks. Can you let go of me now?"

"No," Maddie said, tightening her grip, laughing when Chloe swore.

"We're trying to tell you that we're sorry it took us so long to realize," Tara said. "And that though you march to a different drummer, you have it together just fine."

"Sometimes even more than us," Maddie added.

Chloe narrowed her eyes. "Okay, what do you guys want? You're both going away with your lovers this weekend, right? Leaving me with the inn? Is that it?"

Maddie laughed. "No. We love you, Chloe. That's it."

"Oh, good God." She dropped her head to bang it repeatedly on Maddie's shoulder.

Her sisters both laughed, but Chloe didn't feel quite in on the joke. Her mother had been a free spirit and had flung the L-word around to anyone and everyone, so much so that it had lost its meaning. And then there'd been TV and in movies, and everyone knew *that* love wasn't real either, just an easy antidote to bad stuff suffered in the story. Family betrayed you? I love you. All better. Man ripped your heart to shreds? I love you. Perfect Band-Aid. World destruction imminent and you're going to fly into the asteroid leaving your daughter an orphan? I love you. Buck up.

No, to Chloe it seemed like people used "I love you" when they meant "I'm sorry" or "Could we please forget about what a moron I've been?" They weren't words to be used like a Band-Aid, or to be said to make someone feel better in the moment, like the time Phoebe had left a seven-year-old Chloe at a stranger's house for four days or when she'd spent the entire Christmas money on gifts for her boyfriend.

Chloe might not be the smartest kid on the block, but she'd learned early on that those three words had power. No way she would ever let that power be wasted. That would be a sacrilege. Her sisters could joke all they wanted, but Chloe knew deep in her bones that when it was time to say the words, she'd know. There'd be some cosmic sign. Problem was, she was starting to wonder if her cosmic receiver was faulty.

Wonder if Jax knew a contractor for that?

In any case, she was grateful for what she did have with Tara and Maddie. More than they could possibly know. They were all she had as far as stabilizing forces. They were her only blood ties.

And if she let herself think that way for too long, it made her sad. Lonely.

Afraid.

So she didn't think on it.

Ever.

She just enjoyed having them in her life. And as she'd come to realize in the past year, the more of herself that she gave to the inn, the longer that might be.

"She'll say it when she's ready," Maddie said to Tara. "And we shouldn't be teasing her. Chloe, honey, you're pale. Are you okay? Are you having trouble breathing?"

"It's blood loss from my brain exploding." Chloe jammed her hands into her pockets, suddenly extremely and uncomfortably aware that they were both staring at her with concern. "Not everyone wants to sit around and discuss feelings. Not everyone is in a relationship."

Silence, and she grimaced. When would she learn to stop talking?

"Sugar." Tara's eyes were unusually soft and, dammit, full of sympathy. "Is this about us both getting married?"

"No," Chloe said. "Of course not. I'm thrilled for both of you."

"Is it about you wanting a relationship?" Maddie asked gently.

"If I wanted a relationship, I'd have one."

"Is it about Sawyer?" Tara asked. "Are you're falling for him?"

Yes.

No.

Christ, she had no idea. She shook her head, hoping that covered all the options. "That would be stupid."

Tara let out a breath and nodded. And this, of course, put Chloe in defense mode. "Why are you nodding?"

Tara looked at Maddie, then back to Chloe. "Because," Tara said carefully, "you said it yourself."

"Yes, and *I* know why I said it, but why did *you* say it?"

"Well, there's the whole he-wears-a-badge thing and your whole hate-authority thing. And—"

Maddie put her hand on Chloe's arm. "Honey, what she means is that you've never been all that interested in toeing the line, and Sawyer's life *is* that line, you know?"

Yes, Chloe knew. She knew exactly. And wasn't that just the problem.

# Chapter 18

*"Sex is like air; it's not important unless
you aren't getting any."*

CHLOE TRAEGER

Sawyer's week was an exhausted blur. His counterpart, Tony Sanchez, had been taking a lot of time off because of the new twins, leaving Sawyer overworked and facing too many double shifts. So he wasn't in the best of moods when he should have been getting off duty but instead was heading into an all-nighter and found a car parked oddly on the side of the highway beneath a grove of trees. Sawyer exited his vehicle to check it out, but it roared to life, speeding off, tires squealing, narrowly missing two cars passing by.

Bonehead move. Sawyer jumped back into his vehicle, flipped on his lights, and pulled the car over.

There were two guys in the front seat. Sawyer didn't see anything suspicious inside the car, so he wrote a ticket for reckless driving. The driver bitched about it, then proceeded to pull away, once again squealing his tires and laying down tread, barely missing yet another car.

Sawyer was just pissed off enough to pull him over again, calmly issuing the Idiot of the Day his second ticket.

"Are you fucking kidding me?" the driver yelled. "Another ticket?" He thrust his car into gear.

"Careful," Sawyer warned him. "I have all night."

The guy muttered "asshole" beneath his breath but pulled onto the highway more carefully this time.

From there, Sawyer was called to traffic duty. Construction crews were working on the main street in town and had closed the road. There'd been a flashing sign all week long warning people, and the crew had carefully barricaded the road in several places, posting up "road closed" signs as well as detour signs. And yet several people *still* managed to drive around the barricades and then get angry with Sawyer because they couldn't get through.

"This is ridiculous!" one woman screamed at him. "I can't get out of this mess to save my life. You're all assholes!"

She'd had to drive on the wrong side of the road to get past the barricades—and *he* was the asshole. "See that barricade you ignored and drove around?" he asked her. "You want to drive back the way you came. Go by each of the *road closed* signs that you passed—I believe there were three—and follow the detour directions."

Flipping him off, she turned around.

The next guy to come through the barricades was—oh perfect—Todd. Todd had been questioned after the diner incident as a matter of course and hadn't reacted well. He'd been running his mouth in town, telling anyone who would listen that Sawyer was abusing his power, and that Todd was going to bring him down. The guy wanted a fight, but Sawyer wasn't going to give him one. No way was he going to allow Todd to jeopardize his job or be a menace to innocent people. It'd been *years*; it was time for Todd to get over himself and get his life on track. Unfortunately, Sawyer knew better than anyone that you couldn't make a person do what they didn't want to do. He couldn't save Todd any more than he could gain his own father's approval. There was just some shit that had to be let go.

"What the hell's going on?" Todd said now, not bothering with his usual charm, not for Sawyer. "The road's closed. Why can't you douche bags do this at a more convenient time?"

Sawyer didn't respond to the fact that *he* wasn't actually working on the roads. He was simply attempting to direct the idiots driving on them. Not to mention that it was midnight, how much more convenient of a time could they get?

"How the fuck do I get out of here?" Todd asked.

Sawyer flicked his flashlight into the cab of Todd's truck, knowing he wasn't going to get lucky enough to find a bag of dope in plain sight. "Well, here's the thing, Todd. If you can't follow the detour directions you've been passing, I don't know how you're going to be able to follow the directions I give you to get out of here."

"Fuck you, Thompson. Or maybe I'll just go fuck Chloe."

Sawyer had to work at not reacting at that one.

"Yeah," Todd said, knowing Sawyer enough to see right through him. "She's a sweet piece of ass, and you know what? She's hot for me."

"Stay away from her."

"Or?"

*Or I'll kill you* wasn't exactly the way to keep his job. And he'd never even had this problem before, the urge to say fuck the job and dive through Todd's window and strangle him.

"Yeah, that's what I thought," Todd said on a grin. "Behind the badge, you're all pussy." He shoved his truck in reverse. "Think of us tonight, cozy in my bed while you're out here playing hall monitor on the roads."

Sawyer gritted his teeth and worked the rest of the night, doing his best to remind himself that Todd was just an angry asshole.

An asshole who knew which buttons to press.

Just past dawn, Sawyer drove to the B&B. It was seven in the morning, and he'd been up for just over twenty-four hours, but he told himself he needed some of Tara's coffee.

"You look like shit, man." This helpful statement was from Jax, who was out of his Jeep and putting on his tool belt.

"Damn," Sawyer said. "And I was planning on going straight to a photo shoot from here, too."

Jax grinned and whistled softly. Izzy, his three-year-old brown Lab snoozing in the passenger seat, scrambled to her feet and barked. When she saw that nothing exciting was happening, she collapsed like a wet noodle, closing her eyes again.

"Come on, lazy girl," Jax said.

Izzy cracked open one eye and stared at him balefully.

"Tara'll have breakfast," Jax coaxed. The dog leaped out of the Jeep and trotted to the B&B's front door.

Sawyer shook his head. "You working on the day spa?" He looked around for Maddie's car. "Or you and Maddie just going to play Contractor and the Missus again?"

"Hey, you're not supposed to know about that. Maddie hates it when people know about our sex life."

"You're the ones who got caught in the attic by Lucille and her damn camera phone."

"Fucking Facebook. And I'd lost a bet with Maddie and the deal was I had to strip. It's not like I do it all the time, but hell, when a pretty woman tells you to drop 'em, you drop 'em, you know?"

"Just be thankful Lucille stuck her head into the attic *before* you stripped down to just that tool belt," Sawyer said.

Jax sighed. "She didn't even get Maddie in the shot. Just me doing the strip dance waving my shirt around. Someone should lower her estrogen dose or something."

"Or you could keep your strip tease to your own bedroom."

"What fun would that be?" Jax shut his Jeep door and took a longer look at Sawyer. "Rough night?"

"*Long* night."

"You stopping by to catch a glimpse of Chloe under the guise of getting coffee?"

Sawyer narrowed his eyes.

His friend gave him the same bland stare that Izzy had given Jax a moment before.

Sawyer blew out a breath but admitted nothing. He hadn't been here in two days. He'd told himself that he was cutting back on caffeine, that he was late, that he didn't need to waste the extra gas. He told himself whatever he'd needed to in order to make it work in his head.

But it didn't. Work.

Jax walked into the inn's kitchen with him. Jax got a *very* friendly kiss from Maddie. Sawyer got coffee. While Jax headed to the sunroom, Sawyer looked around the kitchen for signs of Chloe and found none.

"Looking for anything special?" Tara asked from her perch at the stove.

Sawyer glanced out the window. No Vespa.

"She's not here," Tara said dryly. "She's been sneaking away for a few hours here and there, needing to regroup." She paused. "It's because she lets things build up inside of her. She tries to hide it, pretend nothing gets to her. But things get to her. *People* get to her."

"Tara," Maddie said quietly from the kitchen table.

"*He* gets to her," Tara said to her sister, pointing at Sawyer with a wooden spatula.

"What's wrong?" Sawyer asked. "What's happened?"

Tara shook her head. "Nothing. At least nothing specific."

"Any idea where she might be?"

Tara shook her head. "She said she goes somewhere that gives her peace and quiet, a place where she can think."

At that, some of the tension left Sawyer's shoulders. He had a decent idea where she might be.

"Sawyer?"

"Yeah?" Impatient to be gone, he looked back at Tara.

Her eyes were fierce and protective. "Don't make me sorry I told you." There was an unmistakable threat in her voice.

Normally that would irritate the hell out of him, but

he kept his gaze level with hers and shook his head. "I won't."

As he walked out, he heard Maddie say to Tara, "Look at you, meddling like a mother hen."

"She won't thank me," Tara said.

"Depends on what happens next," Maddie said, which was the last thing Sawyer heard as he left the inn.

\*     \*     \*

Sawyer drove through town, hoping he was right about Chloe's location. *Somewhere that gives her peace and quiet.* Hell, if he thought about it too much, that could be anywhere. The mud springs. Lance's house. Hang gliding...

He shuddered. Christ, he hoped she wasn't doing anything like that, but when it came to Chloe, one never knew. Her idea of peace and quiet was decidedly left of center.

But her partner in crime, Lance, had been seen all over town with his new girlfriend, which hopefully meant they'd all been too busy to get into trouble.

So Sawyer headed home. In the middle of the night, with no traffic and no red lights, it took fifteen minutes to get through town and up the hill to his house. This morning, as the sun rose above the tall mountains cradling Lucky Harbor, bathing the town in a golden glow, he made it in seven.

He idled in his driveway, staring at the Vespa parked there. Not wanting to examine the odd feeling in his chest, the one that felt suspiciously like relief and also something more, he got out. He didn't go inside, but walked around the side of the house. He flicked a glance at the outdoor shower, and as it had every other time since he'd been in there with Chloe, his dick twitched at the memory of her pale skin gleaming, water running in rivers down her curves...

He moved to the cliff and took the stairs to the beach. The sun had risen a little more, casting the overhang in black shadow, the rocks indistinguishable from one another.

At the bottom of the stairs, he kicked off his boots and socks and turned to face the cliffs. The sun was in his eyes, blinding him to anything but the outline of the granite. The beach was utterly empty and completely isolated, especially at this time of year. There was a salty breeze but the waves were subdued, soft and quiet. A lullaby, gently rolling against the rocky sand. A bird squawked. Its mate squawked back.

But there was no sight of a petite, redheaded, wild beauty named Chloe.

When he saw the single-track of small, feminine footprints, he sucked in a breath of pure relief. "Gotcha," he murmured, and followed the prints up the beach and around a large outcropping of rock, heading for the cliff.

Where they vanished at the face of the rock.

If it hadn't been for the footsteps, he'd have missed her entirely. Because even tilting his head back as far as he could, she was invisible to him. But he knew she was up there.

He could feel her.

Shaking his head at himself—he could *feel* her?—he began to climb, telling himself that this would be a hands-off talk.

Halfway up, he levered himself over a large, flat rock that jutted out and found her.

Silent, gaze hooded, arms clasped around her knees, her lovely face was in profile but still projecting a loneliness and darkness that called to him.

Because it matched his own.

He crouched in front of her. "Hey."

Chloe turned her head and studied him, from his bare, sandy feet, to his wrinkled uniform, and finally his face. Whatever she saw there had a small smile curving her mouth. "Long night, Sheriff?"

"Jax asked me the same thing."

"It's because you look like shit."

"Yeah, he said that, too."

She nodded and scooted over, a wordless invitation to join her. He crawled in next to her and mirrored her pose.

They watched the waves for a few minutes in easy, companionable silence. He'd gotten the feeling from Tara that Chloe had been upset, but he wasn't getting that vibe from her at all.

No, just that same sense of needing that vague something that he felt deep in his own gut. "Are you all right?"

"Always." She smiled, but it didn't quite meet her eyes. "Same question back atcha, Sawyer."

She didn't often use his given name. He liked the sound of it coming from her lips way more than he should. "Your sisters are worried."

She blew out a sigh and sank farther back against the rock. "They shouldn't be."

"Want me to take you home?"

"Are you asking, or planning on cuffing me and dragging me back?"

"If I cuff you," he said, "the inn is the last place you'll be headed."

She laughed softly. "You're such a tease. You climb up here in uniform often?"

"Almost never."

She looked at him, that damn concern in her eyes again. "You really do look beat."

"I am." He unbuckled his utility belt and set it on a rock.

"Don't stop there," she said.

"Right, and end up on Facebook."

Chloe laughed. "Lucille wouldn't do that to you."

"Only because she knows I'd arrest her."

"Sure you would." Her smile faded, replaced by a thoughtful frown. "Why is that, I wonder?"

"Why what?"

"Lucille loves to shout to the world what you do as Sheriff Thompson, but the private life of Sawyer seems to be off-limits. She never outs you about anything."

"Nothing to tell. I'm always on the job."

"No, seriously. Remember that day you changed her tire? She was telling me all about your younger years, then totally clammed up when she got to your teens."

No, he wasn't tabloid material anymore, thank God. And he owed a big thanks to Lucille for that. "I'm too tired to have that conversation with you right now." Or ever.

"So . . . you're off duty."

"Finally, yes."

"Good." She rose to her knees at his side and tugged at his shirt, indicating she wanted him to lose it.

He shouldn't, but he must have been even farther gone than he'd thought, because he peeled out of his Kevlar vest, his uniform shirt, then the T-shirt he wore beneath, setting everything on top of his growing pile.

She ran her gaze over his chest with frank appreciation. Then he shivered, realizing he hadn't really considered the weather. It was forty-five degrees max, but Chloe was giving him a go-on gesture with her hand.

"All I have left is my pants," he said.

"Yes, please."

"It's cold, Chloe."

She tilted her head. "Are you worried about shrinkage?"

Well, he was now.

"I've already seen the goods, remember? Trust me, Sheriff, you have nothing to worry about."

Sawyer laughed in spite of himself, then went still when she straddled him. Before he could so much as blink, she'd bent and kissed his collarbone. Then a pec. She touched her tongue to his skin, and he shivered again. *Not* from the cold. "Chloe." That was all he managed to get out. His hands were on her hips, gripping her tight as she shifted over an inch and licked his nipple. He sucked in a breath.

"It looked cold," she whispered and blew a warm breath over his damp skin.

He shuddered, the cold air the last thing on his mind now, as she rocked slowly over the obvious bulge behind his zipper.

"I thought I wanted to be alone," she said, grinding on him until his eyes rolled to the back of his head.

"I know," he managed, tipping her face up to meet his gaze. "But I didn't want you to be."

She smiled. "I like that about you. You listen to everyone, but then come to your own conclusions and do whatever the hell you want."

"If you knew what I wanted to do right now, you'd probably be shoving me off this bluff."

"Don't count on it." She rose a little and covered his mouth with hers.

The kiss rocked his socks off. Or it would have, if he'd been wearing any. He pulled back and looked into her eyes. She was definitely no longer feeling lonely or sad, or anything negative at all. Her eyes were soft and...dreamy.

Dreamy was troubling, because it was more than just lust. Dreamy meant things he couldn't deliver, such as his own emotions. It wasn't that he couldn't feel things for her. He could, and did.

God, he did.

He just had no idea what to do with them. "Chloe—"

"I was thinking about your shower," she said, nuzzling her face against his jaw. "I was sort of hoping to find you there."

"We never did finish what we started that day."

Chloe smiled against him. "Maybe 'we' didn't finish, but I sure did."

He laughed. So did she. And then somehow they were kissing again. "Hold on," he said, regretfully pulling back. "We can't."

"Sorry. That word doesn't compute."

He let out another low laugh and tightened his grip on her when she nipped at his throat. "I'm not risking you having another post-orgasm asthma attack while we're way up here on the rocks," he murmured, groaning when she rocked the hottest part of her over the hardest part of him.

"I have a better idea," she whispered.

Oh, good. One of them could still think. "What?"

She pulled her inhaler from her back pocket and waved it at him. Leaning over him, she lightly kissed first one corner of his mouth, then the other. "And I want you," she whispered, her mouth brushing his with each word. "So much. Please? Please, Sawyer..."

This was her idea? To beg? Because first, that really worked for him. And second...hell. He couldn't remember.

# Chapter 19

*"The severity of the itch is inversely proportional
to the ability to reach it."*

CHLOE TRAEGER

Chloe lost herself in Sawyer's embrace. It wasn't a surprise, the man could kiss like nobody's business. She was
floating on waves of pleasure and desire when he pulled
back. "Not here," he said again, putting his gear back
on to climb down. "Not on a sandy rock in fifty-degree
weather."

The weather had actually improved. Everything was
wet and dewy from the rain, and the sky hung low like
a covering tarp, but the sun had begun to peek through.
She inhaled the salty air coming off the water and the
scents of spruce and pine from the woods. Glorious. So
was the man trying to give her the bum's rush down the
hill. "We could just free the essentials," she said breathlessly.

"Yes, but it's my essentials I'm worried about." He was
following her down, climbing with the agility of someone

much lighter and smaller than his size. "I don't want anything freezing off."

She laughed. "It's not cold enough."

"Says the woman who doesn't have a part to freeze off."

"And here I thought you were so tough."

"An illusion." He hopped to the sand and then, because apparently she wasn't moving fast enough for him, snatched her off the rock himself for one more bone-melting kiss. Then he had her by the hand and was pushing her toward the stairs.

Apparently, they were in a hurry. She was on board with that and picked up the pace. But that combined with her undeniable excitement worked against her because after a few steps, she felt her chest tighten. Goddammit. "Sawyer—"

He took one look at her, swore, then lifted her into his arms and took the stairs as if she weighed nothing at all.

Laughing breathlessly, she said, "Don't wear yourself out. I have plans for you."

"You just concentrate on breathing," he said, expression dialed into fiercely intent male. "Inhaler?"

"Got it." She pulled it from her pocket and used it as he carried her through his backyard and past the shower.

"Oh," she said, looking longingly at the showerhead. "But—"

"*Bed*," he said firmly.

She wriggled her gritty toes. "I'm sandy."

"You're going to be hot and bothered in a minute," he promised and shouldered open his back door.

She was already hot and bothered, and a shiver of anticipation racked her as Sawyer carried her through the house so fast that she could barely see. "Hey," she said. "You painted some more—"

This was all she got out before she went sailing through the air.

She landed on a huge bed. Before she'd even bounced once, he was on her. He'd removed his Kevlar vest and shirts again, dropping them to the floor with his other gear. Taking both her wrists in one hand, he raised them above her head and pinned them there as he settled over her. She wriggled and lightly tugged to see if he'd free her hands.

"Not yet," he said.

"No?"

"No." He nipped at her chin. "We need to talk first, and if you touch me, I'll forget what I want to say."

This surprised her. "The big, bad sheriff has a weakness?"

"When it comes to you, more than one," he admitted readily and lightly squeezed her wrists, silently telling her to hold still and stop squirming.

Chloe couldn't help it. He was so nice to squirm against, warm and hard in all the interesting spots, his strength barely held in check. "You don't *really* want to talk right now, do you?" she murmured. "*Really?*"

Sawyer let out a breath and dropped his forehead to hers. "Hell, no. But I have to ask. You said before you couldn't have orgasms."

"Which you proved wrong," she reminded him.

"Yes, at your cost." He paused. "So you don't usually…"

"Not in mixed company, no. I can give myself one, if I concentrate on staying real calm and still."

His eyes dilated black. "That's a hell of a contrast. Trying to come while staying calm and still."

She shrugged. "I manage." Fascinated by the way he was looking at her, as if he wanted to gobble her up whole, she heard herself say, "I could...show you. If you wanted."

"Yes," he said very seriously. "I want you to show me." He backed off of her and sat at her hip.

Suddenly a little shy about this venture that had been her idea, she hesitated.

"Here, let me help." In five seconds flat, he had her out of her shoes, socks, and jeans. He stared down at her sunshine-yellow, boy-cut panties and then ran a finger over the smiley face on her mound. "Show me, Chloe."

Closing her eyes, she slid her hand into her panties. A very rough, male sound of appreciation rumbled above her, and then Sawyer encircled her wrist with his warm fingers. Her eyes flew open.

"Slow," he commanded. "Real slow and easy."

"I didn't say slow," she said. "It doesn't have to be slow. Just calm."

"Lots of calm." His thumb scraped over the pulse at the inside of her wrist. "But let's try slow and easy, too."

She knew that he didn't want an ER run. Problem was, she wasn't a slow-and-easy sort of girl. She was more of a hurry-up-before-she-had-an-asthma-attack sort of girl. "Fast is better. That way I have a shot at it."

"Slow and easy," he repeated firmly and then slid his fingers beneath hers so that he was the one touching her. Gently, so gently that she wanted to weep, he glided his fingers over her core. Back and forth, then again. And again. Teasing.

Arousing.

Her moan echoed around them, and then it was her turn to grip *his* wrist. What he was doing was magic, but she needed . . . "More."

"Shh," he said and kept up that light touch, opening her a little more with each pass of those diabolical fingers, spreading her wetness until she was writhing beneath him.

Then he just stopped.

Gasping, she sat up.

"You okay?" Sawyer asked, eyes on her face.

When she nodded, he put a hand over her chest and nudged her flat on her back again. "Good," he said. "Keep it slow and—"

"If you say easy, I'm going to hurt you."

"I researched asthma online," he said so quietly that it took a moment for his words to sink in. Or maybe it was because his fingers were driving her to the point of madness, affecting her ability to process. But he'd actually taken enough interest to research her problem? It meant something, it had to, but she wasn't sure what. That he liked her? Okay, she could deal with that. She liked him, too. And maybe it'd also been fear based. Her almost dying had scared him. Yes, of course. That made perfect sense.

"I learned that the key," he said, "is relaxation and having a partner that pays close attention to your breathing patterns. I'm paying close attention, Chloe." His smile was both sexy and reassuring and made her chest tighten until she thought she might burst.

"Hey," he said, his gaze narrow with concern. "Are you—"

"*Fine*. It's not the asthma. It's" —she moistened her lips— "you. I don't want to stop."

His gaze immediately went back to her poised hand. "Then don't," he said a little thickly.

She closed her eyes and took a deep breath. Or as deep as she was able. She wasn't feeling asthmatic—yet—but she did feel a little...exposed. "Maybe you could tell me a dirty story," she whispered and heard his soft chuckle.

"Okay," he murmured. "There's this beautiful, gutsy redhead..." He leaned over her on the bed. "She has curves that drive me insane."

"Curves? Is she chunky, then?"

"She's perfect." Sawyer unbuttoned her top and spread it open. She felt his lips on her collarbone, then the swell of a breast. "And she has this way of moving, so confident and sure of herself. It's sexy as hell."

"Sometimes," Chloe whispered, "she fakes the confidence."

"My story," he said and kissed her nipple through the silk of her bra. His mouth was hot, and she arched up into it, moving her hand faster. Her breath hitched, but his fingers settled over hers, stilling her movements, reminding her about the slow-and-easy decree. Before she could object, he tugged down the cup of her bra with his teeth and ran his tongue over her bared nipple. "You were pierced," he whispered against her skin, kissing the pebbled peak.

"Y—yes."

"Why?"

There was no recrimination in his voice, no judgment. Only curiosity. "I don't know." But she did.

Sawyer lifted his head and met her gaze. Not pressing.

Just waiting in that way he had that made her want to spill all her secrets.

"Sometimes, I can't... feel," she said softly.

"Here?" His fingers closed over her nipple, plucking the peak like an instrument, and she quivered.

"No." She shifted his hand to her heart. "Here. I couldn't feel anything, and I needed to."

His gaze dipped to her hand, then rose back to her eyes, his own filled with what might have been understanding.

But she wasn't used to that. And anyway, how could he *really* understand? He didn't give a shit about what anyone thought. He could do whatever he wanted, when he wanted. Run. Climb. Have wild animal sex...

"Did it help?" he asked quietly. "The pain?"

She waited to feel the anxiety build in her chest, festering and clawing at her until she shut down in self-preservation. But she was looking right into his eyes, and there was still no judgment, nothing but a simple acceptance, and she didn't get anxious at all. "Yes, it helped," she whispered. "At the time."

"And now?"

"I don't need the pain anymore."

"Good." He flicked his tongue between her breasts and worked his way south. Her hand was still in her panties, her fingers where she needed them, moving in what felt like tandem with his mouth, making her arch up into him.

"Still pierced here," he murmured against her trembling belly.

"I l-like how it looks with my bathing suit. God, Sawyer."

He settled a hand over hers again and slowed her down. "Easy," he murmured.

"If you say that one more time, I'm going to easy your—"

He hooked his fingers into her panties and pulled them down her legs. Then he wedged his broad shoulders between her thighs, getting up close to all her secrets. A groan wrenched from his throat. "Ah, Chloe. You're so wet. No, don't stop."

She'd always assumed that she could make herself come because there wasn't a lot of aerobic action to a self-serve, at least not the way she did it. No stress or performance anxiety involved, just a slightly boring but gratifying release.

But she was definitely feeling a little breathless now, with him holding her legs open, watching her with such avid fascination. Her chest tightened even more, and she realized this wasn't going to work. "Sawyer—"

"Yeah, I know. You're not very good at following directions." He took her hands in his, pulled them to her sides and held them there. "Don't move."

"I—"

He licked the moisture between her legs, and she gasped.

"Keep breathing," he murmured against her skin. "You're holding your breath. In and out, Chloe. Slow."

Was he kidding her? "I *can't.*"

"Thought that word wasn't in your vocabulary."

She huffed out a faint laugh. But his hot mouth was still working her, making her tremble, and his name tumbled from her lips as she slid her hands from his and fisted them in his hair.

He stayed the course, hummed her name against her, making her toes curl. She tightened her grip, but he couldn't be rushed. Whenever she tried, he merely captured her wrists again, pinning her legs with his heavy body to hold her still. "Shhh," he told her and then continued.

Slow.

Easy.

Driving her right out of her mind. "Please. Sawyer, *please.*"

But her entreaty fell on deaf ears. He did his own thing at his own pace, gently massaging and teasing and coaxing her right into a blissful explosion that shocked and rocked her to the very core.

While she trembled and shuddered back to Planet Earth, he gave her one last soft kiss and moved back up her body to study her face closely. "Okay?" he asked.

"If I was any more okay, you'd have to peel me off the ceiling."

He smiled, but his eyes were still hot, lines of tension bracketing his mouth.

"I really am okay," she said, stunned to realize it was true. She was breathing heavily but not feeling wheezy. "Sawyer?"

"Yeah?"

"Your turn." She pushed him down to the bed. Leaning over him, she took his wrists and forced his hands up to the headboard and curled his fingers around the spindles. She lowered the timber of her voice to imitate his. "Slow," she commanded. "Real slow and easy."

He smiled. "But I don't have asthma—"

"You're not very good at following directions either. I suppose I'll have to take over."

He raised a challenging brow. He was sprawled beneath her wearing only his uniform trousers, his body warm and strong, his every muscle taut. God, so many muscles. Even his feet were sexy. Lord, she had it bad. "I could look at you all day," she whispered.

A flicker of surprise came into his eyes and then heat. "Look all you want," he said. "But first let me—" He let go of the headboard to adjust himself with a grimace.

"Yeah, those pants do look pretty uncomfortable." Batting his hand away, she popped open the button herself.

"Careful," he said when she reached for the zipper.

"Easy, Sheriff. This won't hurt a bit." She unzipped him with great care and then tugged the pants down his long legs, watching as he sprang free. Sitting back on her haunches, she smiled. "Happy to see me?" Leaning forward, she kissed him on the tip of his very impressive erection, making his low reply unintelligible.

He rose onto his elbows to watch her, reaching to glide his fingers into her hair, but like he'd done to her, she shoved him back to the bed.

He gripped the headboard again, tight enough to turn his knuckles white. "Christ, Chloe. You're killing me."

Ditto, she thought, transfixed as the sight of him spread out for *her* viewing pleasure now, so perfectly in proportion from head to toe and all the glorious spots in between. Wrapping her fingers around the base of his hot, silky length, she licked him delicately, then not so delicately, until he shuddered and slid his fingers back into her hair to pull her away. "God, Chloe. You're going to make me—"

"That's the idea."

"Not yet." He grabbed her, hauling her up his taut,

heated body until she was straddling him. She gave a little wriggle to get him right where she...wanted...him—

"Oh no, you don't." Gripping her hips, he held her still. "I want you to stay with me this time."

"I'm with you," she promised. "All the way with you. My lungs are good, see?" She inhaled as deep as she could and let it out.

"Good. Keep doing that, keep breathing," he ordered softly. "I'll do the rest." Biceps flexing, he lifted her up and then allowed her to sink onto him, and exquisite pleasure washed through her as he slid home.

"Your pace," he said. He sounded a little rough and strained, but his hands loosened their grip on her.

Her pace. Normally she'd kick into gear, desperate to get to the finish before it was too late and she couldn't. But he'd already proven that she didn't have to rush. So for the first time, she set an achingly slow rhythm, letting herself get lost in his eyes as she moved on him, feeling each emotion as it shimmered through her.

Love or lust?

Hard to tell. For all she'd done in her life, she'd had little experience with either. But it'd be nice to know which had driven them to this, which was fueling the passion between them, suspending her in a timeless beat. Sawyer's chest was rising and falling quickly, as if he'd just finished a run. Watching him fight to control himself was a huge turn-on.

It was her, she realized, *her* making him pant. Her eyes drifted closed as a sweet climax washed over her. She heard herself cry out, and then Sawyer's low, ragged answering groan as he joined her.

When she opened her eyes, she was lying on top of

him, clinging to him with a quiet desperation that surprised her.

"You okay?" he asked, his incredibly sexy voice rumbling up from his chest where her face was plastered.

Since words were still beyond her, she nodded.

He lifted her head to look into her eyes. "Sure?"

She licked her lips. "*Yes*," she managed in a croak.

"Okay, good. Maybe you could loosen the grip just a little?"

She realized it wasn't just her arms and legs gripping him, but that her fingers were digging into his back. "Oh! I'm sorry!" She started to sit up, but he tightened his grip on her. "Just the nails," he murmured, his hands soothing her, holding her still. "The rest stays."

She relaxed again. Actually, slumped bonelessly against him was more like it. She had no idea how much time passed, but when she surfaced again, he was cradling her against his side, lightly stroking her back from the nape of her neck down her spine, over her bottom and the backs of her thighs, then up again as their breathing slowed.

Love or lust? she asked herself again. And if she asked him, would he have any more of an idea than she? No. She didn't want to know. Because maybe it was a little bit of both. And besides, it wasn't a question that needed answering now. She'd just take their odd mix of frustration, heat, affection, and desire and...enjoy it.

For as long as it lasted.

She lifted her head again to look at him. His eyes were closed, body relaxed, all the tension gone from his face. Feeling her gaze, he opened his eyes. "It's good to be inhaler worthy," he said.

She grinned. "I didn't even need it, not during, not once."

Reaching up, he tugged on a strand of her hair, mouth quirking into a smile. "I noticed."

The joy of it surged through her, and she sat up, unable to contain herself. "I got an orgasm, *and* it didn't cost me a thing."

"I'm a regular blue-light special," he said, shaking his head in amusement. "And you even got a twofer."

This was true. "And no asthma attack," she murmured, still marveling at that. "No ER visit."

Nothing to stop them…

Clearly realizing this at the same time, he rolled her beneath him, pressing her into the mattress, his expression dialed to Wicked Intent.

He was hard, and she shivered with anticipation. "Again, Sawyer?"

"Oh yeah," he said, dipping his head to kiss her breast. "And then again."

# Chapter 20

*"You have the right to remain silent. Otherwise, any-
thing you say might be misquoted and
used against you."*

CHLOE TRAEGER

Chloe slipped out of Sawyer's bed and scooped up her
clothes. Sawyer came up on his elbow to watch her dress,
hair tousled, eyes sleepy, looking for all the world like a
lazy, sated wild cat.

"Gotta get back to the B&B," she told him, torn between getting under his sheets again and facing her responsibilities. "Jax is working on the spa room today.
And I'm bringing Lance some lunch and a chest rub. If
Renee's there, I'm going to spend some time teaching
her how to make it for him. Oh, and we have a guest. A
runaway bride, actually. She's been with us a few days
and I've been giving her spa treatments to cheer her up. I
promised her I'd give her a body wrap today before I head
to Seattle. I'm giving facials at some bachelorette party
thingy at the Four Seasons."

She'd pulled on her panties and was wriggling into her bra when Sawyer rolled out of bed and headed toward her with that singular-minded intent of his.

The wild cat once again stalking his prey.

"Oh no," she said with a laugh, backing up. "I told you I'm busy today." She pointed at him. "Stay."

"*Stay?*"

"Yes." She put a hand to his broad chest, feeling the strength of him beneath her palm. It was ridiculous to think that she could push him around. Except he'd given her all the power she'd wanted in his bed, and at the thought, her nipples got perky.

Sensing capitulation, he reached for her but she evaded. "I don't know what this is exactly," she said on a shaky laugh. "But for two polar opposites, we sure get along in the sack." Turning away, she picked up her shirt.

"We're not all that different, you know," he said.

She turned back to him and saw that he was serious. He'd found a pair of jeans and had them pulled up but not yet buttoned. Buttery soft, they fit him perfectly, lovingly cupping one of her very favorite parts of him. "Okay, so maybe we're both...well, sort of single," she allowed. "Alone."

He looked at her for a long moment. "You like believing that, I think. That you're on your own."

"I *am* on my own."

"And your sisters are what, chopped liver?"

"Noooo," she said slowly, not sure how they'd gotten so off track. "I mean I've been on my own until recently. Sometimes I forget that I have them."

"And not just them," he said. "There's Jax and Ford now as well."

"And Jax and Ford," she agreed, looking around for her shoes, trying not to notice that he hadn't included himself.

"And the people of Lucky Harbor who care about you," he said. "Lance, Tucker. Amy. Lucille."

She nodded again, fighting back... what? A growing resentment, she realized. Which was ridiculous. He didn't owe her anything, certainly no pretty meaningless words that she'd doubt anyway. "Fine. I stand corrected. I'm not alone. But thinking otherwise is a hard habit to break."

"Because you like thinking it."

She shoved her feet into her shoes and turned to him, hands on hips. "Are you suggesting I like being a martyr?"

"No, I'm suggesting that I don't buy the alone thing, and neither do you."

Okay, *definitely* time to go. She turned to the bedroom door again, needing out. She hadn't had an asthma attack when he'd been buried inside her, but she was closing in on one now.

"And me," he said quietly to her back. "Are you going to leave me off your list?"

Chloe dropped her forehead to the wood. "You want on the list?" Her voice was strong. Which was good. Because she felt small. Small and weak, and wasn't sure she could face him. And dammit, when had she become a coward?

She wasn't. She was just a realist.

"I care about you," he said.

Her heart skipped a beat, and she turned to him, letting out the question that she could no longer contain. "What's happening here, Sawyer?"

He drew a deep breath and slowly shook his head. "I don't know."

Well, at least he was honest. "Maybe I need to know."

"Do you?" There was no amusement in his expression, no mockery in his voice. He was asking her to think about how deep she wanted to dig, how much she truly wanted to hear.

She nibbled on her lower lip and fought with herself. A part of her wanted to admit that yes, she needed to know how he felt about her, that she was, in fact, dying to know if he was as flummoxed as she was over what was happening between them. She needed to know that she was more than a good time to him, that he thought about her, ached for her like she was coming to ache so desperately for him.

But the other part of her, the stubborn, cynical part, refused to ask. Because that would be putting herself out there, laying herself bare before him, and she didn't do that. Ever.

"Chloe," he said softly, watching her carefully. "You can't even tell your sisters how you feel about them. If I told you how I felt, you'd—"

"Have an asthma attack?" She put her hand to her very tight chest. "*Dammit.*"

"Take a breath," he instructed firmly, moving closer, stopping when she held up her hand. "You're holding your breath."

God, she was. The air whooshed out of her lungs in one big massive exit, leaving her deflated. She had no idea if that was relief that replaced it, or desolation.

"Now inhale," he directed.

She did. And then again, ignoring him when he

closed the distance between them and cupped her face. "This is panic," he said, studying her features. "Not asthma."

"I know!" She grimaced and pushed free. "I'm working on that. And for your information, I do care about my sisters." At his raised brow, she crossed her arms. "Which means I'm your normal, average woman. A normal, average woman who's just messing around with her local sheriff."

"Chloe." His laugh was short. "You're beautiful, smart as hell, and can make me lose my mind. But you are not, nor will you ever be, *average*."

"Hey," she said, not missing that he didn't correct the "just messing around" comment. "I could be average if I tried."

"That wasn't a put-down." He ducked to make eye contact, his hands on her arms. "I like you just the way you are."

Sweet, but doubtful. "Well, I wouldn't mind a little bit of average, you know?"

"Why?"

"Why? Because…" She trailed off and rubbed her chest, which was still way too tight. Because his eyes were reflecting something far too close to sympathy, she scrubbed her hands over her face so she didn't have to look at him. "Never mind. Just ignore me." She got to the front door before he spoke.

"Chloe."

"What?"

"Average is boring." He came close, pulled her inhaler out of her pocket, and shook it for her before handing it over. "Have you ever thought that maybe your asthma's triggered by emotional responses rather than physical ones?"

"It's beginning to occur to me," she admitted. "Not that it matters in this case. We're just...messing around." She felt the doorknob at her back and reached behind to grip it, desperate to flee. God. She was so full of shit. The man had taken the time to research asthma, for God's sake. If showing meant more than telling, then damn, he'd hit the bull's-eye. She opened her mouth, praying something brilliant would come out, but all she managed was a "bye" before she escaped.

\*      \*      \*

Even after his morning coffee, Sawyer was still thinking about the look in Chloe's eyes as she'd left his bedroom, the look that said he'd somehow disappointed her.

He was good at that, disappointing people, but admittedly, she'd really gotten to him. She'd seemed confused and vulnerable, which had caught him off guard.

He'd felt the same. Christ, they were a pair. And work wasn't the time to think about it or he'd get himself or someone else dead, so he forcibly cleared his mind.

His first not-so-big surprise of the day was to learn that Mitch had been picked up at the crack of dawn, high as a kite. He'd already plea-bargained by naming his drug source.

Todd.

According to Mitch, Todd was doing some heavy dealing for a big drug lord. Unlike Mitch, Todd was smart enough to stay off the crap. Apparently Todd and Mitch were equal partners until Mitch had started caring more about his own consumption than selling for their head honcho, and Todd, worried about losing his meal ticket, cut Mitch out of a deal. Now Mitch was pissed and scared enough to point the finger.

But Todd was only the middleman to the bigger fish, a fish that the DEA was already trying to corner. They were now going to use Todd to lead them to him

Sawyer couldn't say that he was all that surprised about any of it, but he was certainly angry. Especially as he went to Todd's place to try to talk some sense into the ass.

"Christ," Todd said when Sawyer got out of his SUV. "What do you want?"

"We need to talk."

Todd laughed. "Seriously, man? I have nothing to say to you."

"I can get you a deal if you help us out."

"You want me to give you a name," Todd said.

"Yes."

"Not going to happen." Todd got into his truck.

Sawyer let out a breath. He wanted to say fuck it, but he couldn't just walk away. He had no idea why. "It's not too late. If that's what you're thinking. It's not."

Todd's smirk faded, but his eyes stayed hard. "Yeah, it is."

Sawyer watched him drive off, torn between the feeling of fury and failure. He knew Todd, whether Todd wanted to admit it or not. Todd was stupid enough to try to warn his supplier.

Sawyer would hopefully be smart enough to catch him at it. Sawyer shook his head and turned back to his vehicle. It was done, then. Todd had had as many opportunities as Sawyer to turn his life around, and at every single turn, he'd chosen to fuck himself over. Not happy, Sawyer called the DEA and gave the information to his contact, Agent Reed Morris, detailing everything that Mitch had provided and what Sawyer knew about Todd.

All they needed now was for Todd to lead them right to his next big deal.

Sawyer tried not to feel guilty, relieved, or any other useless emotion. No matter what went down, Todd would blame him. And with some effort, Sawyer hoped he wouldn't blame himself.

*Not your fault...*

Chloe had told him that, not even knowing the full story. She was like a spring storm—wild and unpredictable, and yet somehow also a calm, soothing balm on his soul. He didn't understand it, not one bit. Nor did he know what to do about the fact that they hadn't burned out on each other as he'd supposed they would.

He still wanted more of her. And he had a sinking feeling that he always would.

And he was back to thinking about her. Perfect. He shook it off as he was called by dispatch to a house where some drunk guy was allegedly punching out all of his mother's windows. When Sawyer arrived at the house, the front door was open. The woman who'd made the call was standing on the porch. "It's my son," she said, voice trembling. She leaned in to whisper, "Tommy's got a drinking problem."

"Is he still inside?" Sawyer asked her.

"Yes." She was wringing her hands. "What are you going to do to him?"

"I'm going to have Tommy come outside to talk."

"But not arrest him, right? He didn't threaten me or anything."

"Ma'am, he's committed malicious mischief with the windows, and that's domestic violence. Plus those windows are probably at least three hundred bucks a pop. If you add it all up, it's a felony. I have to arrest him."

"Oh, God. He's going to be really mad." She bit her lower lip. "I think he needs rehab," she whispered. "Can you take him to rehab?" ·

Sawyer looked inside the house. Tommy was mid-thirties but looked fifty, like someone right out of a *Cops* episode. He was sitting on his couch in the living room, and in front of him on the coffee table were two rows of at least twenty empty beer cans. On top of one of the cans was perched a pair of sunglasses.

"What are you doing?" Sawyer asked him.

Tommy just kept staring at the cans with the intense concentration of the extremely inebriated. "Isn't it obvious?"

"Humor me," Sawyer said.

"I'm testing my sunglasses. They say they're polarized, but I think the manufacturer is full of shit. I'm gonna sue." He bent, peering through the lenses, then unexpectedly slashed out with his hand, sending the cans and glasses flying against the far wall. "Fuckers."

"Okay," Sawyer said. "How about we go outside?"

"How about I punch you in the face?"

Sawyer hauled him up to his feet.

For the first time, Tommy looked up at Sawyer. And up, taking in Sawyer's size and bulk, exaggerated by the Kevlar vest. The suspect lost some of his aggression. "I was just testing my sunglasses," he said with far less attitude.

Thirty minutes later, he was testing out the bench in lockup, sobering up.

And Sawyer was at career day at the junior high school. God, he hated career day. He didn't mind the no-drugs speech so much, or the kids' questions. No, what he hated were the censorious looks from teachers who remembered him from his own junior high school days.

When that was over, Sawyer had a baseball game, and to his great satisfaction, they kicked the firefighters' collective asses. Then he had a late dinner with Jax at the bar where he pretended not to be watching the front door for Chloe, who didn't make an appearance. At some point, Sawyer was reminded by Jax that as upcoming best man, he'd better be planning a righteous bachelor party.

Sawyer called Ford and told him to get on that.

The next day, Sawyer was trying to catch up on his ever-growing paperwork when dispatch sent him out to talk to a woman who was claiming she'd been robbed. But when Sawyer got to the beauty salon on the pier, the woman wanted to tell him about her twelve-dollar manicure.

"Ma'am," Sawyer said. "You said you were robbed."

"I'm getting to that. The place is all new on the inside, you see?"

"So?"

"So there's no way they can possibly be making it work with twelve-dollar manicures; clearly it's a front for criminal activity."

Sawyer nearly arrested her for being annoying. Instead, he told her if she stopped talking, he *might* see his way to being charitable enough to not ticket her for making a nuisance call.

Then, since he was there on the pier anyway, he went into Eat Me for food, where Amy took one look at him and promptly served him a double bacon blue burger and a huge helping of pie. "Oh, and heads-up—Chloe's here." She hitched her head in the direction of the table behind him, where Chloe was sitting with Anderson, the guy who ran the hardware store.

Amy left Sawyer alone to eat, and he forced his gaze away from the couple. It was no business of his who Chloe ate with. But as he sat there with his burger, Sawyer wondered how he'd feel if she *were* seeing other people.

Shit, he knew the answer to that without even putting his mind in gear. Two months ago, he'd have laughed at anyone who suggested he'd be this attracted and confused and crazy over a woman. But he felt like he was in a fucking tailspin. When he got a call from dispatch, he jumped on his radio so fast he nearly spilled his soda. Used to eating on the road, he grabbed the second half of his burger and ordered himself not to look over at Chloe as he exited the diner.

But he totally looked.

She smiled and waved as if she were truly happy to see him, and his dumb-ass heart lightened. It took some effort to stop picturing her face as he drove to Delilah Goldstein's house. Delilah was eighty-nine, and alone, and once in a while she called in odd reports to 9-1-1. Lucille had adopted her into her posse, but Delilah wasn't as mobile as the other blue-haired hellions that Lucille hung out with.

"What's the matter, Mrs. Goldstein?" Sawyer asked when he stood on her porch.

She peered at him through the screen. "Sawyer? Is that you, dear? Have you been playing doorbell ditch again?"

He bit back his sigh. "No, ma'am. Not in about twenty-five years. I'm a sheriff now, remember? You called in that you needed help."

"Yes, I do need help. I keep hearing Frank Sinatra singing through my TV when it's turned off."

Sawyer paused a beat, then glanced through the screen into her living room. Her TV was definitely off. "Huh." He scratched his chin. He'd seen and heard it all, or so he thought. But this was a new one even for him.

He walked into her living room and squatted in front of the TV, which was at least fifteen years old. The surface didn't have a spec of dust on it, which took a definite talent. But he wasn't hearing any Frank Sinatra. "Do you like Frank Sinatra?" he finally asked Mrs. Goldstein.

"Oh yes, of course. My Stan—God bless his soul—*loved* Frank. We used to listen to him every afternoon at this time of day. Sometimes we'd dance in the living room." She sighed, the sound an expression of grief as she pressed her hand to her mouth.

To give her a minute, Sawyer made a pretense of checking out the back of the TV, but Christ, sometimes this job sucked golf balls.

"Why do you think it happens?" she whispered. "Do you think it's Stan's ghost, or Frank's? Because as fond as I am of Frank's music, I don't want him here in my house, watching me. It feels . . . scary."

Sawyer straightened and looked her right in the eyes. "It's Stan," he said. "Not Frank."

"You're sure?"

"*Positive*. And I think that you should just enjoy the music, Mrs. Goldstein. Don't be afraid."

She smiled at him, her voice tremulous. "You're a good man, Sheriff."

At least she hadn't said sweet.

She made him stay for coffee and a brownie. "Are you ever going to corral in that wild child Chloe Traeger and marry her?" she asked, bagging up a brownie for him to take with him.

He was so thrown by this question that he just stared at her.

"I only ask because Chloe comes over when I get the headaches. She massages my temples with this fantastic homemade balm she creates. It's wonderful. She's wonderful. She'd make such a great sheriff's wife."

Chloe, a wife? The mere thought should've made him laugh, but it didn't.

He knew better. Chloe had to be free to do as she wanted; it wasn't in her nature to be "corralled." And it wasn't in his to try to do so. "I'm not exactly marriage material myself, Mrs. Goldstein."

"Oh, hogwash. That's the silliest thing I've ever heard. You young people have no sense of romance. Why, in my day, if you wanted a girl, you went after her. You made her yours."

Yeah, and wouldn't that go over well with Chloe. She just *loved* it when someone told her what to do. Sawyer moved to the door. "Have a good day, Mrs. Goldstein."

"Don't you mean 'mind my own business'?"

Sawyer grimaced, and she laughed. "Listen, dear. I'm old, and probably far too sentimental, but I'm not dead. Not yet. Don't close yourself off to what could be. Or when you're as old as I am, what will be coming out of your TV?"

Metallica sounded good to him.

It was late afternoon, and he was on the road when he got the call that the convenience store that had been robbed several weeks back had set off their alarm again. He raced over there, lights and sirens blaring, to find the owner and the clerk standing outside waiting for him. When Sawyer got out of his SUV, the owner looked at his watch. "Wow, seven minutes," he said, sounding impressed. He smiled at Sawyer. "We just had a new alarm system installed, and this was our dry run. Nice job, Sheriff. Thank you so much."

Christ. Sawyer did his best to unclench his jaw before pointing out that he wasn't the convenience store's personal security consultant, and they couldn't call 9-1-1 unless there was a true emergency. And then, what the hell, he also took the opportunity to buy two candy bars.

By the time Sawyer pulled up to his house that night, a rainless lightning storm had moved in. Not good. With how dry it had been, it was like playing Russian roulette with lightning-bolt-sized matches on dry timber.

His place looked dark and empty. Empty, he knew, of food, of warmth, of anything remotely welcoming, new paint or not. He walked through his front yard and stopped short at the sight of Chloe sitting on his porch.

She was wearing a long coat and tight leather boots up past her knees but was still huddled into herself for warmth, and without letting himself think, Sawyer pulled her upright and wrapped his arms around her because *she* wasn't dark and empty. She was the opposite, and as she leaned in to him, a feeling surged through him that felt startlingly like relief. And need.

So much fucking need. "You're frozen solid," he said. "What are you doing out here?"

She simply shook her head and pressed her icy nose to his throat, making him suck in a breath. He opened his front door and ushered her inside, where he cranked the heat before turning back to her.

She stood there hugging herself and flashed him a very small smile. "So, um, have you ever done something stupid and then had regrets?"

His heart contracted painfully. If this was where she said she'd just slept with Anderson, he was going to have to shoot the guy, which would suck because Sawyer's department tended to frown on excessive lethal force. "I try really hard not to do anything stupid," he said carefully. "But it happens. Ditto on the regrets. What's this about, Chloe?"

She looked away, but Sawyer hooked a finger under her chin, turning her face back to his. "Me?" he asked. "You regretting us?"

"No. Never."

He nodded like he understood, but he didn't. "You and Anderson?"

Her eyes widened. She looked startled, then insulted. "Anderson gave me his twenty-percent employee discount for materials for the spa, so I bought him lunch."

Sawyer let out the breath he hadn't even realized he'd been holding, pulled her in again, and kissed her, his body reacting so quickly that it caught him by surprise, and he heard himself groan into her mouth.

Chloe lifted her head. "Do you remember when I said sometimes I need to feel? And that sometimes I do stupid things to get there, like pierce a nipple or hang glide or—"

He ran his gaze over her, thwarted by her damn coat. "Are you hurt? Are you—"

·"No." She fumbled with the buttons, then dropped her coat. Beneath she was utterly, gorgeously naked. And beautiful. So fucking beautiful that Sawyer lost his words and his mind. "God, look at you," he said hoarsely.

"Welcome to my latest crazy," she whispered, wearing nothing but those knee-high boots and an unsure smile. "Oh, and you should probably know, I'm quite possibly hypothermic."

"Luckily I've been trained to handle this situation."

Chloe smiled, and he realized she was nervous. He was nervous, too, which made no sense to him whatsoever. They'd been here before, right here. He pulled off his shirt and reached for her at the same moment she leaped at him, wrapping her legs around his hips. He had one hand on her ass, the other high on her back and in her long hair as he carried her to his bedroom. Lying her on the bed, he stepped back only to get rid of his gun and phone, then strip out of the rest of his clothes, which he did in less than five seconds. *Mother of God, let nobody have an emergency tonight, he thought.*

He had a moment where he stared down at her on his bed in nothing but those fuck-me boots, not wanting to take them off. But then she shivered, and he reluctantly tugged them from her feet and dropped them to the floor before shoving her beneath his thick covers and following her in. "Step one," he said. "We conserve body heat."

"Good plan." She turned to him, wrapping her frozen limbs around him.

He hissed in a breath when she pressed her frozen toes into his calves, but her own breathing wasn't anywhere close to even, and he paused. "Need your inhaler?"

She shook her head. "I need you."

He opened his mouth, but she put a finger over his lips. "I'm done talking now."

Yeah. So was he. But when her icy fingers walked their way down his chest and stomach, he sucked in another harsh breath and grabbed her hand, rubbing it between his to warm it up.

She laughed at him, but he knew how to shut her up. He kissed her hard and long and deep, running a hand down her quivering body, sliding it between her thighs. Ahhhh. She wasn't cold here. She was already hot and slick and ready. "You want me."

She smiled. "Yes. Whatever this is that we're doing, I want you. I've always wanted you."

Her softly whispered words staggered him. It hadn't been a confession of love. Hell, he knew that she didn't do confessions of love.

So why did it feel like one?

Because he wasn't doing so well at controlling his emotions with her, that's why. "I want you, too," he said, sure as hell not able to remember a time that he hadn't.

Pulling him down, she kissed him, and he let himself sink into the kiss, into her, willingly drowning in her heat, grateful that he couldn't talk and kiss at the same time because he was dangerously close to spilling his guts.

"Now," she said against his lips.

"No, not yet. I want to—"

"*Sawyer.*"

Like he really stood a chance against the sound of his name on her lips. Cradled by her open thighs, he slid into her.

Home.

Slow, he reminded himself, searching her face for

signs of distress. But he found only desire and hunger and closed his eyes as her hands ran over his chest, his arms, everywhere she could reach, swamping him with pleasure. He pulled back and thrust again, deeper now, groaning at the feel of her, but hesitated when her nails dug into his shoulders.

"No, don't stop," she said, soft and throaty, still showing no signs of trouble. "Please don't stop." Accompanying this sexy little plea, she made a restless circular motion with her hips, and he lost the tenuous grip on his control.

This morning he'd run three miles on the beach, and he'd been in good enough shape not to feel the exertion overly much. Now, here in her arms, buried in her body, his breath was coming in ragged pants. He reared up on his hands, back arched to get as deep as he could as he began to move. When she cried out this time, he recognized it was a plea for more, and he gave it.

She cupped his face, slid her fingers into his hair, and beamed up at him. God, he loved her smile. She felt so good. Her eyes were a staggering, fathomless green, and looking at her made him ache so much that he ran out of air.

Completely. Ran. Out. He struggled to breathe and thought this must be how she felt. But then she pressed her mouth to his and gave him her air. He groaned and continued to move in and out of her, harder now, faster, and then she came, her eyes filled with a faint, endearing surprise as her body clenched around him.

God, she felt so good. Just watching her sent him spiraling. It began deep inside, racing through his body so that his arms trembled, and he dropped his head with a rough groan, burying his face in the curve of her neck as he completely lost himself.

# Chapter 21

*"Anything worth taking seriously
is also worth making fun of."*

CHLOE TRAEGER

The next day Chloe gave a yoga class for one. Allie never stopped talking the whole time, about the amazing burgers at Eat Me, her Cute Guy sighting at the liquor store, how there was never a line at the post office here…She loved the people and wasn't sure she missed anyone from home.

"Not anyone?" Chloe asked.

Allie lifted a shoulder.

"It's okay to miss him," Chloe said quietly. "It's okay to miss John."

And for the first time all week, Allie clammed up.

They were still stretching on the beach when Maddie and Jax pulled up to the inn. Maddie started to get out of the Jeep, but Jax drew her back, buried his hands in her hair, and kissed her.

"He's going to inhale her right up," Allie noted, sounding a little wistful.

"They're getting married. I think all almost-marrieds act like that." Chloe winced as soon as she said it, remembering why Allie was here. "I'm sorry, I—"

"No. Don't be sorry." Allie sat Indian style on the mat and stared out at the water. "I can't hide out from it forever."

"I know you've been in contact with your family. Have you called John at all?"

"No." She closed her eyes and inhaled deeply. "I made a mistake, Chloe. A big one. Things got intense before the wedding. There was so much to do, and everyone was trying to be involved..." She shook her head. "I lost sight of what I was doing, and why. John wanted to be a part of the planning, and I told him I could handle it. A bride should be able to handle it. I pushed him away. And then when he finally took a big step back, I fell apart and pushed him farther." She bit her lip. "And then on my wedding day, I felt alone. So alone. It was all of my own making, but I couldn't see that." She turned to Chloe. "So I ran. When the going got tough, I ran like a little girl."

Chloe understood both the pushing people away and the feeling alone. And hell, if she was being honest, she understood the running too. She'd spent years perfecting all three. "It's never too late to face a regret." She handed Allie her cell phone. "You don't have to tell him where you are or—"

Allie snatched the phone so fast that Chloe's head spun. She rolled up her mat and moved toward the inn to give Allie some privacy, but before she'd gotten out of earshot she heard, "Baby? It's me." Allie's breath hitched audibly. "John, I'm so sorry—in some Podunk little place called Lucky Harbor. Really? You will? You'll come? Oh, John..."

\* \* \*

Sawyer knocked on his father's door but wasn't surprised when no one answered. For three days now, it'd been the same story. Worried, Sawyer let himself in and dropped the two bags of groceries he'd brought with him on the kitchen table.

From somewhere in the house, he heard a toilet flush, and then his father shuffled into the kitchen, scowling. "Nice knock," he grumbled at Sawyer.

"I did knock. And I called, too. You're avoiding me."

"I was on the pot."

"I've been calling all week. Wanted to help you fix the gutters."

"My boy did it."

Okay, last Sawyer checked, *he* was Nolan's boy. "I would have—"

"I hate carrots," his father said, nosing through the bags. "And blueberries. Christ, this is fucking sissy food."

"It's good for you." Sawyer eyed his father. White wife-beater dulled by years of washings, dark blue trousers hitched up to just beneath a beer belly. "You need to eat healthier."

"I've eaten how I want for sixty years."

"Yes," Sawyer said. "Hence your health problems."

"Goddammit!" His father waved a hand and knocked the bag to the floor. "*My* business, not yours."

Whether he'd accidentally hit the food or not, it pissed Sawyer off. He could handle drug dealers and gang-bangers without losing his cool, but five minutes with his father and his temper was lit. "Listen—"

"No, *you* listen," his father snarled, spitting out his

words like venom. "Where in the hell do *you* get off telling me how to run my life?"

"Since your doctor said you were going to die if you didn't change!"

"Well, fuck the doctor!" Nolan bellowed. "He's a twelve-year-old, skinny-ass punk kid."

"Dr. Scott is *my* age," Sawyer said, keeping his voice quiet and controlled with great effort. "Josh and I went to school together." In fact, the two of them had spent many, many Saturdays in detention together, driving the high school teachers insane.

"You mean you were good-for-nothing *thugs* together," Nolan snapped.

"Whatever he was, Josh is a doctor now. And a good one," Sawyer said. "Jesus, Dad! You can't hold his past against him." But then he let out a short, mirthless laugh. "What am I saying? Of course you can hold his past against him. You do mine."

Nolan jabbed a meaty finger to the door. "Get out."

"Gladly." Sawyer strode to the door. "Tell your perfect little gofer boy that the porch light's out."

\*      \*      \*

Exhausted as she was, Chloe did the happy dance around the sunroom. No, she corrected. Not the sunroom—the Lucky Harbor Day Spa.

Well, it was *almost* a spa anyway. It was at least finished enough to have provided a short menu of services for the family of sisters, who as of two hours ago had checked out after a long weekend stay.

The week before, Jax had thrown together a changing room, hooked up the plumbing, and painted the last of the trim an hour before the two massage chairs for pedicures had been delivered, along with the shipment of towels and robes. Chloe already had a portable massage table, so that hadn't been an issue.

Granted, there was still more to do to make it a full-service spa, but she had made it work for now.

Grinning, she spun in a circle and collapsed onto a cushy chair. The important thing was that the weekend had been a huge success. And fun. It'd been a sister-team effort, with Tara making No-Guilt-Here foods and Maddie introducing "chick night" events complete with knitting sessions and tissues-required classic movies. Chloe had given facials, mud skin treatments, and massages, along with yoga classes.

Every single one of the guests had not only rebooked for other treatments but had bought gift certificates for friends and family.

Chloe was extremely aware of how much she'd enjoyed the weekend, and exactly what she was giving up to have, hopefully, many more. She knew offers like the one she'd had from the San Diego spa didn't grow on trees, but she felt committed to Lucky Harbor, to being here. To her sisters as well.

Her heart wanted to add Sawyer to that list, but her brain reminded her that Sawyer was fun and heat and magic—but that he'd not exactly shown any signs of wanting more.

*Neither have you…*

She leaned back in the chair and sighed. It was nine o'clock at night, and for the first time in days, she was all alone. Blissful, she put up her tired feet and closed her eyes.

"Aw, look at her, all plum tuckered out. I guess taking people's money is hard work."

At Tara's soft, teasing Southern drawl, Chloe opened her eyes and found her sisters standing in the doorway. "Hey. I thought you'd both left."

"Not yet, sugar." Tara was carrying a bottle of wine in one hand, three glasses in her other. She set them down on the low-lying counter that Chloe had just cleaned, then plopped onto the spa chair and stretched out her long legs. As always, she was in heels. She kicked them off and wriggled her toes. "Lord Almighty, I should have done that about four hours ago." Thoughtfully, she studied the rack of nail colors.

Maddie sat, too. "Long weekend." She smiled at Chloe. "I had a very lovely time just now adding up all the receipts. You've made our bank account very happy."

Chloe wanted to ask *And how about you two, are you happy?* But she didn't. She was afraid of the answer. "I took a booking for six girlfriends for next weekend. Seems we're going to be known for the girls' weekend out sort of thing."

"There's worse things to be known for," Maddie said, covering Chloe's hand in hers. "Heads-up—mushy alert warning."

"What? No, I—"

But before Chloe had finished sputtering, Maddie reeled her in and hugged her.

"Tell her you love her, Mad," Tara said, still prone on her chair. "It'll make her as wild as a peach orchard hog."

Chloe, laughing now, tried to escape, but Maddie squeezed her tighter. "I *lurve* you," Maddie said with as much sap as she could.

Chloe stuck her finger into her mouth and then stuck the wet digit in Maddie's ear.

Maddie collapsed in laughter while screaming "ewwww" and dropped to the floor.

"A wet willy," Tara said calmly, nodding. "Nice tactic."

Chloe brushed her hands together and smirked down at Maddie. "Round two?"

Maddie rolled to her belly and cushioned her head on her arms. "Hell, no. I'm too tired." She crawled to the spa chair where Tara was still sprawled and pulled herself up, curling to share the space. She eyed the nail colors too, then picked out a baby blue. And then a siren red. She looked at Chloe speculatively, then grabbed a metallic silver, and then also a solid black. "Can you open the windows, Chloe? It's not so cold out, and you'll need fresh air for this."

Chloe dutifully opened the windows.

"Now sit," Maddie said.

Which Chloe did gladly since she was exhausted.

Maddie pulled Chloe's feet into her lap. "Nice toes. You got them from Mom. Mine are short and stumpy from my dad, of course." She painted Chloe's big toe the metallic silver, then painted every other toe before filling in the opposite ones with the black.

"Silver and black?" Tara asked, amused. "Different. Suits her."

"Yeah, I thought so, too. You're getting red, by the way," Maddie said, and proceeded to switch to Tara's feet. "And you have pretty feet too, you bitch. Pour the wine, Tara."

Tara arched a brow in Chloe's direction, like *look at our little mouse now*. But she obeyed and poured three glasses of wine, handing one to Chloe and another to Maddie. Finally she took her own and lifted it. "To a hell of a day and a very pretty bottom line."

Tara and Maddie drank deeply to that. Chloe watched them, an unexpected warmth spreading inside her chest. So much had changed so quickly. Tara and Maddie, Ford and Jax, the spa, and of course, Sawyer, who'd made an indelible mark on her life, more than anyone else ever had. She still didn't know what would become of them, and imagining that someday he'd tire of her hurt like hell, so she let her thoughts spin back to her sisters. They would always be here for her. She knew that now. It wasn't just a concept anymore. It was a fact. They were her anchor in a lifetime spent free-floating.

Chloe set aside her untouched wine. She wanted a clear head for this. But more than that, she also wanted to be able to drive herself to Sawyer's later tonight. Thanks to their very busy schedule, it'd been six nights since she'd last been in his bed, naked in his arms, panting his name, letting him take away everything but what they gave each other. Funny, because she'd gone a whole year without sex, and now six days was too long. Or was it simply Sawyer himself that she missed?

"I can't believe it, really," Maddie said.

Chloe started guiltily. "What?"

Maddie began to paint her own toes with the baby-blue polish. "How far we've come. I can't believe it."

Okay, good. They weren't talking about Chloe's sex life.

Tara nodded. "Do you realize that we've each managed to bring a vital part of ourselves to the inn?"

Chloe stared down at her sparkling toes. "Is that it?" she wondered. "Or is it that this place has given each of us something we needed?" When nobody spoke, she looked up. Both her sisters were staring at her, eyes moist.

"Oh, Christ." Chloe sighed and grabbed some napkins, shoving one at each of them. "I swear, if either of you cries, I'm giving out more wet willies, followed by wedgies. I mean it."

"I have a better idea." Maddie stood up. "Our first night here together we stayed up all night decorating our poor Charlie Brown Christmas tree. Do you remember?"

"Hard to forget," Tara said. "Chloe turned our faces and hair green with her facial and conditioner masks, remember?"

"Hey," Chloe said in her defense. "It improved your skin, didn't it?"

"Excuse me." Maddie tapped a fingernail against the wineglass to get their attention, then cleared her throat dramatically. "I'm trying to recount our adventures here, so pay attention. And I do have a point."

"You going to get to it anytime soon?" Chloe asked.

"Do you or do you not remember when we decided to make this place a B&B?" Maddie asked. "We—"

"*We?*" Tara interrupted, laughing. "If we're remembering, then let's remember how it really happened, shall we? *We* didn't decide anything, Maddie. *You* two corralled me into the B&B thing, specifically the chef part. And you did it by dangling Ford in front of me."

"Oh, and that turned out so awful, right?" Chloe responded dryly. "And let me guess—you *hate* being your own boss. You hate ordering us around in the mornings to do your bidding. Is that what you're saying?"

Tara smiled. "No, I really like that part. A lot."

"Hello," Maddie said sternly. "I'm talking here!" She

paused for dramatic effect, but when Chloe and Tara just rolled their eyes, she sighed. "Don't you get it? We need to do something. We need a ceremony for this milestone!"

"It's too early for a Christmas tree," Chloe said.

Maddie tossed up her hands. "Something *new*! Something unique. To celebrate *you*," she said. "To celebrate the spa thing." She scrunched up her face to think, then grinned wide, and then slumped. "I had something. But I forgot."

Chloe laughed. "That cheap date thing must be hereditary."

"Yeah," Maddie admitted with a laugh. "Half a glass and I'm gone. Wait, I think I remember. Maybe."

"Uh-oh," Chloe said to Tara. "I feel something inadvisable coming on."

"Well, sugar, if anyone's going to recognize it, it'd be you."

"Recognize this," Chloe said and flipped Tara off.

"We need to mark this milestone," Maddie insisted.

"We can go to the mud baths," Chloe said, knowing damn well that they'd both shoot her down, tell her she was crazy, and then she could finally go jump Sawyer's bones.

And he had such *fine* bones, too...

"That's *brilliant*!" Maddie stood up and grabbed them each by the hand. "We're going to the mud springs!"

"Wait—what?" Chloe asked.

"It's a great idea," Maddie said, tugging them both along.

Chloe dug in her heels. "Hold up."

"Why?" Maddie asked.

"Because first, you're drunk. Second, I was totally kidding."

"Tell me that it wouldn't be the *perfect* thing to do." Maddie let go of them to clasp her hands together and jump up and down. "Oh, come on! Do this for me and...and I won't make you get me a present for my wedding shower!"

"But it's pitch-black outside," Tara said.

"Actually," Chloe said, "it's a full moon." Too late, she clamped her mouth shut. *Dammit*, she had plans for Sawyer and his naked bod beneath that full moon.

"Yeah," Maddie said to Tara. "It's a full moon, pansy ass."

"You know what?" Chloe shook her head. "I don't think it's a good idea."

"You suggested it, genius," Tara reminded her.

"Yeah, but I was joking." But it was the disappointment shining in Maddie's eyes that killed her. "Okay, don't do that. Not the Bambi eyes."

"I thought you'd appreciate the fact that I'm willing to do something that's so *you*," Maddie said. "After all, the spa was your baby."

"Yes, and I do appreciate it." And only a few weeks ago, Chloe would've been the first one out the door, not sitting here considering the fact that it was late and not altogether safe to be slipping and sliding around the springs. She glanced at Tara, then back to Maddie, and sighed. "Fine. *Jesus*. Why the hell not?"

"Yay!" Maddie polished off her wine, grabbed another bottle, then pulled them through the inn to her car, tossing Chloe, the only sober one, the keys.

Chloe thought for a second, then ran back inside for

everything she'd wished she'd had the first time: towels, three spa robes, flashlights, and even though it took another trip, she hauled out three big gallons of fresh water to clean off with. When she returned, still laughing at herself a little for being the only grown-up of the bunch—*how scary was that?*—she found Tara still standing outside the car.

"Did she really call me a pansy ass?" Tara asked in a hushed whisper that the people of China could have heard.

"We have to get her a present for her wedding shower?" Chloe whispered back as she tossed the stuff into the trunk. "Because I thought the wedding shower *was* the present."

They got to the trailhead just after eleven, and Chloe felt like a pagan white witch leading her sisters up the trail by flashlight.

Once at the mud springs, they had no trouble seeing. The moon had cast the meadow in a pale blue glow. Steam rose off the mud into the night, and Chloe shivered. "I don't know—"

"And you call yourself the wild child," Maddie chided and stripped down to her tiger-striped panties and bra. "I think we should switch monikers. *You* be the mouse. I'll take wild child, thank you very much!" So saying, she dipped a toe into the mud, then holding the bottle of wine like she was of the highest royalty, waded in up to her waist and sighed in bliss. "Warm."

"Since when do you have tiger-striped underwear?" Chloe asked.

Maddie blushed, her face lighting up like a glow stick in the night. "They were a present from Jax. Isn't it gorgeous out here, all silvery and mysterious? You can almost see the forest fairies."

"Okay, no more wine for you," Tara said. She eyed the mud and sighed. "I must be insane." But she followed suit after Maddie and stripped. Though, of course, *she* took the time to carefully hang her dress over a branch. Her underwear was not tiger-striped but a pale, silky cream and lace that screamed sophistication and elegance. Or at least as much as one can scream sophistication and elegance while standing in your underwear in the woods at eleven.

Chloe was hands on hips staring at them. "For the record, I have never called myself the wild child."

"Come on in, Mouse," Maddie called.

"Nor did I ever call you the mouse." At least not to her face. Chloe kicked off her shoes. "Though I think we should call you Queen Bee-yotch. Damn, it's cold out here!"

"Only until you get in," Maddie promised, tossing back some more of the wine right out of the bottle before handing it over to Tara.

Chloe wriggled out of her jeans, then hesitated there in her panties and sweater. She wasn't wearing a bra.

Tara made the sound of a chicken.

Chloe rolled her eyes and tore off her sweater. When she was up to her chin in the mud, Tara grinned at her. "You took out your nipple ring."

"Last year," Chloe said, watching as Maddie snatched the bottle of wine back from Tara.

"Really?" Tara asked Chloe. "Why?"

"I don't know. It kept catching on my bra." Which was true, but it'd been more than that. Somehow, at some point, she'd realized she'd outgrown the need to be so wildly different. It'd been right about the time that the three of them had agreed to stick together and renovate the inn. They'd been halfway through the renovation when there'd been a bad fire, forcing them to start over. The fire had been devastating in many ways, but by some miracle, they'd survived. And it'd been that night, lying in the ER, suffering from a smoke-induced asthma attack, with a sister on either side of her, that Chloe had known.

She'd been singed nearly to a crisp, lost everything including the clothing on her back, but it hadn't mattered because she had her sisters and she loved them. "I do," she said softly to herself, nodding. "I really do."

"You believe in fairies?" Maddie asked, confused.

Tara took the wine from her. "Shh, sugar. I think Miss Wild Thang's having an epiphany. Let's leave her to it."

Chloe stared at them. Tara was in the middle of carefully streaking the mud on her jaw in order to get the maximum benefit from it. Maddie had done her face already and looked like a zebra. And Chloe felt a smile bloom both in her heart and on her face. "To us," she said softly.

"To us," Maddie said, and drank to that.

\*     \*     \*

Sawyer got the call from the forest service about midnight. It was Matt, reporting flickering lights had been seen on the trails out at Yellow Ridge. Matt was on Mt. Jude, the far side of the county, a good hour away, and couldn't respond to the call. "I'm contacting you," he said, "because the caller gave a description of a hopped-up shiny black truck going off-road, and it sounded like Todd's. I know you're watching him. I can call another ranger, but it might be morning before I can get anyone out there, and as you know, those trails are supposedly closed at nightfall, thanks to the fire season."

"I'll go," Sawyer said, already in his truck, knowing this was it. If he caught up with Todd, he'd catch whoever Todd was working for. It was the break they were looking for. He was already on call twenty-four seven for the DEA until they closed in on their drug case, which most likely involved Todd one way or the other. Twenty minutes later, he was shining his flashlight on the car in front of the mud springs trailhead, shaking his head in disbelief.

Maddie's car. What the hell was she doing up here? He flickered his flashlight in the window and saw a purse on the passenger floor. He thought maybe it was Tara's. There was a phone on the backseat. He was pretty sure it was Chloe's iPhone, which explained why she hadn't picked up any of his calls. "What are you three up to?" he murmured.

No doubt the three sisters would have an explanation that would make him dizzy. Chloe might just be the most impulsive person he'd ever met, but she was also one of the sharpest. She had a reason for most everything she did, although sometimes the reason was to turn the world on its ear. But Tara and Maddie? He'd have figured them more sensible than to follow her up here.

Hell, it was fall. Bears were on the hunt to store up their winter fat. Coyotes were doing the same. Not to mention that in spite of the combined efforts of the forestry service and his own county department, there'd been plenty of illegal camping and hunting going on during this long, late Indian summer.

He needed to let it go. They were three grown women and could handle themselves. His job was Todd. If he was out here, he was up to no good, but the demands and conflicts of his job had never been stronger as he caught sight of the iPhone in the backseat of Maddie's car.

Fuck.

He eyed the trailhead, and the sign there, posted by the forest service.

### TRAIL CLOSES AT NIGHTFALL.

Swearing beneath his breath, he headed up the path. There were several forks, and he methodically worked his way along each until twenty-five minutes later he came to a clearing and stood staring in utter disbelief. Three heads appeared to be floating disembodied in a mud spring by the light of the moon.

"Hey," he said to the three sisters, hands on hips, "if it isn't Curly, Larry, and Moe."

The three faces grinned. Sawyer had long ago schooled himself to be braced for surprise, trouble, danger...anything. And he had a really good blank, cop face. He knew this because it was that face that allowed him to whip Jax's and Ford's asses in poker every single time. But it was a struggle to stay blank at the sight before him.

Far above them, the moon's glow gave off an unearthly feel, and with nothing surrounding them but isolated wilderness, the three women might have been ancient Indians in their war paint.

The tallest one narrowed her eyes and spoke with a Southern accent. "We were thinking more along the lines of *Sex and the City* than *The Three Stooges*," she drawled.

The next one squealed with delight at that. "Oh! I want to be Carrie! I've always wanted to be Carrie!"

The petite one just studied Sawyer meditatively. "I think we should make him join us," she said, her expression angelic, her voice pure devil. "He doesn't always wear underwear, you know."

Six eyes swiveled to his crotch.

Christ. He resisted cupping himself.

"Come on in, Sheriff," the little minx called softly. "We don't bite."

"You're drunk." Perfect. He should arrest them for all for public intoxication *and* public nudity, not to mention being out here on closed trails, but hell if he could make himself do it. Where was Lucille when Facebook needed her? He pulled out his cell phone.

Tara gasped. "What are you doing?"

"Getting a shot for Lucille. You're going to be even more popular than the elusive Cute Guy."

Maddie and Tara squealed and immediately gave him their backs.

Chloe held her ground, watching him. "You wouldn't."

"I should."

"Come in."

"Not gonna happen." If she'd been alone, he'd have been tempted. Which was a sorry thing. Before she'd come along, the thought not only wouldn't have entered his mind but would've appalled him.

He pressed the button on his phone to check for calls from Agent Morris before he remembered—no service up here. "Okay, everyone out." He held out his hand to Maddie first because she was finger-painting Chloe's face and looked to be the most gone. She didn't come out. No one did. Tara was gathering the hair off her neck, her skin gleaming pale and smooth beneath the moonlight, looking like some sort of Greek goddess. Maddie finished with Chloe's face and began humming a song to herself while doing some sort of dance. Chloe grabbed her before she could dance her way farther into the shadows. "Whoa there, Pocahontas," she said, snagging her sister by the arm, surging up out of the mud to her waist to do so.

She wasn't wearing a bra, and Sawyer swallowed hard. "Chloe—"

She sent him an innocent smile and pulled both sisters out of the mud, wrapping them each up in towels before reaching for her own towel.

Sawyer turned his back and stared hard up at the stars. He tried a few multiplication tables, but it couldn't hold up against the images of three gorgeous women covered in mud, washing each other off.

By the time Chloe came up to his side, cleaned and grinning, he was sweating. "You can look now," she murmured.

They were all dressed, thank God. He could stop picturing Ford's and Jax's women, nude by the pale moon's glow.

But he didn't have to stop picturing Chloe.

They walked together down the path, making it in twenty minutes back to Maddie's car. He then followed them down the road to the highway in his truck, getting out when Chloe pulled Maddie's car over to the side.

"Just wanted to say thanks for checking on us," she said when he'd walked up to the driver's door and she'd rolled her window down.

His phone beeped as his cell service kicked in, and he

realized he had messages. From where he stood, he could also hear dispatch trying to get him on his radio. *Shit.* He listened to the first message on his cell and his blood ran cold.

"Sawyer?" Chloe's smile faded. "You okay?"

He held up a hand, listening. Dispatch had been trying to reach him. Agent Morris had been trying to reach him. Everyone and their mother had been trying to reach him. In the forty minutes he'd been out of range, all hell had broken loose. There'd been a reported drug deal before the DEA could mobilize. They had a witness, a hiker, who claimed that he'd seen the whole thing but by the time the authorities had arrived, everyone had scattered.

It'd been only a few miles from here.

The DEA had gone to Todd's place to discover that not only had they missed whatever had gone down tonight, Todd had cleared out entirely, probably holed up waiting until the heat was off.

No doubt thanks to Sawyer going to Todd, trying to interrogate him about his drug source and offering him a deal. Instead Todd had packed up his shit and vanished.

"Sawyer?"

"I've got to go." He strode back to his truck, vibrating with anger. Jamming his key in the ignition, he tossed his cell on the seat, then peeled out of the parking area, furious at himself. He'd known he was the only one on the DEA task force actually stationed in Lucky Harbor, and he'd also known better than to be out of cell service that long, but as always, being anywhere near Chloe stole his good sense.

Not her fault. Nope, this one was all on him, and it'd been at the expense of the job that meant everything to him.

# Chapter 22

> *"Women might not like to admit their age,*
> *but men don't like to act theirs."*
>
> CHLOE TRAEGER

Chloe stared after Sawyer's truck, Maddie's headlights cutting through the cloud of dust in his wake.

"What the hell was that?" Maddie asked. She sat in the backseat, a towel wrapped around her hair. She didn't sound drunk now. "He seemed mad."

"He wasn't angry before," Tara said from her shotgun position in the front seat.

Now that the dust had settled, Chloe pulled back onto the road, replaying the evening in her head. "It wasn't about us," she said. "I think it was about his messages. Something must have happened."

"I hope everything's okay," Maddie said. "I'd hate it if he missed helping someone because of us."

Chloe, too. She'd never seen Sawyer react like that before. It wasn't his style. Usually when things went to hell, he got calm and quiet. Steady as a rock. It had to be something bad. Her thoughts went first to his father, but that didn't hold up. If he'd had a heart attack, Sawyer would have been concerned, not angry.

"He sure was surprised to find us in the mud," Maddie said. "I can't imagine what he was expecting, but I can guarantee it wasn't the three of us in war paint."

Chloe thought of Sawyer's expression when he'd come into view at the edge of the trail and found them. He'd been irritated, then relieved to find them. Then he'd looked right at her and hadn't even tried to hide his affection.

The memory brought an unexpected lump to her throat. Jax and Ford had known Sawyer forever, and yet he hid his emotions from them all the time. His emotions and his weaknesses...

But not from her.

He let her see him, all of him. It was a gift, she realized. The gift of himself.

She'd never had such a thing offered to her before, and she was still thinking about it, marveling at it, when she dropped Tara and a very groggy Maddie at the inn. No one even bothered to suggest cleaning out the car tonight. Jax and Ford were waiting to pick up their women.

Chloe parked and walked around back to the cottage. It was with mixed feelings that she went inside, alone.

She stripped there in the doorway and stepped gingerly to the bathroom, where it took her nearly an entire bottle of her own shea butter body wash to get clean. Afterward, she slid naked between the soft sheets of her bed and listened to the quiet creaks and groans of the place around her. Several months ago, she and Lance had joked about the sounds coming from a ghost, a lonely one.

Chloe knew the feeling . . .

No. Life was good, she reminded herself firmly. She and her sisters seemed to be in sync. The inn was doing well. Her past was her past, and her present was actually moving along.

It was only her future in question. A future she couldn't quite see or imagine. She flopped over and told herself she'd never given her future much of a thought, so why the sudden worry now?

The answer was terrifyingly simple.

For the first time, she was feeling content. And she wanted the feeling to last, even though she knew from experience that nothing lasted.

Sleep didn't come. Just more concern. She debated calling Sawyer, but . . . but she had a bad feeling about whatever it was that had happened tonight. She didn't want to interrupt him from something important.

But on the other hand, he could already be home, and not calling her because he thought *she* was asleep.

Which settled it. She'd go to his place, see if his truck was there. If he was mad, he could tell her in person.

When she pulled into his driveway twenty minutes later, she let out a breath at the sight of his truck. Parking the Vespa next to it, she headed up the walk and knocked softly.

Sawyer opened the door in low-slung jeans and nothing else but a decent amount of testosterone-driven attitude. For the first time since they'd been doing this, he didn't seem happy to see her, and dread enveloped her heart. "Is it too late?" she asked much more mildly than she felt.

"Since when has that stopped you?"

She stared at him for a beat, then turned to go. "I shouldn't have come—"

"Chloe." He sighed and pulled her back around. "Come in. You're cold."

No, she was scared. Not of him, never of him, but of what was going to happen between them.

Or not happen.

With butterflies flying around in her gut, she shut the front door and leaned back against it. She tried to get a read on him, but as usual, his face was giving away nothing. "I didn't think you were upset about the mud springs," she said. "Which, by the way, wasn't my idea." She winced. "Okay, so it was, but I'd been just kidding, and then Maddie was all over it, and—"

"It's not about the mud springs."

"Are you sure, because—"

"Not everything revolves around you, Chloe." And at that, he walked away.

"Well, I know that—" But he wasn't listening. He was gone. Her initial thought was to walk out the door, just let everything go. The old Chloe would've done that in a heartbeat. But she didn't want to be that Chloe anymore, that person who skipped town rather than face hard reality.

So she pressed a hand to her nervous stomach, dropped her purse in the entry, and forced herself down the hall after him. That's when she saw the low wooden coffee table, and against the wall, an entertainment unit.

Sawyer had been busy making the place look more like a home.

She found Sawyer in the master bathroom, reaching through the shower to open the window there. To her surprise, one wall was half painted. It'd been a rather out-dated shade of green, which he was covering up with the wildly imaginative off-white. "How did you decide on a shade?" she asked.

"It was on sale."

She might have smiled if it hadn't been for the knots in her gut. "It's two a.m."

"Yep." He reached for the roller.

Every part of her wanted to run for the door, say what the hell, it'd been fun while it lasted, because she'd known, God, she'd known, that this couldn't last.

But the hell with being a big, fat chicken. She was braver now. She didn't understand. She needed to under-stand. "So what was that call about earlier? More crazy women skinny-dipping by moonlight somewhere?"

"No." He rolled a careful stripe of paint, perfectly even. No crooked walls tonight.

"Your dad okay?" she asked.

"He's fine. Blowing me off, but fine."

"Blowing you off?"

He shrugged. "He told me to stay away, that he'd got some kid to do odd jobs around his place. A really great kid who's always on time and doesn't try to screw him and is a fucking pillar of virtue."

"Well, good for him," she said. "Those pillars of fuck-ing virtue are really hard to find."

He tossed the roller down. "There's no damn kid, Chloe. He's making him up."

"Maybe he's trying to save you the time or save face."

"Save face?"

"Yes, you know, stupid male pride?"

"You don't understand," Sawyer said grimly. "And

how could you? I've never told you about who I used to be."

"So you were a punk-ass kid," she said. "So what? A lot of us were."

"You don't know."

"I know who you are now," she said. "And that's all that matters. You're loyal, strong, caring—"

He snorted and went back to painting. Clearly they were done discussing this. Shock. She stared at his broad, expansive back, watching with avid interest as the muscles there flexed and bunched while he stroked the walls with the roller. "Do you have another roller?"

"No."

She squeezed in between him and the wall. "Hi. My name's Chloe, and you might not have noticed, but we're friends. Naked friends, sure, but friends nevertheless. And friends share. If it wasn't your father tonight that pissed you off, what was it?"

He met her gaze. "We're more than just messing around naked friends," he said.

She did her best to squelch the burst of emotion those words caused. "Then talk to me."

He made a restless movement with his shoulders, like he was to-the-bone exhausted. "If you're mad at me," she murmured, "I think I deserve to know why."

He stared at the wet paint on the wall above her head. "It's not you I'm mad at."

"Then who?"

"Me." He drew a careful breath. "I'm between a rock and a hard place here with what I can say."

"Okay."

"It's DEA business. We've been waiting on a break.

I'm on call now, but thanks to me being out of range tonight, our lead went underground and took any evidence with him."

Chloe closed her eyes, stricken with guilt. This was because he'd been at the mud springs checking on her and her sisters. "Oh, Sawyer. I'm so sorry. Is there anything I can do?"

His gaze swiveled to hers, and he studied her meditatively. "That's your only question?"

"No, I have at least a dozen, but I'm working on not being an impulsive pain in your ass."

With a quiet laugh to himself, he asked, "How is it you're so good for me, and yet so bad at the same time?"

Well, if that didn't reach out and punch her in the gut. "It's a special talent of mine," she managed.

His gaze roamed her face, and she hated this, hated standing here waiting for him to tell her that they were through. Because that's where this was going, she knew it. She *felt* it. Everything about his voice and expression told her so, and she knew that she should have left when she had the chance, left and pretended she'd never found contentment and security in his arms.

"You asked if there was something you could do for me," he said quietly.

She nodded numbly.

"You could come here."

Without hesitation, she moved closer, pressing her cheek against his warm, naked chest, finding comfort in the strong, steady beat of his heart against her ear, as his arms surrounded her hard. "I'm not the man you think I am, Chloe," he said into her hair.

"Wrong," she said and pulled him closer. "You are exactly who I thought you were." She kissed him, hard. He responded by pressing her up against the one dry wall, holding her there with two hundred pounds of solid, hard muscle. And he *was* hard, *everywhere*.

"Feeling better, then?" she whispered.

"I'm feeling something. Where's your inhaler, Chloe?"

"In my purse by your front door. I just used it." She slid her arms up around his neck and again pulled his head down to hers. "As a precaution." The wall behind her was giving her a chill, but Sawyer's mouth was hot and urgent on her throat. The hard curves of his back burned warm against her fingers. "I'm sorry about tonight, Sawyer. So sorry."

"It can't happen again. Not ever again."

The words skittered down her spine, causing a shiver. Because it was going to be over. She'd known that. A part of her had always known that. But it was going to destroy her.

*Tomorrow.*

For now, right now, she still had this, had tonight. He wanted her, that much she knew, and she wanted him.

More than she'd ever wanted anyone in her entire life.

Not willing to waste another second of it, she slid her hand between them to unsnap his jeans. He lifted his head, his gaze searching hers. His expression softened, and he took over, stripping out of his jeans. He was commando, and she took him in, one taut muscle at a time.

Heart-stopping.

Breath-taking.

He unzipped her sweatshirt and groaned at the strip of skin he exposed from the pulse point of her throat to the hip-hugging waistband of her jeans. Then he tugged the

sweatshirt off, letting it fall to the floor on top of his jeans.
Her bra went next. "Turn around."

When she didn't move fast enough, he spun her so that
she faced the mirror, setting her hands on the countertop
like he was going to frisk her. Instead, he pressed up close
behind her.

Together they looked at her body in the mirror.

She could feel his warm breath on her neck, coming
a little faster than his usual hibernation rate of breathing,
and it gave her a little thrill. "What?" he murmured when
she shuddered, bending to kiss her neck.

She gasped as his hands skimmed up her torso to cup
her bare breasts, his fingers plucking at her nipples. "I
make you feel things," she said.

He rocked into her. "Yeah. You sure as hell do." He
unfastened her jeans and nudged them down along with
her panties, kicking all the fallen clothes away from their
feet. His hands settled hers on the counter again, one foot
nudging her legs farther apart. When he had her arranged
to suit him, he put his hands on her hips and met her gaze
in the mirror.

"Are you going to search me now?" she teased.

"Mm." He skimmed one hand up her belly to cup a
breast, the other between her thighs. "I could look at you
all day," he said.

She soaked up the warmth of both his words and his
big body behind hers. "Look later." She wriggled. "Do
now."

He didn't hesitate. He plunged into her, and she cried
out in sheer, mindless pleasure, gripping the counter with
white knuckles as she thrust back against him.

With a groan, he pushed even deeper. "Open your eyes."

She hadn't even realized she'd closed them, but they flew open now and met his in the mirror.

They were hot and demanding, much like the man.

"You want this, Chloe?"

"Yes. God yes."

Cursing beneath his strained breath, he bent her over the counter, one hand on her hip, the other between her thighs, using it to drive her straight to the edge. There were no other words for what he did to her. He controlled their movements, and he knew what he was doing. In no time, she was flying, sobbing his name as she came. Pulling her head back, he kissed her deep as he followed her over.

Her legs were wobbling, and he felt like her only anchor in a spinning world. They sank to their knees there on the bathroom floor, his arms hard around her as if maybe she was his anchor as well.

After a few minutes, he kissed her sweaty temple. "Okay?"

If she didn't let herself think. "If I say no, can we do it again?"

He let out a low chuckle and leaned over her, pushing damp hair from her face. "You're breathing pretty hard."

"Yes, but that's your doing," she said.

"It's okay. It's going to be okay." He rose to his feet in one quick, economical movement, scooping her up in his arms.

"Sawyer—"

"Save your breath." They were on the move down the hallway. He snatched up her purse in the entryway and kept moving, right into the kitchen. Flipping on the lights, he set her on the countertop.

It was icy cold on her bare ass, and she squealed. He merely held her there with one hand and rifled through her purse with the other. Yanking out her inhaler, he thrust it into her hands. She took a puff and held it in, watching him.

He'd gone from her lover to the cop in a blink, cool and calm and completely in charge. "Impressive," she murmured when she exhaled. "You're good in an emergency. But you do realize that I'm not having an emergency, right? I was just…" She let out a low laugh. "You're pretty potent, Sheriff. You sent me out of the stratosphere. I'm still coming down, that's all."

"I thought—" He shook his head. "I thought you were having an asthma attack because I pushed too hard, rushing you—"

"No." She ran her hands up and down his tense arms. "I'm sorry I scared you, but I'm fine."

He stared at her, then backed into a chair, minus some of his usual grace, given that he was naked, too. "I thought you were in trouble," he said.

Oh, God. How was she going to give him up? *Don't go there, not now. Tomorrow…* She hopped down off the counter, walked over, and straddled him, sliding her fingers into his hair.

His hands went to her ass and squeezed.

With a smile, she bent over him, lightly brushing her lips with his. "I actually forgot I had asthma," she murmured. "You know that's only happened with you."

"Yeah?"

"Yeah. You must be special to make me forget such a thing."

Between them, he stirred, and he tightened his grip on

her ass, palming her possessively. Still holding her, he rose and turned to eye the kitchen table speculatively.

"Sawyer," she said on a laugh. There were a few things on the table—a stack of mail, an empty paper plate, his wallet and keys—but with one swipe of his hand it all hit the floor.

A ridiculous flutter went through her belly.

He laid her down on the surface of the table and towered over her, planting his hands on either side of her head. "Let's see what else I can make you forget."

# Chapter 23

*"Just when you think you have
a handle on life, it breaks."*

CHLOE TRAEGER

The next day, Sawyer had just finished reading a kid the riot act for shoplifting his lunch at the convenience store when his phone vibrated. *Chloe*, he thought, his chest squeezing with the painful reminder of how she'd slipped out of his bed at some point in the middle of the night.

But it wasn't Chloe. It was Josh calling to tell him that his father had been admitted into the ER for chest pains.

"It's not a heart attack," Josh said when he'd met Sawyer in the hallway outside Nolan's room.

Sawyer took his first breath in the twenty minutes since he'd gotten the phone call. "So what is it?"

"He said he was trying to mow his lawn early this morning when the chest pains came on. He waited until now to come in because he's Nolan Thompson."

Sawyer gritted his teeth. "He said he'd hired someone to do that for him," he muttered, though why he felt inclined to defend himself he couldn't guess. Nearly everyone in town knew about his rocky relationship with his dad, including Josh.

Josh shrugged. He was looking like it'd been a long day already in wrinkled blue scrubs, a stethoscope hanging around his neck, his dark hair ruffled and dark eyes lined with exhaustion. "It's anxiety. I'm going to prescribe some mild anti-anxiety meds, but he needs to go low stress."

"You tell him that?"

Josh gave a tired smile. "Yeah." He clapped a hand on Sawyer's shoulder. "Try to take it easy on him."

Sawyer walked into the room. His father was prone on his back, hooked up to an IV and oxygen, looking frail, small, and old, and yet he *still* managed to make a sound that perfectly conveyed what he thought at the sight of Sawyer. "Gee, Dad," he said. "I'm happy to see you, too."

Nolan closed his eyes. "You'd be sarcastic to your dying father?"

"You're not dying. You're going to outlive me out of sheer orneriness."

His father's eyes opened and narrowed.

"It's anxiety, not your heart," Sawyer told him, standing at the foot of the hospital bed.

"The fuck it is. I was mowing the lawn. No stress in that."

"And why were you mowing the lawn, Dad?"

"Because I..." Nolan clammed up.

Sawyer was trying his damnedest to ignore *The Fresh Prince of Bel-Air* rerun blaring on the TV behind him. He had no idea how to proceed here without further infuriating his father. "Dad, I know there's no kid."

"He got busy."

"There's no kid," Sawyer repeated.

Nolan frowned. "You're standing in front of the TV."

"I'm trying to talk to you."

"Move."

Sawyer felt the helplessness reach up and choke him. It was a new feeling, but it'd become his best friend since Chloe had sneaked out of his bed, and, he suspected, out of his life. What was it she'd once told him—life was too short? She'd been right on. "What do you want from me, Dad?"

"Nothing. Take your fucking bad attitude and get the hell out of here."

He could have no idea how much Sawyer wanted to do just that. But no more putting this kind of shit off. "Look, I know I disappointed you as a kid. I get that. I disappointed *me* as a kid."

For the first time since Sawyer had walked into the room, Nolan met his gaze.

"And I know," Sawyer went on, "that you did the best you could with me."

There was a long, painful silence during which Sawyer kicked a chair closer to the side of the bed and sat.

Getting the message that Sawyer wasn't leaving, Nolan finally cleared his throat. "Maybe I could have done better with you."

"I don't know how," Sawyer admitted. "I was a complete shit. We both know that. In fact, raising me probably put you in here." He reached for his father's hand. It was the first time they'd touched in years. "But I'm trying to make up for it. It'd be great if you let me."

"How?" Nolan asked warily.

"By eating some pride and letting your sorry-ass son help you out once in a while."

"You're busy," Nolan said.

"Not that busy."

His father said nothing to this. His gaze drifted to the TV again.

Sawyer stood up. "But it can't be one-sided. You're going to have to meet me halfway."

Nolan shrugged noncommittally.

"Do you know how many times you've called me, Dad?" Sawyer asked.

Nolan hunched over the remote, squinting at it since he didn't have his glasses. "Fucking remote needs new batteries. Get the nurse for me, will you?"

"Never. You've called me never," Sawyer said. "I don't even know if you have my phone number."

Nolan aimed the remote and gave it another try.

Sawyer sighed. Maybe he deserved this. He'd been so busy preserving his own pride and playing super sheriff to make up for the past that he hadn't recognized his father's pride. The man was getting old, and Sawyer was starting to get how much it sucked when the world you worked so hard to build fell down around you like a house of cards. He took the damn remote and walked out of the room to find some batteries. He was halfway down the hallway when his phone rang. Sawyer looked at the screen with disbelief. It was his father.

"I have your number because when you bought me the phone last year, you put your number in it," Nolan said. "I never called you before because I had nothing to say."

Sawyer walked back into his father's hospital room and stared at his father, the both of them still holding their cell phones to their ears. "You have something to say now?" Sawyer asked.

"Yeah. Except we have to hang up first because I'm not supposed to have this cell phone on in here." His father lowered his arm.

Sawyer reached up and manually turned off the TV because a new episode was starting, and if *The Fresh Prince of Bel-Air* theme song got stuck in his head, he was going to have to kill himself.

Nolan cleared his throat, his eyes going to the now dark screen of the TV. He looked uncomfortable and embarrassed, but he still spoke. "I saw you in the paper. You caught that guy trying to hurt that pretty waitress at the diner."

"Amy," Sawyer said. "She's okay."

"I know." His father cleared his throat. "Because of you."

Sawyer waited, but he said nothing else. Apparently that was as big an *atta boy* as he was ever going to get, but it was so much more than he'd expected that he found himself speechless. "So you're saying?"

His father scowled, the lines etched deep in his jowls. "That you didn't totally fuck it up."

Sawyer had to laugh. "Wow. That's going to go straight to my head, Dad."

"Watch it. I can still kick your ass." But there was a small smile around the corners of Nolan's mouth when he said it. "Now get out so I can get some sleep." In fact, his eyes were already closed.

But Sawyer knew it was going to be okay. Not great, maybe never great, but at least they could do something they'd never quite managed before—peacefully coexist.

\* \* \*

"You look different, Clo."

Chloe glanced at Lance and then quickly averted her gaze, afraid he'd see her misery. She needed sleep. Even more, she needed to understand what had happened at Sawyer's last night.

Or maybe it was best if she didn't.

They were at the cottage. Lance had caught another nasty cold that had kept him in the hospital for the past few days. His doctors had wanted him to stay, but two hours ago he'd had enough and had walked out, calling Chloe for a ride.

She'd brought him here because his duplex was being watched for the still-missing Todd. Plus Tucker was on a job out of town until Friday. Trying to help make Lance comfortable, she had him stretched out on her bed and was giving him a massage while they waited for Renee to get off work and come get him.

"If Renee ends up with overtime again, you're going to stay here with me tonight," Chloe said. Leaning over him, she worked her special oil blend into the knots of tension in his shoulders and back. "You're like a rock quarry. Breathe as deep as you can. Positive visualization. Picture your lungs all clear and at one hundred percent. Puppies and rainbows."

After a pained laugh, Lance shifted a bit, then turned his head just enough to be annoying. "Puppies and rainbows? What's going on with you? You're off today." He tensed and grunted when she hit a particularly sore spot. "Ouch."

"You're not concentrating on visualizing your good health."

He dropped his head down and was obedient for about fifteen seconds. "It's about Sawyer, right? What happened? It got too real, and you bailed?"

"Hey, I don't do that."

Lance was facedown, but she knew he was also brows up, and she sighed. "Jeez, you go and get laid and you turn into a relationship expert."

He snorted. "Yeah, I'd make a fine shrink. I'd tell everyone to fuck the rules and just live." He paused. "And it's more than getting laid, by the way. We're a thing, Renee and me."

Chloe stared down at Lance's painfully thin, pale, disease-ravaged body. She could count his every rib. His breath rattled with each inhale. "Does she understand—I mean, is she—"

"Okay with me dying?" He sighed. "No. Hell no, not even close. But she loves me." He shook his head, sounding marveled. "And if she can love this body and the man inside it, then you sure as hell can find someone to love your sorry—but fine—ass."

Love hadn't been in Chloe's plans when it came to Sawyer. Wild sex, yes. Love, no. So of course that's what she'd done. She'd gone and fallen. Stupid, stupid, stupid. But what was done was done, and she couldn't unfall. She'd tried. Didn't work. She'd only fallen harder, even hoping that he'd caught the bug, too. But she wasn't sure.

God, she was so confused. One lousy minute of contentment, and boom, everything had fallen apart.

"Smell something burning in there," Lance teased. Shoving up to his elbows, he gave her a terrifyingly gentle look. "I've seen him look at you, you know. He accepts you, Chloe. As is."

Maybe. But could he love her?

"Just promise me you won't waste your time doubting or second guessing," he said. "It's not worth it. Just go for it." His eyes were unsettlingly clear and serene. "Look, we both know I'm no shrink, but I know what I'm talking about here. And I want to know you're okay before..."

Before he was gone.

He didn't say it out loud, he didn't have to. It was the big, fat elephant in the room. Why the hell did it seem as if everyone was saying good-bye to her? "We are *not* having this conversation." Her chest was going tight. "People with CF have a median survival age of thirty-seven years now. You have ten years left before I will even *think* of having this conversation with you."

"Chloe, that's the *median* age. People die at two, or ten, or twenty-seven." His voice was low and rough, and he shrugged his too-thin shoulders. "Shit happens."

"Yeah, shit happens. I could get hit by a bus," she said grimly. "Or smack you upside the head for being annoying."

"Goddammit, Chloe, I want to know you have someone."

Suddenly she couldn't breathe. Just couldn't. She struggled for air, couldn't manage it, and staggered backward, tripping over her own legs to fall to her butt.

"Fuck." Lance leaped off the couch and crouched in front of her in nothing but his boxers. He shoved her purse in her lap. "Your inhaler in here?"

She managed a nod, and he opened the thing like it was a ticking bomb.

"Pocket," she wheezed. "Inside pocket."

Looking squeamish, he rooted past a lip gloss, a pack

of birth control pills, and the latest *Cosmo* to get to the pocket. "Jesus fucking Christ," he was muttering. "If I find a tampon in here, I'm going to hurt you." He opened the pocket, plunged his hand in, and came out with a…*"Argh!"* He flung the tampon across the room like it was a hand grenade, and she was both laughing and sobbing for breath when he finally located her inhaler.

She took a long puff. Then another. It didn't help fast enough, and she felt the licks of that familiar horrific panic gripping her. Lance stayed with her, holding her face. "In and out, baby, that's all you gotta do. In and then out."

Chloe caught enough breath to croak out a shaky joke. "That's what *she* said," she gasped, making Lance laugh.

After a few minutes, she'd caught her breath a little more and glared at him. "Okay, don't you *ever* fucking say good-bye to me again."

"How the hell is telling you that it's okay to fall for someone saying good-bye?"

"It *felt* like a good-bye. *God.*" She felt the tears well up. *Tears.* She never cried. "Goddammit."

Lance let go of her face and sat back on his heels. "Chloe," he said softly. "You know it's coming."

"No, I don't! And you can't think like that!"

"I *have* to think like that." When her phone vibrated, he rose to his feet a little shakily and reached out a hand for her. "But you don't. You have your whole life ahead of you."

She swallowed a sob, ignored his hand, and scrambled to her feet on her own. She read the text from Tara requesting some help. "I have to go," she said. "Renee will be here soon. Call me if you need anything." She refused to look at him as she shoved her inhaler in her pocket and ran out the door. She stepped off the cottage porch and wiped the tears from her eyes. It was all she could do to not drop down to the stairs and weep like a child. Clearly she hadn't gotten nearly enough sleep. She and Sawyer had turned to each other over and over again in the night like...like they were never going to have each other again.

*Don't go there.*

Another sniff, another swipe of the back of her hand, and she was almost at the inn. As Chloe moved, she saw a swirl of dust fade at the edge of the woods, which was odd enough to catch her attention. There wasn't a road there, just an old hiking path.

With a quick change of direction, she followed the dust and caught sight of tire tracks in the still-moist mud. She could hear an engine. A truck, probably. Something with four-wheel drive. It wasn't far, but she was wondering who'd be out there in the first place.

At the edge of the woods, she stopped and listened again. Not one truck.

Two.

Chloe took out her cell and called Tara. "Hey, there's a couple of trucks moving around out here in the woods. I'm going to go take a look, and I didn't want to be the stupid chick in the movies who doesn't tell anyone where she's going."

"Hang on, I'll come out."

"It's probably nothing. Maybe the forest service checking on the fire lanes. I'll call you right back." She disconnected, then headed down the trail. She could still hear the engines ahead of her. The trail wasn't meant for a vehicle so it'd be slow, rough going.

And then the engines cut off. There was the faint sound of male voices. And then a truck door closing. An engine revved, coming back her way. Shit. Chloe dove into the bushes and ducked low.

A blue truck drove past her, going far too fast for the terrain. She recognized the driver and covered her mouth to hide her gasp, even though no one could have heard her.

Nick Raybo.

The forest had come down around her like a theater curtain, surrounding her with mossy pines, spruce, and the scent of Christmas. There was still someone ahead of her, and she made her way a little closer, then went utterly still because there, behind a huge outgrowth of sage, was a truck. New. Black. Shiny.

Todd's.

Todd and Raybo. Oh, God, that couldn't be good.

Chloe shifted behind a large pine and dialed Sawyer this time, watching Todd behind the wheel talking on his cell phone. She took a hit from her inhaler and held her breath as Sawyer answered, sounding distracted. "Thompson."

But Todd was exiting his truck now. Afraid to reply and tip Todd off, Chloe bit her lower lip.

"Chloe," Sawyer said. "You there?"

"Raybo. And Todd," she whispered, hearting pounding, chest tight. Too tight. That half-mile walk had taxed her.

"Todd? He's with you?"

"In the woods. Raybo's leaving." It was all she could say. She took another peek from around the tree. She could see the whole left side of Todd's truck, but not Todd. There was something in the bed of his truck that looked like camouflage netting. She knew marijuana growers used it to hide their crops, which made sense given what Todd was suspected of.

"Chloe," Sawyer said. "I'm on my way. Where are you exactly?"

"I'm half a mile or so in." She pressed a hand to her chest. She was wheezing badly. "Lance knows the trail. I think Todd's hiding his stash."

"I've called it in, Chloe," Sawyer said. "We're all on our way. You did great. Now get the fuck out of there." He paused, then added, "Please. Please get the fuck out of there. For me."

Despite the fear and asthma attack now fully upon her, Chloe smiled as she left her tree and started to head back. "Like the please," she whispered. "Nice...touch."

"Use your inhaler."

"Did." She was a safe enough distance away now that she slowed, then stopped. "Okay, I'm in trouble," she admitted. "I have...to rest." She dropped to her knees, gasping for breath. She opened her mouth to tell Sawyer that she was going to hang up when a hand clamped down on her mouth, and her scream was swallowed before it started.

# Chapter 24

> *"If they don't have good adventures
> in heaven, I'm not going."*
>
> Chloe Traeger

Every muscle in Sawyer's body tightened as he heard Chloe's attempt at a hoarse scream and then the beep of the call being cut off. A dozen horrible images raced through his mind, but he cut them off, swerving around slower cars as he called Morris.

The DEA agent was still pissed at Sawyer for not being available when he'd been needed last night, and when Sawyer told him he wasn't waiting for backup as he raced toward Chloe's last-known location, the man started to tear Sawyer a new one.

Sawyer didn't give a shit. The job, the bust, the drugs, none of it mattered. The whole world could go fuck itself if something happened to Chloe. He waited for Morris's rant to end, confirmed the location one more time, and clicked off.

Raybo—he'd been the missing link, the big dealer the

DEA had been looking to nail. It made perfect sense. Sawyer knew Morris's team would get Raybo on the road or at his compound. Sawyer was certain of it.

What he wasn't certain of, what he was terrified of, was what was happening to Chloe right this very second. He wasn't far from the B&B, but every second felt like an hour. If that fucker touched one hair on her head, he was going down. Sawyer had no more mercy left. He cut the sirens and the lights as he approached the turnoff. When he pulled up at the inn, Tara was standing on the porch holding her cell phone. "Chloe called," she said. "I think she's in trouble."

"Which trail?"

Lance came around the corner. "I'll show you." They moved to the marina building, Lance doing his best to keep up, but he was breathing hard. "There," he said, pointing the way. "That one."

Sawyer knew the trail all too well. It was the same one that he, Ford, and Jax had taken the night they'd seen the odd flare. It was also the trail to the hidden clearing where he and Todd had partied through their high school years. "Stay here," he said to Lance. "More are coming. Tell them which way I've gone." He drew his gun. No matter what happened, Chloe *was* coming out of this in one piece, but he'd make no guarantees about anyone else.

\* \* \*

Todd had his arm across Chloe's throat. Just tight enough that a regular person would have trouble breathing. She'd passed trouble halfway to his truck.

"This is just great," Todd was muttering, dragging her

along with him. "Fucking great. I spent a year trying to get your fucking attention, and you could give a shit. And now that I'm headed out, you want a piece of me."

"I don't—"

He tightened his grip on her, cutting off her words. He smelled of sweat and fear, and his body shook with tension as he walked her forward. There was a gun in his free hand, a semiautomatic, and she hoped the safety was on because he was swinging it around like a laser pointer. "I'm not going back to jail," he said, his jaw pressed to hers. "Not even for your sweet ass. But I can't let you go, either."

"Yes, you can. It's Raybo, right? It's all him. You—"

Again he tightened his grip, and she choked. "Shut up," he said. "Shut up and listen. I'm not taking the fall for Raybo. Hell, no. And I'm not narcing him out, either; the fucker is crazy. He'd kill me for sure."

"No—"

"You should be worried about you, Chloe," he said. "Our fun is over. I could have had you that day at the mud springs. That pisses me off. You were hot for me up until then, but something changed."

"I was never hot for you," she managed.

"Liar. But after that, Sawyer had you. That pissed me off, too. You're not his usual type."

"What's that supposed to mean?"

"I don't know what it is about you, but you jump knee deep in shit all the time and still come out smelling like a rose. I fucked with the boats at the marina," he said. "I told everyone that you were pissed off at your sisters and wanted to get out of this place. I thought everyone would blame you, but no one did, no one even believed the rumors. Nothing sticks to you. Too bad you can't teach me that trick," he said almost wistfully.

"I don't—"

He tugged viciously on her hair. "We're gonna load up now, and then we're getting the hell out of here. Just be a good girl. That's all you gotta do."

Todd marched her past a burnt-out tree, then headed for a wild mass of Manzanita bush canopied by two-hundred-foot pines. There was something about the lush growth. It looked like the rest of the forest, but then it kinda didn't, and she struggled to inhale again. She didn't know what would happen if she passed out. Todd wouldn't lift a finger to help her; she knew that.

"Stay," he said, and the minute he removed his arm from her neck, she dropped to her knees. She was gasping, shaking, sweating, and freaking out in general, but he pointed the gun at her, and she sat back on her haunches.

"Jesus. I'm not gonna hurt you as long as you shut up."

"I...can't help it."

"Do you have to gasp like that? I'm not even touching you. Shut the fuck up."

She was trying. Not that she believed him about not hurting her. God, she hoped Tara wasn't following the trail at this moment, trying to find her. Or Sawyer. She was afraid Todd would shoot anyone who came upon them. Hell, she was afraid he'd shoot *her*. She was going to die, either by Todd's hand or by suffocation, and she hadn't told anyone how she felt about them. She hadn't said the words because she was a goddamn chicken, and now she was gonna die, and they'd never know. Not Sawyer, and not her sisters. It wasn't right, and she was so mad at herself *and* Todd that she could shoot him herself.

"Get up," Todd said. He was holding several bundles in his arms. "Chloe, I fucking mean it! Get up or I'll drag you."

If she could, she would. She'd get up, punch his lights out, and run like hell.

Except she couldn't run. Not even on a good day, which this wasn't shaping up to be.

She couldn't do anything but attempt to inhale. She certainly couldn't get any more terrified, which sucked. She'd thought she'd been afraid of three little words. What a joke.

Todd dropped the load in his truck and turned back to her just as she caught some movement out of the corner of her eye. At first she thought it was a deer, but then she realized it was Sawyer. It had to be.

In front of her, she heard the unmistakable sound of a belt being pulled loose from denim. For a second, she got frightened in a whole new way, then realized Todd was going to tie her up using his belt. Still holding his gun, he moved behind her. Vision wavering, she closed her eyes and concentrated on the little air that she was getting, waiting for an opportunity to help Sawyer. Mostly, she wanted to get Todd before Sawyer shot him. She wanted first blood, dammit.

The snap of a twig sounded loud as a gunshot. Todd grabbed her by the throat and spun her around.

"Let her go, Todd," Sawyer said, stepping right into Todd's line of sight, gun aimed, face so fiercely determined that Chloe forgot to breathe.

Until Todd squeezed her throat again. He hadn't gotten her hands tied, and she clawed at his arm around her neck, her vision graying at the edges.

"Drop your gun," Todd grated out. "Or I'll shoot her dead."

Not going to be necessary, Chloe thought hazily...

"There's no reason to hurt her," Sawyer said, moving slowly but steadily forward. "The DEA is five minutes away. They've got Raybo. They got him on the highway and he's in custody. It's over, Todd. Don't make things even worse."

"Worse? How could it be *worse*? You've fucked me over for the last time, man. I'm not going back to jail. You know what they did to me in jail? You were still seventeen. Why the hell didn't you tell them that you were driving? All you had to do was say you were driving!"

"I was unconscious, you asshole. We both were. They found us in the car. We never should have been drinking and driving. You know it as well as I do."

"Yeah, well, easy for you to say. You got juvie, and I got hard time for second-degree murder. You think I ever had a chance for anything after that? Eighteen, and my life was fucking over."

"It's only over if you don't walk away from this. Let Chloe go, and I'll do what I can for you. I swear it, Todd. I know you didn't mean for Sammy and Cutter to die. Nobody wanted that. I'm sorry it was you driving. I am."

Chloe's eyes drifted shut. She felt Todd look down at her, and she used the last of her strength to twist and bring her knee up hard between his legs.

He let out a strangled, high-pitched cry, and then she was free.

Free to tell Sawyer that she loved the stupid kid he'd once been, that she loved the man he'd become now, that she always would. But free of Todd wasn't the same thing as home free.

She fell, bracing for the hard ground rushing up to meet her, but she never felt it.

\*      \*      \*

Sawyer had spent lots of time in the ER. He'd brought in injured suspects, he'd gone to interview witnesses, and he'd been there not three months ago after a power tool incident when Jax had accidentally stapled his thumb to a shelving unit he'd been building.

But until now Sawyer had never sat in a tiny, cramped ER cubicle with panic gripping him by the balls. He stared at the woman in the bed. Pale and clammy. *Him* not her.

Though Chloe was pale, too.

Her hair still had flecks of dirt in it. The silky strands had long ago escaped the hair band to riot around her face. Sawyer might have stroked it back, but the nurse was hovering, moving like a busy bee around them: giving Chloe a breathing treatment, hooking up the monitors, checking the nebulizer, supervising oxygen levels. And all the while, the nurse's mouth was moving, too, though she may have been speaking Chinese for all Sawyer was paying attention. He couldn't do anything but look at Chloe, because if he took his eyes off her she might stop breathing again.

So he pulled a chair as close as he could get next to her bed and watched her struggle. Even with the nebulizer and the corticosteroids and the Beta-2 agonists, she still wasn't out of the woods. But at least her lips weren't blue, and she was starting to get some color in her cheeks.

Christ, it'd been close, too fucking close, and he'd never been so scared in his life.

The nurse finally left and in her wake were the beeping monitors, hissing oxygen, and the steady patter of people moving up and down the hallways on the other side of the curtain. Chloe opened her eyes, and Sawyer took his first real breath in the past hour of hell. He had no idea what to say. He was still struggling to think of something when she pulled the mouthpiece of the nebulizer from her mouth and spoke first.

"Did I miss the Jell-O? I really like it when they give me Jell-O."

His throat constricted. "I'll get you an entire tray."

She reached out and took his hand, running her icy fingers over his knuckles, which were raw and red and a little swollen from where he'd punched the outside wall of the hospital. His form of stress relief.

"Chloe," he said, but her eyes were closed again.

She'd replaced the nebulizer and fallen back to sleep.

Two minutes later, Tara and Maddie arrived. Tara sat in the chair that Sawyer vacated for her. Maddie moved to Chloe's other side, the two of them staring down into her face.

"She's so damn much a part of me that I feel like I can't breathe either," Maddie whispered, hand to her own heart.

"Luckily, she's stubborn enough to breathe for the both of you," Tara said.

Sawyer nearly smiled at the truth of that statement and looked down at his vibrating phone. Morris was here and needed to talk to him. Code for yell at him. Sawyer rose and met him in a hallway, where he spent the next ten minutes explaining exactly why he'd broken protocol and hadn't waited for backup. Morris listened, both pissed off and acknowledging that Sawyer had nailed Todd.

Of course, it hadn't been Sawyer at all, but Chloe and a well-placed knee, leaving Todd in possession of one dislocated nut and relieved of possession of his entire stash.

The DEA had their case and the drugs, and there were a *lot* of drugs. Raybo had been even bigger than they'd thought, and he was already singing. Todd had been making some side deals, storing most of his own shit in his duplex attic, but when Mitch ratted him out, he'd had to change his plans and quick.

Todd had rigged up some duck blinds in the woods, the way they'd done with their booze when they'd been kids, covering it with the military camouflage netting.

Stupid. But Sawyer was done wasting a single second of his time thinking and worrying about Todd.

Life was too short.

\* \* \*

Chloe woke up with a little start. "I got him in the nuts!"

Tara and Maddie, seated at her side, smiled. "You sure did," Tara said. "Proud of you, sugar."

Chloe smiled, relieved it was over.

"So is it that you don't have enough work at the B&B and the spa that you had to add crime fighting to your résumé?" Tara asked.

Chloe choked out a low laugh. She sat up a little, testing her lungs, and was relieved to find herself in relatively good working order. "I, um, thought of something when I was out there."

"Before or after you spoon-fed Todd his left family jewel?"

Chloe smiled. "Before. Actually, way before. I thought of it a while back, but...well, to be honest, I can't explain the why or how of what took me so long." That's how love worked, she thought. It was confusing and messy and wonderful and real. God, so real. And she'd meant it. It *had* been growing in her for a while. But right here, right now, looking at her hodgepodge family crowded around her, she felt it expanding inside of her even more, like her chest was going to explode. In a good way for once. "In the mud springs last night, Tara teased me for having an epiphany. She was right, I *was* having one."

"You 'bout done with it yet?" Tara asked.

"Yeah, I believe I am. But I want you to know, once I tell you, it's not an all-access pass to any group hugs. Those need to be put on the schedule in advance." She drew a deep breath, or as deep as she could anyway. "I love you. I love you both."

"Well, would you listen to that." Tara's tone was dry, in direct contrast to her suspiciously wet eyes. "You just emotionally compromised yourself and lived to tell the tale."

There was a knock on the open door, and they all looked up at Sawyer standing there, eyes locked on Chloe. Yes, she'd just emotionally compromised herself.

And she was about to do it again.

"The nurse says you'll be out of here in less than an hour," Sawyer said. "Need a ride?"

Chloe looked at her sisters. Maddie jumped up, grabbing Tara by the hand. "Oh, that would be great. We're expecting a few scheduled guests, and..."

"Just say good-bye, sugar," Tara said, shaking her head. "And remind me to teach you how to lie better than that."

And then they were both gone.

An hour later, Chloe was dropped down on Sawyer's couch and gruffly told to "hang on." She sat on the couch, shivering. "I'm n-not c-cold. It's just what happens sometimes after a bad asthma attack and all the meds." Her heart raced, too, like it was trying to get outside of her chest, and it pissed her off.

Sawyer wrapped her in a blanket, then carefully lifted her into his arms. She cuddled in, absorbing his body heat as her eyes locked in on the nebulizer on the coffee table. "What's that?"

"A nebulizer."

"I know that. I mean, what's it doing here?"

"I bought one."

Her heart squeezed. "When?"

"What does it matter?"

"When, Sawyer?"

"A few days ago."

She stared into his eyes. "Why did you buy a nebulizer if you were going to dump me?"

"I believe you dumped me," he said lightly.

She stared at him. "Okay, we're going to circle back to that in a minute. Sawyer…" She looked around at the living room. Painted walls. Furniture. "Up until a week ago, you didn't have anything in here, and now you have a nebulizer. Do you know what that means? It means," she went on without waiting for an answer, "that you like me." She smiled, feeling the warmth of the knowledge chase away the chill. "You really, really like me."

"Don't get excited. I like all my house painters." He settled her head against his chest. She knew he was giving her time to settle. And also, she realized as he stroked a big hand up and down her back, he was giving her his heat, strength, and reassurance—the last of which wasn't exactly second nature to him. She knew his job didn't allow for much softness, or a lot of emotion for that matter. Obviously he'd let that spill over into his life, but she knew he was trying his damnedest to offer her what he thought she needed.

Damn. Damn, she was a goner, and she curled into him, tracing little patterns on his stomach with her fingers, enjoying the hard ridges of his abs. Wriggling to get comfortable, she pressed her face into his throat and inhaled him, then rested her head on his chest. Unlike her, he wasn't trembling or shaking at all. "Sorry," she murmured. "I can't stop shaking."

"Adrenaline letdown."

"What about you?" she asked. "You ever get adrenaline letdown? Because I just can't imagine anything getting to you."

Sawyer tugged her hair until she met his gaze, his own clear and unguarded. "You," he said, shockingly gently. "You get to me. You scared the hell out of me today."

"Makes two of us."

His grip tightened on her. "If anything had happened to you..." He shook his head and cut the words off.

"I'm okay." She touched his scruffy jaw. "You make a comfy chair, Sheriff. Sure you're a little hard in spots, but—"

"Chloe." He laughed and pressed his forehead to hers. "You get to me," he said again quietly. "I want you to know that. You get to me, just the way you are." He leaned in close. "No changing."

She absorbed the words as she'd absorbed his heat and felt a weight lift from her shoulders. "What if being myself isn't always pretty or polite?" she whispered.

"Well, Christ, I hope not," he said. "Polite is fucking exhausting. Chloe, listen to me. You being you is who I fell for. Now, as for who *you* fell for…" He drew in a deep breath. "What Todd said today, about when we were teenagers."

"I don't care. It doesn't change how I feel about you."

"Be sure. Because most of it was true." He ran his thumb over her fingers. She stared down at his large, tanned, callused hand against her much smaller, pale one, which looked almost frail in his. "It's not easy to talk about."

"It's me, Sawyer. You can tell me anything. You know that, right?"

"I do now. But until recently, my life was all about work. Only work. I figured I owed it to everyone here for the second chance the town gave me."

"Sawyer, you do realize that the reason no one talks about your past. And that the reason it's not plastered on that damn Facebook page isn't because they're asking for penance. It's because they're protective of you. They care about you and respect you." She hugged him. "So stop punishing yourself. It's over and done."

He was quiet a moment. "Is everything over and done?"

Her breath caught, and she pulled back to look into his eyes. "I don't want it to be."

"What do you want?"

"To know you," she said without hesitation. "All of you. I want to know what makes you feel good."

"Your laughter," he said without hesitation. "Feeling your hands on me. The way you look at me, whether I've been a complete dumbass, or just made you come—"

With a laugh, she ducked her head, but he dipped his down until she was looking at him again. "You want to know what scares me?" he asked.

"Yes."

He leaned even closer and slid a hand to the nape of her neck. "The thought of never having those things with you again. I'm a little slow but not an idiot, Chloe, and I learn from my mistakes." He cupped her jaw. "I love you, Chloe."

"Dammit!"

He blinked. "That wasn't quite the reaction I'd expected."

"No, it's just that I meant to say it first!"

He stared at her. "You could say it now."

"I love you. God, I love you." She let out a breath. "Whew. That's more exhausting than an asthma attack."

He smiled. A real slow, glorious, sexy-as-hell smile. "Maybe it just requires practice."

She returned his smile, feeling so light and happy she could float to the ceiling, although that might have been all the drugs in her system. "Or confirmation."

"Confirmation?"

She pulled out her phone, and he appeared puzzled. "You say I love you, and it reminds you that you have to make a call?" he asked.

"You knew loving me was going to require patience." She accessed her Magic Eight Ball app. "How about it?" she said to the screen. "Me and Sawyer. Yes?"

"Christ, Chloe." Sawyer straightened with a scowl. "You know what it's going to say, what it always says when it's referring to me."

"It's been right every single time with us." She looked at him. "Are you scared?"

"No. But if it says Try Again Later, it's going out the window."

*Absolutely yes*

# Epilogue

*"A closed mind is a good thing to lose."*

CHLOE TRAEGER

## A month later

On the afternoon of Maddie and Jax's wedding rehearsal, the sisters stood together in the cottage, holding hands at the front door.

"This is it," Maddie whispered. She bit her lower lip, looking pale. Very pale. "I mean this is really it."

"Uh-oh." Chloe turned to Tara. "Lock the back door quick; we've got a flight risk."

"Really, really it…" Maddie whispered, sounding bewildered, like she hadn't been beating them all over the head with her bridal magazines for the past six months.

"No, honey, it's just the rehearsal," Tara said gently, stroking Maddie's hair. "It's not the *it* it."

"Which means you can still make a run for it if you want," Chloe said. "I'll drive."

"Chloe!" Tara scolded.

Maddie just kept biting her lower lip.

"Seriously," Chloe told her. "I'll call Jax right now and tell him we're going out for a bag of chips. He'd totally buy it. We get on the Vespa and just keep going as far as the tank of gas will take us. Which, granted, isn't all that far, but—"

"Stop it," Tara said, covering Maddie's ears.

"We'll leave the Steel Magnolia behind, too," Chloe said, studying Maddie. "Your call, Mad."

Maddie closed her eyes. "I have the pretty dress. It's all ready for tomorrow. I'd sure hate to waste that dress."

"No problem," Chloe said. "We'll Craigslist it. *For Sale: a wedding dress, size eight, almost worn once by accident.* You'll get good bucks for it."

Tara reached around Maddie and pinched Chloe. Chloe pinched her back.

Normally, Maddie would have smacked them both, but she ignored them to peek out the window. Jax was waiting for them at the marina, along with Ford, the two of them standing between the marina building and Ford's docked boat. Sawyer wasn't here yet because he'd gotten held up at work, but Chloe had gotten a text that he was on his way.

Maddie watched Jax tip his head back and laugh at something Ford said, and a soft smile crossed her lips. "I really do want him, you know. As mine."

Chloe smiled triumphantly at Tara. "Good to know."

Tara let out a relieved breath, and they all took each other's hands again. "Ready, Maddie?"

"Ready," Maddie said, not quite so pale now. She squeezed her sisters' fingers. "Let's do this. Let's go get me a husband."

Together they walked to the marina just as Lucille pulled up in her old clunker. "Perfect timing!" the older woman called out. "I've got thirty minutes between happy hour and bingo night."

They all settled on the dock. Tomorrow, the railings would be lined with potted flowers. There'd be a runner for them to walk on. Guests would line the way, lots of them.

But for now, it was just Lucille and the five of them—

Six, Chloe corrected, hearing Sawyer drive up. The sound of his truck made her all warm and mushy on the inside, and she laughed at herself. *Sap*.

Lucille pointed everyone to their places, then looked around for Sawyer.

"Here." He was sauntering toward them with his long-legged stride, eyes on Chloe, a small smile threatening the corners of his mouth at the sight of her.

Jax had taken his place at the end of the dock, the water at his back. Following Lucille's direction, Ford escorted Tara to the end of the walkway.

Watching, knowing she was next, Chloe turned to Sawyer, who offered his arm.

He was still in uniform, still armed to the teeth, still looking a little tense from what had undoubtedly been a long day on the job.

They hadn't seen each other in three days. She'd been in Los Angeles, fulfilling the last of her traveling spa obligations. She looked up at him, trying to keep herself in check when she really wanted to throw herself into his arms. Whether it was the happiness emanating off Maddie, or Chloe's own swelling emotions, she wasn't sure, but she felt far too close to tears.

She had no idea why.

Except she did.

Sawyer escorted her down the makeshift aisle and she moved to stand next to Tara.

Maddie came down the aisle next, beaming, her face radiant. Lucille walked them through the short ceremony, and when it was over, Jax practiced kissing Maddie.

Since that went on for some time, Ford suggested that he should practice kissing Tara.

While they were working on that, Sawyer pulled Chloe in tight. "Hey." He nuzzled at her ear. "You okay?"

Because she didn't know, she cupped his face and pulled it to hers for some practicing of their own. When the kissing was over, everyone was talking and laughing about the wedding, about Ford and Tara's engagement, about honeymoons and futures.

Chloe took it all in, wishing her smile didn't feel congealed on her face. She needed to just suck it up. Truly she was happy for her sisters. So happy. Tomorrow Maddie and Jax would be married.

And then in the next month, Tara and Ford would follow suit.

They'd still be sisters, of course. They'd always be sisters, but it would never again be just the three of them.

Chloe was going to go back to being on her own.

Sawyer took her small hand in his much larger one and squeezed. There was a silent inquiry in the touch, and she looked up into his eyes.

He searched her gaze for a long moment, then brought their joined fingers up to his mouth. "You're not okay," he said, as always, seeing what no one else did. "You're sad."

"Of course not."

"You're sad," he repeated with quiet understanding.

She sighed. "Don't you have to go take Jax out and get him drunk now?"

"What's wrong?"

"Nothing." She closed her eyes. "I'll be alone."

Sawyer waited until she looked at him. "I should be insulted."

"No," she said, shaking her head, her control beginning to slip. "No, I don't mean it like that—"

His eyes never flinching, never leaving her face, he said, "Marry me."

"What?" Her heart stopped. Had she heard him correctly? "Because you feel sorry for me?"

"Feel sorry for you? Not likely." He smiled. "Marry me because we're good together." He waggled a brow. "Especially in the shower."

"Oh my God. Shh!" She glanced around, and his grin broadened, probably because the old Chloe wouldn't have given a rat's ass if anyone had overheard. She still didn't, not really, it was just that clearly he'd lost his frigging mind.

"You could marry me right here, right now," he said.

Oh, God. He was serious. "You like your own space," she told him, trying to give him an out.

He lifted a shoulder, cool as could be, while she was ready to burst something. "I like sharing it with you."

Hope kindled and ignited. "I'll drive you crazy," she whispered.

"Already done," he assured her, "in the best possible way." He ran a finger over her temple, gently pushing back a strand of hair. "I want to come home to you every night, Chloe."

"There will be nights I have to be here, when we have guests."

He shrugged. "Then we'll hire someone to work part-time at night and give you breaks, or I'll come to you. I don't care what bed I go home to, as long as you're in it. Say you'll think about it, that you'll think about giving us a real shot."

She stared at him, knowing she'd never wanted anything so much in her entire life. Which made it simple, really. "For you," she said, "I believe I'd do anything."

His eyes went hot. "*Anything?*"

Her knees were wobbling, but she had enough strength to shove him.

A guy to the very core, he laughed and reeled her back in. Leaning close, he pressed his mouth to her ear and nipped the lobe with his teeth. "Trust me. It'll be good."

"The marrying part, or the—"

"Everything."

Since she did trust him—with her heart, her soul, her life—she wrapped her arms around his broad shoulders, pressed her face to his throat, and kissed him there, loving how his arms tightened around her. "I love you, Sawyer. So much."

"I know." His eyes were serious. "It's my very own miracle, and I count on it every single day."

"It would never be boring..." she said.

"Counting on that, too. Say yes, Chloe."

She lifted her face and smiled. "Yes. To everything."

**Did you know that ancient lore says if you break a strawberry in half and share it with a member of the opposite sex, you'll fall in love?**

### Chloe's Strawberry/Banana Oatmeal Face Mask

This mask can also be used as a face scrub and is excellent at exfoliating the skin.

Use your blender to chop ¼ cup of strawberries and one banana. In a separate bowl, put one cup of ground oats and just enough lukewarm milk to make a smooth paste.

Add fruit mixture. Stir well to make a refreshing facial mask. Apply to your face and let it sit for 15 minutes. Rinse with cold water.

Mallory is a good girl who's been let down by countless Mr. Rights.

A violent storm in Lucky Harbor brings a new option to her door... Mr. All Wrong.

When lightning strikes, will sparks fly?

# Lucky In Love

Please turn this page for a preview.

# Prologue

*If you want to make your dreams come
true, the first thing you have to do is
wake up.*

Lightning sent a jagged bolt across Ty Garrison's closed
lids. Thunder boomed and the earth shuddered, and he
jerked straight up in bed, gasping as if he'd just run a
marathon.

A dream, the same goddamn four-year-old dream.

Sweating and trembling like a leaf, he scrubbed his
hands over his face. Why couldn't he dream about something good, like sex with triplets?

Shoving free of the covers, he limped naked to the
window and yanked it open. The cool mist of the spring
storm brushed his heated skin, and he fought the urge to
close his eyes. If he did, he'd be back there.

But the memories came anyway.

*"Landing in ten,"* the pilot announced as the plane
skimmed just beneath the storm raging through the night.

*In eight, the plane began to vibrate.*

*In six, lightning cracked.*

*And then an explosion, one so violent it nearly blew out his eardrums.*

Ty dropped his head back, letting the rain slash at his body through the open window. He could hear the Pacific Ocean pounding the surf below the cliffs. Scented with fragrant pines, the air smelled like Christmas in July, and he forced himself to draw a deep, shaky breath.

He was in Washington state, in the small beach town of Lucky Harbor. The ocean was in front of him with the mountains at his back. He was no longer a SEAL medic, dragging his sorry ass out of a burning plane, choking on the knowledge that he was the only one still breathing, that he hadn't been able to save a single goddamn person.

But hell if at the next bolt of lightning, he didn't try to jump out of his own skin. Pissed at the weakness, Ty shut the window. He was never inhaling an entire pepperoni pizza before bed again.

Except he knew it wasn't something as simple as pizza that made him dream badly. It was the edginess that came from being idle and unable to work. His work was still special ops, but he hadn't gone back to being a medic. Working for a private contractor to the government was a decent enough adrenaline rush and it suited him—or it had until six months ago when on assignment, he'd jumped out a second story window and reinjured his leg. He stretched it now and winced.

He wanted to get back to work. *Needed* to get back. All he was waiting on was clearance from his doctor. Pulling on a pair of jeans, he snagged a shirt off the back of a chair and left the room as the storm railed around him. Shrugging into the shirt, he made his way through the big and nearly empty house he was renting for the duration, heading to the garage. A fast drive in the middle of the night would be good, and maybe a quick stop at the all-night diner for pie.

But this first.

Flipping on the lights, Ty sucked in a deep, calming breath of motor oil, well-greased tools, and rubber tires. On the left sat a '72 GMC Jimmy, a rebuild job he'd picked up on the fly. He didn't need the money. As it turned out, special ops talents were well compensated these days, but the work was a welcome diversion.

The '68 Shelby Mustang on the right was all his, and she was calling to him. He kicked the mechanic's creeper from against the wall toward the classic muscle car. Lowering himself onto the cart with a grimace at the twinge of pain in his leg, Ty rolled beneath the car, shoving down his problems, denying them, avoiding them.

Seeking his own calm in the storm.

# Chapter 1

*Life is a gift. Remember to open it.*

The lightning flashed bright, momentarily blinding Mallory Quinn as she ran through the dark rainy night from her car to the front door of the diner.

One Mississippi.

Two Mississippi.

On three Mississippi, thunder boomed and shook the ground. A vicious wind nearly blew her off her feet. She'd forgotten her umbrella that morning, which was just as well or she'd have taken off like Mary Poppins.

A second, brighter bolt of lightning sent jagged light across the sky, and Mallory gasped as everything momentarily lit up like day: the pier behind the diner, the churning ocean, the menacing sky.

Then all went dark again, and she burst breathlessly into the Eat Me diner feeling like the hounds of hell were on her very tired heels. Except she wasn't wearing heels; she was in fake Uggs.

Lucky Harbor tended to roll up its sidewalks after ten,

and tonight was no exception. The place was deserted except for one customer at the counter. And the waitress behind it. Her friend: smartass, cynical Amy Michaels. Amy, whose tall, leggy body was a complete contradiction to the tomboy clothes that said she could and would kick ass at the slightest provocation. Her dark, spiky cap of hair was tousled, as always, her even darker eyes showing amusement at Mallory's wild entrance.

"Hey," Mallory said, fighting the wind to close the door behind her.

"Looking a little spooked," Amy said. "You reading Stephen King on the slow shifts again, Nurse Nightingale?"

Mallory drew a deep, shuddery breath and shook off the icy rain the best she could. Her day had started a million years ago at the crack of dawn, when she'd left her house in her usual perpetual rush, without a jacket. One incredibly long ER shift and seventeen hours later, she was still in her scrubs with only a thin sweater over the top, everything now sticking to her like a second skin. "No King," she said. "I had to give him up. Last month's reread of *The Shining* wrecked me."

"Aw," Amy said. "Emergency Dispatch tired of taking your 'there's a shadow outside my window' calls?"

"Okay, *one* time." Giving up squeezing the water out her hair, Mallory ignored Amy's knowing snicker. "And for your information, there really was a man outside my window."

"Yeah. Seventy-year-old Mr. Wykowski, who'd gotten turned around on his walk around the block."

This was true. And while Mallory knew that Mr. Wykowski was a very nice man, he really did look a lot like Jack Nicholson in *The Shining*. "Hey, that could have been a very bad situation."

Amy shook her head as she wiped down the counter. "You live on Senior Drive. Your biggest 'situation' is if Dial-A-Ride doesn't show up in time to pick everyone up to take them to bingo night."

Also true, Mallory thought wryly. Her tiny ranch house was indeed surrounded by other tiny ranch houses filled with mostly seniors. But it wasn't that bad. They were a sweet bunch and always had a story to tell. Or twenty.

And anyway, the house had belonged to her grandmother. Mallory had inherited complete with a mortgage that she'd nearly had to give up her firstborn for. If she'd had a firstborn. But for that she'd like to be married, and to be married, she'd have to have a Mr. Right.

Except she'd been dumped by her last two Mr. Rights.

Wind and something heavy lashed at the windows of the diner. Snow. "Wow, the temp must have just dropped. It sure came on fast."

"It's spring," Amy said in disgust. "Why's it frigging snowing in spring? I changed my winter tires already."

The lone customer at the counter stirred. "I don't have winter tires either," she said. "I'm in a 1972 VW." She looked to be in her mid-twenties, and spoke with the clipped vowels that said northeast.

As Mallory's own tires were threadbare and on their last leg, she gnawed on her lower lip and looked out the window. Maybe if she left immediately, she'd be okay.

"We should wait it out," Amy suggested. "It can't possibly last."

Mallory knew better, but it was her own fault. She'd been ignoring the forecast ever since last week when the weather guy had promised ninety-degree temps and the day hadn't gotten above fifty, leaving her to spend a very long day frozen in the ER. Her nipples still hadn't forgiven her. "I don't have time to wait it out." She had a date with eight solid hours of sleep.

The VW driver was a petite blonde in a flimsy summer-weight skirt and two thin camisoles layered over each other. Mallory hadn't been the only one caught by surprise, though the woman didn't look too concerned as she worked her way through a big, fat brownie that made Mallory's mouth water.

"Sorry," Amy said, reading her mind. "That was the last one."

"Just as well." Mallory wasn't here for herself anyway. Dead on her feet, she'd only stopped as a favor for her mother. "I just need to pick up Joe's cake."

Joe was her baby brother and was turning twenty-four tomorrow. The last thing he wanted was a family party but work was slow for him at the mechanic's shop, and flying to Vegas with his friends hadn't panned out since he had no money.

So their mother had gotten involved and tasked Mallory with bringing the cake. Actually, Mallory had been tasked with *making* the cake but she had a hard time not burning water so she was cheating. "Please tell me that no one from my crazy family has seen the cake so I can pretend I made it."

Amy *tsk*ed. "The good girl of Lucky Harbor, lying to her mother. Shame on you."

This was the ongoing town joke, "good girl" Mallory. And okay, fine, so in all fairness, she played the part these days. But there'd been a time she hadn't, not that she wanted to go there now. Or ever. "Yeah, yeah. Hand it over. I have a date."

"You do not. I'd have heard about it if you did."

"It's a secret date."

Amy laughed. And okay, so that had been a stretch. Lucky Harbor was a wonderful, small town where people cared about each other. You could leave a pot of gold in your backseat, and it wouldn't get stolen.

But there were no such things as secrets.

"I have a date with my own bed," Mallory admitted. "Happy?"

Amy wisely kept whatever smartass remark she had to herself and turned to the kitchen to go get the birthday cake. As she did, lightning flashed, followed immediately by a thundering boom. The wind howled, and the entire building shuddered, caught in the throes. It seemed to go on and on, during which the three women gravitated as close as they could to each other with Amy still on the other side of the counter.

"Now *I* can't stop thinking about *The Shining*," the blonde murmured.

"No worries," Amy said. "The whole horror flick thing rarely happens here in Mayberry."

They all let out a weak laugh, which died when an ear-splitting crack sounded, followed by shattering glass as both the front window and door blew in.

A fallen tree waved obscenely at them through the new opening.

Mallory grabbed the woman next to her and tugged them both behind the counter to join Amy. "Just in case more windows go," she said. "We're safest right here, away from flying glass."

"I'll never laugh at you about Mr. Wykowski again," Amy said, her face pale.

"Yeah, right." Mallory got up on her knees and took a peek over the counter at the huge fallen tree blocking the front door. Several more large pines were lining the front of the restaurant. Any of them could go down as well, maybe across the entire diner this time. Not good.

"I can't reach my brownie from here," Blondie said shakily. "I really need my brownie."

"I'd say we need to blow this popsicle stand," Mallory said. "But it's coming down so bad right now I think we should wait it out. We need to call 9-1-1 though."

Blondie pulled out her cell phone. "Podunk here has some pretty crappy reception." She grimaced, realizing that she was talking to two locals. "Sorry. I just got here today. I'm sure Lucky Harbor is a very nice town."

"It's got its moments." Mallory slapped her pockets for her cell before remembering. *Crap.* "I left my phone in my car."

"And I don't have one," Amy said.

Mallory and Blondie gaped at Amy, who simply shrugged. "What? They're expensive. Besides, the diner has a phone in the kitchen. At least we still have electricity."

Just then the lights flickered and went out. Mallory's stomach hit her toes. "You had to say it," she said as Amy made her way blindly into the kitchen to try the phone anyway.

"Dead," Amy said on a sigh.

Blondie rustled around for a moment, and then there came a blue glow. "It's a cigarette lighter app," she said, holding up her iPhone, indeed lit up like a Bic lighter.

"Can't call for help, but we have light. Only problem, it drains my battery really fast so I'll leave it off until we have an emergency." She turned it off and everything went really, really dark.

Another hard gust of wind sent more of the shattered window tinkling to the floor, and the Bic lighter immediately came back on.

"Emergency," Grace said as the three of them scooted closer together.

"Stupid cake," Mallory said.

"Stupid storm," Amy said.

"Stupid life," Blondie said. "Now would be a great time for one of you to tell me that you have a big, strong guy who's going to come looking for you."

Amy snorted. "Yeah, right. What's your name?"

"Grace."

"Well, Grace, you're new to Lucky Harbor so let me fill you in. There are lots of big, strong guys in town. But I do my own heavy lifting."

Grace and Mallory both took in Amy's low riding, army camo cargo pants, her shit-kicking boots, and her snug, thin, plain white tee. The entire tough, tom-girl ensemble was topped by an incongruous Eat Me pink apron. Amy had put her own spin on it by using red duct tape to fashion a circle around the Eat Me logo, complete with a line through it.

"I can believe that about you," Grace said to her.

"My name's Amy." Amy tossed her chin toward Mallory. "And that's Mallory, my polar opposite and the town's very own good girl."

"Oh, stop," Mallory said, tired of hearing good and girl in the same sentence as it pertained to her.

Of course Amy didn't stop. "If there's an old lady to help across the street, or a kid with a skinned knee needing a Band-Aid and a kiss, or a big, strong man looking for a sweet, warm damsel, it's Mallory to the rescue."

"So where is he, then?" Grace asked. "Her big, strong man."

Amy shrugged. "Ask her."

Mallory grimaced and admitted the truth. "As it turns out, I'm not so good at keeping any Mr. Rights."

"So date a Mr. Wrong," Amy said.

"Yeah?" Mallory asked. "Like who?"

"Like... I don't know. Anderson?"

"The guy who owns the hardware store and flirts with anything with boobs?"

"Yeah," Amy said. "Or that hottie, Dr. Josh Scott. Or—"

"Shh, you." Not wanting to discuss her love life—or lack of—Mallory rose up on her knees to take another peek outside. The gusts were blowing the heavy snow sideways, hitting the remaining windows and flying in through the ones that had broken. The rain water on the ground had frozen up. She craned her neck and looked behind her, into the kitchen and at the back door. If she went that way, she'd have to go around the whole building to get to her car and her phone.

In the dark.

But it had to be done, so she got to her feet, just as the two windows over the kitchen sink shattered with a suddenness that stopped her heart. Grace let out a stifled scream. Dropping back down, Mallory huddled close to her and Amy.

"Holy shit," Amy gasped, and holding on to each

other, they all stared at the offending tree branch waving at them from *that* opening. "Jan's going to blow a gasket."

Jan was the owner of the diner. She was fifty-something, grumpy on the best of days, and hated spending a single dime of her hard-earned money on anything other than her online poker games.

The temperature in the kitchen dropped as cold wind and snow blew over them. Grace's Bic app went back on, and she blinked owlishly at them. "Did I hear someone say cake?"

They ro-sham-bo'd, and Amy lost, so she had to crawl to the refrigerator to retrieve the cake. "You okay with this?" she asked Mallory, handing out forks.

"Very," Mallory said. "Joe will live. This is definitely a cake emergency. Much better than attempting to drive in this freak snow storm."

They all dug in. And there in the pitch black night, unnerved by the storm but bolstered by sugar and chocolate, they talked.

They started with Grace, who told them how when the economy had taken a shit, her hot career as an investment banker had vanished, along with her condo and her credit cards. There'd been a glimmer of a job possibility in Seattle so she'd traveled across country for it. But when she'd gotten there, she found out it involved sleeping with the sleazeball company president. She'd told him to stuff it and now she was thinking about maybe hitting Los Angeles. Tired, she'd stopped in Lucky Harbor earlier today. She'd found a coupon for the local B&B and was going to stay for a few days and regroup. "Or until I run out of money and end up on the street," she said, clearly trying to sound chipper about her limited options.

Mallory reached out for her hand and squeezed it. "You'll find something. I know it."

"I hope you're right." Grace let out a long, shaky breath. "Sorry to dump on you. Guess I'd been holding on to that all by myself for too long, it just burst out of me."

"Don't be sorry." Amy licked frosting off her finger. "That's what dark, stormy nights are for. Confessions."

"Well, I'd feel better if you guys had one as well."

"Mine isn't anything special," Amy said.

"I'd love to hear it anyway," Grace said.

Amy shrugged, looking as reluctant as Mallory felt. "It's nothing special. Just another typical riches-to-rags story."

"What?" Mallory asked in surprise. Amy had been in town for eight months now, and though she wasn't shy and never held back, she never talked much about her past.

"Well, rags to riches to rags I guess is a better way of putting it," Amy corrected.

"Tell us," Grace said.

Amy shrugged again. "It's nothing more than a bad cliché, really. Trailer trash girl's mother marries rich guy, trailer trash girl pisses stepdaddy off, gets rudely ousted out of her house at age sixteen, and disinherited from any trust fund. Broke, with no skills whatsoever, she hitches her way across the country, hooking up with the wrong people and then the even wronger people, until it comes down to two choices. Straighten up or die. She decides straightening up is the better option and ends up in Lucky Harbor, hoping the name of the town is a prophecy."

Heart squeezing, Mallory reached for Amy's hand, too. "Oh, Amy."

"See?" Amy said to Grace. "The town sweetheart. She can't help herself."

"I can so," Mallory said. But that was a lie. She liked to help people. Which made Amy right, she really couldn't help herself.

"And don't think we didn't notice that *you* avoided sharing any of your vulnerability with the class," Amy said.

"Maybe later," Mallory said. Or never. She shared just about every part of her all the time. It was her work, and also her nature. So she held back sharing her "vulnerability" because she had to have something that was hers alone. And thinking about her sister Karen's death, and Mallory's promise to her, was a confession she wasn't ready to make.

"Denial is her friend," Amy told Grace. "She doesn't think she deserves to be happy. I think it's because her siblings are so wild and crazy, she overcompensates."

"Thanks, Dr. Phil," Mallory said, uncomfortable with just how close to the truth that was. She'd had her wild moments. Wild for her, anyway. That people hadn't taken her seriously just added to the reasons why she hated to remember them. "You have a lost and found box around somewhere with extra jackets or something?"

"Nope. Jan sells everything on eBay." Amy sighed. "Look at us, sitting here stuffing ourselves with birthday cake because we have no better options on a Friday night."

"There's always options," Grace said. "There's just a big, fat, mean storm blocking our exit strategies."

"I think it seems like we're all stalled," Amy said. "And it has nothing to do with the storm."

Grace nodded. "Okay, I'll buy that. It's possible I'm a little stalled."

They both looked at Mallory, and she sighed. "Fine. I'm stalled, too. I'm more than stalled. I've got the equivalent of a dead battery, punctured tires, no gas, and no roadside assistance service. How's *that* for a confession?"

Grace and Amy laughed softly, their exhales little clouds of condensation. They were huddled close, trying to share body heat.

"You know," Amy said. "If we live, I'm going to—"

"Hey," Mallory said, straightened in concern. "Of course we're going to live. Soon as the snow lets up, we'll push some branches out of the way and head out to my car, which sounds like our best bet. If not, I have the phone there, and we'll call for help."

"Okay, yes, fine, we're going to live, yadda yadda," Amy said, annoyed. "Way to ruin my dramatic moment."

"Sorry. Do continue."

"Thank you. If we live," Amy repeated with mock gravity, "I'm going to keep a cake just like this in the refrigerator for emergencies at all times. And also..." She shifted and when she went on, she was suddenly serious. "I'd like to let people in more. Ever since..." She blew out a breath. "Well, let's just say I really suck at it and leave it at that."

Mallory squeezed her hand tight in hers. "I'm in," she whispered. "And I'm not going anywhere. *Especially* if you mean it about the cake."

Amy smiled gratefully at her.

"If we live," Grace said. "I'm going to find more than a job. I want to stop chasing my own tail and go after some happy for a change, instead of waiting for it to find me. I've waited long enough."

Once again, they both looked expectantly at Mallory.

Mallory knew what she wanted for herself, but it involved that secret vulnerability she hadn't shared, and a long-ago promise she'd made. Not that she could say so; hell she could hardly think it. So she racked her brain and came up with something else. Something easier to discuss. "There's this big charity event I'm organizing for the hospital next weekend, a formal dinner and auction. I'm the only nurse on my floor without a date. If we live, a date would be really great."

"Yeah?" Amy asked. "And if you're wishing, wish big. Wish for a little nookie too."

Grace nodded her approval, fitting in with them like an old shoe.

"*Nookie*?" Mallory asked dryly.

"Hot sex," Grace translated.

Amy nodded. "And since you've already said Mr. Right never works out for you, you should get a Mr. Wrong."

"Sure," Mallory said, secure in the knowledge that one, there were no Mr. Wrongs anywhere close by; and two, if there were, they wouldn't be interested in her.

Amy pulled her order pad from her apron pocket. "I'm making you a list of some possible Mr. Wrongs, okay? Since this is the only type of guy I know, it's right up my alley. Now, promise me," she said and held up her pinky. "If a Mr. Wrong crosses your path, you're going for him. As long as he isn't a felon," she added responsibly.

Good to know there were some boundaries. Mallory wrapped Amy's pinkie with hers. "I promise—" She broke off at a *thump* on one of the walls out front.

They all went still, staring at each other.

"Okay that wasn't a branch," Mallory said. "That sounded like a fist."

"It was a rock," Amy said. "Let's go with a rock."

They all nodded, but not a one of them believed it was a rock.

A bad feeling came over Mallory. It was the same one she got sometimes in the ER right before they got an incoming. "May I?" she asked Grace, gesturing to the iPhone.

Grace handed it over, and Mallory rose to her knees and used the lighter app to look over the edge of the counter.

It wasn't good.

The opened doorway was now blocked by a snowdrift. It really was incredible for this late in the year, but the snowflakes were big and fat and round as dinner plates, piling up quickly.

The thump came again, and through the vicious wind, she thought she heard a moan.

A pained moan.

She stood. "Maybe someone's trying to get inside," she said. "Maybe they're hurt."

"Mallory," Amy said. "Don't."

"Seriously," Grace said, grabbing Mallory's hand. "It's too dangerous out there right now."

"Well, I can't just ignore it." Tugging free, she wrapped her arms around herself and moved toward the opening, resolute.

Someone was in trouble, and she was a sucker for that. It was the eternal middle child syndrome, and the nurse's curse. Glass crunched beneath her feet, and she shivered as snow blasted her in the face. Amazingly, the aluminum frame of the front door had withstood the impact when the glass had shattered. Shoving aside the thick branch, Mallory once again held the iPhone out in front of her, using it to peer out into the dark.

Nothing but snow.

"Hello?" she called, taking a step outside, onto the concrete stoop. "Is anyone—"

A hand wrapped around her ankle, and Mallory broke off with a startled scream, falling into the night.

When Jill's neighbor decided to have an extension built, she was suddenly gifted with inspiration: a bunch of cute, young, sweaty guys hanging off the roof and the walls. Just the type of men who'd appeal to three estranged sisters forced together when they inherit a dilapidated beach resort . . .

*Meet Maddie, Tara and Chloe in*

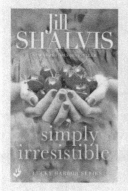

'**Count on Jill Shalvis for a witty, steamy, unputdownable love story**'
Robyn Carr

**headline**
ETERNAL

When the lights go out and you're 'stuck' in a café with potential Chocoholic-partners-in-crime and nothing else to do but eat cake and discuss the mysteries of life, it's surprising just what conclusions women will come to. But when they decide to kick things into gear, they'd better be prepared for what happens once they have the ball rolling . . .

*Here come Mallory, Amy and Grace in*

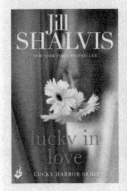  

'An abundance of chemistry, smoldering romance, and hilarious antics'

*Publishers Weekly*

**headline**
ETERNAL

The women of Lucky Harbor have been charming
readers with their incredible love stories – now it's
time for some very sexy men to take center stage.
They're in for some *big* surprises – and from corners
they'd least expect it.

*Really get to know Luke, Jack and Ben in*

  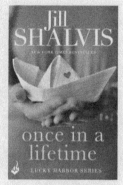

'Hot sex, some delightful humor and plenty of
heartwarming emotion'
*Romantic Times*

**headline**
ETERNAL

$\mathcal{L}$ ucky Harbor is the perfect place to escape to, whether that means a homecoming, getting away from the city or running from something a whole lot darker. Whatever the cause, Lucky Harbor has three more residents who are about to discover just how much this sleepy little town really has to offer.

*Escape with Becca, Olivia and Callie in*

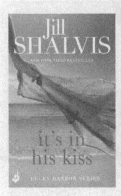 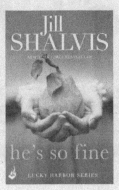 

'Clever, steamy, and fun. Jill Shalvis will make you laugh and fall in love'
Rachel Gibson

**headline**
ETERNAL